Hybrid

By

Angie L Reed

Argus Enterprises International, Inc.
North Carolina***New Jersey

Hybrid

All Rights Reserved © 2009
by Angie L Reed

A-Argus Better Book Publishers, LLC

For information:
A-Argus Better Book Publishers, LLC
Post Office Box 914
Kernersville, North Carolina 27285
www.a-argusbooks.com

ISBN: 0-9823050-8-7
ISBN: 978-09823050-8-9

Book Cover designed by Dubya

Printed in the United States of America

Author's Note:

*I wish to thank my entire family, Wayne, *Emily Caitlin Reed*, Walter (no longer with us), Joyce, Kelli, Michael, Ashley, Itsy Bitsy Teeny Weenie, and Sam. Without their love and support, especially Wayne's, this book *absolutely* never would have been written. I am truly lucky to have them. Also, thanks to all of my friends, classmates, fellow teachers, and students at FWA--especially *Emily Ryann Barron*--for lending me your names--*Hybrid's* characters truly appreciate it!

*Also, a very special thanks to all of my peeps in Lubbock, Texas! Ya'll rock!

Go Fort Worth Academy Warriors!

ALR

Table of Contents:

The Great Wall of China during the Ming Dynasty,
Home of Ursulus, *The Original Vampire, 1368-1644 A.D.*

"The Giaour"

But first, on earth as **vampire** sent,
Thy corse shall from its **tomb** be rent:
Then ghastly haunt thy native place,
And **suck** the **blood** of all thy race;
There from my daughter, sister, wife,
At midnight **drain** the stream of life;
Yet loathe the banquet which perforce
Must **feed** thy livid living corse:
Thy **victims** ere they yet expire
Shall know the **demons** for their sire,
As cursing thee, thou cursing them,
Thy flowers are withered on the stem.
But one that for thy crime must fall,
The youngest, most beloved of all,
Shall bless thee with a father's name-
That word shall wrap thy heart in flame!
Yet must thou end thy task, and mark
Her cheek's last tinge, her eye's last spark,
And the last glassy glance must view
Which freezes o'er its **lifeless** blue;
Then with unhallowed hand shalt tear
The tresses of her yellow hair,
Of which in life a lock when shorn
Affection's fondest pledge was worn,
But now is **borne** away by thee,
Memorial of thine agony!
Wet with thine own best **blood** shall drip
Thy gnashing tooth and haggard lip;
Then stalking to thy sullen **grave**,
Go-and with Gouls and Afrits rave;
Till these in **horror** shrink away
From spectre more **accursed** than they!

by Lord Byron (1788-1824)

Preface

Rose's premature funeral was brief and Mom and Dad requested an open casket service for saddened friends and family. It was unsettling, however, peering into her lifeless face. She wore a floor length, pink satin dress with grosgrain ribbons hand sewn onto the puffy princess sleeves. Grandma Dolan, Mom's grieving mother, purchased a beautiful antique choker with a lone white pearl flanked by two rounded pink sapphires for our lovely Rose to wear. She clutched a tiny white teddy bear and her pink ballet flats were tied neatly above her delicate ankles into perfectly formed bows. Rose's meticulously manicured nails sparkled with the glittery polish she loved so much. Caitlin insisted she be buried with a glass Tinker Bell ornament from the year's previous Christmas--a gift from Aunt Caroline--Rose's favorite relative. I wrote "I love you Rose" on a sheet of fancy lined stationary scented lightly with my favorite vanilla musk and tenderly reminded Dad-- too distraught to remember on his own--to place the heartfelt message inside her coffin before it was permanently sealed. Her petite, porcelain face looked like a delicate cherub figurine Grandma housed inside one of her many cherry curio cabinets. "The quicker Rose made it to heaven"--Mom sang--"the better. This world is too corrupt for an angel like her." We all agreed.

January 9, 2005

Dear Diary:

It's me again. I can't stop thinking about Julian. He's in my thoughts day and night. I feel so guilty. I wrote a poem about him today. Don't tell Max. It would break his heart. Emily Ryan Reed.

Darkened Spirit

His eyes are haunting, dark as night,
my spine tingles, in love with fright.
I cannot forget him. My mind betrays,
Evocative feelings, my body aches.
The night hardens, I feverishly shake.
Will he come? Drink my spirit?
Or will he forget, leaving me delirious?

By Emily Ryan Reed

P.S. How can I ignore my feelings? It's barely been a month!

January 16, 2005

Dear Diary:

I'm scared now. Madison warned me but I didn't listen. I'm scared but my heart is fixated. He owns my soul... Emily Ryan Reed.

Wickedness

Evil is upon us. Here them cry.
Victims of death, an eye for an eye.
Rose is gone. Limbs are buried.
Death searches for me. Long since wearied.
Julian haunts me. Death beware.
He'll have his way, I won't be spared.
What will become of this wayward heart?
For straying a lover, in death we will part.

By Emily Ryan Reed

P.S. What does he want from me? I can't give any more of myself!!! There's nothing left! Nothing!!!

Part One

hybrid: an organism that is the offspring of genetically dissimilar parents or stock...

Chapter 1

Arrival...

November 22, 2004:

In November, Beckley, West Virginia's artic weather is unlike any balmy November day in Dallas, Texas. It is cold. Snowy. And cold. Forty degrees Fahrenheit is the average winter forecast. In Dallas, however, November's routinely include days where grateful residents scurry around town sporting colorful Bermuda shorts and rubber flip flops. *But I'm not in Dallas.*

"Why did I get stuck with the smallest bedroom? I don't even have my own bathroom," I groaned. "I'm the *oldest.* I deserve better than this. *Seriously, people.*"

"Because your stuffed-animal-loving twin sisters require twice--no three times the space!" Mom crudely fired back.

"Just deal with it, *Emily.* You big fat complainer. That's all you do is whine. Get over it!"

Caitlin's menacing words stung. She always had an opinion--forcing it on the entire family. Sometimes I really hated her. Of course she argued just to annoy me. Ashley, on the other hand, was a *little* less mouthy than her two-minutes-older, pain-in-the-butt clone.

Witnessing the birth of a potentially explosive argument, where sharp objects like scissors would be thrown and boxes full of plastic treasures like dollar store figurines and a sordid collection of "I love Texas" memorabilia crushed, Dad reluctantly intervened--like he's done for so many years now.

"Leave each other alone! I mean it! *All three of you girls*. And when *ya'll* are finished unpacking all of your bedrooms and sorting through all that crap--*like you're supposed to be doing*--I could use a hand in the kitchen. There are boxes everywhere in here. Get back to work!"

Suddenly, the "new" house got decidedly quiet with Dad's angry assertion. Frustrated, he'd long since grown weary of the constant bickering between the meddlesome twins and me. And since Rose's death, we were at each others throats even more--the extended and boring drive from suburbia Texas to rural West Virginia did little to ease matters. Trapped inside the packed and soiled *Plymouth Voyager*--unwashed for weeks now--we'd done nothing but come to blows over which CD belonged to whom and what visual masterpiece to play next in the portable *Coby* DVD player Caitlin scored for her thirteenth birthday--another expensive gift from Aunt Caroline. Needless to say, I was sick of watching *Freaky Friday* starring a noticeably chubbier Lindsey Lohan. I wanted to watch *School of Rock* with Jack Black, my favorite comedian--*Rose's too*.

Rose adored cooking. Even though she was only four year's old, she and Mom spent most of their waking hours in our well-equipped, Texas-sized kitchen--complete with honed Brazilian granite countertops and stainless steel appliances. Feeding a family of six required an enormous amount of time and fastidious preparation. Rose loved washing gritty bib lettuce for cob salads and peeling tiny red potatoes for Swedish stew. And she wasn't half bad at it either. After she died, however, our altered family *apprehensively embraced* fast foods. Previously off limits, Mom now seemed lost in the cavernous kitchen without her right hand and take-out food quickly replaced old-fashioned meals like flaky biscuits with chipped beef gravy and hand-battered fried chicken dipped in honey. Similarly, greasy take-out burgers and soggy French fries substituted for homemade chili and spicy meatloaf with roasted bell peppers and a pinch of tarragon--two of Rose's favorites.

"Come on ya'll, stop fighting, we really need your help in here. There must be at least twenty boxes labeled *kitchen crap.* Finish unpacking your rooms. We need you. *All three of you!*" Mom pleaded.

"Mom, have you seen a small box marked *pics and stuff*? I'm missing a box scribbled with hot pink sharpie that says *pics and stuff*. Madison packed that carton. I need it! My whole life's in that box!" I panicked.

"Nope. Haven't seen it, Emily. Keep looking--it'll show up eventually. You just have to have *patience*. Oh, and check the garage again."

At the exact moment Mom stabbed me with her "you just have to be patient remark," the doorbell rang and five curious sets of mostly blue-grey eyes--inherited from my dad's side of the family--headed for the crowded living room complete with a wood burning fireplace and the ugliest wallpaper on the planet. Dad opened the freshly painted crimson door--courtesy of the home's previous owners--exposing a shivering but handsome young male. *He was cute.*

"Hey. Um, I'm Blake. Blake Reynolds. I live about a half a mile up the road in the yellow two-story house. You know, the one with the crashed *Wrangler* parked out front? Mom said to ask you guys if you need help unpacking. Do you? I don't charge anything. I'm just here to offer my help. *Need some help?*"

Dad appeared slightly confused as he spied the at least six-foot-one, chestnut-haired stranger rambling inside our new doorway. Blake's wild-eyed reaction did little to placate him.

"Uh, sure, we could use some *help*. You say you live down the road? So you're a neighbor? Right?"

"Sure am. I knew the folks who lived here before you guys bought the property--the Cook's. And *you all* are in luck. I'm off for a few days from school cuz of the Thanksgiving break and I can help--that's for sure," Blake persisted, reassuring my bewildered-looking father that it was safe to allow him inside our new home.

"Come on in then, son, we could sure use your--uh--*help*," Dad gulped.

It didn't take long for Blake to notice me. After all, he's a sixteen year-old boy with raging hormones--too much testosterone. Besides, we teenagers tend to *smell* each other out quickly--and Blake and I were smelling each other out--that's for sure.

Blake, dressed appropriately for the cold winter weather, was cute--a fact I detected right away. His shaggy brown hair and bright hazel eyes reminded me of my favorite teen star *Robert Daze Holiday* (a cheesy stage name) from a popular sitcom called *In This House*--and that wasn't a bad thing. Staring at him intently, I noticed right away that Blake's otherwise pallid face and neck were tan despite the glacial climate outside. I gathered from the pinkness around his fleshy cheeks--giving him a raccoon like appearance--Blake was probably a skier, especially given that he lived in West Virginia famous for expensive resorts like *Snowshoe* and *Winterplace Ski Resort*. Even with the neon braces concealing his crooked front teeth, Blake's oval-shaped face was handsome--in a wayward, school-boyish way. With such casual but sporty looks, Blake could have modeled for the oober trendy *Abercrombie and Fitch* or the well-established *Calvin Klein* dynasty, respectively of course. A friendly and palatable guy, I liked him already--a detail that didn't go unnoticed by Caitlin and Ashley who stood giggling only a few feet away.

Shortly after our brief but *enlightening* introduction, Blake decided he was going to call me Dallas. I didn't mind his resolution to do so, however. After all, Blake's decision to nickname me so quickly into our relationship only reaffirmed my initial assessment that he's a friendly *and* likeable guy. And one thing's for sure, a boy who's friendly *and* cute *and* likeable means he's popular. Blake's also a jock--a conclusion I came too because underneath his thick black coat--which smelled of wood chips and mesquite--Blake donned a worn out *Woodrow Wilson High School Football* jersey--holes and all. I liked the idea of him being cute, friendly, popular, *and* sporty because with him as an admirer (I was sure he would be soon, if not already), fitting in on the first day of school was bound to prove easier. With Blake accompanying me, I was sure to be a hit. At least I was smart enough to admit I needed

Blake's attention in order to make a favorable impression as I don't exactly have the warmest of personalities. Like most teenage girls I know, in order to make a positive first impression, I rely heavily on what I perceive to be my greatest asset--my *stunning good looks*.

Unfortunately, being new is never easy nor is it particularly enjoyable having dozens of anonymous faces staring you down leaving you wondering if you have food in your teeth or toilet paper stuck inside your fashionable low-riders. I know this because halfway through the fifth grade at *Dallas Academy Prep School*, my parents snatched me and the intolerable twins out of this private haven in favor of the always cheaper public sector. You see, when Rose was born, my belated parents agreed that Mom would relinquish her lucrative title as a school administrator in order to stay home with my newest baby sister. Because money would inevitably be tighter--and it was--public school touted everything private school did. *But for free.* And with the addition of Rose, we needed to slash expenses from somewhere. So my irritating twin sisters and I became the newest members of *Hawthorne Elementary School* (the twins were in third grade) and *Wright Anderson Middle School*. Respectively.

Fifth grade certainly wasn't the worst grade to have be the *newbie* in and I made friends quicker than anyone predicted I would. I must admit, fitting in with the others proved easier than even *I* expected. However, being the novel and clueless teenager in high school was a bit more challenging. With my secret weapon, however, a good-looking, sixteen year old jock, Blake made the horrid situation *slightly* less objectionable.

"Emily, this is Blake," Dad mused, aware of Blake's bulging eyes when he spied me entering the only living area in the not so new house.

"Blake, this is Emily," Dad mused, equally cognizant that I realized Blake's eyeballs bulged when he spotted me entering the muddled room--empty cardboard boxes and mounds of crumpled packing tape strewn across the chipped Indian slate floor.

"Uh, where are you guys from?" Blake stammered with a thick West Virginia accent.

"Dallas, Texas," Dad mumbled. "We're from Dallas. *Texas*. It sure is cold around here Blake. When will the weather change? We just got here and I'm already praying for spring."

"Wow. That's pretty far away. Dallas I mean. *And* spring. It won't warm up for a while though. Why Beckley? What brings you guys east? I thought Texas was *the bomb*," Blake teased while focusing his enamored gaze solely on me. "Why would you leave a metropolis like Dallas for a small town like Beckley?"

Following that *extremely* loaded question, Dad staged his exit; a move I found rude considering Blake's willingness to help a bunch of strangers unpack a sordid collection of miniature horses and no less than eight boxes of Mom's dusty wedding china--*Dresden Rose*.

"Uh, if you don't mind, I've got to get back to unpacking the kitchen, Blake. I'm overwhelmed. I've never seen so many boxes of mismatched salt and pepper shakers and chipped coffee mugs that *should have* been thrown into the trash. Emily will tell you all about it--why we moved to the Appalachian Mountains I mean. And thanks. We *really* appreciate your *help*."

Dad stepped out of the debris filled living area leaving Blake and me to ourselves. Caitlin and Ashley headed back to the cramped space they now unenthusiastically shared--bored by our ineptness. After what seemed like an eternity filled with mindless chitchat about football practice and where I could find a *Dairy Queen*, Blake made an unexpected announcement. "I'm gonna call you *Dallas*. Do you mind if I call you that Emily? You look like a *Dallas*."

"No, um, I guess not. Whatever makes you unpack these stupid boxes faster is fine with me. Did you ever watch the show *Dallas*? Probably not. We were both too young when it first came out. Back home, you can catch the reruns on cable. They play it *a lot*. That show's like our state anthem or emblem or something. Anyway, it's still popular in Texas, they show *Dallas* all the time. You can even tour *South Fork* you know."

"Cool, I've never seen it, but you *look* like a Dallas. Besides, Emily is too, uh, well, common. No offense. It's just that there are quite a few *Emily's* at our school--Emily Becker, Emily Allen, Emilie Price, Emily Blake, Emi...uh, sorry, we just have a lot of Emily's at WWHS. Besides, I like the name Dallas. You look like a Dallas. We've never had a Dallas--at least not that I know of--a couple of Austin's and one Houston--but no Dallas," Blake rambled. "Lots and lots of Emily's though."

"I get it, Blake."

Monday morning, following the short but state-mandated, five-day plus the weekend Thanksgiving break, Blake picked me up for school in his beat up, 2001, gunmetal grey *Ford Mustang. Are You Gonna be My Girl,* by a popular band named *Jet,* was blaring over the detachable *Pioneer* CD player and I could barely hear myself think. I couldn't help noticing, however, that it wasn't a half-bad car--considering his teenaged status. I wasn't sure if Blake was responsible for the multiple dents on his Mustang, however, or if his parents were able to purchase such a car *because* of them. Anyway, I wasn't prepared to ask because I didn't want to embarrass him. Blake wouldn't have heard me over the boisterous music anyway. Despite its crashed up exterior, the interior of Blake's car was remarkably clean and appeared to be well taken care of. Blake was neat for a teenager, at least when it came to keeping the inside of his car fresh. The black and grey, heated leather seats actually looked brand new--he was obviously a fan of leather wipes. I could *smell* them.

"Don't forget to call your mom after school, *Dallas*. I can't take you home cuz I have football practice. Did you bring your cell? I've got my mom's old *Nokia* if you need to borrow mine. Remember, I can drive you to school everyday but I can't pick you up--at least not until football season is over. I don't play baseball or basketball--just football. I'm hoping to get a scholarship to *Marshall*

University. It's in Huntington--home of the *Thundering Herd.* That's the college that had the awful plane crash in the seventies. You know, everyone on it was killed. The players and the coaching staff all died. It was tragic. My parents fell in love with each other at Marshall. They were torn up about it. Very, very sad."

"Yeah, Blake, I brought it--my mobile phone I mean. And yes, she knows to pick me up at three-thirty. Mom's never late. She'll be there," I insisted. "And hey, that's too bad about the crash. I'll have to *Google* it. I've never heard of Marshall University. Is it a good school? Is it a four-year college? How close is Huntington from here anyways? I'm hoping to go to the *University of Texas.* I want to be an art teacher, like Mrs. Wise--she's brilliant. Back home, she taught me to use pastels. If I can't be an art teacher, then I wouldn't mind being a poet like Margaret Atwood--she wrote *A Sad Child* and *The Moment?* Great stuff, Blake. Anyway, *UT's* in Austin--the *Longhorns.* I hate their school colors though--b*urnt* orange and *bland* white--very ugly. Who likes orange anyway?"

"The *Longhorns* have a celebrated football program, Dallas--*very prestigious.* Isn't that school really big? I bet tuition's expensive. Maybe I could get a scholarship there; it doesn't have to be at Marshall--just as long as I get to keep playing ball after high school. That would be awesome. Mom and Dad wouldn't have to pay for anything," Blake quipped. "Some scouts are coming in a couple of weeks to check out the senior players. Even though I'm just a junior, maybe I'll impress them with my quick hands and lightening reflexes," he grinned.

"Maybe."

Despite his incessant babbling about playing football on a hard-to-score scholarship, I was impressed that Blake seemed genuinely concerned about whether or not I'd secured a ride home from school. I found myself appreciating my newest companion. I couldn't help wondering, however, if he was attracted to me. Would we be girlfriend and boyfriend by the end of the week? I *thought* Blake liked me. But you never really know with guys--they can be unpredictable.

"Great," he shot back. "I'm glad she's picking you up. And don't forget about the pep rally this Friday at two-thirty in the gym. There are yellow flyers posted everywhere--even the boys' bathrooms have them plastered inside the stalls. We get to dress up in our school colors--maroon and white. You can pick up plastic pom poms at the front office for fifty cents. *They're worth the investment.* Oh yeah, and we're the *Flying Eagles.* Don't forget *that* part; our mascot is an Eagle. Not a real one though--*PETA* complained. We're the *Woodrow Wilson High School Flying Eagles.* You should memorize that, Dallas. It's really important to know we're the *Flying Eagles*--not the *Falcons* or the *Condors.* The *Eagles,*" he persisted, rattling my uneasy nerves in the process.

"I *know* that, Blake. I *won't* forget. We're the *Eagles*!" I chanted loudly while waving my hands in the air--like any *true* football fan would have done. Blake seemed oblivious to my sarcasm.

The nationally ranked high school was astonishingly large considering the relatively small size of the town. Beckley's stalled population hovered around sixteen thousand persons--all-freezing to death of course. More than fifteen hundred students attended WWHS, ranging in grades ninth through twelfth. Despite its pleasing size, the single-story building's grey plaster exterior was cracked in places and the ancient windows looked like they hadn't been opened or replaced in a long time. Chipped black paint around nearly all of the school's framed metal doors gave the impression that WWHS needed some routine maintenance--not at all unlike the high school I attended in Dallas which also sported peeling latex and broken panes. Outside, the air was cold and damp, a fact I deplored as we headed towards one of the school's two main entrances. I was chilly. *It was chilly.* I'd always heard that West Virginia was a green place. However, at least during the wintertime, Beckley's murky sky was hazy, grey and slightly overcast. Unfortunately, the dead and spindly trees, as well as the dried up rhododendrons out front, did little to offer a much-needed splash of color to an otherwise gloomy exterior. On the concrete parking lot's perimeter--dirty, polluted snow was piled in two feet peaks and the pebbled sidewalks leading to each of the main entrances as well as to the adjoining, cheaply-constructed buildings maintained a near constant film of ice causing many students to slip. One unlucky girl with spiky blue hair and the ugliest purple contacts I've ever seen ended up with a twisted ankle and sprained wrist when trying to break her fall. I felt bad for her; after returning to school--she missed a week and a half--someone had to carry her mound of assorted textbooks for nearly a month. Beckley was nothing like Dallas where the searing Texas sun shined almost perpetually and the average yearly temperature was an enviable seventy degrees.

The wretched weather aside, as a hesitant junior transfer, I hoped the girls at WWHS wouldn't be as evil as those portrayed in cool movies and popular teen books like *Mean Girls* and *Fake*. I needed *these* girls to be laid back and friendly in order to offset my brooding personality. I also *needed* Blake to make the necessary introductions as I wasn't so good at selling myself. I knew I would clam up as soon as I got around a crowd full of unfamiliar faces. *And I did.*

When one creates phantoms for oneself, one puts vampires into the world, and one must nourish these children of a voluntary nightmare with one's blood, one's life, one's intelligence, and one's reason, without ever satisfying them. Eliphas Levi. 1800's.

Chapter 2

New Blood...

"Your schedule sucks," Blake hissed.

"Why?" I shot back, clutching the wrinkled paper inside my taut grip. In a fit of uneasiness, I shook out my long, brown locks--a nervous habit I'd developed after Rose died--when reviewing the schedule's grueling agenda--*Pre Calculus and French.* I felt uncomfortable and my sensitive skin was beginning to chafe because the woolen scarf draped around it was itchy--*should have worn the cashmere one like Mom suggested.*

"Because you're only in two of my classes--math with Mrs. Sheffield and World History with Mrs. Lane. That sucks for you because you won't be able to feast your gorgeous eyes on my irresistible face all day long. It's a tragedy really. I feel for you."

"Oh, I see. That certainly *does* suck for me. And exactly which *obtuse* parent is responsible for your *tasteless* lack of modesty, Blake?"

"That would be my dad Richard," he chuckled and I couldn't help noticing those engaging dimples when he did.

Blake, just as I'd anticipated, accompanied me from his damaged Mustang into the school's musky office and then on to my first class of the day--Honors English with Mrs. Rice. I was glad to leave the cramped surroundings as the view of the dead indoor plants was depressing. One *Boston* fern and a couple of *English* ivy's infested with spider mites were in dire need of water, artificial light, and fertilizer--too bad the gloomy room has no windows.

I was relieved for the escort as my nerves were causing minor eruptions to occur inside my stomach. Because we were running late--due to my required stop at the dank office--Blake and I rushed to our classes. The grimy hallways were empty except for the scattered remains of a few ripped signs on the faded walls touting "*Beat Riverside High.*" I was glad the naked halls were bare. I needed time to prepare myself for the onslaught of unfamiliar faces that would soon be judging me. Despite my reservations, Blake's attitude was casual, and he was either unaware or unconcerned about my trepidation. Of course he had no reason to be anxious himself; he'd been going to school with these kids all his life. Not like my experience in Dallas, however, where migrant faces came and went month after month, year after year. Blake knew everybody at WWHS and everybody knew him. *He was lucky.*

My favorite subject, other than art, was overshadowed by the harrowing fact that as I entered into room 115 A, sans Blake, I suddenly felt twenty-three pairs of probing eyes burning holes through my blotchy skin. I was beginning to suspect my long-sleeved, yellow and white striped sweater bore an "X" on its cotton backside.

"*Who is she?*" I heard them mumbling. "*She's not from around here.*"

"*Obviously,*" I whispered underneath my faint breath. "*I'm the new kid.*"

"Class, please say hello to our newest member. This is Emily Reed. She just moved here and she's from Texas--Dallas I think. Let's all make her feel welcome," Mrs. Rice instructed. *Spoken like a true English teacher.*

"Texas! Can you say *ya'll*?" a yellow-haired boy in the back of the sterile classroom bellowed. Others followed. "*Ya'll* better be quiet for I whip *ya'll's* a...I mean butts."

"Mr. Wright, *be quiet!* I *mean* it, Eric. She's nervous enough," Mrs. Rice scolded the plump boy too large for his metal desk.

"Emily, tell us about yourself dear, and *try* to ignore the locals. And Eric, keep it down. I mean it." Mrs. Rice shot him a burning look meant as a warning. *He looked scared.*

"Um, my name is Emily. Emily Reed. I'm sixteen years old. My birthday is in December--on Christmas Eve. I'll be seventeen. My family is from Texas. Um...I have *three*--I mean two sisters--they're twins--Ashley and

Caitlin. I like to swim...and draw. My dad's a lawyer. He's working at Dwight Hickman's firm." *Oh crap, I'm rambling.*

Sensing my apprehension, Mrs. Rice intervened saving me from myself. "Uh, thanks, Emily. You can sit down now. Class, let's finish our chapter on prepositional phrases. Any questions? Parker, do *you* have any questions? You seemed confused about them on Friday-- the prepositions I mean."

After humiliating myself by babbling, the next twenty seven minutes of class were hell and I had the blood red face to prove it. I knew the kids were staring at me and my entire five foot seven, one-hundred and twenty pound frame shook with dread. My heart-shaped face blistered and my freckled skin--too much Texas sun--tingled all over. My tongue was swollen and my mouth was dry. My blue-grey eyes could focus on nothing but the scuffed linoleum floor beneath me. I was too embarrassed to look up. I could barely breathe and was beginning to feel faint. *God I hate being new.*

By the time second period rolled around I was convinced I'd grown a second head as even more students were feverishly checking me out inside the cramped hallways. Class was equally awkward this time around as seven students from English were glowering at me all over again. The only positive note was that Blake sat only a few seats away and promised to do the introductions. I was grateful for his insistence and prayed he would do a better job assuring the students I wasn't completely stupid.

"Hey dudes and Mrs. Sheffield, this is my new neighbor Dallas--I mean *Emily Reed.* She just moved here from Dallas. She's pretty cool. But she hates math. I think she likes art or something. Oh, and she *prefers* to be called *Dallas.*"

"Hates math, well, that won't do," Mrs. Sheffield sang, with a warming tune. Unfortunately, her two-piece green and white checked polyester suit and stained cream blouse did little to thwart her *teacherly* appearance.

"You can't hate math and do well in my class, Emily. We'll have to do something about that. Or do you *prefer* we call you Dallas?" She tapped her worn-out mules on the soiled floor when inquiring.

"Um, *Dallas* will be *fine,* ma'am," I mumbled--surprised by my answer. I had to admit, I was feeling better. Following Blake's brief but friendly introduction, there were no more rude stares from critical students and the giant "X" on my backside seemed to have disappeared. *At least for now.*

Finally, and just in time for third period, I felt better about being *new.* That is until Maxwell Snow entered the plain but crowded room. Caught off guard by his bouncy blonde locks and tall stature--at least six-foot two--I knocked my black leather purse out of my lap while trying to secure a better look at his perfect face. After spilling its entire contents onto the floor--which included an assortment of pencils and pens, a silver *Lancôme* make-up bag, and one unopened tampon--eighteen World History students laughed at my smashed-up peanut butter and grape jelly sandwich on split whole wheat. Blake included. *Crap.*

"Hey, Dallas, need some help?" he taunted. Blake's dimples weren't so cute anymore.

I forgot he was sitting so close to me. Enjoying my spectacle, he seemed a little *too* eager to laugh at my expense. Trying to ignore him, but failing miserably, I bent over, hiding my crimson face, in order to pick up the scattered contents of my *Dooney & Burke* as quickly as I could. My lunch, however, now smashed into the dirty linoleum, remained on the filthy floor until Mrs. Lane handed me some recycled paper towels from the metal dispenser attached to the grubby wall. I got busy scooping up the buttery mess.

When Max first wandered in, I couldn't help noticing his youthful expression. Despite his boyish looks, his well-built muscular body gave the impression Max was older than his sixteen years. He brushed past me, unaware of my presence, and I caught a whiff of his masculine scent--*woodsy.* Much as I'd sniffed out Blake when he first appeared in my living room (*sporty*), I relied on my senses in order to size up Max. I liked what I saw *and* smelled.

"Lunchtime, come on, Dallas, let's eat!" Blake shouted in unison with the *third period's finally-over bell.* Embarrassed, I rushed to his side and couldn't wait to leave the agony of World History behind. What a joke! The mess I'd made when I'd first laid eyes on Max was on my mind when I followed Blake into the cafeteria--sulking all the way. What a fool Max must think I am for losing my lunch--so to speak--the second he sauntered in. Maybe he hadn't noticed. *Who was I kidding?* Everyone noticed. And Blake, who would have thought he would laugh so readily *and* willingly at my expense? I thought he was my friend--my *only* friend at Woodrow Wilson. My *almost boyfriend*--only if I allowed it of course. *How could he of all people do that to me?* What a jerk!

"Hey, Em.., I mean Dallas, this is Emily Becker-- otherwise known as E.B." Blake's abrupt broadcast was unexpected, knocking me out of my self-pitied daze.

"Uh, hello. I'm Emily Reed. I'm *from* Dallas. Blake *calls* me Dallas. You can call me Dallas if you want. Nice to meet you," I studdered.

Despite being caught off-guard, I was glad for the distraction--I was ready for a change. *A big change.* And Blake's curious act offered just that. Emily B., or E.B as he'd affectionately referred to her, was decked out in a colorful smock and black denim jeans rolled at the ends. She wore a friendly smile exposing what appeared to be naturally straight teeth--a visible gap between the front two clued me in. E.B. was pretty. Her excessively long blonde hair, pulled tightly around her perfectly chiseled face, sparkled against my chestnut locks. Her tresses were curled at the ends and my hair was blown straight; her deep set eyes were crystal blue; mine were blue-grey; her cheery voice was annoyingly enthusiastic; mine wavering and unsure. However, we were *both* attractive young ladies--as Blake would later suggest--destined to be friends. Unfortunately, I wasn't prepared for the next bombshell, as if embarrassing myself in front of Max wasn't enough.

"Uh, Dallas, Emily B. is my *girlfriend.* Why don't you sit here with *us*?"

What did he say? His girlfriend? When did that happen? Blake never mentioned having a girlfriend before. In fact, I got the rather distinct impression--when he was unabashedly checking me out--that he was single.

"Uh, sure, I guess, I'd, uh, be glad to sit with *ya'll*."

I couldn't believe my ears--which were on fire! Blake never mentioned having a girlfriend. I should have known better I guess--good-looking, athletic boys like Blake *always* got pretty, cheerleader girlfriends like E.B.

"So, Emily, I mean, Dallas, we'd love to have you. Here, sit by me. Blake told me you guys bought that cute house down the road from his Colonial. That cream and black bungalow--right? It's been for sale for like forever. I live about five miles away from you guys on Dutch Branch Road--near the interstate. My mom won't let Blake pick me up for school, though. She doesn't trust his erratic driving. Not yet anyway. I'm not sure I do either--you've seen his Mustang--all the dents," she giggled. "Anyway, it's so awkward when we go out on dates. I have to drive!"

After the peanut butter and jelly fiasco in history class, where Max and a host of others discovered what a clutz I can be, I was glad to see the embarrassment welling up on Blake's blushing face instead of mine. He deserved it. Emily's comments definitely struck a nerve.

"I'm trying to be brave you know, when I drive with him. So far, so good," I teased. Blake's body recoiled. *So Blake was responsible for the dents--better not tell my parents.*

"Oh, and thanks for the invitation. I will definitely join ya'll for lunch," I added.

For about the one-hundredth time today, my scarlet cheeks burned as the other students sharing the orange melamine table were zealously checking me out. Four pretty girls and six buff boys--each donning leather football jackets--stared me down. Emily B. was nice enough though sensing my uneasiness--as did Blake. *Finally.*

"Dallas is kind of shy, guys. Go easy on her. She's okay once you get her going. She *loves* to talk about Texas and stuff. That's one of the reasons I call her Dallas."

"Hey, do you like the *Dallas Cowboys*, uh, Dallas?" one of the shorter athletes sitting behind Blake asked. But before I could respond, he rudely fired back. "I don't. *They suck*--big time. I'm an *Eagles* fan. So do you like them--the *Cowboys*, I mean?"

Answering his question in *favor* of the Cowboys seemed like a lame idea after Alex, as I soon discovered his name to be, sat accusing them of sucking. I couldn't say I blamed him, however. They were never the same following Coach Johnson's controversial dismissal in the nineties.

"Uh, they're okay, I guess. I'm not a big football fan though," I stammered--putting my foot into my mouth. I was surrounded by six; make that seven anxious football players with football in their blood and on their pea-sized brains. Realizing my mistake--admitting I wasn't a fan of the brutal game--I backpedaled.

"I mean, I *used* to love football. That is, until Jimmy Johnson left the Cowboys. Dad said that was a huge mistake on Jerry Jones' part--letting him go. They never played the same after he left."

"That's okay, Dallas," E.B. interrupted. "I'm not a fan either. I just like cheerleading because it gives me something to do on the weekends. We're all cheerleaders here," she chatted while pointing towards the four stunning girls sharing the table. "Beckley isn't exactly booming with exciting, extracurricular activities. Plus, cheerleading gets me--I mean us--out of homework when our games are out of town. You should try it--cheerleading I mean. We could use another girl--it makes doing pyramids *so much* easier. Why don't you ask Mrs. Hough if you can join us? Our squad, I mean. We'd love to have you. She's the cheerleading coach--you'll meet her during PE today," Emily purred. Blake couldn't take his smitten eyes off her.

The fact that Emily was willing to include me so soon after meeting made me feel better about the lousy way I'd handled my introductions earlier in the day. *I really liked her*. She seemed like a genuine person and I was glad for having met her--even if she did turn out to be Blake's pretty girlfriend.

"Yeah, Dallas, Mrs. Hough would love to find another girl willing to wear such short skirts in this crazy weather!

After lunch, I'll walk you down to her office--outside in the school's gymnasium. You're gonna like her," a pretty cheerleader with a layered, auburn bob and red-rimmed glasses insisted. I noticed the others sitting around the table calling her Marie Frances--or Frances for short. She was pretty in a nerdy sort of way. Her almond-shaped, emerald eyes gleamed while her copper skin sparkled--too much *Tickle Me Pink* body glitter I guessed.

"That sounds great--I appreciate it--really. Ya'll have been great."

"Hey Dallas, considering the condition of your peanut butter and jelly sandwich, I think I'll pick you up something to eat in line. What do you want?" Blake asked--managing to redeem himself.

"I'll go with you if you don't mind, scope out the selection. Do they have soft tacos or bean burritos? I mean, I *am* from Texas and Mexican food sounds great." I shot a quick glance towards Emily B. making sure I wasn't making her mad by accompanying Blake towards the extensive food court complete with a sprawling salad bar and pizza buffet. Her reassuring grin suggested I was okay.

"Sure, come take a look. Just stay away from the brussel sprouts disguised as cheddar cheese balls--unless you want to spend the afternoon in the toilet," Blake chuckled.

"Disgusting. Thanks for the warning."

"You can even charge your selections to my account. I'm loaded, you know."

"Oh really, Blake, then why don't you pay back the twenty dollars you borrowed from me last weekend, *bonehead*? Since you're so *loaded* and all," Alex quipped as he snuck up behind us.

"Shut up, Alex, you dirt bag. You *owe* me twenty dollars just for being your friend. Nobody else around here can stand your ugly mug."

"Ha. I've got more friends than you, puke face."

Bantering back and forth, Blake and Alex wrestled each other playfully on their way towards the rapidly increasing line. Tagging behind--at a safe distance of course--I tried not to get hurt when approaching the swarm of hungry students.

"They're goofballs, Dallas. Do you mind if I call you that? Blake says it's okay. Don't pay any attention to them. Blake and Alex battle all the time. They've been at it since kindergarten--some things never change. Hang with *us* and you'll be fine--I promise," Emily joked, while walking along side me. *She smelled nice--sugary.*

Standing only a few steps away, the other kids in her popular entourage agreed that I would be okay. And I believed them. Things were definitely going to be easy at WWHS as long as Emily and the rest of the gang accepted me.

When other girls wanted to be ballet dancers, I kind of wanted to be a vampire. Angelina Jolie

Chapter 3

Fitting In...

"Awesome! I *knew* she'd offer you a spot, Dallas, considering we have two leftover uniforms and a couple of sets of maroon and silver pom poms. Since Tara Mason quit to be home-schooled and Zoie Clover got kicked out for bad grades--too many *D's*--we've been short two badly-needed girls around here. We definitely want you on the squad. Especially since state competitions are right around the corner—March, I think. Besides, nobody else tried out when Tara and Zoie left. *Cheerleading's dead*," Emily complained.

I had to admit, I was *finally* in my element since moving to West Virginia. I had the grades as well as the dexterity needed in order to jump and bend like a proud cheerleader. Back in Dallas, I'd been taking gymnastics classes for years, something my athletically-inclined best friend Madison and I did together two nights a week at the YWCA on Remington Court. I also had the slight build required in order to fit into the gently used maroon and white uniform--which barely needed altering thanks to my slim physique. I was tall, thin, and pretty enough to pull off being a varsity cheerleader. There was only one problem, with only a few games left in the *Flying Eagle's* wicked season; I needed to practice--*really* practice--as I'd *never* actually been a cheerleader before.

"We meet Monday through Thursday after school from three-forty five to five-fifteen. No Fridays, of course. *And* we practice outside to get used to this artic weather. *Also,* I can work with you one-on-one at my house on the weekends until you get caught up. If you want to, I mean. You'll be fine, Dallas! Most of our cheers are super easy anyway. And since Tara left, we've cut back on the pyramids and spirals. By the way, Heather's the head cheerleader. She's dating Peyton Clay--last year's most valuable player. He's really, really, good. And super hot. He'll probably get a scholarship to *WVU*. Heather's a senior just like Peyton and she plans on following him when he graduates. They want to get married. Heather can also help you out if you need extra practice. You'll like her. I promise."

Cool I thought, wondering why I hadn't met her before—Heather, that is. One thing was for sure, if Emily liked her I would too. E.B.'s perpetual enthusiasm where cheerleading was concerned was infectious and I couldn't wait to start practicing back flips and hand stands even if it was thirty-eight degrees outside and gloomy as all get out.

Fortunately for me, Tuesday--my second day of class--brought with it an entirely new attitude--thanks in part to Emily's invitation to cheer and Mrs. Hough's willingness to allow me to, despite having no measurable experience. Even though I'd made a fool out of myself during math and World History on the previous day--*maddening Monday* as I'd referred to it at home--I was now a Woodrow Wilson High School varsity cheerleader--a feat never accomplished in Texas because competition was so darn stiff and I was too chicken to try out. Texas football is intense--no matter what age you are. And with that intensity brings millions of stuck-up girls looking up to and wanting to be just like the *Dallas Cowboy Cheerleaders*. Even though I too wanted to be one of the extremely tall; insanely skinny; platinum blonde super beauties cheering on football's biggest named players, I never quite mustered enough guts to pursue a spot on *any* squad--junior varsity or otherwise. Rejection wasn't an experience I necessarily took lightly. Better to avoid it altogether--that was my pessimistic motto. But since I'd been *invited* to cheer and tryouts therefore were not necessary, I was only too happy to accept Emily's invitation. With the pain of rejection conveniently avoided then, I was able to focus on my new found celebrity as a high school cheerleader--maybe impressing Maxwell Snow in the meantime.

"Hey, Dallas, ready for the next game?" Blake pried on our way towards Emily's awe inspiring stucco house.

"Sure, Blake."

During the regular week, after finishing up with football practice, Blake had the privilege of watching Emily B. attempt to re-teach me how to crabwalk, do backbends, and tumble without breaking my neck. *Thank goodness for muscle memory.* With Blake as a willing escort--he just wanted to spend more time with Emily--I was able to practice outside her sprawling, three story mansion for an additional hour and a half nearly every evening. Brianna Ross and Katherine Winguard, senior cheerleaders who were neighbors in this exclusive, gated community, joined us. On my first try, however, and while attempting to land a back flip without the assistance of a mindful spotter, I landed on my backside. Covered in cold, dead grass and flanked by some minor bruising and scraping (I was okay), I realized I definitely needed to rehearse if I was going to be ready by Friday night's game--or any game for that matter.

Blake, cognizant of my struggle, praised my abilities nonetheless, scoring sympathy points with Emily. On the short ride to school the following wintry morning, he continued encouraging me--despite some previous ribbing. I guess he felt sorry for me.

"Keep it up, Dallas. You'll get it. *Really.* You were *born* to cheer! Besides, you've got the world's greatest instructor."

I was relieved that Emily didn't seem to mind my riding in with Blake everyday, it was certainly better than driving to school with my pinhead sisters. And since I didn't have a car of my own--I wanted a black Eclipse convertible with shiny leather seats--accompanying Blake was preferable. In the hectic mornings, however, I could never seem to find my cell phone or a pair of socks that matched and Caitlin capitalized on nearly every opportunity to humiliate me before leaving the frenzied house.

"Oh Emily, Blakie poo is here. Better brush your teeth. Your breath smells like rotten cheese!"

I hate her! She's been a thorn in my side ever since she started babbling at fifteen months. I was sure the first words out of her putrid mouth were "ga ga goo goo--*I hate*

Emily." Mom and Dad had long since learned to overlook her big mouth as punishing Caitlin rarely made any kind of difference in her obnoxious behavior. Blake took it all in stride, however, the bantering back and forth, barely cracking a dimpled smile whenever Caitlin started ripping on me. Himself an only child, Blake was never swayed by the constant sibling rivalry present at my house. Blake was mindful *not* to take sides when the ragging between me and my loathsome sisters got out of hand. He was a good friend, just *not* my boyfriend; and I was starting to feel okay about that--considering my feelings where Max was concerned.

Fortunately, on Tuesday, first period went by quickly despite Mrs. Rice rambling on and on about *past and present participles* and *noun gerunds with "ing" endings. Who could tell the difference between a participle and a gerund anyway?* And second period progressed despite Mrs. Sheffield's insistence upon piling on the math--I hate *Pre-Calculus.* Third period, however, left me nervous and agitated. Sweating profusely, I drenched my favorite baby blue *LL Bean* turtleneck that matched my neurotic eyes. I really wanted Maxwell to notice me. I *needed* him to notice me. But apparently, he didn't notice me. What was I doing wrong?

It would be several days--Friday, December sixth to be exact--before Max looked my way. I didn't understand his disinclination. Everyday, I dabbed my favorite perfume--vanilla musk--around my adorable pointy ears; straightened my hair diligently with the salon-quality flat iron I'd gotten for Christmas the year before; and rocked my best pair of *Sketchers*--the black and white checkered ones with rose and skull appliqués. Still, no forlorn glances or stolen looks my way. No, "*I see you Dallas and you're lookin' good* nod." No, "*Why don't you sit down next to me* wink in World History." And certainly no, "*I wish we had more classes together* plea." Nothing, absolutely nothing. To Max, I was invisible--that is until after Friday's weekly pep rally--in which Emily B. and Marie Frances took the brunt of my out-of-control cartwheels. Rocking my maroon and white polyester cheerleading outfit, I finally got a nibble. *A long awaited nibble.*

"Good luck at the game tonight, Dallas. I hope we win," Max grinned.

His words hit me like a steel pipe. *Finally*, I thought to myself. *He's finally talking to me.*

Caught off-guard before exiting the building, Maxwell Snow--appropriately named considering we lived in the Appalachian mountains and were surrounded by *it*--said good bye and good luck. *To me.* I couldn't believe it. Too shocked to verbally respond, I smiled the most endearing smile I could muster. Flashing perfectly straightened teeth, I grinned from ear to ear making sure Max knew my smile was meant *specifically* for him. Once we exited the aged building, I sauntered towards Max--he was headed for his *Chevy* truck in the bustling gravel parking lot--so I could offer him a *proper* thanks for wishing me luck. In the process of doing so (thanking him) I asked Max whether or not he would be attending tonight's game.

"Um, Max, are you going tonight--to the game I mean? We're playing *Cabell Midland*. I hear they're pretty good," I pried--trying not to appear too obvious. I hoped his answer would be yes of course.

"No. Um, my mom's been kind of sick lately and I promised to come straight home and help around the house. Dirty laundry's piling up and I need to chop firewood. The weather's getting colder and she *hates* chopping wood."

"Oh. I understand. I mean, ever since we moved to West Virginia, we've been burning up the fireplace. Dad loves a fire. We *all* love a fire. It saves on the heating bills--at least that's what my parents say. It's so freakin' cold here. Anyway, I really wish you could come. It'll be fun."

"I'm sure it will be. Maybe next time, Dallas. *Cabell Midland's* tough though. Don't get your hopes up," Max teased--a flirty smile lighting up his welcoming face.

I couldn't believe my luck. Even while facing him, admiring his Caribbean eyes--I couldn't believe I was doing it--having a conversation with Max--and it felt awesome. I even started to ramble.

"You know, the game doesn't officially start until seven p.m. Maybe you could come by for at least part of it? If you arrive at half-time, you don't even have to pay full admission. You'll save like a buck. You should come at half-time, Max. Afterwards, we're all going to Seymour's Pasta House for pizza. Have you been there before? I think it's on Ninth Street. It'll be my first time--to eat at Seymour's I mean, not having pizza of course." *I was definitely rambling.*

"I figured that, Dallas. Pizza is a popular dish," Max chuckled. Suddenly, I didn't feel so comfortable *or* lucky and I could sense butterflies fluttering inside the pit of my stomach. I hoped I wasn't about to make a fool out of myself--*again.* I'd been doing a lot of that lately, especially around Max.

"Well, if you *do* decide to come to the game or to the restaurant, a bunch of us will be there. It'll be fun. It's too bad you're not on the football team cuz you're certainly big enough to play." *Oops.* What was it with me and my *can't stop embarrassing myself* mouth anyway? And why was I always sticking my size seven foot into it? Was I always this goofy around people I didn't know and never realized it before?

Max laughed sensing my uneasiness. "I'm more of a stay-at-home and play chess kind of guy. Besides, my mom is scared I'll get hurt if I play. I'm an only child and she has an aversion to broken necks."

"I see. I live in a packed house with a bunch of girls and none of us plays football either. I'm sure we'd stink if we ever tried. Anyway, if you change your mind, feel free to join us. The more the merrier. I can give you my cell phone number, um, just in case you need directions. I don't mind. I mean--*just in case.*"

"I'm pretty sure I won't be able to make it tonight, Dallas. Like I said, Mom's been out of it lately and she could use the extra help--around the house I mean. Plus, the battery in my old truck's been giving me some problems. I'm going to stop by *Sullivan's* on the way home and pick up another one. Mom says I shouldn't be driving around in this kind of weather with a drained battery. She's right. Thanks again for the invite though. It sounds like you guys will have a lot of fun. Just watch out for the weather, Dallas. It gets *real* cold out here. Especially at night. Ungodly cold."

"Yeah, I've noticed. Not at all like living in the blazing southwest."

After our brief but first *real* conversation--where I batted my eyes incessantly and licked my scarlet lips relentlessly--Max waved a hearty goodbye insisting he'd see me on Monday and we'd discuss the night's victory or loss--whichever occurred. Before heading for his snow-covered ride, however, he turned around wishing me and my cheerleading skills good luck one more time. I was grateful--considering it would be my first time cheering in a game. Before he could take any more steps toward his faded truck, however, I reminded Max not to forget about the quiz over Custer's last stand scheduled for Wednesday. He laughed suggestively thanking me for the heads up--calling me an "*angel.*" It seemed Max had forgotten about the test--claiming to be more of a science guy than a history buff. I was pleased our flirtation ended with Max referring to me as an angel--*his angel.*

Luckily for me, even though it was frightfully cold, my cheering abilities went off without a hitch--or spinal injury. I was finally getting it down. After arriving at the thriving pizza place afterwards, snuggled warmly inside a floor length tufted down jacket and black suede *Ugg* boots, I found myself scouring the swarming teen hangout for signs of Max. No such luck. I guess he really did have to go home and chop wood. *What a waste.*

After the game ended, which the *Flying Eagles* won, Seymour's was rockin. Despite the loud music and even louder teenagers, I heard someone purring into my left ear. "Hey Dallas, wanna dance?" Alex, Blake's obnoxiously persistent best friend, was hot on my heels and ready to party.

"Um, well, I suppose so. Sure, I'll dance with you Alex. Just give me a second. I need to finish this slice of pepperoni."

"Awesome. Hurry up though. I love this song," Alex roared, gyrating his sculpted physique from side to side to the beat of the music. Alex's biceps were thick and I couldn't help noticing the smallish black and red tattoo on his left forearm (a scorpion I think) when he reached for me. Alex was a good-looking guy. Although vertically challenged for an athlete, he was muscular and bulky. His angular face and jutted chin were unusual--yet attractive-- and his jet black hair and coal eyes made Alex appear more mysterious than he actually was. Despite my frequent blow offs, he grabbed my free hand and we trotted towards the tiny but packed wooden dance floor. *Let's Get It Started in Here* by *The Black Eyed Peas* was blaring over the loud speakers and impulsive kids were high-fiving each other out on the glossy oak floor. Ever since *Laguna Beach* aired on *MTV*, *Let's Get It Started...*had become a major hit everywhere and Beckley was no exception. Out on the vibrating floor, every well-dressed girl did her best Fergie imitation--shaking her bottom violently--in hopes of engaging her partner. The trance-like boys accompanying them, on the other hand, jerked around like Mexican jumping beans trying desperately to electrify their dates. Needless to say, I wasn't impressed by the at least twenty or so boisterous males showing off. Unfortunately, Alex proved no exception. Even though he was a cute enough guy with cropped tresses and fleshy pink lips, Alex just didn't do it for me as my thoughts were solely on Max--I still had hopes he would show up despite his earlier assertion not to.

"You did a great job tonight, Dallas. You *didn't* suck as much as I thought you would. Just kidding. Hey, you *really* were good. Practicing with Emily B. everyday after school paid off. You looked *hot* out there," he yelled above the growing crowd.

"Uh, thanks Alex--I guess. Should have been focused on the game instead of me though--you dropped *two* perfectly thrown passes in the end zone. I mean, I'm glad you only dropped *two*--it could have been worse. Much worse," I ribbed. A hint of sarcasm in my strident voice.

"Ouch. That hurts. You're harsh, Dallas--pretty, but harsh. I think you've been hangin' around Blake too much. You know, my incompetent best friend. He's harsh too. By the way, those two *perfectly* thrown passes *he* hurled weren't so perfect--not from where I was standing anyway."

"Chill out Alex. I'm just kidding. Ya'll were great--you included. I mean, beating them by twenty-one points in the first half. That's impressive. Very, very, impressive."

"*Ya'll were great.* Where are you from--Texas or something?"

"Ha. Ha. Very funny Alex--and *so* original. Like I haven't heard that one a million times since moving here."

"Hey, whatever, Dallas. Want more pizza? I'm still hungry. Let's sit down and eat--I could devour a live horse," Alex shouted over the maddening voices of energetic teens. A new selection blared on the stereo and Britney Spear's latest hit--*My Prerogative*--inspired a rush of eager dancers to the rowdy floor. They appeared in droves.

"Sounds good. It's getting hectic out here anyway--I can't even think. And the stench is overwhelming. All these smelly athletes," I joked.

Alex and I headed towards the polluted table where Emily B., Blake, and a mountain of other football players and their ditzy girlfriends sat chomping on greasy pizza and guzzling surgery sodas by the gallons. Nuzzled together in a semi-private corner, E.B. and Blake were carrying on a secretive conversation and I couldn't help wondering what or whom they were discussing. What was even more curious was the way Marie Francis stared at me from behind those trendy red-rimmed glasses. What's that about I wondered. Do I have toilet paper stuck on my *Uggs*? Pizza particles in my teeth? Is my chestnut hair on fire?

"Hey, Dallas. Why don't you sit over here. *By us.* Grab a stool or something," Blake insisted when Alex and I approached the fifties style Formica counter.

"Uh, sure. Okay. Hey, Alex, I'm gonna sit by E.B. and Blake. I'll catch up with you later." I lied. For what it's worth, I had no intention of spending the entire night with him. Heading towards the ratty seat Blake managed to seize when a snotty cheerleader stormed off, I sat down with the conspiring couple. I couldn't help noticing France's damming eyes were still following me. What's wrong with her anyway?

"Um, Dallas," Emily leaned over whispering into my receptive ear, "just thought I'd let you know--not that I care or anything--but Frances and Alex used to be a *thing*. They *dated* for a while. Well, for about a year and a half actually. They broke up on Halloween night. *This* Halloween. They got into a shouting match at the school carnival--near the dunking booth or something. She accused Alex of flirting with Stephanie Grey. Apparently, he was spending all his tickets trying to dunk her. Frances paid for *those* tickets. Anyway, she didn't really want to break up with him but Alex insisted he was sick and tired of her erratic mood swings. She gets kind of crazy sometimes--especially when she's jealous--*PMS* I think. Anyway, she's still obsessed with him. Just thought I'd let you know," Emily warned. A look of seriousness in her guarded expression.

"Yeah, Dallas. *We* wanted you to know," Blake sternly interjected--proud to be of assistance.

"Uh, thanks for the advice ya'll. I guess that's why she's shooting daggers at me. She's been glaring at me ever since Alex and I danced together. What should I do? Should I say something to her? I don't like Alex--he's nice and all, but I don't like him. Not like that. I was just trying to be polite. I didn't want to hurt his feelings. That's why I danced with him. Should I apologize or something? I don't want Frances to hate me. She seems like an okay girl."

"No. I don't think it would help. *Really*. Just give her some space, she'll get over it. No harm done if you don't like him. Besides, Frances will be okay. And you're right, she really is a sweet girl. Just a little insecure sometimes."

"I see. I'll back off then. Just let her know I *don't* like Alex. Not like *that*. And it wouldn't hurt to tell him that either. I don't have the guts to keep hurting his feelings."

"Will do," Blake reassured, wearing an empathetic expression. "He's not a half-bad guy though, if you decide to give him a chance. I know I rag on him a lot, but he's not half bad."

"I get it Blake."

Great, just what I needed; a freaked-out, melodramatic, psycho ex-girlfriend. I'd have to do something--like set up an intervention between the thwarted lovers. Maybe I could persuade Alex and Frances to get back together-- putting their sordid troubles behind them. It was worth a shot and now was as good a time as any to approach them.

*And I knew my vision of the garden of savage beauty
had been a true vision. There was meaning in the world,
yes, and laws, and inevitability, but they had only to do
with the aesthetic and in this Savage Garden, these
innocent ones belonged in the vampire's arms. Anne Rice.*

Chapter 4

Remembering...

Rose Elizabeth Reed had been dead for two years when
we packed everything we owned moving from Dallas,
Texas, to Beckley, West Virginia. And considering the
loss, my sisters and I were doing better than anyone could
have expected. I mean, we definitely missed her, Rose was
the love of our lives. However, adapting to a significantly
smaller house--four plush bedrooms to three--attending
new schools--the twins went to the middle school down the
road from WWHS--and being forced to make new friends
despite my inherently flawed personality, kept the three of
us--mostly me--busy. My heart-broken parents, on the
other hand, were struggling to deal with the death of an
angel.

For as long as I could remember, Mom and Dad had
always maintained a loving relationship and our sizeable
family functioned relatively normally considering the way
some of my friends' family members got along. My
parents claimed to have everything they ever wanted, great
jobs--Mom a respected school administrator and Dad a
successful real-estate lawyer--a beautiful house on a quiet,
tree-lined street (Pecans and Mesquites), and four grateful
daughters who worshipped the ground they walked on.
Following a routine sonogram, however, when my
devastated parents found out Rose was a Down Syndrome
baby, they hesitated to tell us about her condition as Mom
still had quite a few months left of pregnancy. After some
speculative thought and more than just a few conversations
in which they *falsely* assumed were private, they decided
that the earlier we knew about Rose's condition the better.
So, on a sunlit Friday afternoon, Dad gathered us around

the scratched and stained farmer's table in our bright kitchen and proceeded to tell us the daunting news. In a rather casual manner, not like most puffed up lawyers would have done, Dad filled us in regarding Rose's special circumstances.

"We're having a baby girl and we're naming her Rose after my mother. Mom feels great. She's perfectly fine. But the baby has Down Syndrome."

The Texas-sized, fully equipped mega kitchen was uncharacteristically silent for about two seconds. Caitlin, with her irritating voice, broke the unnerving hush.

"Um, okay, Dad. What's her middle name? Can it be Elizabeth? Please? Ashley and me like Elizabeth. Not Hailey--that's Emily's stupid idea. *Please* not Hailey Dad. Can her middle name be Elizabeth?" Caitlin shrilled.

"Yes, Caitlin. I like that name. *Elizabeth*. It sounds great with Rose. *Rose Elizabeth*. No offense Emily. I like Hailey, it's just that I like the name Elizabeth more. You don't mind do you?"

"No problem. Really Mom. Elizabeth is nice. Besides, Madison's middle name is Elizabeth--she'll be thrilled. I'm gonna text her right now. Can I borrow your cell? I'm out of minutes again--even my rollovers are used up. Madison's eating with her mom--*Olive Garden* I think. Angela's got her this weekend cuz her dad's out of town again."

"Tell her Rose and I say hello. The baby's been kicking all morning. I think that *Snicker* bar I ate about an hour ago really got to her. I should lay off of the sugar and caffeine."

Once the brief discussion ended, it didn't seem to matter that Rose had a *syndrome*. I mean, none of us is perfect, right? Look at Caitlin. She doesn't have a syndrome--she's just stupid.

We enjoyed Rose for four glorious years. She was a beautiful child with the sweetest disposition. Her wide eyes were blue-grey just like mine. However, Rose's hair was a brilliant blonde--almost white--like Dad and Aunt Nicole's. When born, she weighed a whopping eight pounds and eleven ounces--Mom's largest baby to date. I think Mom used Rose's *condition* as an excuse to over eat-- just a little. "This baby needs more nutrition if she's to make it in this crazy world," she would argue. Although no one objected her point. Mom got rounder and rounder-- her nearly five foot eight frame hovering around the two-hundred mark by the time Rose was born. Dad didn't seem to mind the extra weight. He was just grateful his two girls were okay. And they were. Mom was never discouraged about the fact that life would be more complicated with Rose around. Not because she had Down Syndrome, she was just getting older and claimed to have a few more responsibilities on her proverbial plate than she'd had when pregnant with any of the three of us. Mom knew her hectic job as an administrator would hinder her. Even though she loved working at the school Ashley, Caitlin, and I dutifully attended, unfortunately, the work was tedious requiring a great deal of concentration. So she did what any loving mother of so many daughters would do in her situation-- she quit.

Dad wasn't upset she'd decided to *retire* early. After all, as a real-estate attorney in a booming Texas market, he made enough money to support the soon to be six of us. He was just glad she wasn't upset about having to leave the myriad of good friends she'd made while working at *Dallas Academy*. Dad knew how much she'd loved being at the school we'd attended since our days as wide-eyed kindergarteners. Mom had liked being there with us; peeking inside our colorful classrooms when she needed a quick look at our angelic faces. She often brought sweets like half-eaten *Krispy Kreme* donuts and *Hostess Ding Dong's* to the cafeteria just in case our blood sugars were low or we needed a quick pick me up. My favorite snacks had been the cut up *Baby Ruth* bars she swiped from inside the employee resource room situated across the narrow corridor of her tiny office. Mom also snuck in an assortment of calorie ridden soft drinks conveniently hidden inside Styrofoam coffee cups--in case we needed an afternoon caffeine buzz--Caitlin always did get sleepy after lunch. I could do without the soda, however, I was more of a pink lemonade kind of girl.

Rose's premature funeral was brief and Mom and Dad requested an open casket service for saddened friends and family. It was unsettling, however, peering into her lifeless expression. She wore a floor length, pink satin dress with grosgrain ribbons hand sewn onto the puffy princess sleeves. Grandma Dolan, Mom's grieving mother, purchased a beautiful antique choker with a lone white pearl flanked by two rounded pink sapphires adorning Rose's vulnerable nape. She clutched a tiny white teddy bear and her pink ballet flats were tied neatly above her delicate ankles into perfectly formed bows. Rose's meticulously manicured nails sparkled with the glittery polish she loved so much. Caitlin insisted she be buried with an antique glass *Tinker Bell* ornament from the year's previous Christmas--a gift from Aunt Caroline--Rose's favorite relative. I wrote "I love you Rose" on a sheet of fancy lined stationary scented with my favorite vanilla musk and tenderly reminded Dad--too distraught to remember on his own--to place the heartfelt message inside her velvet-lined coffin before it was permanently sealed. Her petite, porcelain face reminded me of a delicate cherub figurine Grandma housed inside one of her many Cherry curio cabinets. "The quicker Rose made it to heaven"-- Mom sang--"the better. This world is too corrupt for an angel like her." *We all agreed.*

The weak are the most treacherous of us all. They come to the strong and drain them. They are bottomless. They are insatiable. They are always parched and always bitter. They are everyone's concern and like the vampires they suck our life's blood. Bette Davis, 1908-1989.

Chapter 5

Post-Game Jitters...

"Come on, Dallas. We're gonna be late! Get a move on, girl. E.B.'s waitin!" Blake yelled as soon as Caitlin opened the front door of our single-story, craft-style bungalow.

"Hold your dang horses," I shot back. "And shut *that* door, *Caitlin Millicent Reed!* You're letting the cold air in!"

"Shut your trap, *Emily Ryan Reed!* And get your lazy butt in here ASAP, your smelly boyfriend's waiting. You're such a stinkin' loser."

"You imbecile. I hope you choke on lunch today--or better yet--on breakfast!" I fought back. Meaning every venomous word I spewed.

No more Friday night lights. It was Monday morning and the frosty temperature hovered dangerously around the freezing mark. God, I hoped Blake didn't kill us in his sports car. The uneven roads were sure to be icy.

"Hurry up. Get in before we freeze to death, Dallas!"

Despite the frigid weather, Blake opened my side of the frozen car first--shaking off particles of dirty ice when he slammed it shut. I crammed into the Mustang, glad he'd heated the car's interior before picking me up. At that particular moment, I found myself wondering if I'd ever get used to the arctic temps *wet an' wild* West Virginia offered.

"The roads aren't as bad as they look, Dallas. The street crews got an early start salting them. They started around two-thirty a.m. I saw it on the local news. We should be okay."

"I trust you, Blake. Besides, if you do kill me, I won't have to take that science test over mitosis. And considering I didn't study much this weekend, that's not a bad thing," I nervously joked.

"Well, you could always go to the office and tell Mrs. Lamsens or Mr. Porter that you're sick. You know, to get out of taking the exam. Tell them you have cramps. Emily does when she's not prepared for a test. It works. I promise."

"I'll think about it."

I was pleased when Blake and I arrived at the school's hectic parking lot unharmed. I had to admit, his driving skills weren't as bad as I feared they might be-- considering the multiple dents on his car's haggard exterior. He was obviously used to driving in the snow and on ice. We didn't even skid once. Unfortunately, all this treacherous weather made me afraid of getting my own license. Even after leaving Dallas, where drivers are decidedly more aggressive than those in Beckley, Mom and Dad still insisted I needed to be seventeen before I could take the driver's test. Let's face it--I hadn't even enrolled in a course since arriving here. And they certainly weren't going to let me drive *their* cars with any frequency until a professional deemed it safe--not that I wanted to be seen commandeering Mom's worn out, bus-like minivan or Dad's lackluster, 1998 cream *Chrysler*--boring. Perhaps when the nasty weather improved, I could find a place eager to train inexperienced drivers like myself. In the meantime, I didn't want to think about it--not until the invisible sun reemerged and the treacherous roads were clear again.

"Hi, Blake. Nice shirt," Emily chirped as she slipped a welcoming hug around his willing waist. "Oh, and hey there, Dallas. What's up? You look pretty. You know we're playing *Capital High School* this weekend don't you? I'm sure Blake's already told you. Hope it warms up before game time. It's freezing out there!" Her enthusiasm was catchy.

Every morning as soon as Blake and I walked through the school's streaked metal and glass doors, Emily waited patiently outside of the shabby front office in order to greet us. Today proved no exception. Delighted to see her, Blake and I followed E.B. into the crowded cafeteria--reeking of soggy bacon and egg substitute--for some much needed steaming hot cocoa--a morning ritual for nearly all of Beckley's thriving student population. Emily was dressed casually in loose-fitting black jeans and stained *Uggs*. Almost immediately, I noticed the bright pink gloss covering her friendly lips and made a quick note to ask where she purchased it, when Blake wasn't around to roll his eyes. She looked refreshed considering the moist air that ordinarily wreaks havoc upon a girl's appearance. Her long blonde locks were loose today--no tight pony tail enhancing her European features. I especially liked how she'd made her outfit her own by sewing on a brightly sequenced letter "E" onto the outside of her green v-neck sweater. Both the "E" and the long-sleeved cotton shirt underneath were deep purple just like her quilted ski coat and matching woolen scarf. *She dressed well.*

"It had better warm up," I scolded. "Or I'm gonna turn into a freakin' icicle!" I shouted. Despite wearing Mom's hand-me-down cashmere gloves, my slender fingers still ached from the cold.

"You and me both, Dallas. I *never* get used to this weather. Growing up around here you'd think I'd be used to it by now. But I'm not. And neither is my mother. Daddy loves it though--even if he is a southern transplant like you. He's from Tupelo, Mississippi, but doesn't mind the snow. He's got tougher skin, I guess. Anyway, after the game on Friday night, we're all gonna go see a movie. Wanna come? Blake, Alex, me, Maggie, Shreya, Drezzie, Reagan, Marie Frances--the whole gang's going--about fifteen of us. Too many to name. *Spider Man Two* is showing at the Triplex on

Third. Alex will be there. Did I mention that already? He insisted I invite you. I saw him at *Old Navy* yesterday. He was thinking ahead I guess. *Way ahead.* He really wants you to come and you know what that means?" Emily snickered.

"Um, sure. I'll go to the movie. Just don't tell Alex I said yes or he'll bug me to death until then. He'll insist we sit together and share popcorn. He's a little bit of a pest you know."

"I'll hold off then, at least until after lunch."

"How generous of you, Emily. I wouldn't want you to do me any favors!"

"It's no problem. Really. No problem at all. By the way, I like your sweater, Dallas, turquoise and red look great on you. You should wear that color combination more often. Where'd you get it? The sweater I mean. The *Wet Seal?* I love their stuff. You should *definitely* wear those colors more often--makes your skin glow."

"Oh, thanks. Actually, I got it at a specialty boutique in Dallas--near the West-End. Mom likes to shop there, at least she used to. Half-off, I think. By the way, did you tell Frances that Alex and I are just friends? Did you tell her I don't like him? I mean, not the way she thinks. He's a friend. *That's all.* Just a friend," I pleaded, hoping Emily would note the steadfastness in my voice.

"Yeah. She said to tell you not too worry about it. She was just mad cuz Alex promised to dance with her at Seymour's on Friday night and never did. Anyway, she *swears* she's over him. I don't believe her though, none of us really believe her. And by the way, no, I haven't told Alex you don't like him. If you let me borrow that sweater sometime I'll think about it." Emily was attempting to bribe me. I could live with that-- loaning her my clothes--we were close enough in size, as long as she got Alex off of my back.

"You girls are weird. Besides, Alex doesn't like Dallas. He *can't.* He's a girl--haven't you seen his nails? He might as well paint them hot pink or something--

filing them down and trimming the cuticles is just plain weird--for a guy. That's why he can't play football. Can't catch a ball. His nails are too perfect. He's a girl," Blake mocked.

"What's that, dirt bag? Talking behind my back again? Are you calling *me* a girl? You with your baby-blue, *I Love Dolphins* sweatshirt on. *I'm* the girl?" Alex charged while joining the three of us for hot cocoa with marshmallows and burnt cinnamon toast.

"*Hey*, Emily got me this sweatshirt when she was on vacation at *Sea World* in San Antonio! I love this shirt. It's my favorite shirt! I always wear it after we win big. It makes her happy!"

"Yeah, Alex. It makes *me* happy. By the way, Blake, my baby sister picked that out for you as a joke. She bought it on sale from a street vendor. Apparently, no one else wanted it. She said if I actually got you to wear it she'd clean my room for a week," Emily laughed.

"Did she?"

"Did she what, Dallas?"

"Clean your room for a week?"

"Heck yeah. The Becker's don't lie. And besides, Blake couldn't put the sweatshirt on fast enough once I gave it to him. He loves dolphins! Haven't you noticed that about him?"

"Of course he does, that's because *he's* a girl. Not me. Me Big Strapping Male. Wanna see my muscles?" Alex flexed.

"No thanks," Emily shrugged.

Tired of the mindless chit chat about Blake's dorky sweatshirt, I decided to bail. "Well gang, I'm headed for class. I need to check something out with Mrs. Rice. I'm not sure if I did the right assignment for English. We've moved on from prepositions to participles to transitive and intransitive verbs. *My favorite*. Gotta love those verbs. Anyway, I need to keep my grades up if I'm going to keep cheering."

"Bye, Dallas," Emily and Blake moaned in unison. *So cute together*.

"See ya'll, I mean *you guys* later," I winked.

"See ya, Dallas. Hey, are you coming to the movie Friday night? *Spidee's* showing." Alex's burning question was right on schedule.

Third period rolled around and I was thankful. I had a lot I wanted to say to Max and Emily's generous complements about my turquoise sweater fueled my confidence. I felt good about the way I looked. My lengthy brown hair--layered at the ends--was brushed and straightened and I smelled awesome--vanilla musk again. My curve-hugging jeans were clean and freshly starched (thanks to Mom) and the excess denim was tucked neatly inside the fringed boots I'd elected to wear--hoping they weren't overkill. I made sure the black liner highlighting my smoky eyes wasn't smudged. I borrowed--without her knowledge of course--Caitlin's apricot blusher and lip gloss which complemented my peachy skin. The sterling silver bangles Grandma Dolan gave me for *Easter* jingled whenever I strolled down the congested halls. My second-hand leather bomber jacket completed the edgy look. All I needed was Max to notice me. When he sauntered into class--two minutes late--Blake shot me a curious glance. I suspected he was catching on to the fact that I liked Max and I felt embarrassed by his all too-accurate assumption. A few seconds after Maxwell's anticipated arrival, Mr. Tennyson--our ornery principal--entered the stuffy classroom with developing news. It seemed Mrs. Lane had left the building rather quickly--wasn't feeling too well or something. One of the students saw her puking inside the girl's bathroom. *Disgusting.* Ignoring the unsolicited remark, Mr. Tennyson announced that a senior student aid would fill in. He also recommended we use this time wisely and in order to make that possible, he turned the next twenty seven minutes of history class into a make-shift study session--upon which we were advised to study.

"Can we pair up?" an acne prone boy in the back of the unadorned classroom questioned as soon as Mr. Tennyson left the room.

"Uh, sure. I guess," the aid replied--his squeaky voice slightly agitated. Upset he had to stop reading from his worn out copy of *Shane* in order to answer the boy's burning question, the aid's voice was gruff. "Just don't make too much noise," he grumbled. "I don't want Mr. Tennyson coming back and yelling at me."

"We'll be super quiet," the class unanimously agreed.

Blake shot another probing look. However, he seemed to sense that I didn't want to sit with him, turning his head towards the skinny, red-headed girl behind him instead--Antoinette Wiley or Tony for short. Blake was right. I *didn't* want to sit with him, I wanted to pair up with Max. Not wasting any of the precious time merely *contemplating* doing so, however, I bravely signaled towards Max as soon as the coast was clear. He grinned and waved back. My body quivered at the sight of him acknowledging me. The next thing I knew Max was plopping his statuesque body into the empty desk beside mine and my breathing increased. Since the back of the plastic chair attached to it was cracked and loose, students avoided sitting there--a fact that pleased me--at least on this particular day.

"How was your weekend?" he whispered--leaning in closely. My anxious palms began sweating.

"It was great. I picked pebbles out of my rubber work boots all day long on Sunday. Dad had me shoveling snow and clearing sidewalks. What fun," I joked--leaning in just as closely to him. So close, in fact, I could smell Max's breath on my face--um, minty I thought. His musky cologne wasn't bad either.

"Welcome to West Virginia, Emily, shoveling snow is our national past time," he winked. *For a minute, I had trouble catching my breath.* I was glad he'd called me Emily, as I hadn't quite gotten used to the nickname Dallas yet--although it was starting to grow on me--

much to the chagrin of my parents. But it still felt awkward at times.

"What are spring and summers like around here, Max? *Please* tell me they're warm! I need them to be warm. I miss the hot Texas sun on my face."

"Oh, they're warm all right. And wet. And nasty. Humidity sucks *almost* as much as the snow. You'll see," he laughed--his friendly eyes crinkling when he did. *I loved the peaked arches of Max's flaxen eyebrows.*

"Can't wait. Hey, where do you live?" I questioned-- still leaning in and shocked by my forwardness.

"Not too far from here actually. I live up the road about two and a half miles--close to the New River Gorge. It's frozen over right now. We have a small house on about twenty acres. We grow Christmas trees-- *Snow's Christmas Tree Farm*--and we also raise fresh herbs and vegetables in the summer. That's how Mom makes a living. She also grooms dogs in our basement. Only small breeds like poodles though--a few per week-- not too many. She's too busy with the farm. Since my dad left, she's been growing evergreens and pursuing her grooming business on the side. She works both jobs in order to keep up with the mortgage payments. She didn't want to let the land go when Dad left. So when he did, I was about a year old I think, she quit her job as an LVN to take care of the place. She only started her grooming business a few years ago. She's helping me save for college--med school I hope. I want to be a Cardiologist. I shovel a lot of snow and work in the science lab for extra cash. I try to stash away as much of my earnings as I can," Max explained--in great detail I noticed.

I was surprised by how candid he was. Max didn't seem at all reluctant about telling me his mother and father split when he was young. *Or* that they were experiencing financial difficulties since the breakup. *Or* that he worked feeding animals at the school in order to save for life as an undergraduate. I couldn't believe his honesty--considering we barely knew each other. I had a hard enough time admitting to anyone about the troubles plaguing my own family since Rose's premature death. As a matter of fact, no one in West Virginia knew anything about Rose or that we'd moved here to escape the painful memories surrounding her loss. We'd barely put out any pictures of Rose--just a few generic family photos here and there. Mom wasn't ready. I couldn't say that I blamed her--I wasn't ready either; seeing Rose's innocent face was heartbreaking. Some images were better left in Texas.

"So you're an only child then?" I whispered. Didn't want to infuriate the power hungry aid.

"Yeah. After Dad left, Mom never, uh, got *involved* with anyone again," Max stuttered. I wondered why he suddenly seemed uncomfortable. "She misses him too much I guess. They never speak--we're not even sure where he is. Even his own family doesn't know where he ran off too. Not that we talk to them either--*his parents are dead*. I've never even met them. Mom insists I'm better off. I guess she's right--considering no one else from his side has tried to contact me. Not even the aunt who raised him."

"Oh, I'm sorry to hear that Max, you must miss him a lot. I would. I couldn't imagine not seeing my dad." My sympathetic voice grew louder and the grouchy girl sitting in front of me shot a look of blatant disapproval-- she was almost as mean as the senior. I adjusted the volume in response to her glare.

"I couldn't imagine not seeing Grandpa Reed. *Or* Aunt Melanie. *Or* my favorite cousin Broderick. Our family is close--especially on Mom's side. I'd miss them too much." Oops, there I went again, forcing my wide foot into my narrow mouth. When would I ever learn?

Max continued our dismal conversation despite the awkwardness now present between us--thanks to my unintended bout of insensitivity.

"No, um, not really. I don't miss him. I mean, I don't even remember him. Like I said, Mom disposed of his pictures after he left. She hates to be reminded.

"I understand. I don't blame her for getting rid of those photographs. Too depressing."

For a brief moment, I considered whether or not to tell Max about my precious sister Rose and why I couldn't bare to look at pictures of her either. I decided against it. However, I understood his mother's reluctance to dredge up the past.

"So, what about you, Dallas? Got any brothers or sisters?" Max quizzed, smiling widely despite my insistence that unlike his, my family was tight.

"Unfortunately. They're mutant twins. Ashley and Caitlin. They're three years younger than me. Identical twins. Mirror images of each other, like minds--and all that corny stuff."

"That would be cool--to have a twin. I always wished I'd had a brother or sister close enough in age to hang out with. We could share bunk beds, climb trees, and build a fort. You know, pal around. Plus, it gets pretty tiring chopping all that wood by myself," he joked. I was glad to hear him laughing again.

"I understand. I don't know how you and your mom keep up with twenty acres. We can barely keep up with one."

"Shh. You guys need to keep quiet over there. You're getting way too loud," the ruddy aid scorned.

Max and I continued chuckling underneath our breaths. However, we hated causing trouble.

"Hey, where do you go for lunch, Max? I never see you in the cafeteria."

"Oh, I hang out in the science lab. Mr. Smith lets me do research in there. I don't have a computer at home so he let's me borrow his--I mean the school's. Besides, it's warmer in the lab--have to keep all those exotic animals alive. You should come in sometime--hang out with me. Chinchillas aren't the best lunch partners, especially since they're nocturnal. Although *Franco's* not too bad."

"Maybe I will. You never know. I might surprise you one of these days. *Maybe* even today. And who's Franco?"

"That would be great. Oh, and you'll meet Franco whenever you join me." Max rested his long arm across my delicate wrist and my entire five foot seven frame tingled when he did. I could feel my cheeks flushing as the crimson blood rushed to my weak head.

"You two are going to have to separate. I mean it. You're disturbing the entire class now!"

"We'll be quiet. We're really sorry," Max pleaded with bright, endearing eyes. Had the aid been female, *she* would've easily forgiven him.

The goofy senior (dressed in a bright plaid shirt and khaki pants at least an inch too short), blasted a nasty gaze meant as a final warning. It seemed we were overstepping our boundaries by continuing to talk despite his previous threats. Max and I got the message, promptly shutting our chatty mouths. We didn't want to spoil things for the other well-behaved students and wind up being labeled bad apples. So during the remaining fifteen minutes, we pulled out our raggedy textbooks and proceeded to study. Actually, I spent the final moments of class trying to decide what I would tell Emily and Blake so that I could ditch them at lunchtime in order to dine with Max. After all, I had a date to keep--and I intended to follow through with my plans-- *our plans*. Chinchillas or not.

"*Where'd* you say? The science lab? Make up work? But you haven't missed a day of class since moving here, Dallas. What kind of make-up work is Mr. Smith giving you? What the...? And why lunchtime? That doesn't make any sense. We haven't had homework in over a week. We're reviewing for finals for goodness sakes. I don't get it," Emily drilled. "Can't he give you a study sheet or something?" She wouldn't give up.

"Well, it's not *exactly* make-up work. Mr. Smith wants me to *catch up*. Finals are in a few weeks and he wants to make sure I'm prepared. That's all. No big deal. Besides, he's giving us that quiz over mitosis on Wednesday and I can study while I'm in there."

"Whatever, Dallas," Blake mused, rolling his suspicious yet determined eyes at me. "She's not going to the science lab to *study,* Emily. Are you, Dallas? Tell Emily what's *really* up. Max is in there. *Maxwell Snow,*" Blake oohed and awed. "You know, the braniac extraordinaire. He's always there at lunch, concocting or something. Besides, the school pays him to feed the animals. That's why he's always *in* there instead of *out* here in the cafeteria. He gets paid to help Mr. Smith. And since Dallas likes Max--that's the real reason she's meeting him for lunch--she thought she'd ditch us so they could have a secret rendezvous. I'm smart, girls. I know things. *These* kinds of things. Keep that in mind, Dallas."

"What a pain in the butt you are, Blake. I didn't say I was going to be *alone* in the lab. Mr. Smith already told me Max would be there. He's going to tutor me. Besides, you don't know everything. You just think you do," I shot back--half teasing of course.

"Oh snap, Dallas," Emily gushed.

"Whatever, Dallas. You guys are *sweet* on each other," Blake countered batting his eyes. "I can tell. I have two classes with both of you in them and all you do is stare at each other. You can't wait to get here in the mornings so you can see Max. I'm very observant. I am the eyes and ears of Woodrow Wilson. Fear me."

"*Sweet* on each other. What year is this? 1952? Anyway, whatever. You don't know what you're talking about--you're such a dork. I'll see ya'll later. And, Blake, mind your own business. I'm going to science."

"Hope the leeches don't eat you up--and I don't mean the disgusting ones in Mr. Smith's specimen jars!" he yelled as I quickly exited.

I was thankful to leave.

"Hey, Dallas. Check this out, Franco's cleaning himself," Max grinned as I made my way through the metal door. Max's lucent teeth gleamed against his faultless skin and I couldn't help noticing how adorable his blonde curls were--*again*. Or that his azure eyes were as clear blue as Emily B.'s. They could almost pass for twins.

"I thought those hairy creatures were nocturnal? Why is Franco cleaning himself so early in the day? Shouldn't he be sleeping or something?" I drilled--grossed out by the stench of his dirty, three-story cage. Although the view of Max was excellent from where I stood, the odor permeating the tight space was revolting.

"Franco's on a different schedule than most chinchillas, Dallas. With all the noisy kids running around for nearly eight hours a day, he doesn't get much sleep. And the fluorescent lights above are distracting."

"Oh. I see. Poor little guy--maybe if we eat quietly he'll be able to catch some zzz's. Try chewing silently, Max. We don't want to disturb the little guy," I chuckled--pressing my hands against his wire cage. I pretended to like him.

"Maybe," Max agreed. "Good thing Mom packed vegetable soup and bagels today. Nice and quiet. Unless I slurp the broth of course. I better not slurp." Max paused for a moment before deciding to change the subject. "Hey, I thought maybe we could meet up after the game on Friday night. If you'd like too, I mean. Maybe catch a movie or grab something to eat in town. If you don't already have plans."

"Sure, I'd love to, Max. Some of the kids are going to see *Spider Man II*. We could go--to the movie I mean. Or if you'd rather do something else...," I stammered. I couldn't believe my luck; Max was asking me out causing my knees to nearly buckle.

"Well, I'd kind of like to hang out by ourselves--just the two of us--if that's okay. You know, get to know each other better. Besides, I like your company, Dallas." Max was flirting.

"Um, sounds great. That really *does* sound great, Max. We could meet back at the school gymnasium. I'll be there anyway, helping the players unload equipment.

We could leave from there. It's up to you. Whatever's easier," I insisted as coolly as possible.

"Yeah. That'd be fine. I'll meet you near the western entrance of the gym out in the parking lot around ten. Will that give you enough time to help the team unpack?"

I shook my woozy head *yes*--trying not to hyperventilate. Max noted my agreement unaware that I couldn't breathe.

"We'll grab some food in town. I know the perfect place. Do you have a curfew?"

"Midnight." I was lying of course. My curfew was eleven-thirty p.m. on the weekends. I would have to do some serious begging in the meantime in order to sway my guarded parents.

"Great. There's a Mexican place by *Saint Mary's Hospital*--my mom used to work there as a nurse before she met Dad. You like Mexican food--right?"

"Doesn't everybody? I mean yes, I love it. See you in the parking lot Friday night, Max. Ten p.m. sharp. I can't wait. Really. It'll be fun," I sang in the calmest voice I could muster. However, my stomach was doing cartwheels.

I so very nearly took you then. There was only one other frail human there--so easily dealt with. Edward Cullen

Chapter 6

Night On The Town...

I spent the rest of the humdrum week anticipating my pending date with Max. However, as much as I loved the idea of eating refried beans dripping with cheese and onions deliciously smothered in spicy salsa, the idea of *possibly* becoming gassy freaked me out. I decided I would order tortilla soup with a side of guacamole instead. Another worry was how my overly protective parents would react when I told them about my first date since moving to Beckley. I also wondered how I was going to convince them to extend my curfew by thirty extra minutes on the night of our rapidly approaching date. And while increasing my popularity-reducing curfew from eleven-thirty to midnight wouldn't ordinarily seem like such a big deal, considering I was in a new state, a new town, attending a new school, *and* going out with a boy they'd never met, the task seemed insurmountable.

"Mom, you know on Friday nights how the gang goes out after the football game? Well, uh, this week, we, I mean *I*, am going out with just *one* of the guys--just the two of us--for dinner," I stumbled. "We're going to a Mexican Restaurant in town. Max says it's good--his name is Max by the way. Maxwell Snow. And I was hoping I could stay out a little bit longer than usual--like maybe until midnight or something?"

"Midnight? That's a little late don't you think, Emily? You and Christopher always managed to make it home by eleven-thirty in Dallas. Why midnight? What's so special about *this* boy that you have to spend another half of an hour with him? Is he a movie star or something? Did he win *American Idol*? Is he captain of the football team? It's not Blake is it? I thought he was dating Emily B. Isn't he dating her?" Mom drilled.

"Of course he is. And no, he didn't win *American Idol*. Fantasia Barrino won. Remember? And she's a girl. You know, a female?"

"Oh yeah, of course she did--I remember now. Such a pretty voice. So, midnight, huh? Better bug your dad. I don't mind, but you better get his approval first."

"Awesome! I'll ask him when he gets home from the office tonight. Awesome, Mom! *Thanks*!"

Life in West Virginia was turning out to be sweet. I was a cheerleader with a respectable group of friends--except for Alex, of course, he was *almost* as pesky as Caitlin and Ashley--and I had a date scheduled with an amazing guy. *Life was good.*

Unfortunately, things didn't go over as easily when I hammered Dad to extend my curfew. Needless to say, my request for an extra thirty minutes was getting the ax.

"*No*. Absolutely *not*. What is there to do at midnight that can't be done by eleven-thirty? Same curfew Emily. *Don't* be late."

"Wayne, why can't she have an extra half of an hour? It's just midnight--no big deal. Another thirty minutes--come on."

"The roads are icy around here Kelli. Or haven't you noticed yet? And most of the businesses close by eleven. If they had trouble--car trouble or something--they'd be stuck out in the cold," he grumbled--unaware of the turned shoulder and pointed nose he was now getting from Mom.

"We *have* cell phones Dad. We can always call a tow truck or something. Or 911. Or *ya'll*. I mean, what's the big deal anyway? It's just another thirty minutes--like Mom said. Please?"

"Look at the loser, Ashley. What a stinkin' loser--begging Mom and Dad to let her stay out all night with her stupid boyfriend. *Does Christopher know yet?* She'll get in trouble Dad, losers always get in trouble!"

Caitlin screamed. Then she stuck her disgusting tongue out at me. Dad couldn't see that part, of course.

"Shut up, Caitlin. You're the loser. You and your Freddy Krueger tongue. Stay out of my business *Satan,* I mean *Caitlin,*" I fired--shooting multiple daggers her way.

"Emily, be nice to your sister," Dad quipped. "You're supposed to be setting an example for Caitlin and Ashley. You're the oldest. Straighten up!" Dad was yelling now, something he did quite a bit of lately--or at least since Rose died.

"Wayne, Caitlin started it. *Not* Emily. She's just fighting back. Give her a break. She's been under a lot of stress lately--with cheerleading practice and attending a new school. It's not easy being a teenager. Especially with all she's been through over the last two years." *You know what I mean, Wayne--Mom's redolent look and serious tone insinuated.* "Let her stay out until midnight. It really isn't a big deal. We're talking thirty extra minutes," she persisted.

In addition to losing Rose in a mysterious manner, Mom was also referring to the potentially fatal way I'd chosen to deal with Rose's death in Dallas--after all, *I'd nearly died myself.*

"Jeez. Okay, okay. If it will get *both* of you off of my back," Dad backed down. "But if *anything* happens to her, Kelli, it's on *your* head. I mean it. Not *mine.*"

Ouch. We all knew what Dad meant. He'd always blamed Mom, at least to some degree, for Rose's death. *"Ya'll should never have eaten at that restaurant, Kelli,"* he insisted. *"We should have been waiting for him at home."* Was Dad *also* insinuating that Mom was somehow responsible for the foolish way I'd reacted after Rose passed? *Mom had nothing to do with my momentary lapse in judgment.*

"Fine," Mom snapped, turning her head around faster than Linda Blaire in *The Exorcist.* *"I'll* deal with whatever happens. And if something does go wrong, you can blame me--ag*ain*. All of you," she glowered.

Double ouch.

"You're not coming with us to see *Spidee*? What's the deal, Dallas? Are you grounded or something? What's up?" Alex prodded--nosy as ever.

"No, Alex, I'm not grounded. I've just made other plans. Is that okay with you? Do I need your permission or something--to make other plans?"

"Yeah, actually you do, considering *I* asked you out first. *Who* are your plans with? What's *his* name? Do I know *him*? Does *he* play on the team? Are *you guys* sneaking around behind my back?"

"No, Alex. And no, he's not on the football team but you do know him. I have plans with Max. He's in my third period World History class with Mrs. Lane. We're going out to eat. That's it. Nothing cosmic," I stammered. "Not that it's any of your business."

"What? That *freak?*"

"*What* did you call him?" Before Alex could answer, Blake jumped in defending Max as well as my decision to date him.

"Oh come on, Alex. Max is not a freak. Just because he doesn't play football, that doesn't make him a freak. He likes school--science and stuff. He wants to be a doctor or something like that. He's got ambition. Want me to spell the word? A-M-B-..."

"Shut up, Blake," Alex rudely interrupted.

"You shut up dude. Anyway, Max likes to study. That doesn't make him a freak, you know. Jeez. Come on, we've known Max since kindergarten. He's a good guy. Everyone likes him--especially Dallas. Leave em' alone. They're in *love*," Blake ragged--shooting googly eyes at Alex--he was always doing that.

"What the...since when? Since when are they in love? And why am I the last to know? And *yes,* he is a freak. Any guy who hangs out in a science lab all day is a freak. What? Does he like eating bugs or something? He's weird. That's just weird. Doesn't play sports? Is he some sort of pansy?" Alex crudely persisted.

"He could whip your butt anytime. The guy's got at least three inches and twenty pounds on your girly frame. You look like a wet noodle. And you run like one, too. That's why we lost the game tonight, you idiot. You run like a wet noodle," Blake hissed--a hint of frustration in his miffed voice.

"We did *not* lose the game. We beat them by two points. Just because we didn't clobber them like last week doesn't mean we lost, butt face," Alex angrily retorted. "Besides, if Max is so stinkin' big *and* tough *and* strong, why doesn't he play football? What's he scared of, getting his girly science hands dirty or something? You're right man, he isn't a freak. He's a *girl*."

"No he's not. He doesn't play because he doesn't want to share a smelly locker next to yours. You stink, man. Like a pair of dirty socks. Take a shower, dude!"

"Stop it you two. You're getting on my nerves. Hey, Dallas, brush your hair--he'll be here any minute. It's almost ten o'clock. And put some lip gloss on. Want to borrow mine? I've got cherry flavored *Lip Venom*. It's in my purse. Blake, hand me that *Coach* bag!"

"Yeah, I'll take some gloss. And thanks for the brush, Emily. I forgot mine again. I'm always doing that. How do I look? Better I hope."

"Great, just shake the dead grass off the backside of your outfit. You fell down quite a few times tonight, Dallas. I think we need to practice more. Let's meet up at my house again tomorrow morning. I'll call Brianna and Katherine--let them know we're practicing. You can tell us *all* about your date then," she giggled while spritzing me heavily with *Peach Fuzz* body spray.

"Will do. Hey, I think that's him pulling up--in that truck. Do I look okay? I'm going over there and I *don't* need an escort, Alex. I'll see ya'll later. Wish me luck, Emily."

The look I got from Alex was not favorable and I was glad I'd decided to walk to Max's truck unaccompanied.

"I can't believe you're going out with him. What a bore!" Alex shouted as I quickened my step.

"Good luck, Dallas! Don't mind him. And have *fun* tonight! Don't do anything *we* wouldn't do," Emily yelled, smiling in Blake's direction.

I turned around just in time to catch her winking at him and then at me. But since I'd only known them for a few weeks, I wasn't sure what she'd meant by that last remark. In fact, I didn't *want* to know what Emily and Blake did together--when they were alone that is.

"Sorry about the messy papers, Dallas. I should have cleaned my truck out before leaving the house. I've been kind of busy lately. Between school and the tree farm, I barely have time to sleep." Max groaned. "And Mom's feeling sick again, for a few weeks now actually. She's not running a fever or anything like that. But she's definitely having trouble sleeping. It's happened before. I'm keeping my eyes out--don't want her to get overloaded with work."

"It's okay, Max, about the car I mean. I don't even have one. I can't even drive yet! My parents won't let me. They're worried I might end up killing myself. I'm not sure why they're so afraid; I've never had trouble the *few* times I've been *allowed* to practice in Mom's van. I'll probably drive fine when I finally do get my license. Anyway, I'm sorry about your mom, I hope she feels better soon. Really, I do. She's got a lot on her plate-- with the property and all--especially with Christmas approaching. I bet things are getting busy around there-- families choosing their Christmas trees already. Maybe Mom and Dad can pick one out for us. I'll ask. By the way, I'm glad it finally warmed up a little. I was beginning to think I would turn into a human popsicle. Tonight at the game I could actually feel my lips moving when we cheered. And my fingers didn't feel like they were going to break off when I landed my cartwheels. Hooray for warmer weather," I joked.

"No kidding," Max joined in. "Hooray for heat. Oh, and thanks again about my mom. I'm sure it's nothing. Just stress. She needs a good night's sleep and she'll be fine," Max insisted, trying to convince himself as well as me. "And you're right. Business is *definitely* picking up. People are buying trees from us left and right. I cut down three spruces this morning."

Max's scent was woodsy and I could smell him from where I sat. It was probably from the trees he and his mother raised. He looked handsome--more so than usual. Max was dressed for the occasion; his blonde hair was slicked back--and I could still see tiny curls forming around the ends. His neck was muscular and Max looked like a surfer--odd considering where we lived. His skin, not unlike Blake's, bore a slight tan and his nose sported a red tinge--a mild sunburn from working outside. Max's cerulean eyes were large and crystal clear. He looked healthy. Blake was right when he joked that Max was strong enough to take Alex; he was buff and his biceps were thick. And Max was tall. Incredibly tall--at least six foot two. Wearing skinny-legged jeans--Max's entire outfit consisted of a long-sleeved black turtleneck, a worn black leather jacket, and black and white *Nike* tennis shoes. Only his jeans were a different color. *He looked delicious.* Admiring his angelic face--his perfectly round face--I noticed a slight mark on the outside of his prominent chin. I didn't mind it though--scars were sexy--especially on him. Freshly shaven, his smooth complexion glowed and was blemish free--surprising considering his teenaged status. Some of his bottom teeth were slightly crooked, but they were bright white--just like the capped Appalachian Mountains surrounding us. Even tonight, Max's breath maintained the same minty smell present just a few days prior. I liked him. *A lot.*

Snapping out of my daze, I heard Max chuckle. "Earth to Dallas. Hey, you look pretty tonight. Maroon is *definitely* your color."

"Oh yeah, sorry about that. I didn't have time to change out of my uniform. I wanted to. I even brought some extra clothes with me. I left them in Blake's Mustang. But we got back to school later than expected--no time."

"Not a problem. You look great. I mean it, Dallas. Maroon *is* your color," his voice sounding more insistent this time.

"Thanks. I wish I could have changed though. This uniform is itchy--cheap material I guess."

"I guess," Max beamed--causing my body to tremble. "By the way, we're eating at *Jorge's*. They have pretty good food. I hope you like it. The owners are from Mexico--Mexico City I think. Authentic tasting from what I hear. The restaurant is colorful too--lots of ceramic iguanas covering the hot pink walls and lots of velvet paintings. There's a giant one near the dessert stand with a bull and Matador painted on it. It's kind of funny I guess. Not something you usually see around here."

"Sounds like you've eaten there before, Max. At the restaurant, I mean."

"Yeah. A few times. Not with Mom though. Mr. Smith introduced me to the place. He and Mom--Katie's her name--are old friends. He comes by from time to time to check on her. He's a good friend--to both of us. He's like a surrogate father I guess you could say. He talked Mr. Tennyson into paying me to help out in the science lab. It gives me some spending money--feeding the animals. Things are kind of tight at home."

"I understand. Being a single parent must be difficult for your mom. It's great that he looks after ya'll though. I'm impressed. I'll have to get to know him. Mr. Smith sounds like a great guy. She's lucky to have him and so are you."

"Yeah. She really is. For as long as I can remember he's been coming around. His wife is great, too. Sadie. Too bad they don't have kids--they'd make great parents."

I was always impressed by how forthright Max was--
at least when he was around me. That's why it sort of
surprised me that Max didn't appear to have a whole lot
of friends. I mean, I always saw him chatting with other
students and his face was a constant at our pep rallies.
Max even participated in a short skit once, in which a
few of the male students painted their faces gold and
white parading around the gym *minus* their shirts. It was
funny. They even carried handmade signs reading, "Rip
the shirts off *Cabell Midland*." I laughed when I saw
them--shirtless I mean. So did the rest of the crowd.
What I noticed, however, was that Max didn't seem to
have a *specific* group he ran around with. I'd seen him
with some chess club members--Thomas Weber and a
skinny kid named Andre. But he didn't appear to have a
best friend. Not like Blake did with Alex and I was
beginning to develop with Emily.

"If you'd like, I thought we could stop by the farm for
awhile," Max suggested after finishing dinner. Half-
eaten meat tacos spilled onto the square table and salsa
drippings soiled the standard red and white checkered
cloth. While attacking the generous spread, we'd made a
mess--that's for sure. Our chirpy waiter Trey needed to
remove the dirty plates that were stacking up.
"That would be great, Max. I'd love to see the farm,"
I beamed--excited for the invitation. I didn't want the
date to end. "Will your mom be there too?"
"Um, yeah. But I thought you could meet her another
time. In case she's not up to it."
"Oh sure."
"Besides, we don't have much time. Only about an
hour and a half before I have to get you home. Midnight,
right? Don't want to get you there late. Your parents
might not like that."
Max didn't realize just how right he was.

The ride to his property allowed each of us the chance to pry as much information *from* each other *about* each other as possible. I was only too willing to go first.

"So you don't play football and you like science. And you want to go to medical school after you graduate. Oh, and you like chinchillas and beef tacos. Is there anything else I should know about you, Max?"

"Um, well, hmm. I can't think of anything. I'm a pretty boring guy, Dallas. You might want me to take you home now," he playfully winked.

"Not on your life. I'm not budging. Not until you teach me how to chop wood. I've never chopped wood before. Can you help me?" I teased. "Chop wood, I mean?"

"Uh, sure. No problem. I can't think of a better way to spend a Friday night with a beautiful girl."

When we arrived at the farm, I couldn't believe how lovely it was. The trees were glistening from the solid ice weighing down their delicate branches and the full moon cast a silvery glaze over the noble landscape. Cypress trees, blue spruces, and pines graced the generous property. The view of the staggered vegetation was amazing.

"I love it! Max, it's stunning out here! You're so lucky!" I screamed--excitement fueling my voice.

"If you follow this dirt road, Dallas, all the way up the hill, that's where our house sits. You can't see it from here though. Too far. But it's up there, I promise."

"Oh I believe you. Maybe I'll get to see it sometime-- your house, I mean. I'm sure it's as lovely as the grounds are."

"It is. Mom likes to garden. She's got an herb garden up there. And a rose garden with lots of antique varieties. She likes English roses. Especially red roses. Everything's dead right now, but in the summer, she grows lemon basil, peppermint, rosemary, parsley, sage- -you name it, she grows it. The scents are overwhelming and the Monarch butterflies can't stay away. It's a beautiful garden, really it is."

"I believe you! I believe you! I can't wait to see everything--especially the herbs. Maybe Mom can grow some at our house this year. She doesn't have a green thumb though--not like your mother does. But herbs aren't too difficult to manage. Are they?"

"No, not at all. I'll give you some seeds--Mom keeps plenty around. She's got a green house too--full of hothouse tomatoes and *Boston* ferns. She loves ferns."

"That sounds great, I love fresh tomatoes. I can't wait until the weather warms up! I want an herb garden too!"

The ride up the steep hill was spectacular and Max drove slowly so I wouldn't miss a thing. He pointed out other trees--beeches, maples, firs, and oaks--making the landscape appear even more impressive. As we neared the small house, even though we didn't plan on going inside, I couldn't help feeling nervous. That is until Max grabbed my hand--causing my rigid body to suddenly quake. I hoped he didn't notice. *How could he not notice?*

"If you'd like, we can get out and take a walk around the property. It's not too cold. You can borrow my leather jacket. The lining is wool--it'll keep you toasty. Who knows, you might even see some bunny rabbits scrambling around. Maybe even a deer or two."

"*Are you serious?* A *deer*? I haven't seen a deer since my family camped out at Big Bend over two years ago! I'd love to walk around. It's beautiful out here. An oasis, really. It's like a post card or something."

Max stopped the late model truck and we climbed out. I was disappointed, however, when he let go of my hand. Of course he had to in order to unbuckle his seatbelt. My heart was beating wildly and I wondered whether or not he would reach for it again once we exited the truck. I was thrilled when he did--but first Max draped me in his warm jacket. *It smelled like him.*

"I want to show you something, Dallas--we're close to it. It's just around these trees. Watch your step. We're almost there."

The chill in the air was exhilarating. I clutched tightly onto Max's large hand and his long fingers intertwined with mine.

"Look, see it there. See the sign?"

"I do! Oh Max, it's beautiful! *Snow's Christmas Tree Farm.* It's so big!"

"Yeah. Before my dad left, he painted that sign for my mom. It's pretty much the only thing we have from him," a hint of regret in his deep voice. "I wish he could see the place now. Mom's done such a great job keeping it up. I think he'd be impressed. I guess we'll never know."

"I *know* he'd be impressed. You and your mom are artists--this place looks like a painting. And ya'll make such a great team. You'd have to be in order to keep up with *all* this. Look at it, this property goes on forever. It's incredible Max--just incredible!"

"Thanks Dallas. I'm glad you're finally getting to see it. I can't think of anyone else I'd rather bring here tonight. Uh, thanks, um, for coming," he stuttered. For the first time tonight, Max seemed as anxious as me.

The lump in my throat was huge making it difficult to swallow. I couldn't believe I was here, with Max, on this transparent night. My left hand quivered as he coupled it with his own. His fingers were long and his palms were warm. I felt safe in Max's tight grasp. Lightheaded, I could barely feel my feet resting against the hard, snow-covered ground. The glow among the trees was breathtaking allowing me to discern Max's perfect features in the light. I was in heaven.

Hand in hand, we walked a little farther up the hill, steadily towards his house, and true to his promise, we saw bunny rabbits, lots of them, scurrying in our path.

"They're *so* cute--and tiny," I exclaimed. "Look at them, Max, their teeny tails turned up. How adorable!"

We stopped just shy of his wooden house and I could see the peeling white picket fence meant to enclose the roses and herbs. Two large grey boulders flanked the hand-forged, iron gate only a few yards away from the home's front door painted a welcoming shade of green-- emerald green--just like the evergreens covering his land. A live Christmas wreath covered in red berries hung from the hinged door and two tall juniper topiaries, covered in tiny white lights, lit the entrance. Once again, I reminded Max that his property resembled a post card-- or something out of a *Norman Rockwell* painting.

Underneath a particularly large spruce, branches draped generously with thick snow and ice, Max stopped--rather abruptly--turning his large and powerful body towards mine. His eyes were amazing--twinkling like the far away planets barely visible in the midnight sky. Gazing deeply into mine, I could almost see my reflection inside his pupils. Clutching my chin inside his hospitable hands, Max turned my willing face towards his and kissed me. *Max kissed me.*

Part Two

Blood is thicker than water, and much tastier.
Anonymous vampire.

Chapter 7

The Day After...

Early Saturday morning, I leapt out of my double bed even though the feather down comforter draping my lean body kept me toasty. The temperature outside was freezing--*again*--and I winced as my bare toes touched the icy, wooden floor. But I needed to call Emily B. and tell her about my evening with Max--frigid weather or not. Clutching the tired receiver, I pecked anxiously at the faded numbers.

"Rise and shine, sleepy head! Early bird gets the worm--and all that corny stuff. Just get your butt up! And call me back!" I screamed into her expensive *Blackberry*. She also drives a 2001, *convertible* Lexus-- her dad's *old* ride. He's the only cardiac surgeon in Beckley--hence the fancy phone and wheels. I don't have a luxurious vehicle or a cool cell like Emily's. My crummy old, hand-me-down *Motorola* belonged to my grandmother Rose for what must have been a century ago. Its scratched up, worn out exterior is even cracking in places. Unfortunately, Mom and Dad refuse to replace the piece of crap until it dies--officially that is.

I left a garbled message because teenagers, much like me, rarely rise before ten a.m. unless it's a school day or they're excited following an *extremely* eventful date. It wasn't a school day. I only had to wait a few minutes, however, before the *antique* began vibrating.

"Okay, okay, Dallas--I'm up! What is it? Did the world end or something? Do you have skin cancer from all that *blistering* Texas sun? Did Caitlin run away? *Or did Max kiss you*? He kissed you--didn't he! I knew it. I knew he would! Blake's right, you guys are *sweet* on each other."

"Well, if you get your size zero butt over here I'll tell you *all* about it. My pathetic phone's making that crackling noise again--I can barely hear. Get over to my place so we can talk!" My voice was laced with anticipation and I could hardly breathe. I couldn't wait to tell Emily *everything* and I didn't plan on leaving out *any* of the night's juicy details.

"That restaurant--I mean *Jorge's*--was totally awesome Emily. I mean it; it was *really, really,* good, just like the Mexican food in Texas." I wasn't about to utter anything negative about my date with Max even if the cuisine was mediocre--too much lumpy *Kraft* cheese.

"Who cares about the grub, Dallas? I want details. Details, girl! Spit it out!" Emily gushed. "What happened *after* dinner?"

Spread out on top of my carved walnut bed--sporting a new purple and white polka-dotted cover--Emily and I huddled underneath the yellow afghan Mom knitted when I was three years old. The two of us spent the next few minutes gabbing about boys--specifically Max and Blake--giggling loudly while we did.

"Tell me *everything,* Dallas. I know the food was good, I got that part already--*boring.* But how was Max? Did he hold your hand, wrap his arms around your waist, run his fingers through your hair? Come on--tell me!"

"*Well,* after our *spectacular* feast at *Jorge's,* I pigged out on tortilla soup and guacamole salad--we drove to his Christmas tree farm--which by the way is *amazing.* On the way there, Max reached over and grabbed my hand. He grabbed my hand! I couldn't believe it. I was completely shocked. He just snatched it right up! I *submitted* of course, I mean, who wouldn't let Maxwell

Snow hold their hand for goodness sakes. His skin was warm. *I love his hands.* I felt so safe!"

"*Oh--my--god*--on the first date he snatched your hand--just like that! What a player, Dallas."

"He's not a player, Emily; he just recognizes a gorgeous hand when he sees one. And mine *is* gorgeous. I mean, just look at the perfect body it's attached to. *Can you blame him?*"

"Of course not. Blake did the same thing on our first date, only he squeezed my fingers so hard I thought they'd break. He's stronger than he realizes. Sometimes I think he's an ape--all that extreme football and monotonous weightlifting I guess. So tell me more. Surely you guys did *more* than just hold hands," she cooed.

"Well, actually *we did*. Now that you mention it, Max kissed me. *On the lips.* And I enjoyed the taste of his moist breath tremendously. Under the stars, close to the largest spruce on his sprawling property, he kissed me. Max turned his face towards mine and planted one right on my mouth. I was totally shocked. He's rather forward you know--not at all inhibited. I mean, before this date we'd only spoken a few times and now we've *kissed*. So much for the getting to know you period."

"Oh you guys *know* each other all right, Dallas. Kissing is the best way to get to know anybody! So now what? Another date pending I should be aware of?"

"Not *officially*. But I'm leaving Friday nights open just in case. And Saturdays. Even Sundays if he wants! Whatever Max wants Max gets--you can be sure of that. Anyway, I was thinking about inviting him to the game next week. Is it at home? Maybe we could meet up with you and Blake afterwards--you know, double date. Just don't embarrass me. I will kill you if you do. I mean it, death in the most painful of ways. Excruciating pain. You will suffer!"

"All right, all right, I get it. Chill out girl, Blake and I will not embarrass you guys. We promise. I can't say the same for Alex though. He's going to be angry when he hears about 'the date.'" Emily made air quotes with her petite fingers when she said *date*. "You'll have to break the news to him gently, Dallas. Very, very gently."

"Whatever. By the way, what do you know about Max? I mean, he's chatty enough, but I don't know much about his social life. You've known him since kindergarten; tell me about Max, Emily. *Tell me everything.*"

"Well, I have known him since we were babies practically. We even went to preschool together at *'Baby Genius'*. A lot of us went there--Marie Frances, Alex, Presley Higgins, Brandon Peters, Peyton, Bailey Cox--even Harrison Rice--Mrs. Rice's son. Not Blake though--he's no genius--that's for sure. But Max has always been bright. Top of the class--like you. You're in honors courses---you know what being smart is all about. Well, um, let me see, what else, he's tall, good looking, and sweet. I mean, I know Max, but I guess I don't *really know* Max. Understand what I mean? He's a wonderful guy, but he keeps to himself. Everyone likes him though. I've never heard anyone say anything negative about Maxwell Snow. But I never see him outside of school. I know he and his mom manage that tree farm by the new river gorge--we've bought pines from them before. She's a pretty lady--always has been. But Max looks nothing like her. He must favor his dad-- I've never met him. In fact, I don't think anyone has. Does he even have a dad, Dallas? Does he ever talk about him? Come to think of it, only his mom shows up at school functions. She's *really* pretty. Did I mention that? She's got long dark hair and black eyes and her skin is pasty white--maybe she's *Italian?* Quite a contrast, her murky eyes and pale skin. I don't think she gets out much. And she's vertically challenged. Nothing like Max, he's like six foot three. He should play basketball. His feet are giant--watch your toes, Dallas. Anyway, the last time I saw his mom was last year when Max gave a discourse in history class--Mr. Graves told us to use that word, *discourse*. Max was discussing the

Nazi's--totally wrong what they did to the Jews--how can people deny the *Holocaust*? Killing all those innocent people is just wrong. Anyway, Max's mom was the only parent who showed up to listen to our speeches. Katie's her name. She brought warm cider and a homemade pumpkin loaf for the class. I remember that because it tasted so good and it was like thirty degrees outside so we were glad for the hot drinks. Katie was quiet but pretty. The guys were oohing and ahhing over her-- Blake especially, his tongue was hanging out of his mouth. Such a loser sometimes. It was totally embarrassing, Dallas. *And gross.*"

"Oh, wow. I didn't get to meet her at the farm. Max says she's been sick. She's having trouble sleeping. He promised I'd meet her *next* time though--I'm counting on that next time."

"I get it, I get it! You guys are in love. So sweet, really, I'm pleased for both of you. Max couldn't have picked a better girl to date. Really, Dallas. I mean it. I think you two are perfect together. You have my blessing."

Thanks, Emily. That means a lot. Hey, wanna get some lunch? We can eat here or drive into town. I'll chip in for gas. All this chatter about Max is making me ravenous. I could eat a horse." *Where have I heard that before?*

"Lunch? It's barely ten o'clock. How about *IHOP*? Brunch sounds better anyway. I'm not much for horse meat though. Yuck. And yes, I'll take five bucks for gas--Dad's *Lexus* is a fuel hog and he's ragging on me about my expenses. He's threatening to take the *Visa* away if I don't slow down. Is five dollars too much for a donation?"

"I think I can handle that. And *IHOP* sounds excellent. I could go for some fresh blueberry pancakes and salty grits dripping in butter right now. Let me shower first, I smell like crap. And my hair's a mess! Look at me, Emily. I look like *Medusa*. Why didn't you tell me? Are you purposely trying to sabotage my reputation as West Virginia's newest hottie?"

"Whatever, Dallas. Take a shower and wash the stench of Max off. You're making me envious. He's *dazzling* you know!"

"Okay, okay. Give me fifteen minutes. And while you're waiting, pick me out something decent to wear just in case Max and his mom happen to be dining on Belgium waffles and loads of bacon. God, I'm hungry! Oh, I downloaded Britney's CD onto my IPod if you want to listen to *My Prerogative*. I love that song. Not a bad CD either--it's a shame she broke up with Justin Timberlake. *Now he's hot.*"

I showered quickly using more of the *Cupcake* body scrub Emily gave me (she's very thoughtful) and dusted my face lightly with medium bronzer--compliments my peachy skin tone. Not too much though, didn't want to appear like I was trying too hard--even though I was. Emily's face is similar to that of a famous supermodel's--flawless and perfect. Mine takes a bit more work, however.

On the drive to brunch, Emily and I imagined an entire double wedding--her in beaded white satin and me in yards of cream toile. Our eight bridesmaids--including Madison from back home--wowed attendees with strapless lavender gowns and the church's stage overflowed with pink tulips and wild orchards. Once inside the crowded and smoke filled restaurant, however, our cheerful moods changed. Sitting in a corner booth, knee deep in maple syrup and scrambled eggs, sat Blake and Alex. And despite their aromatic spread, it only took them a few minutes to *smell* us.

"E.B., over here, over here! You guys, hey, over here!" Blake screamed, humiliating us with his rowdy gestures and screechy voice. "Hey, Dallas and Emily, over here!" He wouldn't give up.

The hostess noted our anguish. "It's *okay* if you guys want to join them. I'll let the waitress know."

"Uh, thanks. We will. Sorry they're so noisy. We'll shut them up," Emily snapped--shooting Blake and Alex dirty looks. They didn't care.

"No problem. I'll let Daisy know you guys are ready. What do you girls want to drink?"

"I'll have a glass of two percent chocolate milk--organic please," Emily insisted, conscious of her petite figure.

"I'll take *Coke*. Um, *diet Coke*," I mumbled--trying to appear mindful of my own weight--even though it wasn't an issue.

"No problem. Here, take these menus. Looks like *they've* already ordered." The lanky hostess shot Blake and Alex—too busy pigging out to notice--a disgusted look.

"Sure. Um, thanks again," Emily and I groaned, embarrassed by the smacking sounds emanating from their noisy table.

"Ladies, ladies, have a seat. Grace us with your beautiful faces."

"Whatever, Alex. Eat your scrambled eggs. And Blake, the next time you decide to scream inside a restaurant, make sure it's not at me!" Emily's tone was serious and Blake noted her antipathy.

"Sorry sweetie. Was I that loud? I'm sorry. Here, sit by me-have have some Canadian bacon. You girls look hot this mornin'! How'd you know we'd be here?"

"We didn't, Blake. *Obviously*. Or we'd of eaten at *Owens*. We wanted some privacy. Anyway, I thought you'd be at church. Why are you here so early?" Emily grumbled--the smell of burnt coffee wafting in the stale air.

"Mom cancelled church today. We're sinners. She wanted to sleep in so I called Alex. I was starving. She wouldn't even fix breakfast. I had no choice but to eat out. Dad went to *McDonalds* instead--too cheap for *IHOP*. Anyway, Alex owes me twenty bucks. He's paying for breakfast you know. Order up, girls, he'll get yours too."

Shut up, dude. *I'm not paying c*uz I don't owe you any money. You owe me twenty bucks. Remember? I'll pay for Dallas' though. Whatever you want Dallas-- sky's the limit. Order up," Alex interjected, while sizing me up. *Good thing I wasn't on the menu.*

"That's okay, Alex. I can get my own."

"Awe, come on, Dallas. Let me get breakfast. It's the least I can do. This can be like *our* first date--breakfast at *IHOP*. Scoot in closer," Alex begged, patting the ratty leather cushion beside him. "Come on, next to me. *I've got this, Dallas*. Anything you want. *I've got this*."

"She said no, Alex! Jeez, you're so pushy! Give her a break. Besides, *Max* wouldn't like it if you paid. *She's taken,* you know. Give it up."

"Oh snap, buddy! Dallas is taken! Back to Marie Frances I guess."

"Shut up, puke face!" Alex quipped.

"You shut up, you moron," Blake fired back.

"*Both of you* shut up! You're so lame!" Emily was seriously agitated now.

"It's okay, Emily. Besides, they need to know how my date with Max went. If ya'll can shut up for like five minutes I'll tell you. Can you? Can both of ya'll be quiet for five minutes?"

"Yes," they groaned. Alex's voice was uptight as he slouched in his corner seat.

"Well that sounds great, Dallas. *Really.* I'm glad you like him. Max is a cool guy--quiet, but cool. You guys are good together. *Seriously.*"

"Thanks, Blake. I mean, we're not officially a couple or anything. But I do like him. I'd definitely like to go out again. Me and Emily are thinking about a double date next time. Are you in?"

"Sure. Just tell me when and where ladies," Blake winked in Emily's direction. "You know I'll be there. Anything for my two girls."

"Are you serious, dude? *Dallas and Max*? That's just weird. I mean, Max is a decent guy, but he's boring.

What do you see in him anyway? I mean it. Seriously, what is so special about Maxwell Snow?"

"Shut up, Alex. You're just jealous. Max is awesome. He's *smart*, funny, good-looking--*clean.* He doesn't smell like rotten gym shorts. He's going somewhere in life--he wants to be a doctor like my dad."

"Whatever, Emily. And I'm not the one who smells like crap. That would be your boyfriend Blake. He never showers you know. Besides, I was talking to Dallas."

"All of ya'll be quiet. And nobody here smells bad, not today anyway--not even you, Alex. And it was just one date! We went to a Mexican restaurant and his tree farm. I had to be home at midnight for goodness sakes! We only spent two hours together. It's not like we're getting married!"

Not yet anyway.

Sic Gorgiamus Allos Subjectatos Nunc. We gladly feast on those who would subdue us. Addams Family Credo.

Chapter 8

Back To Reality...

"Mornin', Dallas. Ready for another exciting week at WWHS? Get a move on, girl. Hey, you look *sweet--r*ed is your color. I think Max will like it--the sweater I mean. I certainly do. And you *smell* nice, like cotton candy or something."

"Put your tongue back inside your mouth, Blake. And it's *Summer Cupcake* body scrub you smell. I got it from your girlfriend as a gift for surviving her grueling cheerleading workouts."

"Yum."

"And Blake, don't embarrass me in front of *him*. Okay?"

"Deal."

During the awkward drive to school, Blake sensed my nerves and promised not to make a big fuss about my date with Max once we got to class. He also agreed to double up this weekend if Max was interested in pursuing our relationship further. I hadn't decided whether or not I would approach him about Friday night's game because I hoped Max would come to me first, *begging* for a second encounter. I felt confident he would ask me out again--I just didn't know when.

After we arrived at school, I couldn't wait for third period and my body flinched each time the bell rang. Max was on my brain--as usual--and my stomach quivered whenever I thought about him, specifically our first kiss. Blake's remark about my looking good in red sparked my confidence and I hoped Max would agree with his assessment. It wasn't long before I got my answer.

"Hey, Dallas. You look pretty today. I like your hair that way--pulled up on the side. And your sweater's nice too. And your ears look cute," Max teased, "I like your sparkly earrings. Are those tiny *Christmas trees* or something?"

I melted.

"Yes. Um, what's up?" I couldn't think of anything better to utter and I'm pretty sure I was stuttering.

"Are you ready for the exam, Dallas? I didn't study much yesterday. I chopped trees and then strung holly berries and leftover popcorn on garlands all evening. Mom loves Christmas time--I can't believe it's in two weeks. Every year she decorates the farm with white lights and live topiaries and bay wreaths. The place smells great. I think she went a bit overboard though, especially with the mistletoe. But she enjoys the holiday bustle and the customers like the atmosphere we provide. It's good for business. Mom even serves warm apple cider and homemade sticky buns while families shop for trees. Anyway, I'm glad we get to use our note cards for the test. I crammed as much info as I could onto them. By the way, are you meeting me for lunch? I brought enough for two. Mom packed peanut butter and jelly sandwiches on cracked wheat bread for the *both* of *us*. We've also got split pea soup with ham and carrots. You like peanut butter and jelly don't you? Mom made the jelly--cranberry spice. *Will you join me, Dallas*?"

"Of course I will, Max!" I belted--happy to get a word in edgewise. "And yes, I love peanut butter *and* pea soup. Mom *used* to make split pea soup with ginger and ground turmeric. Anyway, I'll see you later in the lab."

Considering the peanut butter and jelly fiasco that occurred when I first laid eyes on Max, I was surprised by his choice of foods--was he making some sort of statement? Was Max *teasing* me? It didn't matter. I was psyched about his invitation and the fact that Max brought lunch--peanut butter or not--proved he was thinking about me. What kind of sixteen-year-old boy does that for a girl? A romantic and thoughtful one--that's who. Max amazed me and I couldn't wait to snuggle beside him at lunch--munching on whatever else included in that brown paper bag he dangled like a carrot in front of my face. Anxious to join him, I stared at the oversized clock hanging on the cracked wall facing me hoping the hands would move a little faster. They didn't of course. Finally, at eleven fifty a.m., the bell rang and I nearly jumped out of my skin. Max left history class a few minutes early in order to feed the animals and was already waiting for me inside Mr. Smith's lab.

I rushed down the crowded halls toward the room. My books nearly went flying when I ran smack into a dazed freshman. When I got a few feet outside of the lab's front door--the glow of heat lamps radiating--I slowed my pace, didn't want to appear too eager. I caught my breath before entering the warm environment and tugged gently at the wire clip supporting my weighty hair. I wanted to look perfect for Max.

"Hey, Dallas. Over here. Check out Freddy."

"Who's Freddy?"

"Freddy's our newest resident. He's a rat snake. Give him a hug," Max hissed, waving Freddy's slimy body in front of me. "He loves pretty girls, you know. Especially ones from Texas."

"Not on your life. Keep that icky monster away from me!" I snapped--half jokingly of course. I didn't want to anger Max by shying away from Freddy, whom he obviously admired, but I wasn't about to kiss a snake. Not even for him. Thankfully, Max returned Freddy to his artificial habitat.

"So there's another football game this weekend Dallas. It's a home game I hear. We're playing *Lincoln County.* We *should* beat them--they kind of suck. Not unlike Freddy here. If you give him a raw egg he will *suck* it all the way down his narrow belly, crush it like ice, and digest the embryo. He's quite an eater you know. Better not get too close."

Poor baby chicken, I thought to myself.

"Nice. Just what I wanted to hear. Hope you didn't bring egg salad sandwiches for lunch. Wouldn't want to entice Freddy or anything."

"Good one, Dallas. Hey, about that game, wanna meet up afterwards?"

"Absolutely. I'd love to go out again. Same time and place?"

"Yes. But bring a blanket this time; we're dining under the stars."

"Wow! Do you mean it?"

"Yes. The weather is supposed to be clear this weekend and the trees are beautiful in the moonlight."

"I know they are! I'll bring a blanket for sure. Do I need to pack food?"

"Nope. I've got that covered. I'm a rather excellent cook you know. Mom taught me well. I hope you like *Italian*."

"Of course I do. I'll eat anything--except snakes," I teased. "I can't wait--really Max, I can't."

"Me either. So, do you like creamy Alfredo or marina with meat sauce on your linguini *al dente*?"

"Are you kidding? You can fix all that?"

"Sure can. And we're having broccoli and pea salad with *Tiramisu* for dessert."

So much for double dating with Emily and Blake.

The week progressed slowly and I couldn't concentrate on anything other than my pending *second* date with Max. Mom and Dad agreed it was okay to see him again and this time there was no argument over my extended curfew. I ate lunch with Max in the lab every day except Wednesday--I met with Mrs. Lane about some catch up work instead. Emily and Blake didn't seem to mind my hanging out solely with Max. Nor did Marie Frances--she was relieved to have Alex to herself again. Alex stayed clear of me and Max in the halls--didn't want to appear too desperate in front of us I guess--although it was already too late for that. I was pleased for the distance since he got on my nerves. I wasn't sure if Max was aware of the fact that Alex wished he was in his shoes. Alex shied away from him and I was relieved. I didn't want Alex upsetting Max by starting a verbal confrontation. As far as I was concerned, Alex and Marie Frances needed to rekindle their tired love affair leaving me and Max to ourselves.

Friday night's here. *Finally.*

"Too bad we can't double up tonight, Dallas. Blake and I could use a night under the stars. I'm sick of going to the movies or out for pizza every weekend. Where's the romance in that?"

"Don't ask me, Emily. So what movie are ya'll seeing tonight?"

"Don't laugh, Dallas. *Seriously.* We're seeing *Shrek Two.* Blake's so excited he's about to wet himself. He loved the first one you know. Stupid, huh?"

"Are you serious--*Shrek?* I'll have to ride him on that one. Maybe ya'll can take my *baby* sisters!"

"Whatever, Dallas. As long as he buys *two* jumbo buttered popcorns and a super-sized box of *Hot Tamales* we'll be okay. Oh, and lots of *Diet Dr. Pepper.* I love that stuff. I've been consuming it by the gallons lately," Emily gushed.

"I'm more of a *Coca Cola* junky myself. And I prefer *Gummy Bears* over *Hot Tamales* any day."

"Gotcha. Hey, you and Max have fun tonight. The weather's perfect. Did you bring the blanket like he asked?"

"Yes."

Emily and I bounced around like rag dolls inside the tattered interior of the crowded athletics' bus during our conversation. Football players stink. I couldn't wait to get to the school's gym in order to ditch the funky bus-- the odor was overwhelming. Despite the offensive stench, I was pleased we'd beaten *Lincoln* and hoped Max would be in a good mood courtesy of tonight's victory.

"Wow! Dallas, you look great!" Max raved as soon as he saw me--his cheeks blushing. "You didn't have to change clothes though. I don't mind the uniform. Really. Oh, here, let me take that blanket from you--it's heavy! This will be perfect. Hope it's okay if it gets a little dirty. Are you sure it's okay with your parents to use this blanket outside?"

"Yeah. Mom thought the woolen side would be perfect for us to sit on. It's okay if it gets a little smudged, she can wash it."

"Great, I can't wait to eat, Dallas. I'm starving. How about you? Did cheering at the game leave you famished? I bet you burned a bunch of calories, flopping around on the hard field like a frog. At least the weather was nice tonight. Let's head out to the farm. We've only got a couple of hours before curfew. My truck's parked beside the coach's green *Taurus*. Over there," he pointed.

"Awesome, let's go."

On the ride to his property, I wondered if I would meet Max's mother Katie tonight. *Would she be dining with us*? I didn't ask Max about her, however. I'd let him surprise me. Besides, I was too excited to think about Katie for long--I had more important things on my mind--like whether or not Max would seize my left hand *again*. I made sure it was free and strategically placed it on top of the truck's shabby cushion--just in case Max felt romantically inclined. *Killing Me Softly* by *The Fugees*--one of my favorite slow songs--played on Max's FM radio and the music must have put him in the mood. It wasn't long before he grabbed my open hand. *I was thrilled.*

"So, Dallas, are you nervous about my cooking? I made linguini with clam sauce instead of Alfredo and Mom packed homemade yeast rolls with rosemary and goat butter. Oh, and I changed my mind, we're having *cannolis* for dessert. Hope you're hungry."

"Oh, I am. And no, I'm not nervous about your cooking. I'm sure everything will taste great."

"You really do look wonderful tonight, Dallas. I love your cowboy boots. *They're cool.*"

Thursday, one day before our scheduled date, I ditched cheerleading practice in favor of clothes shopping with Mom and the twins. First, the three of us ate at a run-of-the-mill Chinese buffet in town, where Ashley gorged on soggy dumplings and cold sweet and sour soup. Mom, Caitlin and I feasted on overcooked rice and bland *moo shoo pork*. The food sucked. Afterwards, we headed for the packed but minimally-sized mall on Route Two.

"I like this one Emily," Mom chirped. "What about you?"

"It's okay. I'd rather have it in purple. Emily B. wears purple a lot and it looks great on her. I'll take it in purple."

"They don't have this sweater in purple. Better look somewhere else. How about the *Banana Republic* girls? Their clothes are cute. Let's head that way."

"I hate the *Banana Republic*," Caitlin whined. "Their clothes suck."

"Shut up, Caitlin. We're going," I snapped--sick of her constant complaining.

"You're such a pig Emily--or *Dallas*--whatever your stupid name is. You're too fat for their clothes anyway."

"Caitlin and Emily! Zip it! We're going to the *Banana Republic*. That's final!" Mom shouted--seriously perturbed now. Ashley kept silent--a wise choice on her part.

On the way towards the pricey chain boutique, Caitlin and I continued arguing despite Mom's growing frustration. As soon as we got there, however, I shut my mouth. Awed by the navy button-down pea coat and white cotton wrap that was displayed in the store's front window, I couldn't wait to get inside.

"That's it Mom. That's the outfit!" I shrieked. "Can I have it?"

"I don't know yet, Emily. Let's see how much everything costs."

Mom grabbed the nearest sales clerk who pointed us in the proper direction--too lazy to accompany us, I guess. The luxurious coat was marked down an enticing thirty percent and the dressy blouse was red-tagged an additional twenty percent off. The outfit was mine...

Snapping out of my daze, I answered Max quickly. "Oh, um, thanks Max. I love these boots, too. I've had them for a long time. I used to wear them on class trips to the Stockyards in Fort Worth. Rodeos are fun and I love visiting the Stockyards. Guess I'll miss out this year."

"Sounds fun," Max answered. "The rodeo I mean," his dazzling smile almost knocking my fuzzy socks off.

My chestnut hair was blown straight and Mom even splurged for reddish highlights at the mall. The navy pea coat fit perfectly; draped snugly around my rounded shoulders. The tiny brass buttons had miniature sailboats etched onto them. The coat's white piping accentuated the straight lines of the fleece cover. My faded *Calvin Klein's* were loose around my calves and I opted for tucking the excess denim inside my grey leather boots. The wrap-around cotton blouse emphasized my little waist and I added a synched black leather belt for good measure. My pierced ears were adorned with natural pink pearls dangling from white gold chains--an early birthday gift from Madison. Around my neck, a string of costume beads with a sterling silver clasp completed the ensemble. Lined heavily with charcoal liner--my eyes were smoky. The powdery grey shadow, swiped from Mom's messy makeup drawer, drew attention to my upper lids. Red stain highlighted my pursed lips and my teeth were bright--*Crest Whitening Strips.* I looked at least eighteen.

Max was equally handsome. Decked out in a waist-length, black leather coat--different from the one he'd worn on our first date--his plaid, button-down shirt was tucked neatly inside a pair of tan corduroys--they made a scratchy noise whenever he walked. He wore a western style belt with a fancy buckle. His blonde hair was slicked back--again--and his milky skin was freshly shaven. Max's cologne was stronger this time and he smelled heavily of cloves and musk oil. On his left hand, Max wore what appeared to be a white gold insignia ring with a purple stone--perhaps a family crest? I noticed a bottle of coco-butter hand lotion lay on the car's floorboard. *I couldn't wait to clutch his soft hands or feel them against my skin.*

"How about here, Dallas? Under the sign Dad painted. Is this a good spot to eat?"

"It's perfect, Max. There's just enough light from the moon to see what we're doing. It's perfect."

"Great. I'll throw the blanket down then. Would you mind moving those rocks out of the way? I want to be able to stretch out."

"Sure Max. The rest of the ground seems okay. I'm famished you know. I'm ready to eat."

"Awesome. I brought enough to feed the entire football team. Mom helped pack--we've got plenty of linguini, broccoli salad, and rosemary bread. So eat up."

"I plan on it."

The stars were bright allowing Max and I to set up dinner. After placing the thick blanket on top of the hard ground, we dove into the wicker picnic basket, carefully removing its fragrant contents. Since the night air was calm, nothing blew away. Max grabbed the container with the linguini sauce inside so it wouldn't spill out onto the cover. The food in the basket was surprisingly warm and the noodles were cooked perfectly. I couldn't wait to dig in. *I was that hungry.*

"These rolls are awesome Max. Your mom's a good cook. Does she enjoy baking?"

"Yes," he managed--his mouth full of broccoli and pea salad.

"My mom used to bake, but she hasn't done much cooking since we left Texas. We eat out a lot."

"Why's that, Dallas? Is she too busy or something?"

"Yeah, I guess so."

For a fleeting moment I considered telling Max about Rose and how she and Mom used to cook together--but I hated to ruin the moment. I wanted the night to be perfect. I decided the timing wasn't right.

"She's not working yet or anything. She's just busy getting the new house in order. Dad's job requires longer hours than it did in Texas. This firm is smaller, not enough lawyers. Since he's gone more, we eat out a lot. I'm sick of fast food. I miss Mom's home cooking."

"We don't eat out much--too expensive. Besides, Mom loves trying new recipes. And she's part Italian--she enjoys preparing large meals. Of course, we eat a lot of pasta dishes. But she also enjoys making vegetarian dishes and spicy curry like kabobs and lentils. Her tastes are varied--I'm glad. I'll eat just about anything. Except sushi--I haven't developed a taste for *raw* meat or fish. I like my items *well-cooked."*

"I understand. I'm more of a well-done person myself. My dad loves his meat bloody, though. *Gross."*

"Yeah, gross. Hey, eat up, Dallas. We have cannolis for dessert."

"Homemade, I presume?"

"Of course," he grinned.

The scattering of trees were still and, except for an owl hooting in the distance, the night was eerily silent. The smoke from Max's burning chimney was the only substance clouding an otherwise dark but clear sky. Tiny planets and a mix of twinkling stars provided light, and I watched intently as Max's animated features provided the nights entertainment. *He's beautiful I thought to myself.* After we inhaled the array of delicious foods before us, Max pushed the empty contents of the basket to the side and we sprawled out on our backs onto the warm blanket. For a while, we laid beside each other in complete silence just staring at the full moon. My body trembled lying so closely to him.

"I'm glad you're here, Dallas. I've been waiting all week for this night. I want to ask you a question though. I hope I don't scare you off."

"I'm not going anywhere Max. Ask away."

"I know we've only known each other for a short while, but I was wondering, do you think you'd want to keep seeing me? Like this I mean? I guess I'm wondering if you would like to see more of me, Dallas." Max was stuttering and his hands were shaky. I could of sworn I saw beads of sweat forming on his wrinkled forehead.

"I'd like to see you as often as possible, Max. I enjoy our time together."

"Um, what I'm trying to say, Dallas, is that I'd like to see *only* you. I don't want to date anyone else." *He was sweating.*

"Oh. Well, I don't want to see anyone else either. So yes, I'd like to date you exclusively if that's what you're asking."

"It is."

"Well then, it's official, Max. We're dating each other *exclusively*."

"Great, that's exactly what I want. Sorry I didn't say it better. I'm new at this, Dallas. I've never dated anyone *exclusively* before."

"There's a first time for everything, Max," I giggled--aware of his nervousness.

So much to tell Emily...

This world is older than any of you know, and contrary to popular mythology, it did not begin as a paradise. For untold eons, Demons walked the earth; made it their home--their Hell. In time they (the demons) lost their purchase of this reality, and the way was made for the mortal animals. For Man, What remains of the Old Ones are vestiges: certain magic's, certain creatures.

.....Buffy the Vampire Slayer.

Chapter 9

Stop Staring...

"So, how'd it go, Dallas? You two an item yet? Officially, I mean," Blake buzzed.

"Yes, as a matter of fact we are. Max proposed to me last night."

"Huh?"

"Just kidding. But yes, we've decided to see each other exclusively. *No sharing.* I'm happy about it and I think Max is, too."

"Poor Alex, that douche is gonna be mad. Break it to him gently Dallas."

"I will."

As usual, Emily stood waiting for us outside the dreary front office. I'd already filled her in regarding our newly developed status as a *real* couple--E.B. got an ear full Sunday night on her *Blackberry*. I was surprised she hadn't shared the exciting turn of events with Blake yet.

Emily looked gorgeous in a bright coral sweater and matching turtleneck. Her blonde locks were long and curly and her clear eyes sparkled in silver shadow, chocolate liner, and brownish mascara. Emily's *Uggs* were wet from the moisture outside, and her bleached denim jacket fit snugly around her miniscule waist. Her expensive leather *Coach* bag was draped across her tiny shoulders and a *Timberland* backpack graced her enviable backside. Emily's pearly teeth gleamed and her shiny gloss was also peach--complementing the brilliant hue of her trendy sweater.

"What's up you two? Ready for some hot cocoa?" she gushed, unaware of how beautiful she was. *Even her manicured nails were painted peach.*

"Absolutely. I'm freezing. Bring it on, already," I answered. "The cocoa I mean."

"I'm gonna pass today, girls. I need to meet with Coach Delapaz about the football scouts that are coming to watch us play on Friday night. See ya in a few."

"Okay, Blake, I'll see you in math," I shot back.

"Yeah, bye. I'll meet up with you during lunch," Emily grinned--blowing him air kisses.

"You look cute today, trying to impress anyone in particular, Dallas?"

"Maybe," I hissed.

Instead of waking up at six-thirty--my usual time--I jumped out of bed at six instead, anxious to start the day. I needed the extra thirty minutes in order to look my finest for Max. The hot shower shocked my senses and cleared my pores. The revitalizing *Egyptian* sea scrub caused my writhing body to tingle all over. I scoured between my fingers and toes--freshly painted with silver *Opi* polish. I cleansed my long, newly tinted hair with lavender-scented shampoo purchased the same day Mom paid for my red highlights at the mall. When I got out of the steamy shower, I sprayed my alert limbs with lavender body atomizer--*Crab Tree and Evelyn*--and splattered an abundance of creamy deodorant underneath my freshly shaven armpits. *I smelled good.*

Before I could make it to my first class, Max snuck up behind me on my way towards the row of beaten metal lockers lining the inside corridors.

"Dallas, hey, wait up. Let me walk you to English," he grinned.

"Uh, sure Max. Won't you be late if you do?"

"Probably," he beamed. "But you're worth the demerits."

Max wore the same haggard leather jacket present on our first date at *Jorge's*. His creased black denim jeans accentuated his well-defined legs. A freshly pressed *Ralph Lauren* button-down demonstrated that Max wanted to look equally special for me and I appreciated his efforts. As we headed down the halls, Max startled me by grabbing my free hand. The dubious stares we got from puzzled onlookers was nerve-racking. It felt like my first day at WWHS all over again. But I was proud to accompany him and his touch felt spectacular.

"Meet me for lunch," he whispered into my amenable ear--leaning in closely when he did. "I have a surprise for you."

My heart skipped.

"I will," I stuttered. "I can't wait."

The next three and a half hours crawled by as I imagined kissing Max over and over again inside that very lab.

"Don't start without me," I protested. Max was busy setting up the delicious spread when I strolled in. Laid out on top of a red plaid blanket brought from home, Max displayed finger-sized cucumber and cream cheese sandwiches, homemade potato chips, as well as several red *Jell-O* cups topped with whipped cream.

"You brought all of this for us to eat?" I quizzed.

"Sure did. Sit down by Freddy's aquarium. The heat lamps will keep you cozy. And dig in, Dallas. Don't be bashful."

"I'm never bashful around food, Max. You should know that about me by now."

"Here. Have a taste." Max dangled a tiny sandwich in front of me and the smell of cream cheese caught my attention.

"Yummy," I said.

Max sprawled the twin-sized blanket out onto the linoleum floor and passersby ducked their curious heads inside the lab to gawk at our spectacle. We didn't mind.

We were lost in each other's company. I couldn't think of any place I'd rather be.

"I said I had a surprise for you Dallas and I do. Are you ready?"

"Yes Max. I'm ready!" I squealed.

"Well, close your eyes then."

"Okay. They're closed."

"Oh, I wasn't expecting that. It tickled. But I liked it."

Max had leaned over gently kissing me on the lips. It was a brief kiss, but a kiss nonetheless. *And I enjoyed it.*

"Mistletoe? Oh Max, you brought it from your property!"

"Yep. I thought you'd like it. Or at least I hoped you would. You don't mind me kissing you at school do you, Dallas?"

"Of course not. I'll take all the kisses I can get. *Anytime, anywhere.* Can I hold it for a minute, the mistletoe, I mean?"

"Sure."

I grabbed the tiny bush from his extended hand, aiming it above Max's curly head. I leaned in closely towards his tempting mouth and kissed him back--my kiss lasted considerably longer than the peck Max planted on me, however.

"Wow, I should carry mistletoe around more often," Max groaned. His expression suggested he enjoyed the kiss. *I certainly did.*

Unfortunately, the bell rang startling both of us. "Lunchtime's over. Back to reality," I growled.

"Yeah. Back to class, I guess. Mr. Smith doesn't teach science again until two p.m. I'll come back later and pick up the mess. Let me walk you to PE."

"Okay. And, Max, thanks again for lunch and for bringing the mistletoe. I can honestly say I've never had mistletoe for lunch before."

"Me either," he laughed.

"How was lunch, Dallas?" Emily giggled as we passed each other in the halls.

"Very, very, tasty," I countered.

"I'm sure it was."

"See ya at practice, Dallas."

"Bye, Emily."

The exciting day ended and I met Mom and the twins outside in the busy parking lot after French--my last class of the day. The ride to Emily's for cheerleading practice was silent as I refused to discuss Max with my horrible sisters. Caitlin would have teased me relentlessly all the way towards E.B.'s impressive mansion if I'd spilled the beans about our romantic lunch. I couldn't wait, however, to fill Emily in regarding the days exhilarating turn of events. And when Blake picked me up at five-thirty to drive me home, I'd make sure he knew all about Max, the mistletoe, and our passionate exchange. Hopefully, he would pass the revealing information on to Alex.

"Emily, I think it might be Max calling on your cell--I don't recognize the number. It's vibrating," Mom yelled from inside the damp kitchen.

"Okay, I'm coming."

"Make sure you finish your homework. Don't spend all evening on that phone," she scolded.

"It's done. That's what study hall is for, Mom."

"Whatever, Emily. Just don't let your school work suffer because of a *boy.*"

"Hello?"

"Hey, Dallas. Um, are you busy? If you are, I can call back later," Max stumbled. It was our first time speaking with each other on the phone and he seemed nervous. I was too.

"I'm not busy, Max. I was just watching TV in my bedroom. *Dr. Phil* comes on much later here than it did back home. That's my favorite show. My best friend

Madison and I used to watch it every day. He's from
Texas you know--Dr. Phil."

"I know that. Hey, I wanted to ask you something.
You said once that your birthday was on Christmas Eve.
Is that right?"

"Yeah. That's in like ten days. Time flies."

"Well, if you don't already have plans, I was
wondering if you would like to spend your birthday with
me. I know it's the night before Christmas, but maybe I
could borrow you for a couple of hours at least. Do you
think your parents would mind?"

"They won't mind, Max. We usually hold off until
the twenty-fifth to celebrate anyway. My birthday and
Christmas presents are combined--kind of sucks,
actually. But no, I mean, they won't mind if I hang out
with you Christmas Eve. As long as I'm here for
Christmas day."

"Great! I want you to come over. Oh, and I want you
to meet my mom."

"Really? Wow, Max, I can't wait."

"She's ready now, Dallas."

"Um, okay. Should I bring anything with me?"

"No. I'll pick you up around six o'clock if that's
okay."

"Six is fine."

"Mom's going to make us dinner first and then I'm
taking you somewhere special."

"Should I dress up?"

"No, but dress warmly, just in case."

"I'm curious, Max. What have you got planned?"

"It's a secret. But we'll have to keep an eye on the
weather. Hopefully no blizzards are scheduled during
the holiday break."

"Hopefully."

"By the way, I miss you right now, Dallas. I've been
thinking about you ever since lunch. That kiss you gave
me was special. I'm ready for another one."

"Bring some mistletoe tomorrow and you might get
lucky," I blushed.

"I plan on it."

"I certainly hope so, Max."

"Well, hey, I've gotta go. If I keep talking to you, I won't be able to concentrate and my homework's piling up. I'll see ya tomorrow at school. Meet me for lunch again. Mom's packing leftover Chicken Parmesan. Mr. Smith has a microwave in his office. I can warm the food in there. And I'll definitely bring the mistletoe."

"Should I bring something, Max? I mean, I feel terrible. You always bring the food. Let me pack something for us. Dessert, at least."

"Dessert sounds fine. And I don't mind bringing the food, Dallas. I want to--for you that is."

"You're sweet, Max. I'm a lucky girl."

"I'm the lucky one. Goodbye."

"Good bye, Max."

Not all who wander are lost. J.R.R. Tolkien.

Chapter 10

Nightmares...

"Emily! Emily, wake up!"

"Huh, what is it, Mom? What's the matter?"

"You're screaming in your sleep. And look at your neck. You're scratching it to death. I think it's bleeding!" The panic in Mom's voice was unsettling.

"Huh? My neck, what's wrong with my neck?"

"It's bleeding Emily! You're clawing at it! You must be having a nightmare. Get up and let's take a look. I think you need some water."

I struggled to climb out of the cocoon-like bed and my wobbly legs felt like mush. I could barely position myself on top of the sub-zero floor and I felt as if my frozen knees would buckle. Mom steadied my uneven body weight and we headed towards the empty bathroom I reluctantly shared with Caitlin and Ashley. She poured a small amount of tap water into a disposable cup and I drank the icy liquid. I'd been having a nightmare.

"Look at your neck, Emily. It's bleeding. Does your throat hurt or something? Are you getting sick? Maybe your tonsils are bothering you again. Dr. Matheson said they needed to be removed. We should have done that before we left Texas. There was just so much going on at that time."

We both knew what Mom was alluding to--Rose's mysterious death as well as to my nearly fatal lapse in judgment after she died. We just couldn't say the words.

"I'm okay. And my throat isn't bothering me. Could you hand me a wash rag though so I can clean up?"

"Sure. Let me warm it up first."

Mom held the thick terry cloth under the brass faucet until the steaming water saturated the cotton rag. The warm compress felt good against my clammy skin. Why was I scratching my neck anyway? I'd never done that before. In fact, I hadn't even had a nightmare since leaving Texas. Rose was the heart of tonight's disturbing vision, however--her miniature face streaked with crystal tears. *Why was she crying?*

"Emily, why don't you sleep in the twin's room tonight--on Ashley's trundle bed? You can stay in there."

"No thanks, Mom. Really, I'd rather sleep here. I don't want to disturb them."

"Okay. But let me know if your throat starts bothering you again. I'm going to schedule an appointment with an ENT first thing in the morning. You need to have those tonsils removed ASAP. We should never have waited this long."

"I guess. Hey, Mom, shut the door on your way out. The light from the hallway keeps me up."

"Okay, Emily. Try to get some sleep."

Mom closed the weighty door behind her and I couldn't help feeling uneasy. My tonsils are fine, I thought to myself. I don't need surgery. Still jumpy, I snuggled under the tepid covers, thankful the purple jersey sheets were still warm. I fluffed the down pillow before resting my dizzy head on top of its feathery peak. I closed my heavy eyelids anxious for slumber. The electric clock radio on the bedside table read three a.m. I was glad for the remaining three and half hours I had left to sleep.

"You okay, Dallas? You look tired this morning," Blake asked.

"I am. I had a nightmare last night. Didn't sleep well."

"Hmm. I have them sometimes too--nightmares I mean. Especially when we lose a really big game big. Coach Delapaz yells and screams at us, and then in my dreams, he whips us with a metal chain. I hate those kind of dreams. *Ouch.*"

"Yeah, ouch. Hey, Blake, do you think I could look over your review sheet on the way to school? I didn't study much last night--I was on the phone with Max."

"It's in my backpack, Dallas. In the blue folder marked *History.* I haven't even looked at that thing yet. Why don't you read it out loud while I drive?"

"Sure."

Max was waiting beside my locker--again--looking handsome as usual and we hugged each other eagerly.

"Dallas, I brought our lunch. Did you get the dessert?"

"Sure did. We're having oatmeal patties courtesy of *Little Debbie.* Sorry, I ran out of time and couldn't bake anything."

"Oatmeal patties are fine. You look pretty." Max swept his gentle fingers across my left cheek and I could feel my face starting to flush. The delicate stroke of his hand left me feverish, craving more of his precious touch. Max's effect was intoxicating and I could hardly breathe with him standing so close. His clear blue eyes gazed into mine and for a moment I was unaware of the commotion surrounding us. *Our world was soundless.*

"You look nice too, Max. I like that shirt," I managed, despite being heady.

"You must be warm, Dallas. That turtleneck is thick. I guess you don't need to borrow my jacket today, huh?"

"Oh, um, no. I guess not."

I forgot about the heavy turtleneck I'd put on this morning in order to hide the purple marks on my bruised flesh. My neck exhibited deep lines etched into the soft tissue causing tiny blood vessels to burst. Embarrassed by the display, I didn't want Max, or anyone else for that matter, surveying the damage.

Despite worrying about my neck, hand in hand, Max and I floated down the packed halls oblivious to the stares.

"Dallas. Hey, Dallas. Wait up," Emily yelled. "Wait for me!"

We slowed down momentarily, allowing her to catch up. "What's up, Emily? I haven't seen Blake since we got here if you're looking for him."

"I'm not. I'm looking for you actually. Oh, hey, Max. What's up?"

"Not much, Emily. If you guys don't mind, I'm gonna take off. I need to pop into the lab and ask Mr. Smith a question. I'll catch up with you later, Dallas. Goodbye, Emily."

"Bye, Max. I hope I'm not running you off," Emily apologized.

"No. Not at all. I was just about to duck out anyways," Max assured her.

"See ya later, Max. I'll join you for lunch," I winked.

"Yeah, I'll catch you at noon, Dallas."

"I'm sorry. Really, I didn't mean to run him off. Hey, your birthday is coming up right?"

"Yeah, Christmas Eve. Why?"

"Well, I was wondering if you wanted to come over to my house and eat with my family."

"Um, I'd love too. But Max already invited me to his."

"Sweet, Dallas! Things are moving fast between you guys. I'm glad. Really. I'm happy to see him connecting with someone. *Finally.*"

"I'm sorry. Really I am. I appreciate the invite, Emily. It's just that I already promised to celebrate my birthday with him."

"Don't worry about it! I'll bring your present to school. I think you'll like it. As a matter of fact, I'll give it to you early so you can wear it on your date."

"You don't have to do that, Emily. I can pick it up during the long break. Next Wednesday's our last day of class, right?"

"Yep. I'm bringing the gift so you can have it for your date though--I insist."

"Thanks, Emily. You've been really sweet to me since I moved here. I appreciate it. Really, I do."

"I know you do, Dallas. Just promise me you'll wear it to Max's house on Christmas Eve."

"Of course I will."

"Gotta run. I'm going to be late for *Drama Club* with Mrs. Suarez if I don't get my butt in gear. I'm *Dorothy* you know--in the school play. We're putting on the *Wizard of Oz* in January for the entire student body. Blake loves my singing. Can you blame him?" she teased.

"No. Just keep him away from your ruby slippers. I don't know about Blake sometimes," I joked.

Max stood dissonantly tranquil inside the humid lab and chills ran down my spine when I caught sight of him. So beautiful, I thought to myself. *Perfect in every way.* His blonde curls were lightly tasseled on top of his unkempt head and his chiseled face sported a five o'clock shadow--unusual since he was usually freshly shaven. The scar on his chin was strategically hidden by golden fuzz. Max's long-sleeved navy polo was missing the top button and I could see tiny hairs on his ripped chest. His black denim jeans, cuffed at the bottoms, highlighted his stately presence. Max looked like a mythical god. *Too faultless to be human.* He also looked sleep deprived--much like myself.

"Hey, Dallas. Everything's set up. Ready to eat?"

"Yes. I'm starving. Keep that snake away from me though. I want food. Real food for lunch," I giggled.

"Good, because I've already nuked the *Chicken Parmesan* and Mom threw in some glazed carrots with parsley for a side dish. Hope you don't mind leftovers."

"Are you kidding me? Last night for dinner I had *Taco Bell*--for the second time this week! I'd love some homemade chicken and vegetables. Your mom's the best!"

"She's looking forward to meeting you on your birthday. She's gonna love you, Dallas. I think you'll like her too. You guys remind me of each other."

"I'll be on my best behavior Max. I promise. I really do want her to like me."

"She will. *I certainly do.*"

Max and I dove into the abundance of food and the fatigue I'd been experiencing all day abruptly vanished. I gorged on cheesy chicken breasts and baby carrots smothered in buttery sauce and Max and I topped off lunch with *Little Debbie* snack cakes. As far as I was concerned, I was the luckiest girl at WWHS--as well as the best-fed. When lunch was finally over, Max and I exited the lab and didn't see each other again until two-thirty outside of his disheveled locker. I was upset, however, because Max forgot to bring the mistletoe.

"I'll call you tonight, Dallas."

"Okay, Max. Get some sleep. You look as exhausted as I am."

"I know I do. I was up late last night finishing my Spanish project. *Adios.*"

"*Chaos*, Max."

Mom picked me up at three-thirty, concerned about last night's *episode*--as she'd resorted to calling it.

"You're seeing Dr. Howard Walters tomorrow at four-fifteen Emily. He accepts new patients. He's an ENT and wants to check you out. You might be having your tonsils removed over the Christmas break."

"Ha!" Caitlin sneered. "Serves her right. She's a big fat doo-doo head and I hope she feels like crap over Christmas!" Caitlin stuck her disgusting tongue out at me again and I felt like ripping it out of her revolting mouth.

"Shut up, puke face," I shot back. "I'd rather be high on painkillers than have to deal with your putrid face all break."

"Girls, keep it down. I'm trying to drive. I can't concentrate with all of the screaming back and forth. How's your neck, Emily? I've got *Neosporin* at home. It's in the medicine cabinet--put some on your scratches so they don't get infected. You should probably sleep in that turtleneck just in case your throat hurts tonight--don't want you clawing at it again."

"My throat's fine Mom. I told you that already. I had a bad dream--that's all--and I scratched at my neck for some strange reason. I don't need to see a doctor, you know."

"Well, it won't hurt to meet with him. We should have scheduled the surgery when we were still living in Texas. I'm sorry we put it off and now you'll have to spend the entire holiday in pain. I'll stock up on ice cream though--lots of chocolate and that shaved Italian ice you like so much."

"I'm fine Mom. Really. And I don't need that surgery."

"Pipe down, Emily. You're such a baby! Too scared to go to the doctor? Maybe that creepy dude Max can go with you and hold your stinky hand!"

"That's enough, Caitlin! Seriously. Shut your mouth before I punch you in the face!"

"Girls, I mean it. Keep it down! You're getting on my nerves!" Mom rattled.

"Emily, when we get back to the house, put that ointment on your abrasions like I said. Don't want them to scab over and scar."

"I will, Mom. What's for dinner tonight anyways?"

"*McDonald's*."

"Sounds great."

Glad I had a wholesome lunch.

"Where's Dad?" Caitlin bellyached.

"He won't be home until late. His team is working on a new proposal--some big sale of thirty acres of prime land near the turnpike. Finish your homework and maybe you'll get to spend some time with him before bed."

"He's always working late," Ashley groaned.

"He has to dear. It's required by the firm. He'll get some time off over Christmas. Maybe we can all go somewhere--if Emily's up to it, that is."

"Maybe," Caitlin grumbled. "It's just that he's always out late. And when he is home, he just sits in his office staring at his paperwork. He barely talks to any of us. And when ya'll talk, you end up yelling at each other. What's the matter with him anyway?"

"He's still upset about losing Rose. You know that-- we all know that. Just give him space. He'll come around. It's barely been two years since she died-- January 31, 2002. He needs some more time," Mom muttered. "We all do."

On that sad note, I left the three of them as quickly as I could heading for the safety of my bedroom.

"Your phone's vibrating, Emily. I think it's Max calling again," Mom yelled from the cluttered kitchen table--she was busy paying bills. My backpack and purse were on top of the ugly laminate counters picked out by the previous owners. I rushed from my crammed bedroom into the out-dated breakfast area to retrieve it.

"Is your homework finished, Emily?"

"Yes Ma'am. I'll have to call Max back. Looks like he left a message."

"Okay. Just don't be up too long. You need to sleep tonight. Last night was rough for you."

"I know. And I will get some sleep. I won't talk long."

"Good. I'll check in with you later."

"Okay Mom."

I headed towards my messy bedroom nervous about calling Max. I pressed the luminous numbers despite my insecurities.

"Max, uh, hello. It's me. Dallas."

"I know who this is, Dallas. I recognize your beautiful voice. Thanks for calling me back."

"You're welcome. Sorry I missed you earlier. I couldn't get to the phone quick enough."

"It's okay. Hey, I was calling to see if you wanted to go out on Saturday night. I know the game on Friday is an away game, so I thought we could meet up on Saturday instead."

"Yeah, of course. Saturday would be great."

"Good. I'll pick you up at your house around seven p.m. Is that okay?"

"That's perfect. I'll give you directions at school tomorrow."

"Sounds great, Dallas. I can't wait to meet your parents."

"Oh yeah, they're eager to meet you too. See you tomorrow. I'm headed for bed. I didn't sleep well last night."

"Me either, I had a bizarre dream--a little girl was crying in Mom's herb garden. Very weird, I barely slept a wink. Decided to work on Spanish instead."

"That is weird, Max. I better go. See ya tomorrow."

"Bye, Dallas. Try to get some shut-eye. I can't wait to see you. *I miss you.*"

So Max was having nightmares too. *Strange.*

Two pairs of eyes are watching me now, from the couch and the ledge by the window. Faerieland shines in those eyes. And I must leave you, for it's the witching hour and a full moon is rising...

Washington Irving, 1835.

Chapter 11

The Witching Hour...

"Emily, Emily! Wake up dear! Wake up!"

"Huh, what...Mom?"

"You're having another nightmare, sweetie. Wake up. Let's get you some water."

"Where's Rose? She was here Mom. Standing right beside the bed, right here, Mom!"

"What are you talking about, Emily? It was just a dream, honey. Just a bad dream. Let's get you up--to the bathroom. You need some water."

"No! I don't need water. I need to talk to Rose; she was trying to tell me something!"

"Emily, you're having a bad dream. Nobody's here--except me. I'll check with Caitlin--make sure she wasn't bothering you. Maybe she wandered into your room before I did. Now get up, let's get you into the bathroom. Put your slippers on, the floor is freezing."

"Mom, I swear, Rose was standing right here, she was trying to speak to me. Her lips were moving but I couldn't hear a sound. I need to talk to her!"

"Rose is dead, Emily. You know that. Stop it, you're upsetting me."

I shook my head trying desperately to wake from my fog. The spinning room was blurry and my head felt hazy. An image of Rose in her funeral garb was etched into my brain. Her tiny face haunted my confused thoughts. What was Rose doing in my dream, and what was she trying to tell me? The clock read three a.m.--just like the night before. *Hmm, the witching hour I thought to myself.* I remembered that from a horror movie Madison and I watched together late one night in her bedroom. An unsuspecting teen met her demise at precisely three a.m.--the time witches and demons haunt their victims. *Was Rose haunting me?* Seriously freaked out, and too afraid to sleep by myself, I took Mom's advice and headed towards the twin's crowded room. I tugged on the lower portion of Ashley's trundle bed until it opened. I dove into to the icy, pink satin sheets praying for sleep.

"Jeez, Emily. You've got bags under your eyes. Sleeping much these days?"

"Not really, Blake. I keep having nightmares. I don't know what's going on. Mom thinks my tonsils are bothering me again. But my throat doesn't hurt. I'm seeing an *Ear Nose and Throat* doctor today, just in case."

"Wow. That sucks. I had my tonsils removed when I was like seven. It hurt. Good luck with that."

"Thanks for the concern, Blake. Really. It's touching."

"I'm serious, Dallas. I hope all goes well at the doctor's office today."

When we arrived at the high school, Blake and I climbed out of his stalled Mustang entering through the school's dirty glass doors. We passed Emily (she and I said our hello's), and then I headed towards my locker. Max stood waiting.

"Dallas, hey, over here. What's up? You look tired."

"I am, Max. I had trouble sleeping again last night. I had another crazy dream--I woke up sweating at like three a.m. I was so freaked out I had to switch rooms. I slept with the twins. Ashley's mattress is hard as a rock and my back hurts. Hey, you look kind of tired yourself."

"I am. I had an awful dream too--that's funny, I woke around three a.m. as well. Same as the other night, a little girl was crying outside in our herb garden. But I stayed up--decided to study for finals. I'm glad I did. That history review sheet is giving me hives. Look at my neck! I'm worried about all the dates Mrs. Lane expects us to memorize. I can't afford to bomb her test you know. Gotta keep my GPA up."

"Me too. Hey, let me see your neck. It's red. Does it itch?"

"Nope. Mom says it's hives--they'll go away when exams are over."

"Yeah, I guess. Well, I better get to English. See you at lunch?"

"Yes, but I didn't have time to pack anything for us to eat. We'll have to get food from the cafeteria if that's okay."

"That's fine, Max. Why don't I pick it up and deliver it to the lab. I'll meet you there at noon."

"Sounds good. See ya, Dallas."

"See ya, Max."

Before I walked off, Max grabbed my waist pulling me close to his hard body. He smelled great and I became heady at the sight of his crystal eyes peering into mine. In an instant, we were kissing and I didn't want the moment to end. For a few minutes, the reality of nightmares was a distant thought. When he shuffled off, however, things were back to being weird.

Strange, I thought to myself as I headed towards Mrs. Rice's dreary class. The profound marks on Max's thick nape resemble mine. Of course no one can see the whelps covering my flesh because I'm resolved to wearing bulky turtlenecks until they disappear. They aren't any worse; however, they aren't any better. What's even stranger than the mysterious rashes Max and I share is the fact that both of us were awakened at three a.m. by a little girl--*Rose*?

All day long, I couldn't shake the picture of Rose's diminutive hands reaching out for me beside the antique rice bed inherited from a dead aunt on Mom's side. Throughout the day, Max appeared as disheveled as I was. Our tousled hair needed brushing, our wrinkled clothes needed ironing, and we both needed to address the dark circles forming underneath our faded eyes. Max and I were shabby and tired--each of us needing a good night's rest. Too drained to talk during lunchtime, we smiled at each other while munching reluctantly on stale ham and runny cheese sandwiches purchased from the overpriced school cafeteria. For dessert, two slightly bruised apples and one soggy peach pie failed to wet our appetites.

Sometime after lunch, during fifth period study hall, I journeyed into the school's massive library searching for answers as to why Max and I were having nightmares. On a crowded and dusty shelf, I found a book entitled *The Witching Hour* by Jordan Ellis and promptly checked it out. Tucked underneath my left arm so no one could decipher the volume's revealing title, I headed back towards room 153 B embarrassed by the nature of the leather bound manuscript--didn't want anyone presuming I was a witch. I needed to determine, however, why Rose was attempting to contact me--and possibly even Max--at three a.m. The book's contents were revealing. According to legend, the witching hour is "the time of night when supernatural creatures like demons and ghosts are presumed to be their most powerful."

While alive, Rose was never a witch. And in death, she's certainly not a demon. She could be a ghost, however, considering she's gone. But why would Rose's ghost be haunting us? I continued reading from the tattered script intrigued by its implications:

> *Throughout recorded time, peoples have continued to suppose that during the witching hour, the connection between the world of supernatural and mythical creatures and humans is greater. Therefore, in order to make contact with the persons or entities left behind, witches, demons, and ghosts visit the living between the hours of midnight and three a.m. in order to initiate contact.*

Initiate contact? I could understand Rose's insistence to visit me; after all, we're sisters. However, what does Rose want with Max? Rose died over two years ago-- long before Max came into the picture. Eager to learn more about the frightening hour, I scoured the books marred, yellowed pages searching for appropriate answers. On page forty-nine, I found more references to the creepy hour. "In Mary Shelley's frightening masterpiece *Frankenstein,* Shelly wrote, 'Night waned upon this talk, even the witching hour had gone by before we retired to rest.'" I made a mental note to return to the library as soon as possible in order to check out her controversial book. While skimming the volume's lurid text, I found even more references to the infamous hours. Shakespeare wrote in *Hamlet*:

Tis now the very witching time of night, when churchyards yawn and hell itself breathes out contagion to this world: now could I drink hot blood, and do such bitter business as the day would quake to look on.
[Act 3, scene2]

Shakespeare's passage was puzzling. If the witching hour is a time peril (hell itself breaths out), and evil occurs (now I could drink hot blood), why was an innocent like Rose involved in my sordid dreams at this frightful hour? I'm no saint, believe me, but Rose--she's as pure as gold. The witching hour was not the only disturbing phenomenon captured in its weathered pages, however. Tales of beasts, demons, witches, and even *vampires,* flooded it's wrinkled pages.

On page ninety-nine, a disturbing tale of lust, death, and blood thirsty creatures captured my attention. During the late seventeen hundreds, Lord Byron composed a lengthy poem called "The Giaour." The rhythmic passages were distressing. The hairs on my arms stood on end when I read but a few of the disturbing excerpts.

With sabre shivered to the hilt,
Yet dripping with the blood he spilt;
Yet strained within the severed hand
Which quivers round the faithless brand;
A fragment of his palampore
His breast with wounds unnumbered riven,
Fallen Hassan lies-his unclosed eye
Yet lowering on his enemy,
As if the hour that sealed his fate
Surviving left his quenchless hate;
And o'er him bends that foe with brow
As dark as his that bled below.

Severed limbs, dripping blood, open wounds, witches, *vampires,* and spirits communicating with the living--the book was too much. I closed its unsettling pages hoping for a respite as I was tired and overwhelmed by the disturbing content. I wanted to go home, curl up in my warm and comfortable bed, turn out the hot and bright lights, and fall asleep. But it was only two-twenty five p.m.

"Emily, get in the van," Mom snipped. "Hurry up, you're letting the cold air in."
"Okay, Mom. Just a minute. Jeez. I'm moving as fast as I can you know."
"Shut up, Emily. Just get in the car. You're holding up the line--idiot."
"Be quiet, Caitlin, before I punch you in the face," I screamed.
"Hurry up, Emily. Your appointment's at four-fifteen. We need to get there early. Lots of paper work to fill out."
"All right, Mom. I'm in. Just go already."

The drive to Dr. Walter's office was short. The medical district was only a few miles from the high school and we even had time to grab sandwiches from

Chick-fil-et. I didn't realize how hungry I was until the smell of waffle fries filtered through my nose. The stale ham sandwiches Max and I had barely consumed for lunch were terrible, and I'd only managed to eat half. Grateful for the delicacy now before me, I gorged on greasy chicken, *Diet Coke*, and oily fries. The food tasted good.

"Hope you brought a toothbrush, butt face, or Dr. whatever his name is will throw up when he gets a load of your breath," Caitlin taunted.

"Mom, please shut her up. She's getting on my nerves."

"Shut up, Caitlin. Don't get me started today. I mean it. Leave Emily alone."

Wow, I couldn't believe Mom was actually standing up for me. *Shut up, Caitlin--that's a new one.*

"She started it, Mom," Caitlin whined.

"What are you talking about? You started it!" I screamed.

"That's right, Caitlin. Emily's right--you started it this time. And I'm ending it. Keep your mouth shut or I'll ground you--I swear."

"Okay, Mom. Jeez. Just keep her away from me," Caitlin fired.

"Gladly, you moron. I will gladly stay clear of you," I managed.

"Please, girls, everyone stop shouting. We're going into the office now. Behave. Impress me with your self-control--even if you do hate each other," Mom hissed.

After my exam, we climbed back into the van and Mom was perplexed by the diagnosis.

"I told you Mom, it's not my tonsils. My throat isn't even sore. I scratched my neck because I was having a nightmare. I don't need to have them removed."

"I don't know Emily. Dr. Walters is awfully young. Perhaps he's not experienced enough to conduct the surgery. We could always go back home--stay with Madison over the break--she'd love that. You could have the surgery there. Dr. Matheson knows what he's doing. Maybe I should give him a call."

"I don't need to have a tonsillectomy, Mom. Give it up already. I told you, my throat is fine. Dr. Walters confirmed that I don't need the surgery. Maybe Dr. Matheson was the one not qualified to make the call--or maybe he just wanted to yank them out for the money!"

"Emily! Hush. We've known him for a while. He went to *Texas AM* with your father. They got their bachelor degrees in *Biology* together. It's a great university. Too bad your dad went to law school instead of medical school--we'd be rich if he'd become a doctor, you know. Look at Emily B.'s dad."

"We've got plenty of money Mom. How much does a family of five need anyway? Besides, doctors hold even later hours than lawyers--and we barely see Dad as it is."

"I know. You're right, we're managing. But maybe I'll return to work this year anyway. I'm bored at home. Sick of all the cleaning."

"That sounds like a great idea. You should see if any of the private schools around here are hiring. You have tons of experience working in accounting. You really should consider finding a job."

"I will, Emily. Maybe I'll beef up my resume when we get home. As for you, take a hot shower and hit the sheets early tonight. You need the rest."

"I will, Mom. I can't wait to sleep."

They say foul beings of Old Times still lurk In dark forgotten corners of the world, And Gates still gape to loose, on certain nights, Shapes pent in Hell. Cthulhu Mythos.

Chapter 12

Better Days...

"TGIF, Blake! No bad dreams for a couple of nights now. Hurray!" I mused.

"That's great, Dallas. I was beginning to worry about you. You were starting to resemble an old hag or something--bags under your eyes and everything. I thought a wart might sprout on your cute nose."

"Whatever, Blake. You're such a pest. Drive on. I'm eager to see Max. We're going out tomorrow night. He's coming to my house--meeting my parents. I'm kind of nervous. I hope he likes them."

"What if they don't like him, Dallas? You should be more worried about that you know."

"What's not to love about Max? He's perfect for goodness sakes. He stays out of trouble, wants to go to medical school, loves his mom, worships me..."

"You're full of yourself today, Dallas. Your head's getting bigger by the minute. Watch out, it might explode. Wait till we get outside though, I don't want brain juice all over the inside of my Mustang. I just wiped the seats down again. *Smell the leather...*"

"You're weird Blake. How does Emily put up with you?"

"She loves me. I'm better than Maxwell Snow any day. You're missing out."

"Whatever, dude."

"Blake, Dallas, ready for tonight's game? Can you say road trip?" E.B. teased. "We're playing *Mountain State Academy*. Should be a close game. Hope we come out on top."

"Oh ye of little faith--of course we'll scorch them. Look who's quarterbacking," Blake thumped his heavy chest while bragging about his football skills.

"That's the problem, Blake. With you and Alex starting in tonight's game, we're sure to suck," I joked--winking in Emily's direction.

"Good one, Dallas. Stick him where it hurts, I always say."

"Emily, I thought you were on my side? I'm your boyfriend--your hero. Worship me."

"Whatever, Blake. Walk me to class. And here, carry my backpack--like a real man would--like Max does for Dallas."

"Oh snap, Emily," I snickered.

"You girls are sick. Always ragging on me. Bringing me down. I'm better than Max. I'm the king of WWHS you know."

"King of the morons, Blake."

"Whatever, Dallas. You know you love me. *Both* of you girls love me. Oh brother, here comes Max. See you *next year,* Dallas."

"See ya'll!" I ran towards Max, giving him a giant bear hug.

"Wow, what's that for? What did I do to deserve that welcome? I should do it more often whatever it was!"

"I slept great last night, Max, and I feel revived. How about you? Sleep well?"

"As a matter of fact I did. No bad dreams. I feel like a new man."

"Me too. I mean, I feel like a new woman--not a man, of course."

"Well, you look like a woman; I don't know too many men who wear cheerleading uniforms--at least not in public. Or with legs as hot as yours."

"Walk me to English, Max. I'm not ready to say goodbye yet."

"Wow, you really are full of surprises today. I've never seen you this peppy. I'm glad to escort you, Madame. Here, grab my arm."

"Gladly."

Clutching his free arm, I hung on tightly--I wasn't about to let go of Max. Not today, not on any day. I was proud to be by his side.

A vampire lives in a constant state of desire and disgust. His nature often revolts him, but he doesn't have the will to deny his indulgences. There's the killing, but there's also the pleasure, the sensuality, the lust. The sheer ecstasy of it all. Forever Knight, Stranger than Fiction.

Chapter 13

Meet The Parents...

"Okay, whenever he gets here, nobody embarrass me. Seriously. If you do, I will kill you. I mean it; do not embarrass me in front of Max!" I warned the five barren faces curiously staring me down. Caitlin rolled her spiteful eyes. She wasn't about to cooperate with my demands. *What's new?*

"Whatever, Emily. You're such a dork. What makes you think I want to meet your love bird anyway? He's probably a loser like you," she shrieked--annoying as ever.

"Well, since you feel that way, Caitlin, why don't you go to your bedroom now? Hide out or something. Max would bore you anyway--I promise. Ya'll have absolutely nothing in common. Really, you can text Marissa on my cell phone if you want--just go to your room. Say the word and it's yours."

"Trying to bribe me, Emily?" Caitlin nastily retorted.

"Yes. Take the *Motorola* and text Marissa or Kendall or Molly--whomever you prefer. Heck, text all three of them! Just leave the living room!"

"Fine! Just give me the cell phone already. Where is it? In that stupid-looking purse on the coffee table? I don't want to meet Max anyways. He sounds dull."

"What about you, Ashley. Anything I can do for you?" I inquired. Ignoring Caitlin's rude remark about the pink and black velour *Juicy* purse I'd scored before we left Texas.

"Nope. I'm good."

"Okay then. He'll be here any minute. Dad, you answer the door. Shake his hand and be friendly. Mom, you sit over there on the sofa. Don't get up until we leave."

"Chill out, Emily. We've greeted your dates before-- none of them ran out of the house screaming. And they each came back—well, most of them. It's okay, really," Mom assured me with half-way convincing eyes.

"I just want tonight to be perfect. Max is important to me. Don't ruin this ya'll. I really like him."

"I hear a car, Emily. I think he's here. What do you want me to do again?"

"Just answer the door, Dad. And be friendly. *Please!*"

"Will do," Dad blinked. Somehow I didn't quite believe him.

The doorbell rang and Dad followed my barked out orders to the letter--like a robot. After courteously greeting Max--they shook hands and exchanged pleasant hellos--Dad invited him inside our cozy bungalow. The grey brick fireplace--topped with a hand-carved oak mantle--was crackling, warming up the small but tidy space. Mom and I'd spent most of the day scrubbing floors and dusting furniture so the house was clean. Max sat down on our chenille, plaid couch--per Dad's obedient instructions--directly beside Mom who was looking refreshed in a black cardigan and striped beige slacks. Only a few inches separated the two of them. She cordially offered Max a sparkling glass of *Coca Cola*--pre-made in the tiny but efficient kitchen--and he politely accepted. I couldn't help noticing that Max looked grand in starched khaki's and a long-sleeved black button down shirt. Wearing his *nice* leather coat and a black woolen scarf, Max's leather cowboy boots complemented his rather formal ensemble. I liked the way he looked and I could smell Max from where I sat-- on a matching plaid chair and slightly soiled velvet ottoman. His slick pale hair was gelled and perfect--not a strand out of place. His broad but handsome nose was sunburned from chopping trees and firewood all day and he looked like he should be surfing in the Pacific Ocean instead of shoveling compacted snow. Max's all-American good looks reminded me of the chic hot models gracing life-sized black and white billboards back home. Like Blake, he could have made a living off his fashionable face--he was just too genuine a guy to do so.

"So, um, Max, how old are you?" Dad drilled--embarrassing both of us when he did. Max's mortified face turned red. It seemed Dad was no longer complying with my demands.

"Um, sixteen sir. I'm, um, sixteen; I'll be seventeen in April. April twenty-fourth," he stumbled. Max's relaxed posture suddenly stiffened and sweat formed around his furrowed brows. *Should have positioned him farther away from the fireplace. So much for Dad remaining courteous.*

"Sixteen? Do you always date older girls, Max?" Ashley taunted. *What's up with her? She's not usually the constipated one.*

"Be quiet, Ashley. You're embarrassing Emily's date. Go to your room and play with Caitlin," Mom snapped. *Thank goodness she was being reasonable. I could always count on Mom.*

"Um, come on, Max. Why don't we head out? I'll be home by midnight, Dad," I grumbled, shooting him a malevolent look. "Caitlin's got my mobile phone. Can I borrow yours, Mom?" My voice was shaky.

"Yes, Emily. But please don't lose it. I can't afford another one. These cell phones and their confusing plans are costing me a fortune you know."

"I promise I won't lose it, Mom. And thanks, I'll call if there's trouble--car trouble I mean. See ya'll later," I managed, blood rushing to my head.

Max jumped off the couch and opened the squeaky front door insisting he would follow closely behind me. Before exiting, however, Max turned civilly towards my daunting father bidding him as well as the rest of my Stepford-looking family a polite goodbye. Only Mom returned his pleasantries. Dad stood perfectly still, a snarl forming around his tight lips. He looked like a sadistic Rottweiler ready to lunge at its frightened victim. Max noted his disdain.

"Um, well, it was nice meeting you guys. I'll, uh, have Dallas--I mean Emily--home by midnight. Possibly even earlier. We won't be late sir. I promise," Max spluttered. Dad grinned ever so slightly at Max's uncomfortable hesitation. Then he impolitely slammed the heavy door behind us.

"Whew. Sorry about that, Max. I've never seen Dad so hostile. I don't know what got into him. He's not usually like that, I promise. I really am sorry."

"Don't worry about it, Dallas. He's just protecting his oldest daughter. Ashley's right though, I do like dating older women. And you certainly are older than me," he teased.

"Whatever, I'm like three and a half months ahead of you. Big deal. You're not exactly robbing the proverbial cradle."

"I know. I'm just kidding. Hey, watch your step, Dallas--wouldn't want you to get injured under my watch," Max joked. "Your father might murder me."

"Dad would disembowel you if you neglected me, Max."

"I'm sure he would."

Max graciously assisted me when I climbed into his noticeably cleaner truck and I was thrilled to feel his solid arms envelop my appreciative waist. I hoped the rest of our date would feel this amazing. Only time would tell.

Max drove slowly keeping the details of our developing night a mystery. Since I didn't know my way around Beckley very well, I had no inkling where we were heading. I just wished Max would speed up. I couldn't wait to get out of his truck and into his strapping arms. *I wanted Max to hold me.*

"So, Dallas. Do you like ice?" he teased.

"Ice, what do you mean? We're surrounded by it, Max! Look around, there's nothing but ice in West Virginia. What exactly do you have up your sleeve? Should I be worried?"

"Nothing to fret over. You'll find out soon enough what the evening holds for you--for *us*."

I liked that Max referred to me and him as *us*. Together, we were an *us*--like Sonny and Cher, Romeo and Juliet, and Cleopatra and Mark Anthony.

"Well, at least give me a hint. One teeny, tiny, hint. You said ice, right? Are we going to a sculpted ice exhibit? Is that it? Or better yet, are we going out for icee's? I love those things. Cherry flavored icee's are the best. Are we going to *Dairy Queen,* Max?"

"Not exactly. But keep guessing, Dallas; I enjoy your incorrect answers. You have a vivid imagination."

"Hmm. Ice. Hey, I know! I've got it Max. We're going ice skating! That's it, isn't it?"

"What? Hey, how did you come up with that? Did your Mom spill the beans this morning? She promised not to tell!"

"My mom? Am I right, Max? We're going ice skating?"

"Yes, Dallas, we are. I called your mother earlier-- she said you were still sleeping--to see if you knew how to skate. She said you and your best friend Mattie used to skate at the Galleria in Dallas. She assured me that you're pretty good on the ice. I hope you're not better than me. That would be embarrassing."

"I can't believe I guessed it. And yes, I do know how to skate. Madison and I went to the Galleria a lot and we had season passes to skate. We even took lessons together for awhile. We skated at least once a week-- usually on the weekends. Mattie is better than me though. But I'm not half bad. Oh Max, I can't wait! Seriously! I haven't been on the ice since Rose's deat..."
Oops.

"Huh? What did you say? Did someone close to you die?"

Crap. I wasn't ready to tell Max about my dead sister Rose. Not tonight anyway.

"Um, well, I don't really want to talk about it Max. But I will tell you this, I had a younger sister named Rose, she was only four years old, who passed away just over two years ago. That's why we moved to West Virginia. It was too painful to stay in Texas."

As soon as I told him about Rose, Max pulled over onto the shoulder of the busy interstate to console me. He turned off the truck's noisy engine and faced me directly. Before I could think, Max grabbed both of my shaken hands clasping his comforting fingers around mine. He couldn't have been sweeter.

"Dallas, I'm so sorry. I didn't know. We don't have to talk about it tonight if it will upset you. Just please understand, I'm here for you. I will *always* be here for you. Whenever you're ready, say the word. We'll talk about it. I'm truly sorry for your loss. You must be devastated."

Max was so sweet that I decided to dig into my purse and show him a picture of Rose. My hands shook when I removed the tiny image from inside my wallet. "This is Rose, Max, isn't she lovely?" I choked.

Max accepted the tiny picture clutching it tightly in his hands. "Yes, Emily. She's beautiful. Rose is beautiful--just like you."

"Thanks, Max."

Max stared into the photo as if he recognized the face. "Um, she's a sweet looking little girl, how old did you say she is, Emily?"

"Rose was four when she died. This picture was taken about a month or so before she was murdered. What is it Max? Are you okay?"

"Um, yes, I'm fine. It's just that...Oh never mind. Hey, I'm truly sorry for your loss, Emily. You must miss her. I would."

Max's convincing eyes were sincere and I promised him that one day very soon we would indeed talk about Rose and how much I missed her. We all missed her. Visibly upset, I choked back a flood of salty tears and Max realized I was overcome with emotion. I assured him, however, that tonight I wanted to focus on the future instead of dwelling on the past. Tonight was about living in Beckley, West Virginia. Texas, and all of the sadness connected with it, was a distant memory.

I'm the world's best predator, aren't I? Everything about me invites you in--my voice, my face, even my smell. As if I need any of that! Edward Cullen.

Chapter 14

Skating On Thin Ice...

"We're here, Dallas. *Lock and load.*"

"Who are you supposed to be now, Max? James Bond or something?" I laughed--feeling better about our intrepid conversation regarding Rose. I couldn't help noticing how perky Max's affable personality could be-- in the right company of course.

"We're here, gorgeous, *let's rock.*"

"Now you're seriously acting goofy. I've never seen *or* heard you like this before. Are you trying to cheer me up with your silly slang? I'm okay you know. You don't have to worry about me anymore."

"Yes. Now get a move on, *chica.* Before the ice melts." Max was on a roll.

We gathered our snug-fitting jackets, put on our thick, cozy gloves as well as our chunky knit scarves, and headed towards the western entrance of the chilly hockey rink shared by the middle school and the high school during hockey season. Unfortunately, ours was a losing team.

"Wait a second, Dallas. I need to go back to the truck. I forgot something. I'll join you inside."

Hmm. Must have forgotten his wallet. I saw it on top of the dashboard.

I entered the massive, state of the art facility alone, impressed by its overall size and relative newness. The innovative arena couldn't have been more than a couple of years old boasting the best of everything. Inside, although a nippy forty-five degrees, the colossal stadium offered rows upon rows of palatial seating as well as an imposing concession stand complete with frozen pickle juice and freshly popped corn. Something was off though. Except for an aged, silver-haired man collecting nightly admission, the enormous place was empty. Max and I were the only skaters in sight.

"Uh, hello, sir. My um, boyfriend and I will be skating tonight. You're open, right?"

"Sure am pretty lady. Come on in. *Is Max outside?*"

"Uh, yes. He's getting something out of his truck. You know Max?"

"Sure do. My wife Margaret and I've been buying Christmas trees from his mother's farm for years now. He's a sweet boy. Said he needed the rink tonight cuz he was bringing a pretty girl. I thought he meant his mother. I guess he had someone else in mind," Jasper winked.

"I guess so," I stumbled. Just then Max wandered inside, breaking the awkwardness only I seemed to be experiencing. *Must've found his wallet.*

"Hey Jasper. How's life treatin' ya? Did you and Margaret decorate the spruce yet? You guys picked the prettiest tree on the property. You always do."

"Hey, Max. I was just talking to your nice-looking lady friend here. She sure is sweet. When you inquired about renting the rink for a couple of hours, I thought you planned on bringing Katie out to skate. What's this one's name?"

"Jasper, this is Dallas. Dallas, this is Jasper."

"Uh, nice to meet you, sir. You have a great place here. The rink is lovely."

"Thanks, honey. Hey, let me guess--you need a size seven narrow boot. I'll see what I've got in the back."

"Yes, sir. You're a pretty good guesser."

"I've been doing this for awhile. I owned a popular skating rink in Huntington before my wife and I built this huge place. I managed it for nearly twenty years. Raised a family of six while I did."

"Oh. There are five of us at my packed house. I know all about large families. I've got twin sisters."

Max strolled by, interrupting our unceremonious conversation.

"Size twelve and a half for me Jasper. My foot keeps growing and growing and growing."

"I know Max, you're part giant," Jasper serendipitously grinned. "Just like my oldest son Mason."

After acquiring our appropriate sizes, Jasper Jones headed for the tidy office in search of leather skates. When he was no longer in plain sight, Max appeared perceptibly nervous--pacing fretfully on the grey cement concrete.

"Um, Dallas, I'll be right back. I need to, uh, pay Jasper," he stuttered.

"Sure Max. I'll wait here."

Max headed anxiously in the old man's direction. When the two returned from the administrative facilities in good spirits, I found myself wondering what was up with the grinning duo. I felt as if they were in on a covert secret I wasn't privy too. What were Max and Jasper concealing?

"Lace up, Dallas. I'm ready to skate."

"Me too, Max. I'll try not to make you look bad-- wouldn't want to bruise your fragile ego."

"Whatever, Dallas. Do your best to keep up. I'm fast you know. *Remarkably fast.*"

"Is that so?"

"Yes."

The rock music Jasper had chosen to play while we twirled across the solid ice blared over the arena's invisible and imposing sound system--it must have cost a fortune. I was rather surprised, however, by Jasper's choice of fast paced songs. Max and I skated to Journey's *Don't Stop Believing* and Def Leopard's *Pour Some Sugar on Me.* Intrigued by the night's unusual play list, I laughed out loud when Max finally landed on his defenseless backside during Led Zeppelin's mega hit *Whole Lotta Love.*

"Showing off again, Max?" I cooed.

"Who, me? I would never do that, Dallas. My blade just got stuck in the ice. Otherwise, I'd of landed that jump just fine."

"Is that so?"

"Yes. Hey, why don't I ask Jasper to tone the music down a little? Perhaps he could play some slower songs."

"Sounds like a plan."

"I'll be right back."

Max headed towards the warm office--courtesy of Jasper's ceramic space heater--and I couldn't wait until we'd be able to skate hand in hand. I was tired of twirling by myself. He'd only been gone a few short minutes when Etta James' *At Last* revived the newly darkened arena. Poised just outside the center of the rink, Max made his way towards me on the rock-hard ice. As he glided in my direction, my heart was pounding. So much so, I thought my heaving chest would explode. As soon as he reached my welcoming side, Max looped his powerful right arm around my tiny waist and we galloped in unison towards the center of the ice. Red and white lights illuminated our path and a mirrored disco ball hanging from the rafters above sparkled like diamonds. Staring intently into each other's imploring eyes, Max hummed along with the song's seductive words and I couldn't get enough of his silky voice.

"You look beautiful tonight, Dallas. *As always.* I can't take my eyes off you. *I'm spellbound.*"

Max's romantic sentiments manifested themselves into a giant-sized lump in my throat. I could barely swallow. Clinging to each other's receptive bodies, we floated atop the crystal floor oblivious of the world surrounding us. Ours was a perfect world. Absorbed in each other's inviting limbs, we were mesmerized.

"I don't want this night to end, Max. It's too perfect. I can't breathe."

Before I could say anything else, Max scooped me up inside his immense arms kissing me passionately on my sympathetic lips. We lingered in each other's embrace for the rest of the song.

When the tempting ballad finished, I prayed desperately that Jasper would rewind the song as I didn't want our dance atop the unyielding ice to end. Is this what Max and Jasper had been conspiring when they left me alone in the rink? Finding the perfect melody in which to woo me? If so, their scrupulous plan to sway me with its lurid lyrics worked. *I was persuaded.*

The next song to play was a ballad Mom and Dad used to listen too--long ago before Rose died and our family was permanently altered. When I first heard the haunting melody over the loud speakers, I was sad. Sad because Mom and Dad had done nothing but fight since Rose's tragic passing. Sad because the six of us used to be a happy family playing putt putt golf on Saturdays and renting family classics like *Bambi* and *The Goonies* from *Blockbuster's* on Sundays. Sad because I was having nightmares in which Rose appeared to be trying to tell me something horrible. And sad because I would never see her in the flesh again. Perhaps sensing my melancholy, Max pulled me closer when *Nothing Compares to You* echoed in the large room.

"Are you okay, Dallas? You look kind of lost."

"I'm fine, Max. I was just thinking about my baby sister. I'm okay though. Really. I'm just happy to be here with you. This is a wonderful night. I can't believe you planned all of this for us. You're so romantic--not a silly teenager like Blake or Alex. I'm impressed by you, Maxwell Snow. Very, very impressed."

"Well I'm glad to hear that, Dallas. And I feel the same way. You impress me--I mean, everything you've been through lately--leaving Texas and moving clear across the United States--that's impressive. And I'm sorry you're having to deal with the loss of your sister. You've been through a lot. And yet look at you. You're a survivor, Dallas. You have a new home, new friends, new responsibilities, *a new boyfriend,"* he chuckled.

"And you're managing everything perfectly. I'm the one who's impressed."

"How can I argue with those sentiments? You make me sound so strong, Max. I don't know if I really am though. Maybe I'm weak and just haven't cracked yet. Maybe I will soon. I don't know. I'm just trying to manage, that's all. You're right about one thing; I do have a new boyfriend. And I'm glad about that. You mean everything to me. Everything. I hope I never let you down."

"You won't, Dallas."

I hope not, Max. Maybe I should tell him about nearly dying myself. He deserves to know that I'm weak--that I did crack once. That I let my entire family down the night I took those pills. I'm not so perfect Max. Not nearly as perfect as you think I am.

The romantic night at the skating rink waned and Max and I danced as closely as possible atop the solid ice before our time at the arena expired. Max promised Jasper we'd be out of there by eight p.m. so the gray-haired manager could open up the facility to everyone. One last slow song lit up the speakers and we snuggled together on the center of the ice, our bodies entwined. I made sure this time that Max knew my thoughts were solely on him.

"I can't say it enough, Max--this night has been great. I still can't believe you planned all of this without my knowledge. And my own mother knew about the evening and didn't even tell me!"

"I made her promise not to. Sorry Dallas. I just wanted tonight to be special. You deserve it."

Max ran his gentle fingers through my fine hair and I could feel his warm touch against my scalp. A jolt of electricity surged through my body each time he stroked my long locks. Max's head was bent over and he rested his strong chin on top of my bowed head as I'd opted to lay it across his thick chest. In doing so, I could hear and feel his heart pulsating. My lips trembled and I longed for him to continue kissing me. This time, however, our bodies swayed gently to the slow beat of the soft music. My chest was pressed against his and our shallow breathing was in unison. Max's belt buckle tickled against my stomach as we rocked back and forth. His free arm graced my waist as Max held me tightly in his grip.

"You're beautiful, Dallas. You know that. Right?" he whispered.

"You're the beautiful one, Max. I can't take my eyes off you tonight."

When the song ended, Max scooped up my quivering chin, planting a long kiss atop my malleable lips. Once again, I was in heaven.

I am a night bird, I am not much good in the daytime.
Dance of the Vampires, 1967.

Chapter 15

Mesmerized...

"Are you okay, Dallas? You look kind of funny. Feeling alright?" Blake pried, as I entered his Mustang.

"I'm perfect! Extraordinary! Couldn't be better! Wanna touch my forehead? See, no fever. *It's all good.*"

"Whatever you say, Dallas. You just look a little weird. Nightmares again?"

"Not at all, Blake. My weekend was perfect," I purred. "Max and I went skating at *Jasper's Ice-o-rama.* We had a blast. He's fast on the ice, you know. *Surprisingly fast.* Max should run track or play on the hockey team. Maybe they'd score some more goals. He's one tough guy. *Indestructible* even. One time he hit the ice hard on his bottom and wasn't even fazed. He's a machine."

"Wow. Max is a lucky dude to have such a pretty girl bragging on him like you are right now. I'm happy for you guys. You make a great couple. Really. Emily's right. You're perfect for each other."

"Thanks, Blake. That means a lot. You and Emily are great together too. She's a lucky girl. You know you're not half bad, Blake. Of course Max is better," I beamed.

"I get it, Dallas. I always wondered why Max didn't play sports though. He's big, built like an athlete, and his heavy legs are like tanks. He could've been a linebacker or a point guard or even a quarterback like me. He's never played on any team that I know of. Not even a little league squad. It's kinda weird really. You'd think that, not having a dad, his mom Katie would've signed

Max up for sports. But she never did. I guess she's worried he'll get hurt."

"Maybe, Blake." *Maybe.*

"Finally! You guys are late today! What the heck took you so long? Now we don't have time to drink hot cocoa in the cafeteria. Class starts in like five minutes!" Emily groaned. Her innocent voice simply oozing disappointment.

"It's Dallas' fault, E.B. She's *mesmerized* by Max--couldn't get her out the front door this morning. She kept running back to her bedroom--adjusting her makeup or something," Blake insisted, while contorting his facial features uncontrollably.

"What? You look great, Dallas. You're glowing! You always look pretty--that's why Max and Alex are obsessed with you," Emily countered.

"Thanks, Emily. I just wanted to look perfect today. Our date at the ice rink on Saturday night was awesome, I don't want to disappoint Max by looking all raggedy. I need to *shine*."

"You are shining, Dallas. So shiny in fact I could spot you from the crowded parking lot before you guys walked through the plate glass doors. You're shining like diamonds."

"Thanks Emily, Max thinks I'm shiny too."

"Speak of the devil, Dallas, here comes your knight in *shining* armor."

"Good one, Blake," Emily chuckled.

"Max?"

"No, it's Alex," Blake teased.

"Oh brother. What does he want?" I wondered out loud.

"You, Dallas, Alex wants you," Emily uttered.

"Perfect. The feeling is definitely not mutual," I shrugged.

"Hey, people. What's up? Too late for hot chocolate today. Cafeteria just closed. Hey, Dallas, can I escort you to English?"

"Uh, sure, Alex. I suppose so. I don't see *Max* around anyway. Let's walk."

Alex's tight and faded *Levi's* accentuated his beefy thighs and the white button-down he sported underneath his weighty coat revealed a tuft of jet black chest hairs. His murky, cropped hair bore slight indentations on the moussed sides from what appeared to be a brand-new *Texas Rangers* baseball cap he'd politely removed once in my presence. *I didn't realize Alex was a Rangers fan. Trying to impress me again?* His worn out, black suede *Puma* sneakers were messily colored in with a dark sharpie and he desperately needed a new pair of running shoes. He claimed those to be his lucky sneakers, however, and wouldn't replace them until the thinned rubber soles wore completely off. Alex proudly donned his familiar leather football jacket and a pair of slightly weathered gloves. I guess he'd forgotten to remove them from his frozen hands when he entered the frosty building. WWHS administration failed to keep the structure warm enough as the price of natural gas was rising considerably. As a result, chilly students routinely wore layers upon layers of bulky clothing in order to stay warm. I was no exception. Today, I'd elected to wear a ribbed black turtleneck (again) underneath a chunky hunter green and maroon woolen sweater. My trusty black rayon down coat hung loosely around my adorned calves. The excessively long cover kept my writhe body toasty. My brown mane was left somewhat messy when I hastily removed the hand-knitted, cable ski cap Mom bought me at *Kohl's*. A matching black and white striped scarf and black mittens complemented the heavy ensemble. Black suede boots enveloped my legs and I had to admit, I was warm. I wanted to see Max though. Alex was a bore. *As usual.*

"Hey, Dallas. Um, wait up. I'm over here," Max shouted.

I spun my head around as soon as I heard his soothing voice.

"Max! Hurry up! We're going to be late!" I yelled. Thrilled to see him.

"What's he doing here, Dallas?" Alex whined.

"It's a school day, where else would he be?" I shot back.

Alex was furious when Max approached and his disdain was obvious. Max seemed oblivious to the risk, however. At least initially.

"Hey, Dallas and Alex. Nippy out there, huh?" he sang.

"You're too late, Max. I found her first. I'm walking Dallas to English class. Back off," Alex barked.

"You back off, Alex, I don't need an escort you know. I can navigate the route myself," I scolded.

"Um, it's okay, Dallas. I can meet up with you later," Max countered, suddenly keen to Alex's threatening posture. "We'll see each other at lunch. I brought brownies."

"Brownies? What's your problem, dude? Can't Dallas eat in the cafeteria with her friends? You hold her up in the science lab like she's some sort of hostage. Let her out once in a while, man. She's eating with us today!" Alex puffed. His stiffening position even more foreboding.

"Shut up, Alex! I'm eating with Max. You don't tell me what to do. Back off!" I lunged. Surprised by my fit of forcefulness.

"Whatever, Dallas. The dude's a pansy. You're better off with us. He's got you brainwashed or something. You can't think of anything but Max," Alex sniffed.

"Um, it's really okay, Dallas. If you'd rather eat with your friends, I understand. We can meet another time, maybe tomorrow. I'm sorry Alex."

"What are you saying, Max? I want to eat with you. Alex doesn't know what he's talking about. Do you? You can leave now, you know. Max is here, everything is fine," I quipped.

"Whatever, Dallas. Maybe I'll see you around sometime. That is if Max allows it."

Alex stormed off in a fit of rage and I was glad to see his backside heading south. What a jerk, I thought to myself. Then I turned towards Max.

"I'm really sorry about that. I don't know what got into him. Alex is a real jerk sometimes. Such a pain the..."

"Don't worry about it, Dallas," Max coolly interrupted. "He likes you--that's obvious now. I guess I never really noticed before. Can't blame the guy. You are irresistible, that's for sure," Max cooed in a reassuring voice.

"You're too nice, Max. Really. Alex doesn't deserve to have someone as kind as you defending his caveman actions. He's a first class jerk as far as I'm concerned and I don't care to ever speak to him again. I mean it."

"It's okay, you know, I'm not trying to steal you away from your friends. I just enjoy your company, that's all. You can eat lunch with the gang. I don't mind. Really, I don't."

"Not on your life! I'd rather be with you. I could never give up our lunch dates. Besides, Franco and that creepy rat snake would miss me too much if I bailed. I'll see you at noon. Just like always. And forget about everything Alex said. He's a jerk. A first rate jerk."

"See ya at noon then, Dallas," Max laughed. Before he walked off, however, he bent forward tenderly kissing my bare forehead. His warm breath and supple lips wisped across my clammy skin and I felt heady. I longed to grab Max's idyllic face. I wanted to kiss him convincingly on his alluring mouth. In my wandering imagination I did--pursed my eager lips atop his. Max returned the pungent kiss that lingered for nearly a minute. Of course this fantastical exchange existed only in my shocking thoughts. Maybe at lunchtime my fantasy would be realized. A girl could always dream.

"Tell me everything, Dallas. What happened? I heard Max and Alex got into a violent shouting match in the packed hallway this morning. Is it true? Did they fight?" Emily buzzed outside of my newly organized top row locker. "Everyone's saying they did."

"He's such a loser, Emily. Really. I could kill Alex. There was shouting all right. Except the yelling only occurred between me and Alex. Max was a gentleman. He never raised his voice--even though Alex deserved it," I huffed.

"You're right, Dallas. He is a loser. But I have to admit, I've never known Alex to act like that before-- even when he and Marie Frances were hot and heavy. He really likes you--you're right about that. But he needs to back off. You're with Max now."

"Yes I am. I have no intention of breaking up with Max in order to placate Alex. He needs to disappear from the face of the earth even."

"Don't worry about *him*, Dallas. Alex will get over it. He's just attempting to mark his territory--like any vigorous dog would."

"He's a dog all right, Emily. And he's lucky I didn't kick him where it hurts this morning. I certainly wanted too. I can't stand that loser. He's on my hit list now. *Seriously*. Keep Alex Samuels the Third away from me! Or heads will roll! At least one head anyway."

"I hear you, Dallas. I'll yell at him during lunchtime-- embarrass him in front of the gang. He won't bother you again after I get through with him. At least we only have two more days of school left to suffer through. Christmas break starts on Thursday. I'm bringing your birthday gift on Wednesday. You promised you'd wear it on your date with Max. I'm holding you to that!"

"Of course I will, Emily. And you shouldn't have bought me anything. You've done enough for me already. You're a great friend you know. Really. I don't need anything else but your friendship."

"I know that, Dallas. But you still have to promise to wear the gift on your date with Max."

"I will! I will! Now get to class! And don't forget to embarrass the heck out of Alex when you see him at lunch. I'll be in the science lab with Max!"

I love the night. It's the only time I really feel alive.
Helen Chandler, Dracula 1931.

Chapter 16

Here Comes Santa Claus...

"Emily, it's gorgeous! I mean it! You shouldn't have spent so much money! I love it!" I squealed.

"Put it on, Dallas, let's see it. I want you to *shine* on your date with Max over the holidays. Put the darn thing on!"

"I need your help. Can you clasp it?"

Emily centered the at least two carat, cushion cut purple stone strategically around my healed throat and the amethyst bauble sparkled as if it were a genuine diamond. The sterling silver, heart-shaped pendent hung delicately around my nape and I loved it already.

"It's gorgeous, Emily. It must have cost a fortune. You went overboard!" I gushed.

"Don't worry about it, Dallas. I got it on sale. One of my dad's ex-Angina patients owns a hand-made jewelry store near the mall on Route Two and he promised my dad a giant discount if he purchased Mom's Christmas gift from him this year. Dad saved his life, I guess. Anyway, I went with him to pick out Mom's surprise--he got her a fancy four carat, Emerald cut diamond tennis bracelet--and I saw this thing gleaming at me from inside a velvet box. I thought it would make a perfect gift for you. Do you really like it?"

"Of course I do! I love it! Hurry up though and take it off me. I don't want Max to see it yet. He'll be here any minute. I want to wear it on my birthday to his mom's place. It's beautiful. I know just what to wear it with too--a purple satin blouse I wore to a sports banquet once in Dallas. My date was a bore--Charlie O'Brien--but the glossy top was a hit. It was stunning--the blouse

I mean. Anyway, it matches this brilliant stone perfectly. I can't wait!"

"The blouse sounds pretty, Dallas. Purple is my favorite color you know. Purple is the color of royalty. Anyway, Max will be *mesmerized*. He won't be able to take his doe eyes off you!" she frolicked. "I'm jealous!"

I gave Emily a giant bear hug and thanked her repeatedly for the extravagant gift. I was worried, however, because all I'd gotten her was a simple pair of gold-filled, dangle hoops I'd found while scrutinizing *Mervyn's* half-off jewelry section. I'd have to rush to the mall and pick out something more substantial for my generous companion. Perhaps I'd give the unadorned earrings to Ashley instead. Emily deserved better. She was a thoughtful friend supportive of my relationship with Max. I already had something special in mind...

"Hey, can I join you girls? This looks fun!" Blake wailed while wandering aimlessly in the thinning hallways.

"You're so cheesy, Blake. We're finished hugging now anyways. You're too late," Emily ragged.

"Dang. I would've given anything to be in the center of that cozy embrace. Just my luck. A day late and a dollar short."

"It's Wednesday, guys, last day of classes, we better take off, Blake. Max will appear around that corner any minute. He'd rather die than not walk Dallas to English class," Emily winked.

She was right of course. Everyday Max greeted me hungrily outside of my beat up metal locker--214--just so he could proudly escort me to my first class of the day--Honors English. A true gentleman, Max always carried my mass of tattered textbooks no matter how heavy the giant load. Outside the busied classroom, in plain sight of course, Max would gently peck at my all too-willing left cheek and inquisitive onlookers--mostly female--would sigh impetuously at the sight of our spectacle. The brood of envious girls were jealous. Why couldn't their crummy, uninspired boyfriends stare at them as pensively as Maxwell Snow gazed at me? I felt bad for them. *Truly.* They had no idea what real love *felt* like. Gut-wrenching love. I can't bear to live without you love. Put your arms around me or I'll die love. Unlucky fools.

"See you at lunch today, Dallas," Max smiled coyly as he exited.

"See you at lunch, Max," I teased--licking my lips in order to tempt him.

Wednesday, December 22, our last day of classes before the Christmas break, flew by faster than a flock of frozen geese heading south for the winter. Lunch with Max--curried lentils and basmati rice with almonds and gooey rice crispy bars for dessert--was delicious. At three-fifteen, however, we parted ways--kissing each other passionately before reaching the crowded parking lot where Mom and the horrible twins sat in the stale van, waiting. On the ride home from school, despite being famished, the four of us unanimously agreed to stop by a local *Hallmark* store in order to purchase an assortment of colorful foiled wrapping paper, green and red curly bows, and a collection of humorous greeting cards for family and friends. The not-to-be-taken-seriously cards would arrive shockingly late, of course. While surveying the store's various collection of overly-priced holiday merchandise, I selected an early gift specifically meant for myself. On a ransacked shelf marked "clearance items," I uncovered a slightly tattered 2004-2005, leather bound journal complete with a tiny metal lock and yellow-feathered writing pen. I had to have it. For Max's mother Katie, I scored a four by six crystal heart frame with dark matting and a black velvet backing. For Max, a handsome photo album in a masculine print seemed sufficient. Earlier in the week, I'd already picked up a generous and expensive bottle of *Guess* cologne for him at *Dillard's* as well as a hand knotted, red and green cable sweater for my dad. For Mom, I'd grabbed a pair of tiny freshwater pearl earrings and the twins got matching hot pink *Hannah Montana* short-sleeved tee shirts--Caitlin hates *Hannah Montana.*

"I'm paying for this, Mom," I announced clutching the fancy journal inside my cupped hands.

"Okay, Emily. I can get it if you want me to, though. I don't mind."

"It's okay, Mom, I've got it. I still have some leftover birthday money from Aunt Caroline anyway."

"Is that photo album for Max?"

"Yep. He asked his mom for a digital camera for Christmas. Thought he'd need an album to house all the nature pictures he's sure to take."

"It's a thoughtful gift, Emily. I'm sure Max will love it," Mom insisted.

"Hope so. He deserves something nice."

"He's a special boy, Emily. I like him--I really do. Dad does too. He's just worried about you--doesn't want you getting hurt *again*. We both worry about you. All of you. You and your sisters have been through a lot. We want ya'll to be happy."

"I know, Mom. There's nothing to worry about. I'm fine--*now*. I would never do anything that stupid again--you know that. I'm okay. Even Dr. Brothers insisted I was okay before we left Texas. There's nothing for you and Dad to worry about. I would never do anything stupid again. *Ever*."

"I know, Emily. I trust you. Just let me know if things get hard on you again. We can always consult another psychiatrist. I've already looked around. Beckley has some notable physicians."

"I'm okay, Mom. Really."

"Well, come on then, girls, let's get this mound of stuff paid for and get the heck out of here before ya'll bankrupt me! We need to get home and wrap some presents!" Mom roared.

As soon as we got back to the stuffy little house complete with the ugliest white plastic Christmas tree the world's ever seen--Mom and I unloaded the hodgepodge of treasures we'd scored earlier, choosing to wrap each other's gifts inside of our locked bedrooms so the others couldn't spy. Caitlin was dying to uncover what I'd gotten for her and Ashley when perusing the swarming mall last weekend. I couldn't wait to see her disappointed face when she realized I'd purchased matching *Hannah Montana* outfits for the dubious pair. *They hated matching outfits. So cliché...* After finishing up--leaving remnants of gaudy holiday paper scattered across the hard, wooden floor--I carefully removed the hand-bound leather journal from inside the clingy plastic bag housing it undoing the fragile lock with the dainty silver keys cleverly attached. I wanted to write. Something I hadn't done in ages.

Daily Journal 2004-2005

December 23, 2004

Dear Diary, or journal, whatever you are:

I'm bored so I thought I'd write. I haven't written much since Rose died. In fact, I'm not even sure what happened to my old diary. Mom probably hid it. Anyway, I don't have much to say. I mean, a lot's been going on. Let's see. In November we left Texas--finally. Things were getting too intense. Dr. Brothers said it was time for us to leave. She thought I needed a new start. A fresh start, somewhere else. After I took those pills--my so-called "suicide attempt,"--she thought it would be better if we got out of Texas. Too many painful memories of Rose, I guess. I was the one who begged Mom to go to that restaurant you know. The one where Rose got snatched. I couldn't believe they found her body so close to where that crazy man grabbed her. Dead. The doctors said she'd been drained or something sick like that. Anyway, Dad blamed Mom immediately of course. Said we should have eaten at home. It wasn't her fault you know. I picked that crowded restaurant. That stupid restaurant! Whoever snatched her should have stolen me. I wish the creep that took Rose had been found. I would have killed him myself. Anyway, we're here now. In Beckley. Too bad she's not with us. I miss her terribly. Rose was the love of my life. She was too innocent to die. She had Down Syndrome, for goodness sakes! Couldn't he have picked on someone stronger? Someone who could have fought back? She was too small to fight. Too innocent. I hate that man! That brutal man! So tall, so strong. I saw him grab her. His blonde hair and scarred face. I told the police everything. His long arms and crooked teeth! Everything! I told them everything! That cruel man, who took our Rose. What did he want from her anyway? She had nothing to offer an evil sort like that. I hope he's dead now. Like Rose. I hope he's dead. Emily Ryan Reed.

P.S. I feel like writing a poem. I'm surprised. But I need to keep writing I guess. Here goes. Haven't written a poem in ages. Hope it doesn't suck.

Crooked

Cruel teeth, crooked and faded,
running amuck, the city is inundated.
This killer, who is he? What does he want?
We've nothing to offer. Yet still, he hunts.
Rose is the victim. Her face speaks volumes.
We'll find her dead. She's no choice but to follow.
His hands are strong, his grip is ferocious.
She's dead now, Mom. Her body is lifeless.

P. S. S. I hate him! I hate him! I hate him! I hate him!

December 24, 2004: Christmas Eve

"Caitlin, you baboon! Seriously, you're sitting on my ski jacket! I can't even get out of the car. Get up, fart face! I need to get inside the house. Max will be here in less than an hour. I need to get dressed for our date!"

"Shut up, vomit breath! You smell like *Taco Bell* anyway. We should have gone to *McDonald's* again, Mom!" Caitlin hounded.

"It's Christmas Eve, Caitlin. A lot of restaurants are closed today. *Taco Bell's* the closest to us anyways," Mom retorted. "And get off Emily's coat! She needs to get ready for her date with Max. He'll be here soon. You shouldn't have eaten so many tacos, Emily. Isn't his mom fixin' dinner for ya'll?"

"Yes. But I was hungry. I always get hungry when I'm nervous. Food calms my nerves," I insisted.

"If you say so. Just be sure to eat what Katie offers. It's impolite to turn away food from a gracious host. Eat everything on your plate--no matter what."

"I will Mom, I will. I would never be rude to Max's mom. I want her to like me. Hey, have you seen my khaki skirt? The one with the pleats in front? I want to wear it with my purple blouse. Can you help me find it?" I begged.

"It's in my closet. I borrowed it a couple of weeks ago when I went on that job interview in town— '*Baby Genius*'. They haven't called me back yet. Anyway, I had it dry-cleaned. The skirt looks good."

"Awesome, Mom. I need my black riding boots too. Max said to dress warmly. It's not too bad out there right now. I'll wear my long black coat and boots with my khaki skirt and purple shirt. I shouldn't get cold."

"You'll be fine, Emily. It's a clear night. Enjoy your date with Max."

At six o'clock sharp, I painstakingly straightened my caramel locks with the flat iron, pinning the loose sides upwards with borrowed silver hair clips. My pointy ears--inherited from Uncle Hoot--looked "precious" Mom beamed. I placed the satin chemise gently over my provocative hairdo and proceeded to wrap the extravagant amethyst necklace around my fragile nape. I was glad I'd gone back to the mall, purchasing a dainty freshwater pearl anklet for Emily. While getting dressed, I saved the nearly floor length khaki skirt for last, didn't want the cotton to wrinkle while adjusting my makeup and finishing my hair. My taut, even complexion glowed from the meticulously-applied dusting of warm, metallic bronzer. I selected silvery-grey shadow for the lids of my bluish eyes. The dark mascara and eyeliner complemented my dark and giant pupils. Shimmering peony blusher and matching lip gloss tinted my lightly flushed cheeks and lips. I made sure to cover my splattering of freckles generously with matte foundation. Rose-colored polish adorned my manicured nails and pedicure--an early birthday gift from Mom--the only parent supportive of my relationship with Max. *Betsy Johnson* cologne, splashed generously across my torso, smelled like apple blossoms, jasmine, and cinnamon. No vanilla musk tonight. Madison sent the succulent-smelling perfume meant to be a birthday/Christmas gift. I was grateful. When I finished painting my face and primping my hair, I stood up from the marble vanity, slipping on my elongated skirt. For a brief moment, I considered changing outfits. However, Mom assured me the sophisticated look was more than satisfactory. I grabbed my black leather riding boots, completing the elaborate look. Later on, when the doorbell finally rang, I seized my freshly-oiled black leather bag and nearly floor length coat, heading for the front entrance. I couldn't wait to see Max.

"I'll get it!" I shouted.

I opened the squeaky door revealing my inspired date. Max was awed when he laid his bedazzled eyes on me.

"Uh, wow, Dallas. You look lovely. I don't know what to say. Really. You take my breath away."

"I do?"

"Of course. You're stunning. I've never seen you look this incredible before."

"You look great too, Max. Come inside. I'm almost ready. I just need to let my parents know we're heading out. Dad's asleep in his bedroom. He's been under the weather for a couple of days. Hey, Mom, I'm leaving now! See ya'll at midnight!" I yelled. She was in the spotless kitchen rearranging the canned goods for the second time this week--still bored I guess.

"Goodbye, Emily. You and Max have fun tonight. See ya'll later," she answered--peeking her snooping head out at us from behind the breakfast nook.

"I guess we're all clear now, Max. Let's go. I'm ready when you are."

Max didn't argue as we made our way out the front door, hand in hand. My body sizzled when the heat of Max's palm nearly scorched my own. The chemistry between the two of us reached a boiling point after Max and I climbed inside his truck. Before he started the antique, Max reached over scooping my unsuspecting face inside his warm hands. Staring intently into each other's eyes, Max and I began kissing each other passionately. Lightheaded, I nearly forgot that we were on our way to his house to have dinner with his mother. I wanted to stay inside that balmy truck forever.

I told you, I feed erratically, and often enormously.
Max Schreck, Shadow of the Vampire. 2000.

Chapter 17

The Perfect Night...

The exhilarating drive towards Max's ample property in the lush, West Virginia hills was liberating and I couldn't wait to finally meet his elusive mother Katie. A twinge of panic, however, wracked my keyed-up body when I introduced myself to her over and over again inside my dramatic imagination. Would she like me? I certainly hoped Katie Snow cared for me as much as I anticipated appreciating her.

"You're not nervous are you, Dallas? You shouldn't be you know--Mom will love you. You're an awesome girl. She'll fall in love instantly," Max purred, while gently stroking my available wrist.

"I hope so Max. I really do. Your mom is special to me already--even though we haven't met. I feel like I already know her. I mean, I see so much of her feminine qualities in you--your kindness, your tender nature and, of course, your positive manner. Your mother is responsible for all those noble traits you know. It's her matriarchal influence, I guess. That's why you're so darn magnificent."

"She raised me, Dallas--that's for sure. I mean, without a father figure--a masculine influence I guess you could say--I've never really felt aggressive. Mom's always insisted I remain composed. I think one of the reasons she didn't encourage me to play sports is because she didn't want me getting too worked up or antagonistic. She's always been adamant I remain calm and collected-- no matter what the circumstance--to never lose my cool. I've never been much of a fighter, you know. She keeps me grounded I guess. That's why I prefer my school studies to the stresses of sports and the tranquility of nature to the aggravation of the city. I suppose that's why I want to be a small-town doctor--I'd rather help people than hurt them. Anyway, I hope you like her. I think you will. I know she'll fall desperately in love with you. I don't doubt that for a minute," Max poured.

"You're awesome, Max. You really are. I'm lucky to know you."

"Thanks, I feel the same way. I mean, not about my awesomeness," he chuckled. "I feel lucky to know you, too. Very, very, lucky."

The rest of the ride towards his glorious tree farm was equally revealing. Once we pulled into the gravel road heading towards his verdant property, Max squealed like a pig at the sight of a mischievous raccoon frolicking by himself in the snowy drifts.

"Dallas, hey, look up! Over there! See the raccoon? Over there, see it?"

"I do! It's so cute! It looks like a baby! I thought they only came out late at night?"

"Usually. But since it's so quiet out here, no cars or traffic, sometimes they sneak around foraging for food. There it goes. Back into the thicket. I guess my truck's bright headlights scared it off. Too bad--it was cute, huh?"

"Very cute. I bet there's more of those tiny creatures hiding in the trees. A whole family even."

"Yep. Hey, we're almost here. Are you excited?"

"Are you kidding Max? I can't wait to meet your mother. I've been waiting for this moment for a while now. Hurry up and park!"

"Okay. Hey, before we go inside, I want you to know that I'm happy we're going out. I mean, I guess I'm trying to tell you that I'm glad we're dating. You mean a lot to me, Dallas. Keep that in mind tonight."

"I will."

Like a true gentleman, Max courteously opened my side of the antiquated truck, graciously assisting me when I exited.

"Watch your step--snow's slippery, you know. Wouldn't want you falling down and ruining that beautiful outfit of yours."

"Thanks Max. For the hand, I mean. I think I'm ready. Let's go inside."

"After you, my lady."

"After you, sir."

Max and I ambled up the freshly salted, curved sidewalk leading to his cozy front porch clutching tightly to each other's hands. Even though I was nervous about meeting Katie, I felt safe in Max's protective grip. I knew he would never allow anything unpleasant to occur between us. Not that I anticipated anything terrible happening when the belated introductions finally took place. I just knew that Max cared enough about Katie and me to ensure the meeting would be amiable.

"Mom, hey, Mom, we're here! It's us, we're here!" Max roared once inside the petite but meticulous wooden abode.

"I'm coming, Max. Be there in a second," Katie returned the fervor, her voice silky as butter. I heard the patter of fragile footsteps on the solid oak floors as she got closer and closer to us.

"I'm right here, Max," Katie beamed--her lucent face illuminating the shadowy room.

Max's adoring mother made her way inside the miniature living area and her striking Italian features lit the diminutive space the second she laid eyes on her indulgent son.

"Mom, this is Dallas," he proudly announced.

"Dallas, this is my mom--Katie," Max dotingly sang.

"Dallas, oh my goodness, it's so good to finally meet you. I'm sorry it's taken so long! I've been under the weather. But I'm so very glad to meet you!" Katie crooned. Her unwavering and enthusiastic voice seemed sincere as she assured me she was indeed thrilled to know me.

Katie took my uneasy hands gently into her own and then warmly reached out around my slender neck kissing my left cheek tenderly. Her cozy lips felt honest against my unsullied skin.

"It's nice to finally meet you too, Ms. Snow," I politely offered.

"Please, oh please dear, do not call me *Ms.* Snow! It makes me feel so old! To you I am Katie--always Katie. Okay, Dallas?"

"Uh, okay, ma'am. I can live with that. Katie it is," I agreed, looking at Max somewhat apprehensively.

"Mom is only thirty-six Dallas. She hates being called Mrs. or Ms. or ma'am. It's fine to call her Katie--I promise."

"Yes, Dallas. Always call me Katie. Never be afraid it's too casual. I insist. I truly do insist."

"Yes, Katie. I will. And thanks for allowing me to."

"You're welcome. Oh my goodness, you are so beautiful, Dallas! As beautiful as Max insists you are! And I am so glad to know you."

"Hey, Mom, guess what we saw outside, on our drive up the hill? A baby raccoon. I think there's more. Hiding in the trees."

"Really Max? Show me where you spotted him tomorrow--I'll leave out some seeds or peanut butter. They love granola cereal you know. I'll take him some granola."

"Sounds good. Hey, um, is everything, uh, set up? I mean, are we ready, you know, for tonight?" Max stuttered. He always did that when he was nervous.

"Oh, well, yes we are, Max. Um, the food's ready and I think everything else is good to go."

"Great. After we eat, I want to take Dallas outside. You know, show her some more of the property."

"I understand," Katie winked. "*Everything's* good to go, Max. Why don't you kids head for the kitchen. I'll be right in."

Once again, I felt like Max was conspiring against me with an all-too-willing accomplice. What was he planning *this time*?

"Sure, Mom. Come on, Dallas. Chow time!"

"Okay. I'm as hungry as you are, Max."

Katie Doreen Snow looked fetching in her knee-length, black velvet dress and elegant white lace wrap. An expensive looking Victorian style broach with a beautiful purple stone--similar to mine--accentuated the dress' ruffled collar. Her sumptuously long, jet black hair fell casually below her miniscule, belt clad waist. Her pallid skin was free of premature wrinkles like crow's feet or laugh lines. Katie's black eyes complemented her ebony hair and her delicate, subtle lips were left bare--no heavy lipstick or gaudy stain. Katie's flawless and makeup-free face glowed in all its natural beauty. She was stunning to look at.

"Sit down kids. Here, you sit here, Dallas--beside me, I want to get to know you better. Sit here, sweet child."

"Absolutely. I'd love to."

"Max, over there--next to Dallas. You two are so cute together. Can't separate such a beautiful couple!"

"Whatever you say, Mom, can't argue with that logic!" Max proudly gushed.

Katie and Max treated one another fondly while dining at the small but substantial oak table. Their wide, affectionate eyes flashed each other adoringly throughout our *mostly* pleasant dinner. Katie prepared a hearty rack of lamb with a tart cranberry and fresh mint sauce; cheesy garlic mashed potatoes topped with dried parsley; and baby spinach salad garnished generously with thinly sliced purple onions and balsamic vinegar. Before the delicious main course, however, a satisfying bisque wet our hungry appetites.

"Jeez, Max, you slurp beef consommé like a vampire slurps type A blood," I rattled.

"Whatever, Dallas. You're just jealous cuz I got a bigger bowl than you," Max grinned. Max and I were joking with each other of course, however, I couldn't help noticing that Katie seemed a bit put off by our brief exchange--even if we were only teasing.

"Max, mind your manners. Use your spoon. You're not an *animal,* you know. Respect your food. Be glad you *crave* it."

"Huh Mom? What are you talking about?"

"Uh, I just meant that you should employ your manners when dining at the table--especially in the company of two females. Only animals slurp their meals, Max--and you, son, are no *animal.*"

"Sorry, Mom. I was just playing around. I wanted to see if Dallas was paying attention to me or her tasty broth."

"Okay, you two. Finish up the soup, supper's waiting." Katie seemed eager to change the subject. I found myself hoping that our temporary bantering hadn't offended her too much. Leaving the heavy table rather abruptly, Katie headed towards the cramped kitchen. When she returned, a good-natured beam lit up her features--I guess she was over it.

"Eat up, you two! That rack of lamb won't eat itself," Katie mocked, when carefully steadying the silver-plated platter atop the deep wooden table.

"Glad too, Mom. Hey, Dallas, pass the mint sauce. *Please.*"

"Much better Max. You're more handsome when you mind your manners, son," Katie smiled. I was glad to see her happy again.

"So, Dallas, tell me about yourself. Anything you want. I'd love to hear everything about you sweet girl."

"Well, I'm sixtee--oops, I mean seventeen--now."

"Of course you are, dear," Katie politely interrupted. "That's why you're here. To celebrate your marvelous birthday of course!"

"That's right. Anyway, now that I'm seventeen, I hope to be driving soon. Mom and Dad promised I could take the driver's test after my seventeenth birthday. I'm holding them to it. I want a car! I hate having to rely on others to pick me up all of the time and I hate it that Max had to drive all the way out to my house tonight just to pick me up. If I had a car--I could be more independent. Know what I mean?"

"I do, Dallas. Although, sometimes I wish life was simpler and we still rode around on horseback. Cars create so much pollution--I fear we are damaging our environment. All this drilling for oil--I shudder to think about the undue harm we are inflicting unto our defenseless planet," Katie vigorously interjected.

"Mom's an environmentalist, Dallas. She belongs to an organization called *The West Virginia Highlands Conservatory*. It's the oldest activist organization in the state."

"I understand, Katie. It's difficult you know, determining just how much off-shore drilling our planet can endure. It's a balance, I guess. A very delicate balance."

"You're right about that, Dallas. It's good to see young people so passionate about the natural world these days. Still, I can't help but worry about the Earth's future. Let me change the subject though, to something more pleasant. This meal is a celebration, not a funeral. Eat up kids--we've seven-layer chocolate cake for dessert!"

"Sounds great, Mom. You did too much though. I think you went overboard!" Max screeched, patting his bulging Buddha belly when he did.

"This is a special occasion, son. Dallas needs a cake, you know. It's her birthday after all."

"Katie, really, you shouldn't have. You've done too much already. I'm stuffed! You really did go overboard--Max's right!"

"Nonsense, I'm bringing in the cake. Max, clear these dishes. Make room for the piece de resistance."

"Let me help Max. I'll clear the salad plates, you get the soup bowls," I kindly offered.

"I'll grab the larger plates. Just situate them on top of the kitchen counter," Katie insisted. "I'll rinse them later."

Max and I cleared the disheveled mess, making sure there was enough room for the massive dessert resting atop an etched crystal cake stand. Katie lovingly baked the mouth-watering treat earlier in the day. A gracious host, she made sure our first dinner as a trio was memorable. Sporting no less than seventeen hot pink candles, the liberally layered confection smelled awesome. I couldn't wait to dig in.

"Katie, it's magnificent! You shouldn't have!" I howled, delighted at the sight of the enormous mound of gooey chocolate fudge facing me.

"It's perfect Mom. I can't wait for a slice. Make it a giant one, please!" Max begged--too hungry for his own good.

"I thought you were too full for any more food Max," Katie teased.

"I changed my mind."

Katie and I chuckled simultaneously--looking into each other's amused direction.

"Blow out the candles, Dallas. But don't forget to make a wish first," Katie lovingly reminded.

"Okay, here goes nothing." I stood perfectly still for a brief moment before shutting my overwhelmed but giddy eyes. For about thirty seconds, I mentally envisioned my wish--then blew out the smoldering candles.

"Good job Dallas--you got them all!" Max bellowed--grinning widely from ear to ear.

"Sure did, Dallas. Your wish is sure to come true now. Hope it was a good one!" Katie sang.

That black convertible Eclipse was mine.

After greedily devouring the sumptuous heap of chocolate heaven, each of us wobbled towards the feathery couch in order to rest our swollen bodies.

"Oh my god, I can't eat anything else. I mean it, ya'll. I'm done--stick a fork in me!"

"Me too, Dallas. I never thought I'd say this, but Mom, I don't ever want to eat another piece of chocolate again!"

"Me either, Max. I have to agree with you, son!"

Crowded on top of the mocha, velveteen sofa, our rounded bellies extended, each of us were beyond full--stuffed like three little pigs--who weren't so little anymore.

"I'm going outside to collect some firewood. The blaze is dying out."

"Thanks, son. Grab some pieces of seasoned oak--it burns better than maple or beech wood, you know."

"Will do."

Max exited the friendly room. Although markedly undersized--no larger than one-hundred and fifty square feet--the collection of cozy mahogany antiques and plump brown furniture gave the pocket-sized room a giant feel. Max's mom Katie enhanced the earthy decor with a variety of fluffy pillows and an assortment of indoor plants--mostly ivy's. She chose to adorn the pale butter walls with a splattering of colorful landscapes and stills. Her preference was for oil paintings, clearly. However, several imposing watercolors graced the interior's plaster facade. Above the roaring fireplace, a well-done portrait of Katie in her early twenties clung elegantly to its boastful resting place. In the painting, Katie donned the same purple broach gracing her elegant outfit tonight.

"The painting's beautiful, Katie. Who's the artist?"

"Max's father, Sam--he painted it when we were still together. He was an excellent artist--his medium of choice was oils. He painted most of the landscapes in this very room. Throughout the very house, in fact. I miss him terribly, I'm afraid."

Like her adoring son Max, Katie was resoundingly forthright--an inherited quality they unquestioningly shared. Katie also told me she was raised in an orphanage after her parents died in a car crash. She'd had a hard time, that's for sure.

"Max has told me a little bit about his father. I'm sorry he isn't, um, here. I'm sure you miss him terribly."

"I do. He left when Max was just a baby--barely one years old. Max has no memory of his father. Sam took off during the night. *I couldn't stop him.*"

"I'm sorry about that. Truly, I am. I wish I could meet--Sam," I stuttered. I didn't say anything more because I didn't want to upset Max's mother any further.

"Out of the way, girls, I've got a heavy load of wood to drop!"

"Max, you're back! Thank goodness. The fire's almost out!" Katie declared.

Max removed the hang-forged metal screen--similar to the iron gate outside--from atop the worn brick hearth. He piled the four pieces of skillfully hacked oak atop the fiery embers. "We have fire again, ladies," he smugly announced.

"Thank goodness, Max. My feet were starting to chill. Even though the weather's not too cold outside--it's still a chilly forty-five degrees. Be careful when you take Dallas into the woods, son--don't want her fingers and toes becoming frostbitten." Katie briskly warned.

"It's too warm outside for frostbite, Mom. Besides, I would never allow Dallas to freeze. We won't be too far from the house anyway. I just want to show her the back of the property--all the evergreens. And the frozen pond is beautiful in the light."

"I know, Max. Just be careful out there. She's not used to this climate yet. The warmth of Texas is a far cry from the frosty nights we suffer in West Virginia."

"I'll be okay, Katie. Thanks for your concern though. You and Max have been so nice to me tonight. I've got gifts for each of you. I left them out in the truck. Max, would you mind bringing them inside?"

"Sure. Be right back ladies."

"I'm so glad to know you, Dallas. And I'm thrilled for Max. You have brought new energy into his life. He's infatuated with you. I understand why. You own his heart now, Dallas. And he's better for it."

"Thank you, Katie. I'm better off knowing him too."

Max returned from the cold clutching two colorful bags and one poorly wrapped green and red package inside his bulky hands. I passed out the thoughtful gifts praying the owners would appreciate them.

"This one is for you, Katie. I hope you like it. I wasn't sure what to get. And here are your gifts, Max."

"Oh, Dallas. You didn't have to get me anything, you know. Let's see what it is though!" she playfully teased.

Katie carefully removed the fragile, heart-shaped crystal frame from inside the--*striped like a candy cane*--gift bag. Red tissue paper cluttered the bare floor.

"It's beautiful, Dallas. I love it! Oh, I can't wait to put a picture of you and Max inside. I'll place the picture frame on top of the mantle. Right here." Katie headed towards the lit fireplace situating the breakable gift atop the rough hewn cedar mantle. "It's perfect here, just perfect. I love it, Dallas."

After placing it deftly on top of the exposed wood, Katie sprung towards me giving me a giant bear hug. She planted another liberal kiss atop my flushed but pleased left cheek.

"Open yours now, Max. I hope you like them."

Max removed the large photo album first--covered in dark brown linen--from inside another decorative bag. This time, however, a silly picture of Rudolph and his infamous red nose graced the glossy paper.

"Cool, Dallas. I like it. I can't wait to fill it up with pictures of the tree farm--and you and Mom, of course. I love it. Thanks."

"It's perfect, Max. I'm sure you'll get a lot of use out of the album--considering you begged me to buy you a digital camera for Christmas this year. I hope *Santa* complied with your unrelenting demands," Katie laughed.

"I hope he did too, Mom! I can't sign up for the photography class without a camera you know!"

"I know that, son. You've told me at least a hundred times!"

"I'm sorry Mom. It's just that Mr. Smith is heading the photography elective next semester and we're going to be taking a lot of pictures when we hike at Cranberry. I really want to go."

"I know Max, I know. If Santa thinks you've been good this year, I'm sure he'll drop a camera down our hot chimney tonight," Katie winked specifically in my direction.

"That's right, Max. Santa's coming--hope you've been extra special. Wouldn't want him switching out your fancy camera for a lump of coal."

"Chill out, Dallas. Santa would never do me dirty like that. I'm a good boy. Always have been," Max snickered. "Anyway, grab your coat, I've got your present outside--bundle up."

"What have you got up your sleeve, Max? Should I be worried?"

"Of course not, Dallas, it's all good. You're gonna love your *surprises*. Now do as I say and bundle up. Don't forget your gloves. It's nippy outside."

"Okay, okay. I'll be ready in just a minute--let me find my scarf. I think I left it by the front door. And Max, you forgot to open the other gift."

Max grabbed the smaller box ripping the holiday paper into shreds."

"Awesome Dallas! I need some new cologne. Thanks!"

"You're welcome. Now let me grab my coat and mittens. Where are they?"

"I hung everything on the brass coat rack in the hall, Dallas," Katie interrupted. "Let me fetch them for you. I'll only be a moment."

"Thanks. Oh, Max, do I need a hat? I didn't bring one."

"You should be okay. It's not snowing right now. Anyway, your black coat has a hood, right?"

"Yeah."

"You'll be fine then. Come on, let's head out before it gets any colder."

After putting on my outerwear, Max grabbed my restless hand and we headed impatiently out the kitchen's screened back door. The wave of fresh but frozen air was invigorating, enlivening my warm but staled skin.

"Come on, Dallas. Follow me closely. I know the path well--even though it's covered in snow right now. We don't have far to wander--the pond is close by. Watch your step though, I couldn't shovel away all of the tiny pebbles before the snow fell. Don't want you twisting your girly ankles."

"I'll be fine, Max. Besides, I've got my trusty riding boots on. I won't slip."

"Let's bolt then. The pond is less than a quarter of a mile from here. That's where your *surprises* await you know. Get a move on, Dallas. I can't wait until you see them," Max insisted.

The daunting walk through the nearly two inches thick snow heap left me surprisingly breathless. As soon as we reached our destination, however, the sight of the at least eight foot tall Douglas fir--sparkling incessantly in the light of the bright moon--captured my attention. I was overwhelmed by its magnificence.

"Oh my god, Max. It's beautiful! What have you done? This must have taken hours! I love it. Oh my god, I absolutely love it!" I squealed as the willowy branches of the giant conifer swayed gently in the placid breeze. "I can't believe this! When did you do it? *How* did you do it? This tree is glorious Max! It's spectacular!"

"Do you really like it? I mean, it's not your only birthday gift--but it's part of your present."

"What's not to like, Max? I've never seen a lovelier Christmas tree before. It's gorgeous. Really. I can't believe you did all this for me. It's amazing--the best birthday gift I've ever received--and certainly the most creative. I love it," I gushed--marveled by the giant spectacle before me.

Max decorated the ancient fir by piling on layers upon layers of glitzy gold and silver garland while also draping the feathery branches with red and silver satin ribbons. The tiny bows, skillfully crafted, accentuated the brightly colored silken balls flanking the tree's delicate stems. Dozens and dozens of multicolored ornaments bejeweled the majestic tree. While examining the specimen in its splendid entirety, at the base of the giant fir I spotted a tiny package wrapped in rich, red foil resting atop the lacey snow. Aware that I'd spotted the meagerly sized gift, Max reached over, grabbing the trinket inside his cupped hands.

"Here you go, Dallas. Open it. This is your birthday present--the tree is your Christmas present--but this tiny box, my lady, is in honor of your seventeenth birthday. *Enjoy*."

"What have you done Max?"

"Open it, Dallas. Enjoy the moment."

"Okay, I will then," I grinned.

I carefully removed the miniature silver bow resting atop the shiny gift, then ripped into the crimson hued paper uncovering a black velvet box. I opened the small package which housed a white gold insignia ring Max had worn on one of our previous dates.

"It's beautiful, Max! I've seen this ring before--on you! Is this your ring?"

"Yes. It was left behind by my father--Sam. The letter "U" welded in gold onto the stone is probably a family crest--although my father's last name is Knight. We aren't sure who the amethyst ring originally belonged too--but Dad left it behind when he took off. Mother gave it to me when I turned twelve, and now I would like for you to have it."

"Oh Max, I can't accept this. It's too valuable--I mean the sentimental importance alone is immense. I can't accept this extravagant gift Max, I simply can't."

"Yes you can and you will, Dallas--I insist. This ring is yours--I absolutely, positively, insist."

"I don't know what to say. I've never received such an elaborate present before. I really don't know what to say Max."

"Just tell me you love me, Dallas. I want to know that you love me as much as I love you."

"Are you serious? Of course I love you! I've been wanting to tell you that for a while. I've just been too scared to admit my feelings to you. *I love you, Max.* I really do."

"That's why I'm giving you this ring Dallas. Every day I want you to remember how much I care for you--enough to gift to you the only remembrance my father left behind. Mom thinks he did so on purpose. That's why she gave the ring to me. She felt as if Dad wanted me to have it. Now I want you to have it."

"I really am overwhelmed, Max. I promise, I will put it on one of my gold chains as soon as I get home and I won't remove this ring from around my neck!"

Clutching tightly onto the extravagant gift Max generously lavished on me, I stood directly on top of my boot clad tippy toes rewarding him with a zealous kiss. Max's delicious lips hungrily devoured my passionate "thank you." When our earnest embrace commenced--Max and I stood back once again admiring the ornamented Douglass fir--amazed by its engaging presence. When gazing at the decorated tree--hand in hand of course--I couldn't help replaying Max's tender words over and over again inside my mind. Max loves me I thought to myself. Maxwell Snow loves me--and I've got a beautiful ring to prove it!

On our way back towards his temperate house, Max and I indulged ourselves in some additional light kissing. Upon entering the freshly cleaned kitchen, I couldn't help wondering, however, why the antique jewel Max gave me bore a delicate "U" crest instead of a "K" on its elegant exterior. Max said his father Sam's last name was Knight--shouldn't the crest begin with the letter "K"? What did the embossed "U" stand for then? Even though I wanted answers, I decided not to ask--I didn't want to upset Max or his caring mother Katie by prying. I decided to reserve my questions for another day. This moment was too perfect to spoil.

I will eat you. I mean that literally. The Dark Ages Quote. 2001.

Chapter 18

The Not So Perfect Night...

The oh-so-short drive back to my monotonous, one-story bungalow left me glum because I didn't want my astonishing night to end. So much had happened--I'd shared a wonderful dinner with Max and his attractive mother Katie--was overwhelmed by the sight of a one of a kind bejeweled tree--and spoiled with an extraordinary ring. The night produced more than I'd ever dreamed.

When Max and I entered the recently shoveled driveway--Dad busied himself when I was away in order to pass the time--I turned towards him planting what I believed to be one final kiss atop his pursed lips. Impatient for more, Max held my enamored face inside his masculine grip kissing me with more fervor than any of my previous boyfriends ever dared. *I was thrilled.*

"I hate to leave this truck, Max--I don't want tonight to end. But I better let you go. You have a long drive ahead--I'm sorry for that."

"There's nothing to be sorry for, Dallas. You're worth every mile I spend on that winding road. Every single mile. *I mean it.*"

"I know you do, Max. I just wish I could drive--you know--to help out a little."

"Even if you had a car *and* your license, I wouldn't let you do it. I'd rather pick you up--I know these snowy roads better than you. I've been navigating them for awhile. I know every inch of this highway--you're safe with me behind the wheel. Besides, I would never risk anything happening to you--*ever*."

"I know that, Max. You're an admirable guy. That's why I'm so darn crazy about you."

"Well I'm crazy about you too, Dallas. *I always will be.*"

"I hope so, Max--or I'd have to kill you!"

Max and I broke out into simultaneous laughter at my blunt confession before exiting the truck.

"I better get inside--it's two minutes before midnight--wouldn't want to be late you know--or Dad might kill us both!"

"I really enjoyed your company tonight, Dallas. I know tomorrow's Christmas Day--but maybe we could meet up this weekend? Maybe even on Friday?"

"Of course! I'll call you tomorrow. Or you can call me as soon as you get your fancy camera."

"I will. Here--let me walk you to the door, Madame--wouldn't want you to slip and fall. I have to protect you Dallas. It's my duty *now*."

"Whatever you say, Max. By the way, I really did enjoy our evening together. Please thank your mom again for everything--she's a sweetheart--just like you."

Max walked me up the salty, limestone pathway all the way to the brightly painted front door. When we reached our destination, he bent over kissing me softly on the folds of my lips. Dazed, I floated inside our warm house eager to write in my new journal. I couldn't wait to pen my innermost thoughts as I was hopelessly in love with Max.

Daily Journal 2004-2005

December 24, 2004

Dear Diary:

Okay. Pinch me--I must be dreaming! I had the best evening of my life! Tonight, while surrounded by brilliant stars, and in full view of one extremely well-dressed Christmas tree, Maxwell Snow told me he loves me! Can you believe it? Max and I are in love. It's real love, too. I know it is. I've never felt like this before. I can't wait to call Madison tomorrow in Texas. She'll be shocked! Oh, and Emily too. I can't wait! For now, Emily Ryan Reed-aka-Dallas.

At twelve-thirty p.m.--give or take a few exhausted minutes--I climbed appreciatively under my weighty covers eager for sleep. Although my mind was electrified--thanks to Max's confession--my haggard body craved slumber. As soon as my pulsing head rested itself on top of the fluffy pillow, my heavy eyes closed. I fell deeply into a sleep induced coma.

"Emily, Emily, wake up! wake up!" Mom shrieked as she shook violently at my exposed shoulders. "Get up right now! You're having another nightmare! Get up!"

"Huh?"

"You're having a bad dream!"

"Okay Mom, okay, I'm up. What is it? What's going on?" I moaned, still groggy from the crude interruption.

"You tell me dear--you were screaming again. I ran in here as fast as I could manage."

"Oh. I remember now. You're right--I was having a bad dream. I don't know what's going on Mom. I keep seeing Rose. I'm scared!"

"I know honey. I am too. Get up, let's head for the bathroom. You're scratching at your neck again. It's bleeding pretty bad. Come on."

Mom pulled my limp body out from underneath the cozy comforter and we headed towards the mostly pink Jack and Jill bath I shared with the twins. As soon as we entered the colorful bathroom, sporting pink and white tiles on the gaudy floor, my brain reacted to the intenseness of the cold as well as to the brightness of the overhead lights. I was awake.

"What's happening, Mom? Why do I keep having these horrible nightmares?"

"I don't understand it, Emily. Maybe you need to see a shrink again. I'll make some calls when the Christmas break is over. I don't know what else to do. I mean, look at your neck. This is serious. We have to find out what's going on. And soon," she panicked.

"I'll be okay, I don't need to see another specialist. Please--no more creepy psychiatrists prodding inside my head!"

"Let's don't worry too much about it right now. Let's get you cleaned up and back to bed. I'm glad you don't have school for a while. You can sleep in during the Christmas break. We'll delay opening presents in the morning. It's no big deal. I want you to get some sleep. *It's three a.m..* You need to sleep."

"What time did you say it is, Mom?"

"Three a.m. Well, three-eleven actually. Do you want to sleep with the twins again?"

"Yeah, I guess."

After situating myself snugly under the cool satiny sheets gracing Ashley's bumpy trundle bed, my mind was stuck on rewind. The fact that I was being visited by my dead sister Rose during the wee hours disturbed me. That it happened during the witching hour seriously freaked me out. While snuggling under the flimsy covers, I tried to visualize the events of the disquieting dream--probing my shaken memory for answers. Let's see, I remember Rose standing at the foot of my double bed, her miniature hands outstretched. This time, however, her beautiful satin dress was soaked heavily in blood that appeared to be oozing from her neck and underneath her fine, blonde hair. Rose looked scarier in this dream--more sinister. Her small eyes were menacing--as if Rose was angry. Is she mad at me? Am I truly responsible for her death? Bright, red blood wasn't the only thing I noticed on or around Rose's body. I remember a feather-like silhouette hovering ominously above her head--a murky shadow of some sort. What does Rose want? And what is she trying to tell me?

Too sleepy to worry about the nightmare anymore, I rested my drained head atop Ashley's hand me down pillow--which smelled musty and old--shutting my weary eyes tightly. I slept without interruption for nearly seven hours.

Christmas morning, around ten a.m., I was rudely awakened by my troublesome twin sisters--Caitlin especially--both dying to unearth the assortment of half-priced treasures purchased by Mom and Dad. The mound of sale item gifts appeared to double in size overnight. Needless to say, Ashley and Caitlin weren't disappointed.

"Cool! Ashley, look! It's an iPod Nano!" Caitlin squealed.

"Awesome! I got one too. Look, mine's hot pink! I love it, Mom and Dad!" Ashley gushed.

When the twins were finished oohing and awing over their assortment of treasures, four sets of inquisitive eyes focused their relentless gaze upon me and I grabbed the nearest colorful package bearing my name that I could find. I opened the shiny, red box with as much fervor as I could muster.

"Hey. This is great. I love Britney Spears perfume. Thanks ya'll," I managed--still shook up about last night's gruesome dream. Mom sensed I was depressed--and she was right.

"Come on, Emily. Here, take this one. I think you'll like it. I picked it out myself. Go ahead, open the darn thing!"

"Okay, Mom." I shook the medium-sized box pretending to be interested. Truth be told, I didn't really care what the poorly wrapped package contained inside it's golden shell.

"Wow, it's a blue sweater. Thanks, Mom and Dad. I love it."

"Oh shoot, Emily, that's not the one I meant to hand you. Here, let me look. Oh, there it is. Hand me that box with the green bow on top of it, Wayne. Here, open this one instead, Emily, I think it will cheer you up."

"Okay. Well, let's see," I moaned as I ripped off the sparkly paper. "Oh, hey, wow, Mom. I like it. It's awesome in fact. I'll wear it on a date with Max." I felt much better when I spotted the black leather jacket from *Hot Topics*. A colorfully embroidered eagle graced the backside. "This jacket is really *hot,* Mom. Thanks. I mean it. I can't wait to try it on."

"I'm glad you like it, dear. I've been worried about you lately. I know you've been having trouble sleeping." Mom didn't go into too much detail as I'm sure she hadn't enlightened my distracted father about the chronic nightmares yet. "Well, anyway, come on, girls. There are still a few more presents left to tear into. Get busy," she roared. Caitlin wasted little time following her orders.

After the *present-opening party* ended--Mom shooed us into the hygienic kitchen for hot chocolate and *Hostess* donuts. She'd been cleaning the house persistently all week and the room smelled like ammonia and bleach. The five of us gathered around the antique farmer's table sipping warm cocoa from mismatched mugs while munching on stale donuts from a cardboard box. Caitlin was first to break the unnerving silence.

"So what's up with you anyway, Emily? Why do you keep waking up in the middle of the night screaming at the top of your lungs? You're getting on my nerves, you know. I need my rest."

"Shut up, Caitlin. It's none of your business anyway," I yelled.

"Whatever, loser. And what's up with the book about witches hidden under your bed? Are you casting love spells over Max or something? Is that why he's so ga ga over you?"

"Caitlin! That's enough," Mom howled.

"What are you doing searching under my bed, puke face? I told you to stay out of my room! I hate you!"

"I didn't find the book, loser! Mom did!"

"What's she talking about, Mom? Are you spying on me too?"

"Of course not, Emily. I was sweeping the wooden floor and knocked the book clear out from underneath the bed frame. I put it back as soon as I finished. And Caitlin, Emily's right, mind your own business!" Mom was practically screaming--shooting her a fierce look.

"Whatever. She's probably a witch by now, Mom. That's why she's having nightmares. Emily's summoning up the devil or something. Better be careful. She might put a spell on all of us."

"That's it, you little brat! Stay away from me. Seriously! I can't stand you! And if I catch you near any of my things ever again, I'll kill you. I mean it! Keep that brat away from me, Mom! I hate you, Caitlin. *I wish you'd been the one to die!*"

"Emily!" Mom and Dad yelled in unison.

"Don't you dare talk to your sister like that!" Dad finally interjected. "I mean it. Why in the world would you ever say anything like that to Caitlin? *Are you crazy?* No one in this family should have died! No one!" Dad jerked the table so hard while exiting that Caitlin's chocolate milk spilled everywhere. We were all shocked by his outburst.

"Where are you going, Wayne?" Mom pleaded. "Come back here. We need to talk about this! Don't leave this table!" she demanded.

"Well I'm certainly not staying around here, Kelli. I need to leave. I can't take it--I miss my family. Since Rose died, I don't even know these girls anymore. Especially Emily," he glared. "I need to get out of here. We'll talk about this later." Dad grabbed his car keys heading straight for the back door. Still wearing his plaid pajama bottoms, an old college tee shirt, and shabby leather slippers, he didn't even bother changing. Dad was that upset. And I was the reason.

Mom was stunned as Dad slammed the heavy door behind him. She didn't even bother hiding her emotions as she turned her angry gaze directly towards me. "Emily, what have you done? Why would you say such a thing to your sister? Especially in front of your father! Rose's death crushed him. You know that. He misses her the most--if that's possible. Their bond was special. She was daddy's little girl."

"Uh, I don't know what to say, Mom. I'm sorry. I didn't mean it you know. I was just mad. I'm sick of

Caitlin pestering me--you know that. But I didn't mean anything by what I said. I'm sorry, Caitlin. You know I didn't mean it. I just want her to stay out of my room. That's all."

"It's okay, Emily. I know you didn't mean it. I'm sorry, too. I'll try not to bother you anymore," Caitlin whispered. I halfway felt sorry for her.

"Oh, girls. We're all sorry. Even your father. He's torn up about everything. He's been through a lot--losing Rose and then nearly losing Emily. He needs more time, I guess. We all do. Of course it doesn't help that he blames me for everything. Perhaps more family counseling would help. I'll see if I can get him to agree. But let's don't worry about it anymore today. He'll be back soon. How far can he go? He forgot his wallet and the *Chrysler* is almost out of gas," she suddenly mused. Mom even started laughing. We all did. The thought of Dad running out of gas wearing nothing but ratty old slippers and a tee shirt full of holes in this cold weather was amusing. Still, I couldn't shake the feeling that I was solely to blame for the somber mood. I ruined Christmas morning all because I was sleep deprived and in a bad mood. Feeling terrible about the mess I'd made, I needed cheering up and I knew just who to call. *Max*.

"Um, hello, Katie. I, uh, wanted to speak with Max. Is he available?"

"Of course he is dear. It's so lovely to hear your voice. Let me call him. I think he went back to his bedroom. He's trying to decipher his camera's confusing instructions. He's must be reading them in French. Hold on just a second. Oh Max, Dallas is calling."

I heard him respond, excitement fueling his deep voice. "I'll pick up in here, Mom. Thanks. Is that you, Emily?"

"Yes. Hey. How was Christmas? Was Santa good to you and your mother?"

"Santa was awesome. I got a camera. You can even dive underwater with it. It's pretty fancy. Mom, I mean *Santa*, went overboard. It's incredible!"

"I'm glad to hear it. What about Katie? Was he good to her as well?"

"Sure was. Mom got a new cell phone. She needed one. Her Razor crapped out last month. Hey, what about you? What did you get? Everything you asked for, I hope. *You deserve it,* Dallas."

"You're sweet Max. But I'm not sure I deserve anything right now."

"What are you talking about?"

"Oh, nothing. I'm just thinking out loud I guess. Anyway, I just wanted to call and wish you and your mom a Merry Christmas. Will I see *you* anytime soon?"

"Of course you will. How about tomorrow morning? I'll pick you up around ten. I've got some ideas. See you then."

"Perfect, Max. That sounds perfect. I can't wait to see you. I better go. I need to clean my disgusting room. I'll be ready. *I love you, Max.*"

"I love you too, Dallas," he moaned softy into the receiver causing goose bumps to rise on my skin. "Sleep tight. I need to get some rest myself. I had another nightmare last night. I don't know what's going on. Maybe I'm eating too late or something." This time, however, Max refrained from mentioning the little girl who looked just like Emily's dead sister Rose.

"Really? You had bad dreams last night too? Um, did you happen to notice what time they started?"

"No. Not really. It had to have been well after midnight though. I stayed up late with mom watching *Van Helsing.* Pretty sickening movie. He was a *vampire* slayer. Mom thought it was a zombie flick--that's why she rented it. Didn't read the package too well, I guess. Anyway, she was disappointed when she found out vampires were attempting to rule the world. Personally, I thought it was rather entertaining--gory but good. Well,

I better run, Dallas. I need to get this camera figured out. It's driving me crazy!"

"Okay, Max. It was good to hear your voice. *Really.* I'm cheered up now. And I'll see ya tomorrow. Okay?"

"Okay."

So Max had another awful dream last night. What's going on? Was Rose in it? Did the nightmare scare him as much as mine scared me? So many questions to ask. Where do I begin?

Part Three

Jeez, Max, you slurp beef consommé like a vampire slurps type A blood. Emily Ryan Reed.

Chapter 19

Something Wicked This Way Comes....

Dad returned home shortly after noon--full of apologies, of course. Mom was first on his short list of persons needing to forgive him. I was second.

"Kelli, Emily, could you girls come in here? *We need to talk.*"

"Sure, Wayne. I'll be right in--just give me a minute. I need to put this leftover ham in the freezer," Mom replied from the confined kitchen as if nothing had happened. "Why don't you call Emily again. I don't think she heard you. She's cleaning up her bedroom--I think Caitlin's actually helping her this time."

"I'll grab her--just meet us in the living room. We *all* need to talk," Dad sheepishly repeated for the second time.

The three of us faced each other silently near the roaring fireplace for about thirty seconds before my guilty looking father finally interjected.

"I'm sorry, girls. I shouldn't have exploded like that--it's Christmas, for *Christ's sake.* He seemed oblivious to the irony in that particular statement.

"It's okay, Wayne. You've been under a lot of stress lately and the end of January is fast approaching--we all know what that means. It'll be the third anniversary of Rose's passing. It's hard to believe she's been gone that long. She'd be seven years old by now," Mom regretfully acknowledged, tears welling up in her large, brown eyes.

Dad gulped back a flood of tears himself. "We all miss Rose." His muffled voice nearly cracked. "But I'm not the only one suffering--I need to remember that. She meant the world to us--*all of us*. I was feeling sorry for myself this morning and I apologize. I need to be strong for my family. I'm afraid I've let ya'll down. Especially you, Emily--you've been through so much. You need me right now. I promise to do better. Please forgive me," he begged and his earnest words seemed sincere.

"It's okay, Dad. Life just sucks without her. I miss Rose. I want her back." I also felt like crying.

"We all want Rose back," Mom interrupted. "But that's not going to happen. I don't mean to be grim, but our family needs to pull itself together--without Rose. We are a team who needs to start acting like one."

"Mom's right, Emily, we are a team. I really am sorry honey. I never meant to hurt you. Let's start over today. Hey, why don't you and your sisters get dressed and we'll go for a long drive in the country. The scenery in West Virginia is gorgeous right now. Let's don't lock ourselves up in this dreary house all day long. I want to go for a drive--take in the mountains. The air is so much fresher here than in Dallas. Tell Ashley and Caitlin to get dressed," Dad suddenly beamed--delighted by his idea.

"That sounds great, Dad." I didn't mean it of course. I was just trying to be agreeable. "Give us about thirty minutes give or take an *hour*. You know how Caitlin is--slow as molasses."

Mom and Dad chuckled while nodding their heads in agreement. Even though I didn't feel like being cooped up inside the car with my rattle-brained sisters and miserable parents all day long, I didn't want to disappoint my wounded family. Besides, tomorrow I'd be with Max all day--a delicious thought that made me incredibly happy. So happy in fact my stomach did cartwheels and the tiny hairs on my arms stood on end. First, however, I needed to spend some time with *them*--whether I wanted too or not.

"Where are we going, Dad?" Caitlin pried, as she sashayed into the kitchen--eager to show off her new outfit. She'd taken nearly an entire hour to pull herself together--just as I'd argued she would. I was shocked, however, when she and Ashley pranced into the breakfast area donning their matching hot pink *Hanna Montana* shirts I'd given them for Christmas. They also wore rolled up *Apollo* jeans and pink high top sneakers with purple laces.

"You girls look adorable," Mom proudly gushed. "I knew you'd love the shirts Emily got for you. Ya'll look great!"

"Yeah," I unenthusiastically added--somewhat surprised by their sudden show of unity. *Dad must be proud.*

"Thanks," Caitlin ruminated. *Such an attention monger.*

The five of us crammed into the dusty *Plymouth Voyager* imitating the chirpy Brady Bunch when they headed for the sunny island of Hawaii on an amazing two-week stay. Only it wasn't sunny outside and the nearest beach was several hours away.

"Where are we going, Dad?" Caitlin bugged.

"I'm not sure. I thought we'd do some exploring--see what West Virginia has to offer. The light dusting of snow is beautiful and I'd like to get some pictures of us enjoying the white countryside. Let's just see where the day takes us."

"Whatever, Dad," Ashley interrupted. "I've got my Ipod just in case I get bored."

"Put that thing away Ashley," Mom buzzed. "This is family time--we want everyone's attention. No ear phones, no loud music, no DVD's, no fighting--we're all going to enjoy the fabulous scenery together."

"Yeah butthead, put that thing away," Caitlin shrieked. *So much for their surprising show of unity.*

Each of us strapped in and Dad, true to his word, took off without a map of the small but beautiful state. *We're on an adventure, he kept moaning.* Dad didn't even turn on the portable GPS attached to the marred, vinyl dashboard--*we're on an adventure--remember?* In a matter of minutes, our family of five was heating up the icy roadways supposedly enjoying the landscape. All I could think about, however, was my dead sister Rose.

What I remember most about the terrible day she died, is shuddering at the sight of a vile looking creature--approximately thirty year's old--appearing out of nowhere and grabbing her in the hectic *Denny's* parking lot. Rose's thunderous screams were piercing as he clutched her tiny and vulnerable body inside his murderous grip. Before I could scream, however, the monster and Rose were gone.

The shadowy figure had a mouthful of crooked teeth and I passed this information on to the disheveled Dallas Police Department when they finally arrived at the bloodless crime scene. Pulling from my dazed but accurate memory, no detail went unreported as I hysterically filled them in regarding the criminal's morose appearance and sickening actions.

The killer's blonde, pony-tailed locks were lightly streaked and appeared to need a thorough washing. His entire body looked as if he hadn't bathed in weeks. The murderer's skin was scarred and pitted. His yellowed fingernails were long and the points looked razor sharp--although no gouges were found on Rose's body. He was a horrible looking man--if you could call him a man--the shady type anyone would be fearful of if they ran into him alone on a murky night. It was daylight, however, when he unmercifully snatched Rose, who was following no more than ten feet behind me and my twin sisters. Rose was giggling innocently as a gust of wind caused the purple balloon she'd scored at *Denny's* to nearly fly out of her teeny hands. None of us feared any danger, however, as this was a popular family restaurant where everyone knew everyone else. Nothing bad ever occurred here--no gang activity, no murders, no kidnappings. Rose should have been safe.

Upon taking her, the ruthless killer left behind no traceable clues and the confused police were baffled.

Not a single strand of flaxen hair littered the grimy asphalt and no threads from his tattered clothing were detected on the scorching blacktop. As for DNA evidence at the unblemished scene or on Rose's unresponsive body, there was none. No fingerprints on her pale skin were present either. The coroner did discover two miniscule holes on the back of her fleshy neck underneath her fine, white hair. Nothing became of the unexplainable marks. Unfortunately, Rose's mysterious assailant remained just that--a mystery. As did her shocking death.

Rose's petite body was found about two miles away--dumped in a wooded area beside the noisy highway. Police officers and no less than one hundred volunteers quickly combed the surrounding area fearing they would uncover her remains close to the crime scene. An African-American father of six boys was the first to discern a small pink tennis shoe separated from its owner's precious foot--Rose's lifeless and bloodless body was discovered only inches away.

Recalling the worst day of my life while trapped inside the cage-like van was upsetting--to say the least. I needed some fresh air and was pleased every time Dad spotted a particularly gorgeous tree or rock formation he simply had to snap a picture of. On a narrow and winding road, several miles from the interstate, our family happened across a beautiful one-story log cabin complete with a smoking river-rock chimney and what appeared to be an old-fashioned well on the generous front landscape. This time, however, it was Mom who wanted a photo.

"Oh look, girls, isn't it beautiful?" she gushed. "I wonder if the owners are inside. I'd love to have a picture of this place. It would make a great post card for our friends back in Texas. The snow heaps surrounding this cabin are spectacular--so clean and fresh. Can I knock on the door, Wayne, see if anybody's home?"

"No way, Mom! How embarrassing. Just take the shot and let's go," I yelled.

"Chill out, Emily. Mom wants a picture. I'll go the door with you. Let's knock. Please, Mom," Caitlin begged. She just wanted to annoy me.

"I think it will be okay, Kelli. If they refuse, we'll leave. We aren't asking much. Just a quick snapshot," Dad interjected.

"Come with me then, Caitlin. Maybe the sight of a lovely young child will persuade them," Mom laughed.

"Awesome!" she chirped. Caitlin turned her menacing head towards mine making sure I was perturbed by her obvious act of defiance. I was, of course.

Hand in hand, the two of them headed towards the rustic facade and Caitlin rapped lightly on the forged iron entrance--*the intricate pattern and attention to detail looked oddly familiar.* In a matter of seconds, a puzzled-looking teenager opened the ornate door. Watching intently from inside the warm van, I was intrigued by the young man who now stood facing them. *Why haven't I seen him at school before?* The look on his pale face was stern while Caitlin and Mom-- somewhat taken aback--made their request. For a moment, I thought he would run them off his property. He didn't, however, agreeing they could snap a photo. Perhaps weary of the their intentions, the young man with dark eyes and even darker hair, followed them outside closer to the van. And that's when our eyes locked. Taken aback by his brooding looks and powerful stature, I could barely breath as his shadowy eyes pierced mine. *Who is he? I thought to myself. And where did he come from?*

Whoever fights monsters should see to it that in the process he does not become a monster. And when you look into an abyss, the abyss also looks into you. Nietzsche

Chapter 20

Mysterious Stranger...

Mom, Caitlin, and the dissonant stranger now stood only a few feet away from the parked van. Snapping away, Mom aimed the digital camera towards the tall fir and oak trees flanking the picturesque cabin. Even though I realized I was staring, I couldn't keep my eyes off *him*. And the feeling appeared to be mutual as his gaze was solely on me. The enigmatic male was tall--at least six foot two--sporting dark chocolate tresses and even darker eyes. His uneven hair barely touched his intimidating shoulders and his choppy bangs were loosely parted to one side. His pale skin resembled alabaster and his fleshy, red lips seemed swollen. His crooked body was long and lean and his elongated arms were toned but slender. The stranger's thick, brown eyebrows furrowed as if he were angry, and his intimidating expression was intense. Although he made me nervous--almost frightened even--I couldn't take my eyes off his unfriendly but memorable face.

"Thanks a lot," Mom beamed--reaching out to shake his extended but cautious hand. "Your place is extraordinary. I appreciate your willingness to allow us onto your incredible property. Have a nice day, *Julian*."

"No problem," he gruffly replied--nodding once specifically in my direction. Our licentious eyes never separated and I flinched uncontrollably as he unapologetically stared me down. I couldn't have looked away from this powerful stranger even if I'd wanted too. I was hypnotized by Julian's wild and disturbing expression. His vociferous hold over me was strong. *Like nothing I'd ever experienced. Not even with Max.*

Mom and Caitlin climbed into the minivan only after Julian reluctantly opened the passenger side for them. A jolt of electricity surged through my body when he did-- as he was situated so closely to me now. Our curious eyes still locked, Julian signaled goodbye as Dad gently pressed on the accelerator. I turned around to face him one last time before the dusty van took off. Once we started moving, Julian and I watched one another until our strained faces were no longer perceptible.

"Wasn't he gorgeous, girls? I couldn't take my eyes off him!" Mom mused. Dad watched as she acted like a giddy teen in love for the first time.

"How'd you know his name, Mom? He barely talked," I drilled--trying not to appear too obvious.

"I asked him."

"Oh."

"He was cute, Ashley. Did you see him? His sexy eyes...What a hottie!" Caitlin interjected.

"Alright, girls, settle down. *All of you*," Dad mouthed. "Especially you, Kelli. You're spoken for," Dad teased. "And you as well, Emily. Max wouldn't appreciate you ogling other fellows."

"Fellows? What's a *fellow,* Dad? That's a funny word," Ashley joked.

We all laughed at her wrinkled face when she teased Dad about his outdated lingo.

"That was no fellow, Wayne," Mom interrupted. "Julian's one hundred percent male--full of testosterone. He's no ordinary *fellow,*" she argued. "He's on fire."

I was taken aback by Mom's capricious attitude where Julian, and specifically his unforgettable appearance, was concerned. She was obviously mesmerized by his commanding presence and riveting looks. Who could blame her? We all were I guess--with the exception of Dad, of course.

Needless to say, the drive back to our little house was warm--at least for me--as I was sure my body temperature had risen well above one hundred degrees-- if not higher. And when we entered the house, all I could think about was Julian. Who was this ghostly figure with the haunting eyes and smoldering looks? Where did he come from? Why didn't he go to school at WWHS? He looked my age--at least sixteen. I needed answers but didn't know where to find them. Julian wasn't a friendly person--I couldn't just drive back to his isolated property demanding answers. He looked as if he'd run us off his land at any moment. Julian did not want us there--that's for sure. Clearly, he and whoever he lived with wanted to be left alone.

For the rest of the evening and well into the chilly night, I couldn't shake the image of Julian from my scattered thoughts. Before hitting the sack, I decided to write a poem about him. Specifically, I wanted to immortalize the moment we first locked eyes.

Daily Journal 2004-2005

December 25, 2004

Dear Diary,

I had the weirdest day ever. While driving in the country with my family, we stumbled across a log cabin in the woods. A stranger answered the door, allowing Mom and Caitlin to take pictures of his property. He was handsome--a perfect specimen of white flesh and red lips. His writhe body was toned but harsh. Something about this boy scared me though, but I couldn't stop staring despite being intimidated. All I could focus on was Julian's forceful presence. His limbs were long and lean, his hair was wispy and dark, and his gaze was penetrable. I couldn't take my eyes off him. I need to find him. Julian's presence is hypnotic--and I am hypnotized. For now, Emily Ryan Reed.

Perfect Stranger

Standing before me, his presence is strong.
This demon boy, will scare us all.
His eyes are dark, his gaze is harsh.
I cannot forget him, he stole my heart.
It's lust I fear, not love at all.

My heart is spoken for. I must not fall.
Should Max find out, his heart would break.
For in loving Julian, I'd make the greatest mistake.

Emily Ryan Reed

By the time my heavy head hit the malleable pillow, all I could think about was Julian. And then it donned on me. I had a date with Max in the morning and I'd hardly spent any of the day thinking about him--all because I couldn't seem to shake the unforgettable image of Julian from my brain. I needed to focus, however, on my loving boyfriend. The one to whom I'd promised my heart only a few short hours ago in front of a sparkling Christmas tree. I had a disturbing feeling, however, that after encountering Julian, my weakened soul was spoken for. And I felt very guilty about that. What would Max think if he knew I was pining for another boy? I didn't want to answer that question.

I woke up around three a.m. sweating profusely. I must not have screamed, however, as Mom was nowhere to be found. My unstable body was shaky and my stringy hair was a mess. The cotton sheets on my bed were soaked from perspiration making it too cold to sleep on them any longer. I staggered into my sisters' dark bedroom and carefully yanked on the trundle. Oddly enough, in tonight's bizarre dream, my dead sister Rose had not been the luminary.

Julian's snarled mouth flared--exposing a mound of razor sharp teeth--as he lunged convincingly for my vulnerable neck. His thick, yellowed nails resembled tiny jagged swords ready to rip into my insubstantial flesh. Frightened and cold, I dashed into the moist woods trying to escape his murderous grip. Somehow, I managed to hide inside a frozen cave until daylight. Julian gave up the lethal search despite wanting to rip into my exposed skin. When I woke from the terrifying dream, I felt more horrified than I'd ever been when visited by Rose--even when she was a bloody mess.

Exhausted, I managed to fall back asleep despite being afraid. I slept for several additional hours. When I woke up in my sisters' room, despite still being drained, I wanted to look as fresh and revived for Max as I could. I owed him that much.

"It's nine a.m. Emily. Don't you have a date with Max today? You better get up and take a shower. He'll be here in an hour. Where are ya'll going anyway? Why's he picking you up so early in the day?" Mom pried.

"I don't know. He just said he'd be here early. Max is surprising me I guess. He's like that, you know--full of surprises."

"Better wear that beautiful ring around your neck, wouldn't want to disappoint him. He's a thoughtful and romantic guy. Easy to be around. Not at all intimidating. I really like Max. I'm glad you two are a couple."

I piled out of Ashley's warm trundle bed, heading straight for the shower. I was sure I smelled badly from perspiring throughout the long night. Before I climbed in, I replayed the unsettling dream one more time inside my uneasy head. Let's see, I remember being alone near his cabin when Julian first approached. Initially, he seemed harmless. The closer he got to me, however, the more wicked he became. When he was no more than an arm's length away, Julian's repulsive mouth opened exposing two rows of twisted teeth and a long, serpent-like, blood red tongue. His charcoal eyes were large and demoralizing and his pupils were nearly indefinable. Julian looked like a crazed monster--much like the creature that killed Rose.

After my hot shower, I grabbed a pair of faded *Levi's* topping them with a worn-out *Texas Tech* sweatshirt and white turtleneck. I put on my trusty black boots and pulled my wet hair into a pony tail. Even though I wanted to look fabulous for Max, I just didn't feel like primping. I was still freaked out.

I decided to leave my freshly scrubbed face au natural—ditching my overflowing makeup case and putting on a lightly tinted foundation instead. I then proceeded towards the empty kitchen. Before Max arrived, I hoped to inhale a couple of blueberry pop tarts and a tall glass of *Hershey's* chocolate milk--I had about seventeen minutes to do so before Max showed up.

At precisely ten a.m., the doorbell rang. Max beamed when I opened the front door wearing a giant smile. I threw my arms around him and felt truly happy to see him. All thoughts of Julian quickly vanished when I spotted my handsome mate.

"Hey there, Dallas. Ready for some outside time?"

"What do you mean, Max?"

"We're going hiking today. I'm glad to see you in boots and warm clothing. Grab a heavy coat though, in case you get cold."

"Will my black jacket do? It's definitely the thickest one I own."

"Sure will. You'll need gloves too. And a scarf. The temperature's not too bad. But you're so skinny—I'm afraid you might catch a chill if the wind picks up."

"Alright. Just give me a second. Did you bring your new camera?"

"Of course I did! That's why we're hiking. So I can get some interesting shots."

"I figured as much. I think I'll bring some ear muffs too--don't want to get an earache. Do you have enough bottled water, Max? I can grab some out of the kitchen before we leave if you don't."

"No need. We're fine Dallas. I brought some beef jerky too. Protein always helps when you're climbing steep hills."

"Steep hills? Are you sure I can do this, Max? I'm not exactly the outdoorsy type. I'm a bit of a weenie when it comes to anything physical. Are you sure you wouldn't rather see a movie or hang out around here watching TV all day? It's nice and toasty inside--and I make a mean grilled-cheese sandwich."

"Not on your life, Dallas. I brought a thick blanket we can snuggle under once when we make it to the top. That sounds a bit more romantic than watching the History Channel or *In This House* reruns all day long," he teased. "Besides, I need the exercise. I'm eating too much now that we're out of school. I've put on at least two pounds—my jeans are snug. I need to work off some calories."

"Me too. I've been eating a lot of ice cream with my sisters. I could stand to burn a few myself."

"Let's hit the road then, Dallas. Time's awastin'."

Max and I piled into his truck and true to his word, a bulky blanket covered the ripped back seat. Water bottles and a first aid kid were visible as well. Max was prepared.

"I brought a couple of flares and some flashlights just in case. And Mom lent me her new cell phone. She knows exactly where we're headed and I told her we'd be finished around five or five-thirty. I've hiked these trails before so I'm familiar with how long they take to complete. I've also got matches if we need to light a fire. We'll be fine as long as we don't come across any bears."

I couldn't tell if he was teasing or not. I decided to keep quiet about the bear remark.

The drive towards the hilly trails was much like the one I'd taken yesterday with my annoying family. Much of the landmarks looked the same. After exiting the hectic interstate, we made our way onto a narrow dirt road that seemed oddly familiar. It didn't take long before I realized we were traveling on the same road and heading in Julian's direction. My spine tingled. We'd only gone a few miles before the rustic cabin came into sight. Two shadowy figures were chopping wood outside.

"Looks like those guys have a busy day ahead of them," Max laughed. "Glad it's not me. I've chopped enough wood this winter. I'm ready for springtime."

"Uh, yeah. They're busy--that's for sure," I mumbled--trying to get a better look.

I squinted my probing eyes until Max and I were close enough that I could recognize one of the lofty figures was Julian. A slightly older man, perhaps his brother or father, assisted him. He looked nothing like Julian, however. Even though this man was tall, his hair was blonde.

Max slowed down as we approached the busy pair and waved at them. Neither waved back. However, as soon as Julian realized it was me in the passenger's seat, he targeted his gaze solely on me until Max and I were out of sight. I felt slightly more uncomfortable this time when we made eye contact. An eerie feeling came over me as soon as I spied Julian gawking at me.

Max didn't seem to notice the sharp look Julian shot my way. As for me, I couldn't shake the feeling of uneasiness that flooded me when running into him for the second time. When Max and I got closer to our destination (and farther away from Julian), I was able to center my concentration on Max once again. Thank goodness. I was already feeling guilty about my uncontrollable attraction to him. Why was I drawn to this stranger? We were like magnets it seemed--unable to disconnect from each other's stare. I felt sure Julian was attracted to me as well. I couldn't explain how I could possibly know this. I just did. I sensed that Julian was as intrigued by me as I was by him. And although I felt guilty for betraying Max's unquestionable trust, I was thrilled to know I'd made as big an impact on Julian as he'd made on me.

The walls of my castle are cracked, the shadows are many. But come in. Feel yourself at home. Dracula.

Chapter 21

The Long Winter Break...

Max and I returned home from our grueling six-hour hike at around five thirty--just as he'd promised. I was worn out. Every obscure muscle in my tired body ached. My unsteady legs felt like mush and I could barely climb out of his old truck.

"I'm beat, Max. You wore me out today. *Seriously*. I don't think I can make it inside the house. I need some assistance."

"Come on, Dallas. Grab my shoulders, I'll help you. I didn't realize you were so puny. I thought you'd be able to keep up with me. You shouldn't have continued climbing, you know. We could've turned around. All you had to do was say the word," he grinned. Clearly, Max was not in nearly as much pain as I was.

"I know. I didn't want to disappoint you. You were having so much fun in the snow. I think you got some great shots of the woods. I can't believe we saw so many bunny rabbits on the trails. And the snow peaks were amazing. I had a great time. I really did, Max. Sorry I'm so out of shape. I need to start lifting weights or something--build some muscle tone. I told you I'm a weenie."

"Your not a weenie, Dallas. You're just a girl. You can't help being tiny and fragile," Max playfully teased. "It's part of your genetic makeup."

"Whatever. And you can't help being an overzealous male--it's in your DNA," I fired back, just as playfully of course.

Once we made our way inside my warm but empty home--*where is everybody?*--I noticed the fireplace was still roaring and both Max and I were pleased for the abundance of heat radiating from it. Today, I'd been chilly while sauntering up and down in the virgin snow with Max. Even though the thick blanket he'd thoughtfully provided kept us from freezing to death when enjoying the views atop some of the trail's many rock formations, the temperature was still nippy. It did feel awesome, however, snuggling inside his strong arms. And besides, I was glad for the respite when Max embraced me. I needed to stop obsessing over Julian and the best way to do that was to cuddle with Max.

The rest of the three weeks long winter break flew by. I spent most of my available time with my doting boyfriend and his wonderful mother. I always had fun when visiting their cheerful place. Katie baked fresh bread daily, and taught me how to make Italian favorites like chocolate chip gelato, fresh fruit tarts, lemon biscotti, and scores upon scores of pasta dishes laced with shredded zucchini and smoked mozzarella cheese. The three of us ate so much I thought we'd burst. Katie was also mindful to create solicitous care packages for my needy family that included jars of homemade peach preserves, Italian cream cakes, and spinach and basil pesto. Dad loved gorging on her leftover spaghetti with green olives and garlic and giant pasta shells stuffed with ricotta cheese and parsley.

Fortunately, and much to my surprise, my parents were getting along slightly better and Mom even started experimenting in the modest-sized kitchen. She made old favorites like spicy meatloaf with a pinch of tarragon and gourmet hamburgers with shitake mushrooms and tiny pearl onions. Our family was starting to come together and I was feeling reassured about that. Even the pesky twins and I were fighting less. I still hated Caitlin--especially her sharp tongue and nosy nature. She spied on me and Max relentlessly. We could hear her bouncy footsteps as she scooted up and down the wooden halls on tippy toes. Caitlin was too stupid to realize we knew every move she made. Max and I even pretended to yell at each other sometimes just to get her riled up. She'd always run and tattle of course. She couldn't wait to get us in trouble with my parents.

I called Madison, my best friend in Texas, several times over the wintry break. I rambled on and on about Max and the one-of-a-kind Christmas we'd shared. I left out any references as to coming across Julian in the woods, however. I was trying desperately to forget him. I also refrained from mentioning Julian in my journal or writing disturbing poems about him and never spoke of Julian again to my parents. Mom still remembered him, though--mentioning often how good-looking and mysterious she found him to be. I pretended to be uninterested whenever she brought Julian up in our spirited but embarrassing conversations.

Fortunately, the ghastly nightmares ceased and I was finally able to sleep peacefully through the night. I hadn't dreamt of Rose or Julian in a couple of weeks. I decided that as soon as school started back on January fourth, I would return the leather bound manuscript *The Witching Hour,* as I didn't seem to need it anymore.

During the long and much needed break, I also called Emily B. and Blake, wishing them both a very Merry Christmas, and they gushed incessantly about a wonderful ski trip they'd taken together--with parental supervision of course. E.B.'s stylish mom accompanied them and the lucky trio stayed at a palatial suite inside a fancy resort overlooking the spectacular mountains. E.B. and Blake had a great time and their enviable relationship was as strong as ever. Once again, I abstained from mentioning Julian to either her or Blake. Emily would have scolded me interminably for being attracted to him. She and Blake were convinced Max and I belonged together for all of eternity. I thought they were probably right. However, I still couldn't shake the feeling that something was now unexplainably different between us.

Sunday night, the last day of the holiday break, I ironed my pink and white striped, cotton button-down and carefully laid out my new *Hot Topics* leather jacket and *True Religion* jeans I'd scored for Christmas. I wanted to look hot at school considering it was our first day back. Even though I told myself I was dressing up specifically for Max, secretly, I wished Julian would somehow come across me in my expensive new clothes. He wouldn't of course. Julian didn't attend WWHS. Just the same, I made sure my elaborate get-up was perfectly accessorized. And then faithfully headed for sleep.

That morning I was not yet a vampire, and I saw my last sunrise. I remember it completely, and yet I can't recall any sunrise before it. I watched its whole magnificence for the last time as if it were the first. And then I said farewell to sun light, and set out to become what I became. Louis. Interview with the Vampire.

Chapter 22

We Meet Again...

"Come on, girl. Get in already! Or we'll be late," Blake wailed.

"Alright. Just chill out."

I climbed into Blake's *dirty on the outside but clean on the inside* Mustang surprised by the miniature gold box resting atop the leather passenger's seat.

"What is it, Blake? Is this gift for me? Can I open it?"

"Of course it's for you. I sure as heck ain't giving it to Alex--although he'd probably love what's inside that box. He's so dang girly. Open it, Dallas. It's all yours."

It didn't take long to remove the tiny lid from the petite cardboard container that didn't even have a name on it.

"Blake, they're awesome! I love them. Are you sure you picked these out? Or did Emily do it? I bet she chose these didn't she!"

"Of course she did. I'm no good at stuff like that--*I'm not girly*. Emily said you'd know what to pair them with."

Inside the miniature treasure, two round amethyst stone's, set in delicate sterling silver, amazed me. They weren't large gemstones--but they were gorgeous nonetheless--matching both the necklace Emily gave me for my seventeenth birthday and the antique ring I'd scored from Max for Christmas.

"They're perfect, Blake. Thanks. Um, I'm afraid I don't have anything for you though. I'm kind of embarrassed."

"Don't worry about it, Dallas. E.B. and I spotted them inside the resort's swanky gift shop. They weren't much—fifty percent off. But she, I mean *we*, thought you might like them. Hey, try them on. They match that shiny ring around your neck. A gift from Max I presume?"

"How'd you know that, Blake?"

"Cuz I've seen it on his hand before. It looks old and expensive. Don't lose it, Dallas. You'd break his heart."

"Shut up and drive, Blake. And not too fast, I want to put my new earrings on."

"Whatever, Dallas. You guys are in love. It's written all over your pretty face."

"What the...,*OMG*. It's him. *Oh My God*."

As soon as I spotted *his* somber face and guarded posture, my mouth nearly dropped to the dirty floor. "*It's Julian*," I mumbled underneath my shaky breath. *"What the heck is he doing here?"*

"Dallas, hey, over here. Over here," Max shouted--shocking me out of my stupor. "Hey, I've been calling your name. Didn't you hear me?"

"Um, no, I mean yes. I mean, I, uh, thought I heard you. I'm sorry. I was daydreaming I guess." I watched helplessly as Julian began stuffing a large pile of used textbooks inside his rusty, metal locker. I couldn't take my eyes off him. Julian was dressed in a pair of frayed jeans, a faded black tee-shirt, and black riding boots. His black leather jacket and black motorcycle helmet were shiny and both looked new. Julian's loosely pony-tailed, windblown hair was messy. His outfit was uninspired--to say the least--and Julian's informal appearance insinuated that he did not care to impress his peers. He still looked good, however.

"Are you okay, Dallas?"

"Um, yes. I am. Really, I'm fine. I'm just a little surprised. I was thinking about first period. Um, I hope Mrs. Rice doesn't sneak in a pop quiz," I rambled, in a silly attempt to redirect my muddled attention towards Max. "Um, we're reading *Romeo and Juliet*. Only I didn't get much reading done over the holidays. I'll have to catch up during study hall. So, um, how about you? Are you okay?" I still couldn't take my eyes off Julian or his body. Julian hadn't noticed me yet.

"I'm fine, Dallas. And I'm thrilled to see you!" Max snatched me up in his firm grip squeezing me against his thick chest. *It felt nice.* But I was preoccupied. I kept wondering why Julian was standing only a few feet away from me. *How could that be? Is he new here?*

"Come on, Dallas. I'll walk you to English. Hey, are you sure you're okay? You seem distracted this morning. I think you need some coffee," Max teased.

"I'm fine. Um, let's walk. Tell me about your evening. I missed not seeing you." I was still captivated by Julian and he was still stuffing books inside his locker. *How long would it take, I wondered--before he stared me down too?* I got my answer quicker than expected.

At eight-seventeen, Julian entered into Mrs. Rice's cozy honors English class as if he hadn't a friend in the world. My entire body was ablaze as soon as we locked eyes. Julian was surprised to see me--and neither of us said hello to the other. The warmth radiating off his body heated up the entire room--me included.

"Class, this is our newest student--Julian Knight. He's a transfer. Where did you say you're from, Julian?"

"I didn't. But I'm from Chicago," Julian grunted--still staring at me.

Mrs. Rice seemed taken aback by his coarse attitude as did the rest of the suddenly quiet class.

"Um, well, okay. Julian, there's an unused desk beside Emily--I mean Dallas. Oh, which is it, dear?"

"Um, Emily is fine Mrs. Rice," I stammered--hooked on Julian's gaze. "He can sit here. It's fine," I managed. I felt my face and neck fluster as he continued staring me down. Julian looked mad at the world.

"Is that okay, Mr. Knight?"

"It's fine," he grumbled--still staring at me. *Nobody dared argue with him.*

As soon as his lean body enveloped the wooden desk, the electricity between our bodies sparked. My entire jelly-like form quivered and my dizzying head felt faint. And for some strange reason, my neck started to throb as a rush of blood pulsed through my veins. Only the scorching liquid kept me from passing out. I was breathless as he took his place.

Oh My God--he's staring. What should I do? Look at the board Emily. Don't tilt your head. Focus on Mrs. Rice's blue and yellow plaid dress and ugly black shoes. Whatever you do, don't look at Julian!

I could feel his hungry eyes, however, roaming the curves of my body. Julian started with my long legs, which were crossed, moving his gaze toward my tiny waist. He continued his stare until his eyes rested on my nape--still burning. I was definitely in pain. I tried scratching my neck, but nothing dulled the ache. The pain was unsettling.

"Um, class. Listen up. Please, listen up. Because we are reading Shakespeare's classical drama *Romeo and Juliet,* I thought we'd head to the library and watch a film about the romantic but tragic play. Please be quiet when marching down the halls--don't want to disturb the other classrooms. As soon as we get there, find a desk or table and have a seat. No more than three students per table please. And no chatting once the movie begins. I mean it. If you talk, you get a pink slip and it's off to Mr. Tennyson's office that you go. Well, come on then. Line up single file, ladies and gentlemen."

Julian and I stood up at the same time pushing our way towards the increasing line in an attempt not to be trampled by the other students. When we made our way to the front door—there were about six or seven students ahead of us--Julian hovered directly behind me. So close in fact, I could feel his warm breath on the back of my tender neck. Without turning around to acknowledge him, I followed the mound of eager students thrilled to ditch the crowded classroom for one day. Nobody said a word. Nobody wanted a pink slip. When we arrived at the old library, students fervently attacked available tables and desks hoping to sit next to their friends. Only two spots remained in the back of the sizeable room. Julian and I were forced to share the melamine table as we were the only students left standing.

"Sit down everybody. I'm going to get the DVD player. I'll be back in a moment. Nobody talk!"

As soon as Mrs. Rice exited the cavernous room, the muffled chatter began. Surprisingly, Julian and I were no exception.

"So what's your name--Emily or Dallas?" Julian droned. His fleshy lips and pale skin were intimidating. *Julian was intimidating.*

"Um, it's Emily--*Emily Reed*. But the kids around here call me Dallas." I covered my neck when answering Julian's question, as if that would quiet the pain.

"Mind if I call you Emily?" Julian grumbled. *So unfriendly.*

"No, um, of course not. Whatever's best," I replied. Julian alternated his menacing glances between my eyes and neck.

"You're not from around here are you, Emily?"

"No," I quipped, while nervously shuffling through my heavy notebook. *Don't look at him, Emily.* Julian seemed put off by my reproachable attitude.

"You've got a southern accent. Let me guess. You're from Dallas."

"Um, yep. I just moved here. I haven't been in West Virginia long. What about you. Where are you from?" I managed, trying not to appear too interested.

"Chicago," he grunted. Now Julian seemed uninterested.

"Oh yeah, Mrs. Rice said something about that. What brings you to West Virginia?" I countered--rummaging through some old papers. Too afraid to look into Julian's eyes.

"My dad's from Pocahontas County--near Droop Mountain. But he prefers living in Beckley. The economy's better. He's a welder and an artist. *He's lived here before.*"

"Oh. Um, my dad's a lawyer. He works at a small firm in town. We live close by. But you, I, um saw you in the woods on Christmas day. Is that your cabin my mom and sister were snapping pictures of?" *Still fumbling with an assortment of old papers.*

"Yeah. It's been in our family for awhile. Dad's trying to fix it up."

"Oh." Julian's lips were so tight I could barely see his teeth. And then Mrs. Rice turned out the lights.

Thank goodness, I thought to myself. Let the movie begin.

Because the colossal room was now dark, Julian and I had difficulty making out each other's features even when sitting so closely to each other. I could feel his tepid body, however, as he continued shifting nearer to me. Since first setting eyes on Julian today, my emotions had run the gamut. Initially, I was shocked when I spotted him outside of his newly assigned locker. When Julian entered Mrs. Rice's classroom, however, I was frightened--his looming presence nearly scared me and half of the class to death. Now, sitting so closely beside him and despite the obvious pain in my neck, my body felt excited and slightly aroused. Oddly enough, I didn't want to get up from the table.

"Are you bored yet, Emily?" Julian groaned. I could barely hear the words oozing from his guttural, monotone voice.

"What do you mean?"

"Moving from a fast paced city like Dallas, to a small town like Beckley, must be boring," he countered. My body flinched every time Julian uttered my name.

"No, um, not really. I miss my friends back home. But I'm okay. Beckley's not so bad."

Julian smirked and I heard a rasp of air exiting his lungs. Suddenly, I wished I could see his face.

"I miss Chicago. It's too quiet out here. I miss the traffic."

"I don't. Dallas is horrible. So many wrecks. I don't miss the terrible drivers. Neither do my parents."

I felt Julian's body quake as he smirked once again. His rugged shoulders twisted and his hands clenched tighter. We were so close to each other now. I wondered if the other students found our shrinking distance inappropriate.

"No more talking, students. I've found the DVD. Everybody watch. It's too dark to take notes. But there will be a quiz tomorrow over the movie. I suggest you pay attention. No falling asleep, Thomas," Mrs. Rice scorned the always-in-some-kind-of-trouble boy.

Julian and I stared at the reflective screen. However, all I could think about was the fact that he was sitting so close. So close, in fact, I could feel his rising chest expand and contract with each labored breath he took. *Why am I so struck by this guy? I have a boyfriend, for goodness sakes. A marvelous, wonderful, handsome boyfriend. Focus Emily. Watch the darn movie. Forget about Julian. He's too scary--good-looking but scary. He's definitely got a shady past. Not like Max. Max is clean-cut, studious, polite to my parents, and treats me like a princess. Focus Emily. Julian's nothing but a big bag of trouble...*

I couldn't focus, however--no matter how hard I tried. My mind was racing and my heart pounded inside my burning chest. I hoped Julian was oblivious to the turmoil going on inside me. I didn't want him aware of the disturbing effect he maintained over my body. That would be embarrassing.

"Time's up guys. Let's head to our next class. Push your chairs in. Leave the library just the way you found it," Mrs. Rice instructed. None of the students obeyed, however, as they sprinted towards the exit nearly mowing each other down. Thomas even knocked my leather purse off of my shoulder. Julian picked it up-- while shooting him a nasty look. Thomas appeared frightened of Julian. I understood his hesitance. With the lights turned back on, I couldn't help being drawn to Julian's startling features--his harsh but exciting face-- sharp but tempting eyes--and firm but luscious lips. Julian was gorgeous.

Now you know what we are, now you know what you are. You'll never grow old, Michael, and you'll never die. But you must feed! The Lost Boys, 1987.

Chapter 23

Stay Away From Me!...

After the sappy movie and first period finally ended, Julian lagged a safe distance behind me on the way towards our lockers. He was quiet, however--back to his brooding self. I was glad as my weary mind needed a respite from Julian and his all consuming presence. Also, with Julian far behind, the relentless pain in my neck was beginning to ease up. *What's that about? I wondered.* And after what seemed like an eternity without him, Max and I spotted each other ambling down the crowded hallway.

"Dallas, hey, what's up? How was *Romeo and Juliet?*" Max quizzed. A huge grin illuminating his sweet face. *So different from each other I supposed. Max's hair is curly and blonde while Julian's is long and dark. Max's eyes are welcoming, Julian's are gloomy and intimidating. Max's grin is genuine and Julian never smiles. He's always grimacing; a constant scowl on his foreboding face. Julian is darkness, while Max is light.*

"Oh, hey there to you too, Max. The movie sucked-- boring. And the sound quality was horrible--barely audible. How was your first class of the day?" I beamed, I was truly happy to see him.

"Boring too. I hate Spanish--should've taken French with Mrs. Uhr. We could've sat together. Anyway, are we dining with each other at lunch? I brought strawberry cupcakes with homemade butter cream icing. Hope Alex doesn't mind. He might rip my head off if I don't share you with the gang."

Before answering Max's predictable question, I stared while Julian crept towards his top-row locker, conveniently situated on the other side of the busy hall. With his back finally turned, I was able to shift my concentration towards Max again. Since Julian's intrusive stare is hypnotic, I fare much better when I'm able to avoid eye contact with him all together. A feat that's easier said than done.

"Lunch sounds great. And let me guess--those are *lovingly baked by mom* cupcakes--right? No stale, packaged sweets for you. You're spoiled, Max."

"I know. Mom's very considerate. She thought we'd enjoy a sugary treat on our first day back at school. By the way, have I told you how stunningly beautiful you look today?"

"No you haven't. Let's hear it, Max."

"You look stunningly beautiful, Dallas. And you *smell* irresistible too. Vanilla musk again? And that gorgeous necklace you're wearing around your tempting neck is spectacular. Someone must really love you," he crooned.

"What, this old thing? Just kidding, Max. It is lovely. Thanks again for intrusting me with such a lovely piece. This stone is priceless. I'll guard it with my life."

"That's not necessary. *I'll* guard *you* with my life. Nothing bad's going to happen to you as long as I'm around. I promise, Dallas."

"I believe you Max. But I'm okay you know. The worst is over for me and my family. Besides, what could possibly happen that would hurt more than losing my baby sister Rose? The Reed's are definitely in the clear. Nothing but blue skies from here on out. Come on Max, walk me to math before I'm late."

What the...He's in my Pre Calculus class too? Am I being punished?

"Dallas, hey. Guess what? We've got a sub today--hooray!" Blake sang as I made my way inside the stuffy classroom.

I could hear Blake celebrating from where I stood. However, my mind was numb. Sitting only a few desks behind mine was Julian--looking wicked as ever. I stumbled towards my wobbly desk and nodded ever so insignificantly at him. Julian grimaced. Unfortunately, the back of my neck started throbbing again.

"Um, hello, class. I'm Mrs. Elliot--your math sub today. Mrs. Sheffield wants you guys to finish this worksheet on algebraic equations. You should know this stuff already. You've been reviewing these types of problems all year. If you want, you may work independently or in pairs. I must warn you, however, this assignment must be completed before you exit the classroom. Keep that in mind when choosing partners."

Blake, I thought to myself. I need Blake.

Before I managed to grab his attention, however, Julian's seriously warm hands latched onto my shoulders--the stabbing pain in my neck increased. I cringed as soon as I realized it was him. *Oh please go away...*

"Need a partner, Emily?"

No.

"Uh, sure. I guess so, Julian. Um, scoot your desk over here--mine's kind of shaky. The metal leg's broken. Anyway, let's get this stupid worksheet finished. I don't want an incomplete. Mrs. Sheffield's tough." *Oh crap. Why didn't I say no?*

Julian inched his stable desk closer to mine. Blake shot a strange and puzzled look at us. I rolled my eyes as if I didn't understand what he was implying.

"Long time no see, Emily. Was that your boyfriend just now? The tall, buff blonde that dropped you off at the front door?"

"Um, yes. His name is Max--Maxwell Snow. Are you ready to start?" I cleverly avoided Julian's imposing eyes when answering his peculiar question. Julian was acting nosy.

He twisted his lean and faultless body in my direction and suddenly Julian and I were sitting directly opposite of each other. This time, however, I couldn't resist looking up from the empty worksheet into his eyes. I smiled faintly and then quickly refocused my attention back on our unfinished assignment--I didn't want to linger too long in Julian's gaze.

"This stuff's easy Emily. Here, I don't even need a calculator. Let's see...."

"I can help too you know," I managed, wincing in pain. Julian didn't notice. He was busy scribbling on the blank page.

"Don't need it. I'm a math whiz. That's why I'm in here with you."

"Oh. Well, I just barely made it into Pre Calculus. I've got a low "B" average. I struggle with it sometimes. I probably need a tutor."

"I'll tutor you, Emily."

"Huh?"

"I said I'll tutor you, Emily, are you deaf?"

"Um, I should probably get Max to tutor me," I stuttered. "Besides, he's a genius. Wants' to go to medical school. But thanks for the offer." *Is this guy serious?*

"Max looks like a bore, Emily."

"What did you say?"

"I said the guy looks boring. You really are deaf."

"No I'm not. And Max isn't boring. You don't know him. You know nothing about my boyfriend."

"I know he looks boring," Julian scowled--a teeny but eerie smile forming around his ominous mouth.

"You need to mind your own business. If you'd rather work separately, that's fine with me. I'll figure this stuff out," I interjected. *Who does he think he is calling my boyfriend boring? He doesn't even know Max! Max is awesome! He drives an old truck, studies science formulas most of the day, feeds rat snakes and*

*chinchilla's named Franco at lunch, likes to take
pictures of cute bunny rabbits, and brings strawberry
flavored cupcakes to school--Max is not boring! Is he?*

"Chill out, Emily. It's not that big of a deal. You
don't look like the most exciting girl in Beckley either.
I'm sure you guys are perfect together. Like Tom and
Jerry or Britney and Justin--oops, they broke up didn't
they? My bad. Anyway, I'm sure your weekends are
filled with loads and loads of fun activities like picking
wildflowers and *taking long hikes in the snow-covered
woods*."

"What? How'd you know...Oh, never mind. Leave
me alone. I'm trying to calculate. At this rate, we'll, I
mean *I*, will never finish."

"It's okay. You can copy mine."

"What are you talking about? We haven't even
worked the first problem yet."

"I have. I'm on number twelve. You're slow, Emily.
You're lagging behind. You need to focus on your work
and less on being engrossed with me," Julian annoyingly
chuckled. He appeared to be teasing me.

"You can't be on number twelve. And I am not
enthralled by you. To be perfectly honest, I find your
bad boy image redundant and dull. You need a new act,
Julian. You should try smiling once in a while and being
nice to people."

Julian laughed more candidly this time. The
prudishly dressed sub shot a dirty look.

"I didn't say you were *enthralled* by me Emily--I said
engrossed. *You* used the term *enthralled,* not me.
Anyway, I'm sorry," he giggled. "I just find you
amusing. You get flustered easy, don't you? Every time
we make eye contact your *pedantic* face turns red. Do I
make you nervous, Emily?"

"No. As a matter of fact you don't. You do make me
angry though--criticizing my boyfriend and making fun
of me--and I'm not *pedantic,* I'll have you know. I'm
quite a lot of fun to be around. You need to learn some

manners, Julian. The quicker the better. You're not a nice person."

"Nice doesn't get a guy very far these days. Besides, nice is boring--just ask Max."

"That's it. I'm turning around. I'll do this assignment on my own. I don't need a rude and vulgar partner. Find somebody else to torment. You're on your own."

I whipped my livid body around choosing to stare in the direction of the unused chalkboard instead. *I will not turn around. I'm done playing games with that egghead. Julian's an obnoxious, stuck on himself, bore. I will not waste another minute of my time on him! I absolutely will not!*

I heard Julian snickering and my red blood boiled--increasing the pain in my splotchy neck. Unfortunately, I couldn't stop myself from turning around one last time. And that's when I let him have it. "Leave me alone, Julian!" I screamed. "And stay the heck away from me! You're such a jerk!"

Mrs. Elliot snapped. I've never seen a sub get so angry. "Come here, girl. What's your name? And where does your teacher keep her pink slips?"

"Um, they're in that second drawer, Ma'am. Underneath the yellow post-it notes."

I couldn't believe I answered her. *That was dumb. What was I thinking? I should be defending myself. Julian's the problem here!*

Mrs. Elliot handed me the pink slip--not interested in my excuses. "Here young lady, fill out your proper name and then go and explain to Mr. Tennyson why I'm kicking you out of class. I won't have *your kind* disturbing the others. You need to be respectful. We don't need any rebels stirring up trouble. I'm sorry young man--um, what's your name?"

"Julian. I'm new here. This is my first day at Woodrow Wilson. My name is Julian Knight," he innocently replied--engaging Mrs. Elliot with his stabbing good looks. *How convenient.*

"Well Julian, I apologize for her discourteous outburst. It was rude and insulting. She'll have to think about her dreadful behavior when she confronts Mr. Tennyson in the office. Now leave young lady, and don't return until you can conduct yourself appropriately inside this classroom!"

Are you kidding? I'm being sent to the principal's office? Me? I didn't do anything wrong! I'm innocent! It's that pig's fault--not mine! That rude, arrogant, condescending pig! He should be heading for the office not me. I'm going to kill him. I've never been sent to the principal before. I'm boring-remember? That's it Emily. You will never, and I mean never, ever, speak to that conceited, egotistical pig ever again. Forget about Julian Knight! That's it! No more Julian. He's dead to me.

Dead-To-Me!!!

Daily Journal 2004-2005

January 4, 2005

Dear Diary,

I hate him! I hate him! I hate him! I hate him! I hate him!

p.s.   I   hate   him!

p.s.s. I--HATE--HIM!

No, no master! I wasn't going to say anything. I told them nothing! I am loyal to you master! Renfield. Dracula, 1931.

Chapter 24

Stay Away From Her!...

The following day, Tuesday, January 5, 2005:

"Are you okay, Dallas?"

"I'm fine Max. Couldn't be better," I brusquely huffed--a cloud of steam emanating from my precious, elf-like ears.

"Are you sure you're okay?"

"Couldn't be better I said. I'm perfectly well. Now walk me to my first class. Hurry up. I'm ready to go."

"Okay, Dallas. Whatever you say."

A fresh, new day and I still have to face that arrogant, pig-headed, jerk staring at me from across the hallway. Well, he won't get to me this time. I won't allow it.

Honor's English:

"Mornin', Emily. Try not to upset any ugly dress-wearing substitute teachers today. Wouldn't want you earning another pink slip," Julian grimaced.

"Whatever, Julian. Your not that funny you know. Besides, I'm not talking to you anymore. *You suck.*"

Pre-Calculus:

"Hey there, Emily. Mind your manners in class today. *If you can.* Mrs. Elliot's back," Julian devilishly grinned.

"Leave me alone, Julian. Seriously. *You suck.*"

End of day:

"See you tomorrow, Emily. Have a great evening with Max. Maybe you guys can chase rainbows through the enchanted forest or make pixie dust," Julian smirked.

"Whatever, Julian. *You suck.*"

The next day, Wednesday, January 6, 2005:

"What's up with you and that creepy dude Julian? He's all pale and thin and spooky looking--like a teenage vampire or something. He's always staring at you in math class and in the hallways. He's kind of weird--scary looking. He's got a nice ride though--he drives that shiny black *Triumph Thruxton* parked outside behind the gym. Those motorcycles are fast. I mean, really, really fast. I need to get me one. Chicks think they're cool. Hey, what's wrong with you, Dallas? You're not saying much. You okay?" Blake drilled on our drive towards school--getting on my already frayed nerves in the process. *I wished he'd stop yakking on and on about Julian. He's wearing me down.*

"I'm fine, but Julian keeps bugging me. I wish he'd leave me alone. I don't know what his problem is," I grumbled. At the ridiculously fast speed Blake was driving, I'd be seeing Julian in less than five minutes.

"Tell Max about it. He'll deal with Julian. That's what extremely large, six foot-two boyfriend's are for. Max has got at least twenty pounds on that scrawny dude. Besides, Julian's a punk. Steer clear of him, Dallas. He's trouble," Blake warned. For the first time in his life, Blake was right.

"I know he is, Blake." *I know he is.*

As soon as we arrived at WWHS, against my better judgment of course, I took Blake's advice telling Max about the dark-headed stranger hassling me. He wasn't happy. However, true to his gentle and courteous nature, my incessantly pleasant boyfriend decided to approach the erroneous teen in a friendly manner in order to kindly suggest he focus his ill-advised attention on someone other than me. Needless to say, the confrontation did not go as smoothly as planned.

"Excuse me? You want me to stop talking to Emily? Whatever, dude. Get out of my face," Julian scoffed. His stiffening posture and scowled expression was imposing, threatening even. Wisely, Max took a few steps back.

"You can talk to her. Just stop messing with her Julian. It's not polite. You guys can be friends, but you shouldn't be disrespectful. She's asked you to leave her alone. And now I'm asking you to leave her alone. It's not rocket science, dude, just give her some space," Max warned--this time with a little more oomph in his tone. The veins in his muscular neck started to bulge and it was the first time I'd seen Max irritated. "You're new here. You should try getting along with the students, not antagonizing them. You know--make some friends." Max was definitely annoyed.

"Who are you? The school counselor? Get out of my face. You're pissing me off." Julian's commanding presence was slightly more threatening as a slew of snooping students gathered around the two opposing forces--hoping for a nasty, gut-wrenching fight to break out.

"Listen, I've asked you nicely, Julian...um, whatever your last name is--to please, leave my girlfriend alone. She's asked you politely to mind your own business and I'm asking the same."

"The name's Julian Knight. And if *Emily* wants me to leave her alone, she can tell me that herself. She's a big girl--doesn't need an overzealous bodyguard. I'm sure *Emily* can manage on her own. Isn't that right, *Emily?*" Julian shot a look of disgust my way and I knew he was angry at me for involving Max. I was embarrassed and worried, as I watched my feeble plan go horribly wrong. Now, Mr. Smith was forcing his way down the crowded hall in order to break Max and Julian up.

"Max, what's the problem buddy? Why don't you step back son. I'll handle this," Mr. Smith firmly interjected.

"Um, well, I was just asking Julian--*Julian Knight*--to give Dallas some space. He's new so I don't want to cause him too much trouble, but he's bothering Dallas." Max never took his eyes off of Julian's hostile stare.

Mr. Smith's slightly wrinkled face turned white as soon as he heard Julian's name. It's almost as if he'd seen a ghost.

"Um, well, you and Dallas head to class now son. I'll handle this. Julian, why don't you follow me to the lab. Perhaps we should talk. I'm not blaming you for the confrontation. I just think it might be good if we sit down, get to know each other a little better. Follow me son."

"Whatever. I didn't start this. But I'd be glad to finish it. That is if Max wants to take it outside," Julian threatened. Quite a few of the students backed up when he did.

"Come on, Julian. Let's go talk. Everyone else go to class. There's nothing to see here. Go on. Party's over."

The crowd of nosy onlookers scattered--disappointed heads weren't going to roll, and Max and I headed for our respective classes, glad the confrontation was over.

"I'll see you later, Dallas," Max managed to grin. Trying to placate me I guess.

"Okay. Hey, I'm sorry about all of this. I should have kept my mouth shut. I really am sorry, Max."

"Don't worry about it, Dallas. It's not your fault. Julian's the one causing problems. Mr. Smith will take care of things. It'll be okay. *I promise*."

I felt slightly better, however, I still worried about Julian's ominous threats. Would he challenge Max again? I hoped not. I didn't want the two of them fighting over me. I just wanted Julian to pick on somebody else. He made me nervous. In fact, Julian made a lot of the students nervous.

"So, um, Julian, you're new here. When did you start? I haven't seen you around yet, son," Mr. Smith was cautious--suspicious of the rebellious newcomer--but checking him out nonetheless.

"I've been in class for three days," Julian huffed--mad at the entire student body for rejecting him.

"So, um, where do you live?"

"Near Shay's Creek. My dad owns a cabin. We've been here almost a month now. Am I in trouble? Cuz if I'm not, I'm missing Social Studies. Can I go?"

"Yes. But, son, listen, we don't have a lot of problems at this school and we'd like to keep it that way. Next time a student gives you a hard time, come see me. I'll handle it--we want you to feel welcome. Oh, and Julian, Max is a good guy--he's just a little protective of Dallas. She's *new* here too and she's had a bit of a rough time--family problems--cut her some slack. And let me know if there's anything I can do to make your transition smoother. Don't hesitate to come by my office if you need help, son," Mr. Smith persisted. "I'm here for you. I'll help any way I can."

"I'm fine. I don't need any assistance. Just keep Maxwell Snow away from me. Can I go?"

"Yes, you can. Have a pleasant afternoon, Julian."

"Yeah, see ya around," he jeered. Julian's disdainful voice reeked sarcasm.

As soon as the troubled teen exited the messy office, Mr. Smith grabbed his cell phone pecking anxiously at the hard numbers. Frantically, he dialed an old friend, hoping for some answers.

"Katie, it's me. Listen, we need to talk. Let's meet for dinner--without Max. We have a problem. A very serious problem. I'll see you at seven. Bye."

Part Four

Word to the wise-immortality is no excuse not to floss.
Forever Knight 1992.

Chapter 25

What's He Doing Here?...

Katie Snow arrived at the small, family owned diner on Fourth Street eager to speak with her long-time friend, John Smith. They had much to discuss. Since receiving the harried phone call suggesting Max's long-lost father as well as his dangerous twin brother Julian had returned to Beckley, she could barely breath.

"John, are you sure it's *Julian*?" Katie pried--terrified by the idea the hazardous duo might possibly be living so near her gentle, unassuming *hybrid* son.

"Yes. It has to be. Julian claims that he and his father live near Shay's creek. That's where the old cabin is, remember?"

"How could I forget. I gave birth to Max and Julian inside that very cabin--afraid the rest of the world would realize what *they* are--what *we* are. What should I do? I don't know what to do, John," a despondent Katie worried aloud.

"You must visit Sam tonight. Tell him to leave. They can't stay here, Katie. It's too dangerous for Max. He doesn't know about *them--or us*. We're *hybrids*--half human and half vampire, for Pete's sake. Sam and Julian must leave. It's not safe for Max! It's not safe for the people living in Beckley either!"

"I know, I know. But how can I convince Sam to leave *again*? He promised he wouldn't come back. He promised John! Why now? Max is nearly grown. *Why now?*"

"I don't know what Samuel's thinking. My own twin brother and I don't understand! He and Julian aren't like you, me, and Max. They cannot fully embrace their human natures. It's not possible for them. Samuel's already proven that--*he's a murderer*--and Julian--well--he's always been different from Max. We knew that even when he was a baby. Julian always tried biting anyone he came into contact with. He craved blood--almost from the moment he was born. *And look how that turned out.* Living as a vampire for all these years with his father, it's too much for him to give up now. Julian cannot deny who he is or what he hungers for--he's part vampire, Katie. Just like Sam--blood is their life source now--they are *immortals.* *They're killers.* They're not like us. We choose to live as humans. We do not feed--we've *never* fed. Max either--you've done a wonderful job with him, Katie--he doesn't even realize he's a hybrid. The most important thing to remember here is that Max can never be alone with either of them. It's too dangerous. Especially near Julian--he could kill Max. I can't stand this. It's too much. I'm going to visit Samuel myself. He needs to listen. If he's ever loved either of his sons or *you*, he and Julian must leave!"

"I'm scared, John. Max is unaware of the powers he possesses. He's never used them--*they're latent*--but present nonetheless. Max is good boy. He doesn't fight or get angry. He's not intense or controlling...like vampires and most hybrids. *Max is a mortal--he's never tasted blood.* And if he does, well, he'll *come back again*--more terrifying than before. *Just like Sam and Julian will return after they die--reborn in other bodies.*"

John Smith interrupted. "Katie, Max and Julian nearly fought inside the hallway at school today. I had to break them up. It's only a matter of time before they come to blows. Max is strong--but Julian's more experienced. He's been developing his powers for sixteen years. Julian's a killer--he'll crush Max. We have to separate them. Max cannot return to school until Julian is gone. You cannot allow him to come back to class. That's final."

"I know that, John. But I'm not sure what to tell Max--I'll think of something I suppose. *I have too.* You're right, Max and Julian can't be near each other. And Dallas, she's not safe either. As long as Sam and Julian are in town, no one is safe. *No one.*"

"Hey, Mom, it's me. I'm home," Max yelled as soon as he entered the front door of his welcoming house nestled atop the magnificent West Virginia hills.

"Um, I'm in here, Max. I'm not feeling well. I've been sick all day in fact. I haven't gotten much done. I'm sorry, son," Katie moaned--worried about the lies she would be forced tell her doting son in order to convince Max to stay with her until Sam and Julian were gone for good.

"You're sick again? You seemed fine this morning. I thought you were feeling better? Why don't I call the doctor. He said he'd make a house call if you needed him."

"Um, no, Max. I just need to rest. It's okay. Come in here son. Talk to me. I missed you. How was your day?" Katie was anxious and her petite hands trembled.

"Not that great really. There's this new kid named Julian--Julian Knight--same last name as Dad's, in fact. Anyway, we almost got into a fight. Not that I wanted too. I tried speaking to him nicely. But he won't leave Dallas alone. Julian keeps picking on her. Anyway, I tried to intervene, but it only made things worse. But Mr. Smith broke us up before anything bad happened. You don't need to worry about it, Mom. I think Julian got the message. Besides, Dallas is fine. She's not going to let him get under her skin again."

"I see. Well that's too bad, Max, but I don't think you should be arguing with Julian. You have a perfect record at school--don't want you blowing your chances of getting into medical school. Stay away from boys like that. *They're trouble.* Besides, it's not worth it. You and Dallas don't need to involve yourselves with troublemakers. I hopes she's okay—and, Max, I love you, son."

"I love you too, Mom. Hey, want some soup or something?"

"Sure. But if it's alright with you, I'm going to turn in early. It's been a long, long, day, Max. And I'm wiped out."

"I'll heat up that clam chowder you cooked the other night. How's that sound?"

"Perfect, Max, that sounds perfect."

Before Blake arrived at my hectic and noisy house-- Caitlin and Ashley were arguing over a stupid pair of *Converse* high tops again--my barely working cell phone began vibrating. It was Max.

"Hey, um, Dallas. Listen, Mom's not feeling well. I won't see you today. Maybe for the rest of the week. I promised to stay home with her in case she needs my help. Mr. Smith agreed to speak to the teachers and gather my assignments so I don't lag behind."

"Oh shoot, Max. I mean, I'm sorry Katie's sick, but I'll miss you. Guess I'll have to eat lunch with the gang-- Alex will be thrilled," I teased--disappointed I wouldn't be getting a giant bear hug or stolen kiss from my thoughtful boyfriend.

"Hey now, don't be flirting with Alex," Max joked. "I don't like to share. Remember?"

"I know, I know. Is there anything I can do for your mom?"

"No. Not really. She just needs to rest. I did take her blood pressure this morning. It was high. I'm watching her--I'll call the doc if she gets too worked up. I better let you go, Dallas--Mom needs breakfast. I just wanted to let you know I won't be around to walk you to class or feed you lunch. I also wanted to tell you how much I love you. I'll miss you. Call me when you get home from school," Max gushed.

"I will. Ya'll take care, okay?"

"Okay."

"I love you, Max. Have a great day."

Even though I was worried about Katie's condition, I was concerned that without Max defending me, Julian would continue stalking me at school. I knew I was being selfish, but I didn't want to face him unprotected.

"*What up,* Emily? What? No big, bad wolf following you around today? Did I scare him off or something?" Julian mocked once I entered into honors English--*Maxless* of course.

"Leave me alone, Julian. Max's mother is ill. He won't be in today," I huffed--trying desperately to avoid his charismatic stare. Almost immediately, the pain in my neck returned.

"Okay, class. Settle in everybody. Alright, listen up. We've read *Romeo and Juliet,* watched the DVD, and now it's time to write. I want you guys to pair up. One girl per boy. Girls, you are the Juliet's. You'll be writing your dialogue's from her perspective. And boys, you are the Romeo's. You'll be writing from his perspective. This is homework guys. I want a three page script by next Friday--and it better be good. It counts for thirty percent of your semester grade. Also, you may not copy Shakespeare's words--that's called cheating. Make up your own text. This is a love story people, make sure your dialogue includes a love scene or romantic commentary of some sort between the two main characters. *Make it good, Thomas--you need a decent grade.* You've been goofing off this year. Also, because there are more boys than girls in this class, two boys--Jonathan and Colin--will have to work together. *And,* Colin, you are Romeo," Mrs. Rice advised.

The entire classroom filled with laughter and both Jonathan and Colin were visibly flustered.

"Hush now. It's no big deal. Keep it down, class. Now, are the instructions clear? You will not have time to finish this assignment in class. You'll need to pair up outside of school in order to create your script. We will read your assignments *out loud* in front of the entire class when finished. The best passages will be posted on the bulletin board for the other students to enjoy. Remember, I need these turned in by Friday of next week. Any questions?"

"Yes, Mrs. Rice, who do we pair up with?" a thin girl wearing a navy sweater and designer jeans in the front row inquired--she had her eyes on Gage Williams--a hunky football player.

"I have the list right here, Andrea. Please listen as I call your names. No booing, hissing or shouting. Take what you get and do not pester me to switch partners. Let's see, Ted and Alexis, Thomas and Railynn, Colin and Jonathan, Miles and Avisha, Emily and Julian..."

Julian nudged me as soon as he heard our names--his fingers were on fire. "Looks like I'll be coming over to your house tonight, Emily. What time should I be there?" he mused--his wide lips exposing a row of perfect teeth.

"Leave me alone, Julian. Perhaps Mrs. Rice will make an exception in our case."

"Better not make her angry, Emily. She said she'd take off points if anyone complained about their partners."

"I heard her, Julian! Jeez! Leave me alone. Let me think..."

"It's okay Max. Really, I can take care of myself. Besides, my parents will be here if Julian gets out of hand. Mrs. Rice insisted that if any of us complained, she'd dock ten points off our final grade. It's okay, really--the assignment is due next Friday and today's already Thursday. We'll only meet up a couple of times. No big deal. I'll probably end up doing most of the work. Julian's a dud. He'll never take this assignment seriously. Don't worry about it. Okay?"

"I'm worried about you, Dallas--Julian's a punk. I wish I could come over tonight. I just hate leaving Mom. She's been in bed most of the day."

"You don't need to come over. I'm fine. Julian won't be here until seven. My parents won't let him stay long. I've already told them he's a trouble maker. I'm sorry Max, but I really should hang up. I need to eat something before Julian gets here. Mom actually prepared a chicken and rice casserole for dinner and chocolate mousse for desert. She's been cooking again lately. I'm glad. For awhile, I thought I was going to turn into a giant bean burrito--all that *Taco Bell* we've been consuming. Hey, I'll check in with you and your mother tomorrow. Take care, Max. *I love you.*"

"I love you too, Dallas. And be careful, there's something about that guy I don't trust," Max warned. "He's like a negative vortex--moody and temperamental. The guy's *shady.*" *Tell me about it.*

"Emily, or somebody, could you please answer the door, I've got my hands full in here!" Mom shouted from inside the busy kitchen.

"I've got it, Mom," I yelled, while exiting my tiny bedroom. "I really do need to hang up, Max. Someone's at the door. Probably a salesman."

"I love you, Dallas."

"I love you too, Max."

"What the...What are you doing here so early? You're not supposed to be here until seven o'clock!"

"Didn't your mom tell you? We talked outside while she and your sisters waited for you in the van--after school. She was shocked to see me. Anyway, I told her you and I were partners on an English assignment and that I was coming over tonight. She made me promise to come early and have dinner. I thought you knew about it, Emily..." Julian persisted--a malevolent smile forming around the corners of his succulent mouth. A black leather jacket and shiny helmet accentuated Julian's long and lean body. *He looked good.*

"No, um, she didn't tell me. Well, come in, I guess," I mumbled--mad at her for inviting him despite my warning that he's trouble. *He just needs a hug, Emily.*

The poor boy doesn't have a mother--how'd she know that? Whatever, Mom. Julian's a punk.

"Oh, there you are, Julian. It's good to see you!" Mom interrupted--a friendly smile lighting up her indulgent face. She shoved past me in order to hug Julian. Her enthusiasm towards him was disturbing-- Mom was like a school girl in love whenever she laid eyes on Julian--another victim of his hypnotic presence. *Disgusting.*

"Hey, Mrs. R., good to see you again. How'd the pictures turn out?" Julian beamed--oozing friendliness. *Such a chameleon.*

"They're awesome. I downloaded them onto the hard drive this morning. Check them out--there in Wayne's office. I can email some to your dad if you'd like. Maybe you could use them as Christmas cards this year? I'm going to. Oh, um, Emily. Would you mind taking the casserole out of the oven while I show Julian to your dad's office?"

"Of course not. Whatever I can do to help," I smirked. *So he's got mother under his devilish spell. What do you want from us, Julian Knight?*

"Thanks, Mrs. R, I'd love to see the pictures. Don't let the casserole burn, Emily," Julian teased as he brushed past me. His uncharacteristically relaxed body was warm. And for the first time since meeting Julian, my neck felt okay.

"Wow. That was awesome, Mrs. R. I haven't had food that good in a long time. Dad and I usually grab something out of a can. We're not big eaters you know. *Never have been.*"

"That's probably why you're so slim. Muscular, but thin. And pale--much more so than when we first met-- out at your dad's cabin. You need to eat more home cooked meals--you need some iron in your diet, Julian."

"You're probably right Mrs. R. I need to eat more meat I guess," Julian grinned while patting his stomach.

"You're welcome here anytime, Julian. I just started cooking again. I took a temporary hiatus from my duties I guess you could say. But my kitchen is fully stocked and I'm digging through some of my old recipes. Why don't you join us tomorrow night? Emily, you're not going out with Max this weekend are you? You shouldn't be around him or Katie if she's sick."

"No, um, I guess not. I'll be here all weekend, working on school stuff."

"Awesome, since you and Julian need to finish that project, and it counts so much towards your final grade, Julian can come early on Friday and eat dinner with us. How does that sound, Julian? I make a mean beef stew with small red potatoes."

"Sounds awesome, Mrs. R. Thanks for the invite. Same time?"

"Same time, Julian."

"I'll be here. And thanks again. The chicken casserole and mashed potatoes were awesome," he beamed. Julian seemed genuinely attached to my mother for some reason. *What's that about I wonder?*

"Well, um, come on, Julian. I guess we should get busy. Can we work in Dad's office, Mom?"

"No honey, I need to access his computer--I'm beefing up my resume again. Can you and Julian use the *Apple* inside your bedroom instead?"

"Uh, yeah, I guess so. Um, let's head for my room then, Julian. We need to get started."

"Ooh, Emily's takin' a boy to her bedroom! Don't be kissing!" Caitlin ragged. "Her breath's disgusting Julian! And she's a witch!"

"Shut up, Caitlin!"

"Caitlin Millicent Reed, for goodness sakes. Leave your sister alone. Julian and Emily are going in there to study," Mom scolded. "Help me clean up this kitchen-- and I'll ground you if you embarrass your sister like that again. Ignore her, Julian, she's just a little pesky sometimes," Mom chided.

"A little! That's an understatement. She's a brat!" I yelled.

Caitlin stuck her disgusting tongue out and Julian laughed.

"She's cute Emily. I bet you guys have a lot of fun together," he joked.

"Come on, Julian. Let's get this over with. I want to finish this wretched assignment as quickly as possible."

I led Julian inside my disorganized room annoyed at Mom for inviting him to dinner and angry at Caitlin for embarrassing me. I'd have to get her back. I just didn't know when.

"So this is your bedroom, huh, it's um, girly, just like you," Julian smiled. *Julian's smiling?*

"Well, what did you expect? I'm not exactly a Goth. And I don't cruise around town in the slush and snow on a shiny black motorcycle--exuding teenage rebellion. Don't you get cold on that death trap?"

"No. Not really. I'm *hot natured*. Feel my skin." Julian swept his long, creamy fingers against my cheekbones and I blushed.

"You are warm, Julian. Are you sure you don't have a fever?"

"No fever, Emily. Like I said, I'm hot natured--just like my dad. *We're two of a kind*."

Flustered by his touch, I knew I was losing the ability to fight off Julian and his not so subtle advances. "Well, um, we should probably get to work. I'm shooting for an A+ on this project. English is my best subject. No slacking off okay? We need to put our differences behind us. Please? And we need to concentrate, Julian."

"Of course, Emily. By the way, I have no quarrel with you. It's your boyfriend Max I'm angry with. He needs to mind his own business and stay out of my way," he scowled. It was the first time Julian appeared mad since arriving early for dinner. It made me nervous.

"What's your problem with Max? He's a great guy. Nobody ever has trouble with him," I stammered.

"Whatever, Emily. Let's change the subject. Hey, have you ever been on a motorcycle?"

"No. Why?"

"Well, the temperature isn't bad right now. Why don't we ride for a few minutes?"

"Are you serious?"

"Of course I am. We won't go far--just around the block a couple of times. I've got a spare helmet in the panniers attached to my bike. It's small enough for your head..."

"No way! It's too dangerous! What if we wreck? Or I fall off?"

"Emily, you'll be fine. I've been racing motorcycles for awhile. I know what I'm doing. Just a quick spin around the neighborhood."

"I don't know, Julian. Besides, I don't think my parents would let me get on that thing with you."

"Your mom said it's fine."

"What are you talking about?"

"I asked her when I saw her in the school's parking lot this afternoon. She said you'd probably enjoy riding."

"Are you serious? My own mother--what a traitor!"

"Come on, Emily--it's just for a few minutes. I promise. I'll drive slowly and cautiously. You'll be fine--I swear."

Julian's face softened when trying to convince me. The wispy bangs of his dark, brown hair framed his pale but handsome face, and Julian's chestnut eyes sparkled when gazing into mine. He was hard to resist.

"If I ride on that thing with you, will you quit bugging me so we can tackle our homework?"

"Yes. Now come on. Let's ride." Julian was positively beaming--and my neck still felt fine.

"Okay, okay. Give me a second. I need a warm jacket and some gloves. I can't believe I'm doing this. I've never been on a motorcycle. I must be completely stupid to get on that thing with you. I swear, Julian, you better not crash. I'll kill you if you do. Hey, maybe you should take Caitlin instead. I won't hate you if she gets mangled. You have my permission."

"I'll take my chances Emily. Besides, like I said, you'll be fine."

Julian and I headed outside towards his intimidating bike. Before we made it out the front door, however, I shot Mom a dirty look for giving her permission without my knowledge. She grinned.

"Have fun on that thing. Emily--it's my turn next!" she squealed.

"I seriously cannot believe I'm doing this. Am I on drugs?"

"I told you, Emily, you'll be fine. Now here, let me fit this helmet on top of your head properly. It should feel snug. Does it?"

"What? I can't hear you, Julian."

"The-Helmet-Should-Feel-Tight!"

I nodded my noticeably heavier head yes. The silver and grey *Shoei* helmet was snug and weighty. It felt like a ten pound bowling ball was mashing against my squishy brain.

"I'm going to climb on first, Emily. You jump on behind me, okay?" he yelled.

I gave Julian a thumbs up letting him know I understood his command. When he signaled a thumbs up in return, my heart softened. *So sexy in that leather jacket and black helmet. Too faultless for words.* When he caught a glimpse of my sincere smile, a brilliant grin lit up Julian's face. He was excited and handsome--an appealing combination.

Before I had time to worry about the risk I was taking, we were spinning out of the smooth driveway--tires screeching. Julian's noisy motorcycle purred loudly as we ventured around the frozen block at least a half a dozen times. Even though I was cold, the surprisingly smooth ride was invigorating. The icy wind whipped through my long hair and I felt a sense of freedom and independence not present before I climbed on. I grabbed tightly onto Julian's waist as he twisted and turned around the familiar roads in my small country neighborhood. We zoomed past Blake's two-story colonial, and I waved--even though no one was outside. I hated admitting to myself that despite my previous protests, I was enjoying the ride tremendously. I should be hating this, I reasoned. Riding on the backseat of a dangerous motorcycle with a rebellious teen is insane. I should be forcing Julian to return to the safety of my home. But I didn't want to go back. I wanted to cruise around on his motorcycle for as long as he would let me.

Julian was surprisingly cautious--treating me as if I were a valuable object in need of safekeeping. He stopped slowly and methodically at every speed bump and stop sign we encountered, guardedly waiting to ensure no out of control drivers were speeding our way. I was impressed. Unfortunately, after about twenty minutes or so, Julian and I arrived at my boring house and I felt disappointed when I saw smoke from the chimney clouding the air. *I don't want to be home, I thought to myself. I want to ride. This is fun.*

I motioned for Julian to go around once more and he obeyed. He knew I was enjoying myself and made every effort to accommodate me. After riding an additional fifteen minutes or so, Julian pulled up onto our flat driveway and we exited the bike. I was beaming. So was he.

"Well, Emily. What did you think?"

"That was awesome Julian! I can't believe I've never ridden before! That felt spectacular!"

"I told you it would be fun. You should listen to me more often, huh?"

"Yes!"

Julian reached for my helmet with friendly hands. Laughing, it was the first time Julian and I appeared comfortable together since meeting. We were enjoying each other's company.

"Um, as much as I'd love to keep riding with you, Emily, we really should be studying. We've got three pages of typed dialogue to tackle. Are you ready?"

"*No!* Oh, okay, I'm as ready as I'll ever be I guess, although I'd rather ride. Come on," I whined. "Let's go inside and warm up by the fire before we head back to my *girly* bedroom."

"Sounds good. Hey, thanks for uh, accompanying me on my bike. You're the first girl ever to ride with me."

"Are you serious, Julian?"

"Yep."

"Then where did the spare helmet come from?"

"Um, well, after your mom promised you'd ride, I, uh, stopped by a motorcycle shop in town and picked one up. I knew it would fit because your head is so small."

"You bought that helmet for me?"

"Well, um, yeah. I guess I did. I certainly didn't have anyone else in mind when I picked it out."

"Wow, that's cool. I'm surprised--but I appreciate it. You're right though--we better get inside. It's getting nippy out here--the temperature's dropping. Are you sure you'll be okay driving home tonight?"

"Are you worried about me, Emily? Don't be. I told you, I'm hot natured. But thanks for asking."

"You're welcome."

Julian and I entered the cozy living area, each of us feeling relaxed and content. A pleasant change from our usual negative experience with each other. *I couldn't help wondering, however, why Julian would purchase such an expensive item for me. I thought he hated me?*

You must excuse me, but I have already dined. And I never drink wine. Gary Oldman in Bram Stoker's Dracula.

Chapter 26

Romeo, Romeo, Where For Art Thou?...

"Ready to get started, Julian?" I was definitely feeling less irritable. The freeing sensation I'd experienced while cruising around the neighborhood on the backside of his *Thruxton* was incredible. So was Julian.

"Um, sure, I guess. Hey, did you really like riding with me?"

"Are you kidding? I loved it! I had a blast. In fact, I'm hoping you'll take me for another spin sometime."

"Of course I will. I'm ready when you are." Julian's long, dark lashes and even darker eyes were difficult to resist. "So different today," I mumbled. "What's gotten into him?"

When I first encountered Julian at school this morning, he was a monster exuding rage and anger. Right now, however, in the confines of my hot pink and neon purple bedroom, Julian was responsive and gentle. *I liked it.*

The two of us were huddling around my computer agonizing over what to write about for our pressing English assignment when Julian suggested rereading some of the play's most inspiring passages in order to familiarize ourselves with Shakespeare's beloved piece of literature. His idea had merit. Julian even agreed to read from the romantic play--*out loud!* As soon as he began reciting from the idealistic passages, my hands and feet went numb. Julian looked exactly as I'd envision Romeo to be--tall, lean, muscular, and drop dead gorgeous.

"Here goes, Emily. Don't laugh." Julian cleared his raspy throat and immediately stiffened his lanky posture. I liked that Julian was nervous--I wasn't used to seeing him that way. Before starting, however, his dark eyes met with mine. Julian wanted my undivided attention. *And he definitely had it.*

> *But soft! what light through yonder window breaks?*
> *It is the east, and Juliet is the sun!--*

Julian's voiced cracked. "Um, should I keep reading Emily? I mean, we need to get this scene down, cuz it'll probably be on the nine weeks test. But I feel kind of stupid standing here all by myself." Julian's translucent face darkened as the rush of blood flushed his hallow cheeks--*hmmm, so he is human--blood does run through his veins.* He was embarrassed. However, I didn't want him to stop. I was mesmerized by Julian--his uneven, chocolate locks and haunting eyes. At this very moment, Julian was the epitome of Shakespeare's dreamy words and romantic hero. Julian was Romeo.

"Keep reading, Julian," I insisted.

"Okay," he shrugged. "Are you sure..."

"Yes," I interrupted.

> *Arise, fair sun, and kill the envious moon,*
> *Who is already sick and pale with grief,*
> *That thou her maid art far more fair than she:*
> *Be not her maid since she is envious;*
> *Her vestal livery, is but sick and green,*
> *And none but fools do wear it; cast if off.--*

Julian cleared his tight throat again and I watched as his visibly nervous hands shook while gripping Shakespeare's thick anthology. He looked at me sheepishly. I nodded for him to continue despite his being uneasy. Whether he knew it or not, Julian brought Shakespeare's enchanting words to life.

> *It is my lady; O, it is my love!*
> *O, that she knew she were!--*
> *She speaks, yet she says nothing: what of that?*
> *Her eye discourses; I will answer it.--*

Julian glanced at me again--searching my eyes for approval--and my heart raced. "Keep reading, Julian. You're doing a great job," I managed--entranced by his smooth voice and subtle gestures.

> *I am too bold; 'tis not to me she speaks:*
> *Two of the fairest stars in all the heaven,*
> *Having some business, do entreat her eyes*
> *To twinkle in their spheres till they return.*
> *What if her eyes were there, they in her head?*
> *The brightness of her cheek would shame those*
> *   stars,...*

"More, Emily?"
"Yes, Julian, more."
"Okay. Whatever you say," Julian shrugged.

> *As daylight doth a lamp; her eyes in heaven*
> *Would through the airy region stream so bright,*
> *That birds would sing, and think it were not*
> *   night.*
> *See, how she leans her cheek upon her hand!*
> *O, that I were a glove upon that hand,*
> *That I might touch that cheek!* [Act. II, scene I]

When he reached the end of the quixotic scene, Julian's body shifted uncomfortably as he closed the anthology laying it on top of my bed. "Well, um, that's it, Emily," Julian winced. "It's the end of the scene."

I smiled widely, thrilled that Julian decided to continue despite initially being nervous. "That was incredible! *Really.* For a moment, I was convinced Romeo was standing right inside this very room. You seem familiar with the play Julian--you didn't have any trouble reading the lines. The language isn't always easy for us mere *mortals* to understand."

"Oh, well I've read it before--at my old school. I've always enjoyed Shakespeare's works. Especially his tragic plays, you know--like *Macbeth, Othello,* and *Richard the Third.* I can relate to the bad guys I guess. So what should we do now, Emily?"

"Well, um, I suppose we could include a scene where the lovers fight--that could be interesting."

"Yeah, maybe. Hey, Emily, what do you think about Shakespeare? Do you really like his work?"

"Of course. I mean, the language is complex, but his stories are timeless--especially the romances. People fall in love and society or other forces don't always support them being together. But you can't always help who you fall for..."

"Yeah," Julian interrupted. "It's just that everybody roots for the good guy--no one ever wants the bad guy to get the girl."

"That's not necessarily true, sometimes the bad guy does get the girl--just look at Hollywood--especially in books and films like *The Outsiders* and *Grease.*"

"I guess so. What about you, Emily? Would you ever consider falling for the bad guy?"

Now I was the one who was uncomfortable. Julian was definitely putting me on the spot with his nosy questions.

"Um, well, I don't know. It depends how *bad* he is I guess. How bad are we talking?"

"I don't know. I mean, how bad is too bad? Some of us...I mean *some people*...are genetically different--they're predisposed towards certain behaviors..."

"Hereditary sucks sometimes--that's for sure. But *everyone has a choice*--they can choose to be good or bad. I truly believe that," I insisted.

"Maybe. But some people...Oh, I don't know. Never mind. I'm just thinking out loud I guess."

"I would never count someone out just because they've made mistakes. No one's perfect, Julian--"

"Except for Max of course." His lips suddenly tightened and the brows above Julian's dark eyes furrowed when referring to Max. Julian was angry again. *What's new?*

"What's your problem with Max? He's a great guy. I don't understand why you hate him so much. You've known him for like three days. It's not natural to hate someone you barely know..."

"I know enough Emily. I know his type--spoiled, judgmental...I don't need to *know* Max to *know* Max. Understand?"

"No I don't, Julian. You're not making sense. And Max is anything but spoiled. He and his mother work hard for what little they have. Her husband *Samuel* left when Max was just a baby. They've had a rough time. You should cut Max some slack," I argued.

"Samuel Snow, huh, that's a funny name."

"Max's father's last name was not Snow. He and Katie never married--Max inherited his mother's name. Samuel's name was *Knight*. Hmm, just like yours."

"*Samuel Knight*?" Julian seemed confused as soon as he heard the familiar name.

"Yes. But Max never met him. He left when Max was barely a year old--and hasn't contacted him since. Not a very honorable thing to do. Behavior like that is hard to forgive. I told you, Max has been through a lot. He's definitely not spoiled."

"I highly doubt that. Keep him away from me, Emily. I mean it."

"I don't get it Julian. You barely know Max. What's your problem?"

"You wouldn't understand." Julian's shoulders slumped and he refused to look at me. His white face blistered and his hands shook. "I'm gonna take off now-- I've lost my motivation. I'll see you tomorrow," he huffed. Julian's rigid posture as well as the near permanent scowl on his creased face was worsening--and for the first time this evening, the back of my neck started pulsating. The burning sensation was painful.

"What? Just like that and you're leaving? We haven't decided what to write about yet! Julian, you can't run away whenever you're angry--we have to finish--I need your help!" I was furious at Julian for threatening to bail.

"I need to get out of here, Emily. This isn't going to work."

"What are you talking about?"

"You, me, this assignment, Romeo and Juliet--it won't work. We're too different. I'll tell Mrs. Rice I'm the problem so you don't get a bad grade. I'll make sure you get another partner..."

"Don't you dare, Julian! Don't you dare bail on me! This is *our* assignment. You promised to put your negative feelings for Max aside so we could work together. You promised!"

"Whatever, Emily. It'll never work, it just won't work...Besides, I always break my promises. That's what bad guys do." Julian grabbed his helmet and leather jacket off the floor and his distressed eyes conveyed hurt. He was genuinely upset.

"What won't work Julian? What are you talking about? I don't understand what you're saying!"

I edged closer to Julian and the energy between us was insane--we could have lit an entire room with the sparks emanating from our hyped-up bodies. Salty tears welled in my blue-grey eyes when meeting his. I was angry and confused. Julian was angry and confused. When the tears finally came--stinging my skin--Julian backed away, and then something inexplicably changed between us. Before I understood what was happening, Julian threw down his riding gear and grabbed my soaked and streaked face. I hurled forward and Julian cupped my face inside his tight but careful grip. The next thing I knew, Julian and I we were kissing. My head whirled and my legs felt unstable. I kissed him back, however, not willing to part from his forceful lips. We held onto each other for what seemed like an eternity, and Julian felt good in my arms. But then he backed away again. I was crushed.

"I'm sorry Emily," Julian poured. "I shouldn't have done that--I shouldn't have kissed you."

"Don't apologize Julian," I choked. "I wanted you to kiss me. I certainly didn't try to stop you."

Still in each other's arms, we collapsed onto the double bed clutching one another tightly. It felt good to sit down--allowing my unsteady legs to rest. Julian stroked my moist face with his slender fingers and his hot touch lingered on my skin. We stared into each other's eyes and I felt happy--bewildered, but happy. Suddenly, I didn't want the evening to end.

"Emily, Julian? It's eight o'clock. Time to wrap things up," Mom insisted when knocking on the door.

"Okay Mom," I stuttered, "Julian was just packing up. He'll be out in a few." Both of us scrambled off the bed, wiping our faces. "I better go now Emily," Julian strained. "I hope I didn't upset you too much--I'm really sorry if I did."

"I'm fine, Julian! Please, don't worry about me. I wanted that kiss to happen--I wouldn't change tonight for anything."

"Me either," Julian smiled.

I smiled right back.

After gathering his things, Julian left my house, each of us feeling exhausted but blissful. He seemed truly happy and I was glad to see Julian smiling again. I walked him to the front door and we said our goodbyes, however, there was no kissing this time--too many curious eyes watching. We did hug, and I felt a genuine connection with Julian. Before falling asleep, I decided to write in my journal about the night's strange turn of events.

Daily Journal 2004-2005

January 7, 2005

Dear Diary,

What a shocking day--or evening I should say. Julian just left--wow. So much happened while he was here. Where do I begin? When Julian first arrived, I was angry--why did Mom invite him to dinner? I told her he's trouble. Anyway, Julian was happy and polite--I was shocked by his unusual demeanor. Julian seemed genuinely happy to see me--he even brought me a helmet to wear on his motorcycle! Oh, yeah, that's the other thing. We went riding. So much fun! Julian's motorcycle is awesome--and he loves riding it. I can tell, he seems so relaxed when cruising around. I'm glad. Julian needs to relax once and a while. He's so intense, so foreboding at times. Julian scares me, but at the same time I'm drawn to him. I can't explain it. He and I are like night and day. But still, he fascinates me. Julian is intriguing. So unpredictable--entirely different from Max. They are definitely opposites. We kissed. I know that's bad-- Max would be heartbroken. But I couldn't resist Julian. He seemed so vulnerable tonight--so at ease. I'm glad he came over. I hope to spend more time with Julian. Anyway, here's a poem. Emily Ryan Reed.

Souls in the Night

Will you have me on this dark night?
I offer my soul, ready for flight.
Wherever you take me, it will follow behind.
To the glories of heaven, or the truly sublime.
It follows without question; in you it trusts.
Break not the bond that transcends us.

Emily Ryan Reed

By the time I climbed into my warm and inviting bed, all I could think about was Julian. What would tomorrow bring for us? More tears, kisses, smiles or turmoil? Whatever the day offers, I will gladly embrace.

"Emily, Emily, wake up! Please, wake up!" Mom screamed, her voice laced with panic. "Please, oh please dear, you must get up!"

Mom shook my limp body violently as blood spilled from my mouth, soaking my pajamas and silky pillowcase.

"Oh dear God! Wayne, call an ambulance, I think she's choking!"

Dad grabbed the nearest phone, but before he could dial 911, my eyes suddenly widened. "I'm okay, Mom," I moaned--spitting blood from inside my mouth. "I just bit my tongue--I'm not choking, I'm okay," I managed.

"Oh thank God. Emily, I was so worried! You were screaming, and by the time I made it in here, I saw the blood and your eyes were closed..."

"I'm okay. I must have bitten it in my sleep--ouch. I was having another nightmare. Oh Mom! It was terrible! It's Rose. She's haunting me!"

"Emily, please, not that again. I don't know why you're dreaming about Rose, but she's not haunting you. They're just dreams, dear--that's all. Rose is dead, she's no where inside this bedroom," Mom argued.

"I don't believe you. She was here. I swear--standing right in front of me--reaching out."

"Come on, Emily--get out of bed. Let's clean you up. Let me see your tongue--do you think she needs stitches Wayne?"

Dad looked inside my bleeding mouth before making his verdict. "No, it's just a small cut. She'll be okay. Come on, Emily. Do as your mother says--let's get you cleaned up. I'll grab some more pajamas and a fresh pillow."

I stumbled out of bed into the bathroom hoping to get Mom and Dad out of my hair as quickly as possible. This time, however, I wasn't going back to sleep without answers. *What do you want from me, Rose? What are you trying to tell me?* I mumbled underneath my faded breath--hoping my parents wouldn't hear of course. *And you, Julian, why were you with Rose?*

As soon as Mom and Dad were convinced it was okay to leave me alone, I scrambled out of the warm bed towards my computer. It was three-fifteen in the morning--no surprise there--and I wanted answers. I logged on, searching websites dealing specifically with the occult--especially the witching hour. What I found, startled me.

Rose died on January thirty-first. Today is January eighth--and the third anniversary of her brutal murder is fast approaching. According to one of the many websites I researched, ghosts and apparitions are keen to what day of the week, month, and year it is. Therefore, it is not unusual for loved ones to witness restless spirits in or around their birthdays, wedding dates, or even the anniversaries of their deaths. *So that's why you're contacting me, Rose. But why haven't you done so before? You've been dead almost three years--and this is the first time you've visited me in my dreams.*

Tonight, Rose *and* Julian looked scary--thick, red blood dripping from their necks and mouths--feathery shadows above their heads. However wonderful I may have felt about Julian earlier, I felt entirely differently now.

In my latest nightmare, Rose's white hair was soaked from the rush of blood spewing from her open mouth and swollen neck. Rose's almond eyes oozed the gooey liquid as well. Rose looked evil--nothing like the precious four-year-old I loved so much. Still wearing the pink dress she was buried in, Rose's exposed flesh bore strange markings--dark blue veins and busted blood vessels--and her sharp nails protruded from her tiny hands. Julian was equally ominous. The only notable difference is that Rose did not sport a mound of razor sharp teeth snapping at me--thank goodness.

Dr. Karen Jenson--So what do you use then? Stakes? Crosses?
Whistler--Crosses don't do squat. Blade. 1998.

Chapter 27

I'm Sorry...

The next morning, even though I felt guilty about our kiss, and disturbed about my dream, I still had difficulty forgetting our embrace. And that's when Julian snuck up and startled me. "Don't suppose you told Max about our *first* kiss after I left last night. Did you, Emily?" Julian grinned. He seemed relaxed again.

"Of course not. It would crush him--you know that. And just so you know, that was our *first* and *last* kiss. It won't happen again."

"So you regret kissing me? Why the change of heart?"

"I'm not sure. I mean, I never should've betrayed Max--and I certainly won't do it again--that's what I regret. But kissing you, well, I don't know, even though it was wrong--somehow--it felt right. I can't explain it. It's as though we were supposed to connect--like fate or something. What about you, Julian? How do you feel today?"

"I feel great. I mean, I'm sorry you feel guilty about last night, but I don't care about Max. He's not my problem. I was upset because you were crying--that's all. I felt bad for you--*not him*--I never felt bad for Max, Emily. I'm the bad guy--remember?"

We stood outside of my muddled locker, dodging awkward stares from puzzled students perplexed as to why we were actually talking to each other. *I was a bit confused myself.* While rewinding the night's strange turn of events, Julian leaned in, his firm body dangerously close to mine, and my heart began racing.

Instantly, my fingers and toes tingled and my head felt dizzy. I wanted to grab Julian and kiss his fiery lips. But I couldn't. *He's not my boyfriend, I reasoned. Julian's not my boyfriend.*

"Still want me to come over tonight?" Julian knew his presence was intoxicating--and continued gazing into my weakened expression. I didn't want to get lost in his stare, but I couldn't help myself.

"I don't know. Remember, I have a boyfriend Julian--and we shouldn't be kissing," I whispered, afraid someone in the crowded hall would hear us. "I can't let it happen again. Understand?"

"I can't make any promises, Emily--you're hard to resist. I'll do my best--but not for Max--I don't care about him."

"I know you don't. But he's my boyfriend. He trusts me. We're promised to each other. Look, Max even gave me this beautiful ring over Christmas as a reminder of our commitment to each other." I unzipped my heavy jacket yanking on the gold chain twisted around my slender neck. Julian did a double take as soon as he saw the purple-stoned ring floating across my chest.

"What the...where did you get that, Emily? I don't under..."

"Max gave this ring to me over the holidays. Max and I are serious Julian--we're promised to each other. I told you that. I don't want to betray him."

"Too late for that, Emily." Julian clutched the intriguing heirloom inside his tight grip staring intently at the ring. "Where did Max get this?"

"His father Samuel left it when he took off. It's been on his side of the family for a while. Katie thinks he left it behind on purpose--so Max would have a reminder. She's probably right."

"You said his name is Samuel Knight. Right? And he left when Max was a baby. What else does Max know about his father?"

"Not much. Why, Julian? What's it to you?"

"Nothing. Um, I need to do something Emily. I'm gonna take off."

"Why? You can't ditch class Julian. You'll get in trouble. Mr. Smith's already seen you today. He knows you're here."

"I'll try to make it back by lunch. But it's important. I'll tell you about it tonight. I'm sorry, Emily. But I've got to go."

"Don't apologize to me, Julian. You're the one who'll get in trouble if the teachers find out you're ditching school."

"I'll see you tonight--at six o'clock. Okay?"

"Whatever, Julian. Hey, be careful."

"Are you worried about me, Emily?"

"I'm not sure. I told you, I'm confused."

Julian's dark eyes widened and the look on his troubled face suggested something serious was up. But what could have Julian so anxious? And why is he so interested in the ring Max gave me? I didn't have answers, but I knew Julian was up to something. *Guess I'll hear about it tonight, whatever it is.*

I had seen my becoming a vampire in two lights: The first light was simply enchantment...But the other light was my wish for self-destruction.
      Anne Rice, Interview With the Vampire.

Chapter 28

Reflection...

During study hall, and with the absence of Julian and Max, I had time to reflect on my confusing life. I came to some startling conclusions. Before Rose was born, my family of five was happy. After Rose was born, my family of six was happy. After Rose died, however, my family fell apart--especially me. And I was beginning to crumble again.

When Rose was murdered, my entire world collapsed. I couldn't breathe. Afraid of spending my days without her, I did the unthinkable--I tried to kill myself. On a particularly depressing day, when I no longer felt like existing, I paid a visit to my best friend Madison's house. Without her knowledge, I snuck into her neurotic mother's heavily stocked medicine cabinet and swiped some prescription sleeping pills--forty-four to be exact. At around seven p.m., I said my goodbyes to my best friend, after pretending to enjoy the scary movie we watched together, and jumped onto my ten-speed bicycle--peddling home as fast as I could. When I got there, I told Mom and Dad I was sleepy--and headed for bed. No one suspected a thing--at least I didn't think so. After showering and brushing my long hair out, I climbed into my favorite pair of silky pajamas, taking all forty-four pills with a *diet Coke*. And then I snuggled inside my warm and comfortable bed--waiting for sleep to take over. I wanted to die.

Initially, my body felt tense. I was nervous, afraid I would throw the tiny white pills up. But I didn't. After about thirty minutes or so, my anxious body began to tingle and my eyes blurred. I felt dizzy and lightheaded and I'm sure my legs were unstable. Then I drifted off to sleep. The next thing I knew, a multitude of doctors and nurses stood over my limp body shoving a long, plastic tube down my throat. It hurt.

Several hours later, I woke up in the psyche ward with black stuff all over my face, hands, and pajamas. I was a sticky mess. According to Dr. Maddox, head of ICU, my stomach had been pumped. I wasn't dead. *Darn.* After I was transferred, my excessively plump and annoyingly cheerful psychiatric nurse Adrian Knowles explained to me that Dr. Brothers thought it best I be admitted and not leave the hospital for a while-- two and half weeks to be exact. My heartbroken parents agreed. And so there I was, still alone, still depressed, and still missing Rose. Nothing had changed.

The days passed and I ate as little of the overcooked hospital food as possible--it was disgusting--I was disgusting. What kind of failure consumes forty-four *Rozerem* pills on an empty stomach and lives? *Me.*

Eventually, the insurance company cut me off and I was released back into the world of the living--even though I still felt dead. Unfortunately, not much had changed on the outside as my broken family still struggled with the loss of Rose and no amount of family counseling fixed us. That's when Dr. Brothers suggested the Reed family move--start over fresh.

Since arriving in West Virginia, my family has made progress. Before, we were a heartbroken crew unable to imagine life without Rose. Now, however, Mom's cooking again, Dad's beginning to enjoy his job as a real estate attorney, Caitlin and Ashley are adjusting to teen life, and I have a boyfriend. Life's better--except for the disturbing nightmares about Rose, and the fact that I'm attracted to a guy who isn't my boyfriend. Oh, and I'm a terrible, cheating girlfriend.

During my forty-five minutes of required study hall, I continued reflecting on the two men in my life--Maxwell

Snow and Julian Knight--trying to decide what each meant to me and why. I started with Max of course. When we first met in November, I fell for him instantly. Max's all American looks quickly captured my attention. His curly blonde locks, sparkling blue eyes, and sun-kissed skin give Max a sporty, healthy look--every girl's dream. Physically, Max is strong and muscular--a typical, strapping teenager. That's why I'm attracted to him.

What I love about Max, is that his gentle nature makes him an ideal boyfriend. He's never argumentative, always in control of his emotions, and of course, Max is cheerful and happy. What makes him an even greater catch is the fact that Max loves his mother. Katie's matriarchal presence has definitely influenced Max--in a good way. He's comfortable expressing his softer side. Max is also honest--which is why I feel so guilty for betraying him.

When we first began dating, Max was careful not to push me--taking his time before holding my hand or kissing me. He took me on thoughtful dates, like ice skating and picnicking under the stars. I will never forget the night at his property--the first time Max kissed me. The warmth I felt when he cupped my face inside his tender hands--staring deeply into my eyes. Max is romantic and he makes my skin tingle. I love him. And then there's Julian...

Julian unexpectedly entered my world on Christmas day--and it's been mixed up ever since. I can't explain his uncontrollable influence over me--it's as if we are supposed to know each other--but aren't able to fully understand our puzzling relationship. We fight, kiss, fight some more, and definitely do not understand one another--who is Julian and what does he want from me? We are connected but separate. It's weird and it doesn't make sense. But then again, Julian doesn't make sense. He's an anomaly.

What I know for sure about Julian, is that I know nothing about him. Why did he move here? Why do

Julian's emotions toward me run hot and cold? Why am I afraid of him? More specifically, why do I crave Julian's hypnotic presence and fiery touch--why do I dream about him? And why are those dreams nightmares. For all of these burning questions, I have absolutely no answers. And that terrifies me.

"Emily, get in the car. Come on, I need to stop by the library and return these books. They're overdue," Mom yelled from inside the parked van.

"I'm coming. Jeez, hold your horses," I shot back.

"Get in the van, witch--and make it snappy. I'm hungry, Mom! I want *Burger King*."

"Shut up, Caitlin. I can't stand you. And I swear, if you call me a witch one more time..."

"Stop shouting, girls. And no *Burger King,* Caitlin," Mom interrupted. "I've got stew simmering in the crock pot. Julian's coming over for dinner. Remember? Let's get home so I can make banana pudding. He'll love my pudding--I make the best pudding in the world..."

"Whatever, Mom," I moaned.

I am neither good, nor bad, neither angel nor devil, I am a man, I am a vampire.
                    Michael Romkey. I, Vampire.

Chapter 29

Father Vs. Son...

Julian's half-human, half-vampire heart pounded as he raced from the school parking lot towards his peaceful, rustic cabin. His retro *Thruxton* motorcycle hugged the slick West Virginia curves with amazing speed and accuracy. The freedom he normally exhibited when riding, however, was hampered by the nervous vibe he was currently experiencing. *Something's not right, he wondered to himself.* Julian couldn't shake the image of the brilliant purple stone from his memory and knew his father Sam would have answers--whether Julian was prepared for them or not. *Dad has a ring similar to the one Max gave Emily--the same "U" crest-- the same intricate carvings. What's going on? Where did Max get that ring?*

While cruising towards his wooden cottage, Julian couldn't shake the image of Emily from his mind. *So beautiful, I understand why Max loves her. But he can't have her, I won't let him...*When he finally arrived, confused and determined, Julian threw his sturdy helmet onto the snowy ground, stormed inside the small log cabin--and demanded his father Samuel cough up the truth--Julian would settle for nothing less than the truth-- *this time.*

"Dad, we need to talk! Now!" Julian ordered after slamming the hand-forged metal door shut.

"What? Where did you come from? You should be at school. You know how important it is...you can't drop out now. We're trying to fit in, Julian..."

"Not now, Dad," Julian snapped. I have some questions. And I want the truth! Do not lie to me!"

"What is it, Julian? Spit it out."

"Who is Katie Snow? And why does she claim Samuel Knight left her sixteen years ago?"

Samuel's pallid face reddened and his curled mouth dropped to the heart pine floor. "What are you talking about, Julian? I don't understand..."

"Of course you do. I can tell when you're lying. You don't blink your eyes. You've lied to me before, Dad...is Katie my mother? Answer me!"

"Um, I don't know what to say, Julian. We shouldn't be talking about this. I..."

Julian's long arms pumped tighter as he lunged towards Sam's alabaster neck--ready to rip into his exposed flesh. It wouldn't kill him of course--he'd recover--in ample time for Julian to shred the tissue again. Julian's dark eyes told the story, however, and Samuel knew not to keep lying. *Never lie to a vampire...*

"Yes. Katie is your mother--I left her when you and your *brother* were babies. I took you with me. You were different from *Max*--whom you've already met. Mr. Smith paid me a visit last night--he's your uncle--I know about the fight in school, Julian. Mr. Smith--I mean John--is a hybrid. So is your mother and so is Max," Samuel answered flatly.

"You told me my mother's name was Kate White."

"I couldn't tell you the truth son, or you would have looked for her."

"If Katie's a hybrid--why did you leave her?" Julian hissed--large, blue veins bulging from his neck and limbs. Julian's nails grew longer and his retractable teeth were sharp--Julian wanted to attack.

"Your mother, my brother, and Max are different from us Julian. They don't *feed.* They are *mortals.*"

"So! We could've stayed! We've lived as humans before. We're doing it now. We haven't fed in months. You said we would start over in Beckley--a new life. Live as humans. You said we'd steal blood from the hospitals--like you did when Katie was a nurse. We had a chance at a normal life before we ever left, Dad--and we blew it! Why did you separate me from--*my mother-*

-we should never have left! Look at Max! He's human--he's never even changed. Max didn't even challenge me. I mean, it's so obvious--his tanned skin, his clear eyes, he's never fed. *Never shadowed."*

"You and Max were different from each other, son. From the moment you were born, you tried to feed. You'd bite your mother, me, John, even Max. It was obvious what you were becoming...But Max...he, well, he seemed normal. He accepted Katie's breast milk, didn't bite, his eyes stayed clear. Max is like your mother and my brother--he's been able to embrace his human instincts. Max will live a long life and then die--just as he's supposed to. So will Katie and John. Even though Katie's pale and has dark eyes like you, she's never *killed* a human. She drank blood when she was a child, but was forced too. Her father thought it would make Katie stronger--but she's never *killed* a human; she's still mortal. Katie will die, son--that's why I left. Not like us Julian, we will live forever. Not in these bodies of course. But we'll come back. Hybrid's who *feed* always come back."

"So why did you bring me back here then?"

"I don't know son. It was a mistake--I see that now. I thought we could live close to them without interfering. I love Katie. I always have. But I see I made the wrong decision...I understand that now, Julian."

"My grandparents, Katie's parents...Where are they? *Who* are they?"

"Katie's father is *Ursulus*--you've heard of him of course. Every vampire knows who Ursulus is. He's been out of her life for awhile--she refuses to see him. Katie's mother was human--someone Ursulus cared about but never changed--one of many females I might add. But he loved Anna Brett--that was her name--too much to turn her into a vampire--she didn't want that anyway. She became pregnant with Katie and Ursulus stayed around for awhile--tried to be a father. But he is what he is--couldn't stop feeding. When Katie became a teenager she ran away. She always hated Ursulus, and the fact that he was a killer. She couldn't accept that Ursulus was a vampire or that her mother loved him. I met Katie a few years later. And then we fell in love--she gave birth to you and Max when she was just twenty years old. Ursulus never found out--if he had, he would've killed you and your brother. Ursulus is not to be defied."

"You told me my mother left us and you couldn't stand to stay in West Virginia. That the memories were too painful."

"I know, Julian. I couldn't bare telling you the truth. I'm the one who left--not Katie. She wanted you, son--but she was afraid. Katie was frightened that if you and I stayed in Beckley and *continued* to feed, Max wouldn't have a chance at a normal life."

"She ditched me so Max could have a life? Are you kidding me? It's all about Max, isn't it? My mother turned her back on me, forcing me to live on the run--as a killer--all because of Max!"

Julian was furious and the anger caused his mouth to snarl and his penetrable fangs to flare--Julian wanted blood--Max's blood. He wanted to destroy him.

"It's not Max's fault, Julian! He's not to blame--neither is Katie. I had to get you out of there, if we'd stayed, eventually the townspeople would have tried to kill us."

"Kill us? How's that possible? We're immortals," Julian scoffed.

"Oh, we can die, son. It's possible--although difficult--we are strong and fast. We're half human, remember? Our hearts beat, blood flows through our veins. We can die. The only problem is, we continue returning and returning. And every time we do, a newborn--sometimes even a fetus--inherits our psyches as we take over their bodies. Hybrids are a strange phenomenon--that's why there are so few of us. Vampires shun us because we outgrow our human bodies--a sign of weakness. We age--they do not. We are inferior in the eyes of true vampires. We are outcasts.

But that's why Katie and John never killed or *voluntarily* fed. They want to die--never to be reincarnated-- immortality is not appealing to them. I can't say that I blame them. When you and I die, Julian, and return again, we will still be hybrids--half-humans who crave blood--shunned by the vampire world--we don't fit it."

"I'm not coming back, Dad, I refuse. I will not come back over and over again just to be an outsider. I'll find a way to end it--I'll seek out Ursulus. There must be a way to undo this curse."

"If there is, son, I don't know of it. I wish I did--I'm not looking forward to returning either--forced to live without you, Katie, Max. I wish I'd never killed. I wish I could take it back."

"If you're so miserable, then why did you let me feed? Why did you *allow* me to become a killer?"

"I couldn't stop you, Julian. It happened so fast..."

"What are you talking about, Dad? What happened so fast?"

"It doesn't matter now, son. It doesn't matter..."

Julian couldn't take anymore. He needed to leave, and knew just where to go.

Take me from this earth...and endless night--this, the end of life...From the dark I feel your lips...and taste your bloody kiss.

Type O Negative.

Chapter 30

Son Vs. Mother...

"I'm out of here, Dad. I need to think--I need some fresh air," Julian droned--angry at his father for deceiving him all of these years.

"You can't leave, you're too upset. Let's talk--please," Samuel begged his fuming son.

"I'm done talking and I'm done with the lies."

"Son, I'm sorry. I know you're shocked and upset--I don't blame you for being mad at me and your mother. But I love you--Katie loves you--we did what we thought was right. If you had stayed in West Virginia--if we had stayed--things would only have gotten worse for our family. We had to leave son...there was no other choice."

"There's *always a choice,* Dad," Emily's words resonated inside Julian's muddled head. "Besides, I don't want to hear anymore of your excuses! We could've stayed--Mom should have insisted that we stay! She abandoned me--and for what? So Max could have a normal life? It's not fair! It's not fair!"

"I know, son, I know."

"No, Dad, I don't think you do."

Julian stormed out of the living room not even bothering to grab a helmet or protective riding jacket. Julian was too distraught to stick around--he needed to ride..."

Julian hopped onto his stalled motorcycle heading for town. *I need a phonebook he thought to himself. Emily*

*said Max and Katie own Snow's Christmas Tree Farm.
Where is it? Where are you--Mother?*

Weaving recklessly in and out of traffic, Julian sped
towards a familiar gas station--oblivious to the freezing
temperatures outside. *I'll find you guys--both of you.
And when I do...*

It didn't take long for Julian to come across the tall
hill full of oak trees and evergreens lightly dusted with
snow. When approaching the giant tree farm, Julian's
adrenaline peaked--the gravel road was no match for his
slippery bike. Julian zipped through the sharp curves,
dodging loose rocks and busy squirrels. As soon as he
caught sight of the large, hand-painted sign in front of
him, Julian recognized the distinctive brush strokes
immediately. *Dad painted that sign. I'd know his work
anywhere.* On his way towards the petite but welcoming
house, Julian's anger intensified--he hated his mother
and brother for turning their backs on him when he was
barely a toddler. But mostly he hated Max..."*I'll kill
him,*" Julian threatened underneath his clenched
breath...."*and her too.*"

As soon as he reached the front entrance, Julian
parked his motorcycle underneath a large blue spruce. It
wasn't long before he stood pounding on the door--fists
bloodied from the amount of force being exuded.

Max was somewhere out on the sprawling property
chopping wood leaving Katie to fend for herself. Her
heart stopped when she heard the pounding. *It's him.
It's Julian. He's come back for me.* She gathered the
nerve to answer his cries--and nearly fainted when she
saw her son for the first time in fifteen years.

"Julian?"

"It's me, Mother. Let me in," Julian ordered--his dark
eyes never parting with hers.

"Okay, son. Okay."

Katie opened the door and her irate son dodged past
her. "Where is *he,* Mother? Where's Max?"

"He's not here, Julian. Son, please, leave him out of this. Max means you no harm. I'm the one who abandoned you. Please, Julian, it's me you should punish, not him," Katie begged.

"Why? Why did you let Dad take me away? How could you turn your back on me? I was a baby! I needed you!"

"I know, Julian, I know. It's my fault. I was scared--I didn't know how to protect you..." Katie winced.

"Protect me? I was a baby...I needed you! I needed you Mother!"

"Yes, you did. And I let you down, son. Oh, Julian, please, I'm so sorry. Please, come here..."

Katie reached for her lost son only to have Julian rebuff her. "Oh please, Julian, let me hold you. I've missed you!"

"Hold me? Are you serious? You think after all of these years I want you to hold me? I don't think so, Mother. You have Max for that. I'm the *killer*--remember--I'm not worthy of your love. Isn't that right?"

"Oh, Julian, please stop. I know you hate me. But your father and I agreed--you couldn't stay--you couldn't. Not after..."

"Not after what?"

"You really don't know do you, Julian. Your father never told you. I'm not surprised. Perhaps I shouldn't either..."

"Tell me what? Come on--be honest with me. You owe me that much. Tell me why you turned your back on me. Tell me now!"

"Julian, you were just a baby--barely a year old. It wasn't your fault. *It wasn't your fault...*"

"Spit it out Mother! What wasn't my fault?"

"Your grandmother, Julian--you killed her. You killed *my* mother."

"What? What are you talking about? I don't under..."

"My mother--Anna Brett--she left my father when you and Max started walking. She loved you both so much. She chose you and Max over *him*. My mother trusted you--both of you. And then one day, your father and I were working outside--we thought she'd be okay. And then the screaming, we ran inside the house as fast as we could...but it was too late...it was too late!"

"What happened? Come on, Mother, what happened?"

"By the time your father and I were able to get into the house, my mother lay on the floor in pieces--blood soaking the ground, worn furniture, and you. Her limbs discarded, my mother's chest was ripped open and her heart lay on the Persian rug covering the wooden floor. She was dead."

"What? I killed her? How could that be? I was a baby...it's not possible."

"I know, son. Your father and I knew you were strong, but we didn't think...we never imagined...The coroner was suspicious. It was difficult convincing him that a stranger had wondered into our home killing her. The town grew insensitive--the crime didn't make sense. Your father and I feared for our safety--so he left, taking you with him. We didn't want anything like that to happen again. Oh Julian, we were so scared! We only wanted to protect you! I'm sorry, son, I'm so very sorry!"

"I killed her?" Julian couldn't believe the words he was hearing.

"Yes. And then, well, it was too late--we couldn't stop the *change*. There was nothing we could do to save you--you'd tasted human blood and *killed* for it. It was too late, Julian."

"And Max? Where was he?"

"In his crib--sleeping. Max was different, Julian. Max was indifferent to the smell of blood--to the texture. He was physically strong like you, but different. It's not your fault. Hybrids are difficult to predict. Oh, Julian, I don't know what to say. I should never have left you unattended. It's my fault. I should have known better. I should have known..."

Julian didn't know what to think. *Had he really done that? Killed his own grandmother? Was it possible?*

Max finished chopping down a dead tree, loading the pile of oak wood into his old truck. Whistling, he was thinking about Dallas and glad he would be visiting her on Sunday--his mother assured him it was alright to do so. When the truck was finally full, Max headed towards the warmth of his cottage--eager for lunch. Max was hungry.

"What the...? Is that Julian's motorcycle? What's he doing here?"

Max entered through the back door curious as to why Julian's motorcycle was parked on the side of the house under a spruce. "Mom, Mom, it's me. I'm back," he yelled. For a few seconds, the house was eerily silent. And then he heard the hesitation in her panicked but firm voice.

"Um, Max. In here, son. I'm in here," Katie responded.

"Mom, what's up? What's going on..." Max entered the living area stunned at the sight of Julian standing so closely to *his* mother.

"What are you doing here, Julian?"

"Well, if it isn't my privileged, twin *brother...*"

And at that moment, as if by miracle, the sick no longer died, and the stifling shadow of the vampire vanished in the morning sun.

Nosferatu, The Vampire, 1922.

Chapter 31

Brother Vs. Brother..
.

"Are you okay Mom? Is *he* bothering you?" Max glared at Julian and the concern in his unadulterated voice was genuine.

"Um, I'm okay. Come here, Max," Katie calmly directed--hoping to avoid inciting a violent confrontation between the thwarted brothers. "I need you to say hello to your *brother*--Julian is your *twin,* Max." Katie still couldn't believe Julian was standing so closely beside her--ready to lunge at any moment.

"What are you talking about? My brother? I don't understand," Max balked. "What's going on here?"

Max edged closer to Katie and his body suddenly stiffened. His biceps bulged and Max's grip tightened. His heart pumped erratically inside his heavy chest and his fists clenched. Max was defensive--his posture threatening--it was all so new to him.

"Mom, I don't understand. What the heck is going on? What are you talking about?" Max's voice was shaky-- but firm. His tone was disconcerting.

"We're brothers, Max," Julian scoffed. "Oh, sorry, didn't *she* bother telling you that all of these years? I mean, it's kind of an important detail to leave out don't you think--*brother*?" Julian smirked.

"Mom, is it true?" Max looked pensively at his heartbroken mother Katie. She hated seeing him this way--she hated feeling this way.

"Yes, Max. It's true," she managed--still trying to remain stoic--while quietly falling apart. Her voice wavered, "You and Julian are twins--he and your father

Samuel have returned. I've known for a few days now. I'm so sorry, I should have told you. I am so very sorry, son," Katie mouthed--tears running down her sullen face.

"Awe, how touching. *Katie* actually cares that you're upset. Aren't *you* lucky? Mommy loves *you*. She's always loved *you*. Too bad she turned her back on me!" Julian shrieked.

"Julian, please. I told you, I didn't want to lose you. But...Oh please, Julian, please," Katie begged with hurt, pleading eyes. "There was no other choice..."

"What's wrong, Mom?" Julian gawked—totally unsympathetic towards his mother's suffering. "Don't want me to tell Max our little family secret? Afraid he won't be able to take it? You're so weak, Max! So freaking weak!" Julian screamed.

"Shut up, Julian. Why don't you just leave! You're upsetting *my* mother..."

"You mean *our* mother...Katie gave birth to me, too! Oops, I guess you didn't know that. Not until today of course."

Max looked towards Katie entreating for answers. *This isn't true. He's lying. Julian must be lying!* Unfortunately, Katie didn't have any--or at least none that he cared to hear.

"Come on, Mom," Julian howled. "Tell him the truth--tell him everything! He needs to hurt just as much as I do right now! Stop protecting him! For once in your dishonest life, stop protecting Max!"

"Tell me what? What's he talking about?"

"We're brothers Max, and we're *hybrids,*" Julian snapped--a depraved curl forming around his wicked lips. He enjoyed stabbing Max with his hurtful truths.

"*Hybrids*?" Max had never heard the term before.

"Vampires, Max. We're vampires--only you aren't a killer--just me. I'm the killer son," Julian mocked, while looking anxiously at Katie. He wanted a reaction.

"Don't say that, Julian--you *couldn't* help it. You *can't* help it. It's not your fault. I should never have allowed Sam to leave with you...I'm sorry for that,"

Katie wept. "I should have protected you." Max put his arms around her despite being confused by Katie's unexpected admission.   However, he still couldn't believe what he was hearing--*hybrids? How can that be? We aren't vampires--they don't exist. Vampires are not real.*

"I know what you're thinking Max. And I'm sorry I never told you. But Julian's right. We're hybrids--half-human, half-vampire. My father--your grandfather, is Ursulus. He is a vampire--he is *the* vampire."

"Ursulus? You never told me my grandfather's name was Ursulus. You told me your parents were dead Mom--Anna Brett and *Uric* Snow. You told me they died when you were young--in a car accident. And you were raised in an orphanage. Was that a lie?"

"Yes, Max," Katie replied--sad about having been untruthful with her son.

"And my Dad, Samuel--he's *here*? How long have you known?"

"A couple of days now. Mr. Smith told me...he's your uncle Max. John and Samuel are *brothers*."

"Mr. Smith? My uncle? Is he a hybrid too?"

"Yes. But he's like *us*. He doesn't feed. John lives as a human..."

"And his wife Sadie?"

"Sadie is human. But they refrained from having children--didn't want to risk..."

"Risk what, Mother? Giving birth to little killers? Like me?" Julian squawked.

"What about my other grandparents--Dad's parents. Are they really dead?"

"Yes *and* no. Your father's mother Clara was a pure blood vampire--she fell for your grandfather--Graham Knight. She got pregnant, gave birth to John and Samuel--and then took off. She couldn't handle the responsibility of raising children. Samuel's father couldn't take the pain of losing her so he killed himself by drowning. John and Samuel were raised by their human aunt--Madeline. She rejected them, however.

She hated what they were. Both ran away when they were teens. John was able to live as a human--he's like you, Max. He doesn't crave blood. He's passive and in control of his emotions. John's temperament is like yours," Katie explained--oblivious to Julian's glare.

"So your father--Ursulus--is alive. What about my grandmother--Anna Brett?" The room was suddenly quiet.

"Tell him, Mother. Tell Max the truth!" Julian barked.

"No! Son, it's enough already! Enough!" Katie screamed.

"Where is Anna Brett?"

"I killed her, Max. She's been dead for years," Julian answered.

"What?"

"Everything you've ever been told is a lie, Max. Face it--our mother is a liar," Julian snapped. And so did Max.

Max was on top of Julian's twisted body in a matter of seconds--his powerful hands wrapped around Julian's pale, bulging throat. Max had never experienced hate or rage like this before. He wanted to kill his *brother*.

"Max, please, get off him!" Katie shrieked. "Max, you'll kill him!"

Julian shifted his feet, managing to stand despite Max's crushing weight. After prying Max's grip from his neck, Julian pushed his irate brother against the plaster wall destroying an antique hutch housing an array of beautiful china. The plates and cups smashed to the floor, and shards of glass penetrated Max's fleshy skin. Julian lunged for his brother--he wanted Max to bleed. *He needed Max to bleed.*

Katie grabbed Max, steadying him to his feet. Dazed, the larger of the two brothers had never fought another *being* before. But there was a first time for everything. Max charged Julian whose teeth were retracting and lips were sneering. Julian's nails grew sharper and his eyes glowed--tiny red specks inside his flaming pupils. Julian resembled an animal--eager to kill. Max had never seen a vampire changing. And then it happened. Max's eyes grew sharper, and the pain inside his mouth intensified. *What the...?* He could feel his fangs protruding. Max's mouth enlarged, and his tongue swelled while his nails lengthened. Katie looked on in horror.

"No Max, no! Don't do this! Stop before it's too late!" she cried.

"What's happening Mom? I don't understand..."

Before he could finish, Julian was pouncing towards him with snarled teeth and a scaly tongue. Julian ripped into his exposed flesh--shredding the delicate skin around Max's thick, muscular neck.

"Get off of him, Julian! Now!" Katie roared.

The pain was excruciating as the blood poured from Max's ripped flesh. His long-sleeved shirt was covered in the rich, red liquid as was Julian's face. For the first time since moving to West Virginia and meeting his mother and brother, Julian felt avenged.

The pain was brief, however, as the wound began to close. Blood dried up and Max's neck healed. It would take much more than that to bring him down. Julian was furious.

"Oh God. Please, stop them! Stop them!" Katie pleaded.

Max grabbed a poker from the hot fireplace targeting Julian's face. He flinched, however, avoiding the sharp object. As he did, Julian fell to the floor, losing his balance. Max aimed the poker towards him again--nearly piercing Julian's heart. And that's when Samuel barged through the front door.

"Max! No! Stop it, son! You'll kill him!" Samuel screamed.

Max flinched as soon as he heard his name. "Dad? Is that you?"

It was like looking into a mirror--almost.

To survive, we must take from the living. They fear us greatly, but we cannot change our ways. We cannot live without the living. Each passing generation, a little more of us is worn away, our bloodline growing thinner and weaker. Soon, we will be nothing but mere shells, husks of our former selves. Growing ever more vulnerable, we wane into the night. We are the scourge of the earth, the undead amongst the living, the cursed among the blessed.

Konya651.

Chapter 32

Samuel...

"Samuel? Is that you?" Katie couldn't believe her damp, swollen eyes. *Max looks so much like him.*

"Katie, what's going on here?" he demanded.

"You have to stop them, Samuel, before they kill each other! Max knows everything--everything!"

Julian looked towards his parents in disgust while his bewildered brother Max was stunned. The on-edge room was calm for a few seconds. And then the hostility commenced--so did the fighting.

"I'll kill him, Father--I'll rip him to shreds! Everything's his fault! Max is to blame for everything!" Julian shouted over the cries of his hysterical mother.

"Julian, son, you don't know what you're talking about! It's not Max's fault. Your mother and I are to blame for this mess. We should have told you both...so much earlier. Please, stop this. You don't need revenge! Let's talk about this--all of us--together. Before someone gets hurt!"

"It's too late for that, Dad," Julian leered. "I'm going to kill him."

"Dear God, Julian. We failed you--*both* of you. But please, stop this. We can move on from here--I'm sure of it son. Just give our family a chance--we can make things right again," Samuel pleaded.

"*Again*? Things were never right, Dad. I killed my grandmother. I'm a murderer! And Max, well, he's an innocent--isn't he? It's not fair, Dad! Why did I have to be born a killer!"

"It isn't your fault, son. You didn't ask for this. Your mother and I should have protected you. We should never have left you alone with Anna Brett..." It had been years since Samuel had uttered her name. Even today, he felt guilty. "It should never have happened, son, but it's not your fault. Your mother and I were young--we thought it would be okay to step outside for a few moments. We failed you, Julian. I am so sorry, son. And Max, I'm sorry to you too. I should never have left. You needed a father. Please forgive me."

Max looked on as his father pleaded. He was puzzled. Katie's caring glance eased the tension in Max's stiff, defensive posture.

"Your father loves you, Max. He always has. He left to protect you--*and* Julian. It was better that way. *Really.*"

Julian hated the way his mother was still trying to protect Max. In anger, he lunged towards his privileged brother again--knocking Max into the heavy TV stand. Max and the TV crashed onto the floor and Julian was pleased--Samuel was not.

"Julian--it's enough already. I can't stand this! I love you, son--but it's enough! Get off your brother--he's done nothing to you--nothing!" Samuel edged.

Julian backed away, but not without cutting into Max one more time. Julian sliced into Max's altered face-- slashing his fleshy cheek--blood ran down Max's blue shirt. It was covered--he was covered.

"Julian, no more I said! No more!" Samuel lunged towards his attacking son pinning Julian's long arms around his slender waist while Katie comforted Max. "It's okay son. You will heal--the wound will close in a matter of minutes. It's okay, Max," she wept.

"Get off me, Dad! I'm done. Get off!"

"Are you, son? Have you gotten your revenge?" Samuel retorted.

"Yes. Now let me go. I'm leaving," Julian huffed.

"What?"

"I'm leaving--let me go, Dad. I'm done, *it's* enough."

"Where are you going, Julian? We need to talk," Katie implored her distant son.

"There's nothing more to say. I need to be alone--I need some space. Please, grant me this, *Mother*. I need to be alone for awhile."

"It's okay, Katie--let him go. He'll be okay *now*. Give him his space," Samuel insisted.

Katie nodded her distressed head yes.

"Where will you go, son?" Samuel inquired.

"To the mountains. I need to think," Julian huffed.

"Okay," his father agreed.

Katie didn't argue--nor did Max.

Julian mounted his rugged bike eager to see Emily. *She needs to know everything about Max and me. Everything. No--More—Lies!*

*Psychos do not explode when sunlight hits them,
no matter how crazy they are.*
                              Seth From Dusk till Dawn.

Chapter 33

Don't Leave...

The ride towards Emily's bungalow was invigorating. Even though Julian was still angry at his divided parents and alien brother Max, the thought of being around her cheered him up considerably. Emily's sweet smile and feminine smell were always enough to perk Julian up. *She's beautiful,* he thought to himself while riding. *I can't wait to see her.*

At age sixteen, Julian had already experienced more than anyone his age ever should. He'd killed the only grandmother who loved and accepted him, had been abandoned by his hybrid mother Katie so his twin could live a normal life, and feasted--*often*--on human blood. Julian had killed--so that he might live and live again-- an idea that didn't please him. And all in the name of vampirism.

When his father and Julian settled into Chicago (Julian was almost two years old), life had been fairly normal--for a vampire that is. He attended school, made perfect grades, and lived in a cozy brick house on the outskirts of town. The only difference between his life and those of his human classmates, was that Julian and his father Sam drank blood in order to survive. And while they did not over feed, in order to remain strong, the two hybrids roamed the dark alleys of Chicago feasting primarily off passed out drunks and petty criminals--shady persons no one would miss. For the most part, Julian and Samuel were scavengers.

As a child and a teenager, Julian was a loner. Generally, he kept to himself--afraid humans would discover that he and his father were hybrids. While the world around him seemed to believe in the existence of vampires--blood drinkers remained elusive in order to survive as self-preservation is key if you are born of the underworld--born of Ursulus.

"What are you doing here?"

"Um, I was wondering if we could talk, Emily. Would you ride with me?" Julian sheepishly asked as soon as she answered the front door.

"Well, you're a little early. You aren't supposed to be here until six. It's four-thirty now. Hey, you never came back to school today. Is everything okay?"

"Well, that's kind of what I wanted to talk to you about. Emily, can we head out somewhere on my bike?"

"Yeah, sure. Let me tell Mom first. Come inside for a minute."

"Mom!" I yelled. "I'm leaving with Julian. We'll be back in time for dinner! Okay?"

Mom entered the living area with a potato peeler in hand. "Hey, Julian! So good to see you!" she sang.

"Mrs. R, it's good to see you too," Julian beamed. He reached over gently hugging her.

"Um, Mrs. Reed, would you mind if Emily and I rode for awhile before dinner?"

"Of course not! You two have fun. Be back around six, okay?"

"No problem. I promise we won't be late," Julian smiled.

"Well, okay then, Mom. I guess were heading out. See ya in a few."

"Ya'll have fun," Mom winked.

"Yeah, witch, have fun!" Caitlin mocked.

"You stupid brat, mind your own business. And stay off of my cell phone when I'm out! I mean it!"

"Shut up, Emily! Wouldn't you rather ride on your broomstick instead?"

"Caitlin, behave! Go into the kitchen and peel potatoes. Now!" Mom ordered.

"Whatever. She's a witch, Mom--I can feel it," Caitlin sneered.

Caitlin followed Mom inside the kitchen and I was glad to see her leave. *Such a pain the butt she is. I wish I really was a witch...*

"So, where to, Julian?"

"I know a beautiful spot--near my Dad's property. I'd like to take you there. Is that okay?"

"Sure, as long as we make it home in time for dinner. Mom will kill us if we're late. She's been cooking all day. I think she's trying to impress you."

"I promise we won't be late. Put your helmet on. Need some earplugs? The engine's loud--I've got some extras."

"Sure, Julian. Hurry up though. I'm ready to ride!" I squealed.

"Alright, alright. Just give me a second. Hold your horses!"

"Hop on, let's go," he beamed.

On the way towards the cave, all Julian could think about was Emily. Inside his head he wondered, *what will I tell her? Can she handle the truth? Will she turn her back on me...on Max? Am I doing the right thing?* So much to think about. Julian was confused and scared--for the first time in his life. Only Emily brought out these sides of him. Julian could live without a mother--he'd done so for fifteen years. But could he live without Emily--the only girl he'd ever truly cared for? Since meeting her, Julian had changed--he could feel it inside his gut. Emily made Julian want to do the right thing--no matter how difficult that was for him.

The icy wind against my exposed face was nothing compared to the chilly feeling I experienced whenever I thought about betraying Max. *Why am I doing this-- again? Why can't I stay away from Julian?* All I could do was hold on tighter and tighter to his waist. *He needs me. Julian needs me--I don't know why--but he does.*

When we finally arrived at the cave Julian loved exploring when he wasn't in school, somehow it seemed that today was a significant day.

"We're here, Emily--give me your helmet. I'll stash everything underneath this tree. Our stuff will be safe. I don't think anyone's ever been out this far. I've never seen any evidence of hikers near this cave. It's not even on the map."

"It's awesome Julian! How'd you ever find this place? It's definitely hidden from the main road. All of these trees are spectacular! They're so tall!" I embarrassingly gushed--excited about exploring the interior.

"I know. I love it out here. It's peaceful. And the inside is warmer than you'd think. Someone could actually live in this thing. Come on. Let's check it out." Julian was excited. He grabbed my hand while clutching a flashlight in the other. His fingers were firm and his palms were warm. Julian seemed to like holding my hand. And I liked it, too.

"Are you sure it's safe?"

"Yep. I've been here a million times. I've even slept inside before. The temperature's very comfortable. And there's fresh water close by. I swear, it's the perfect place to live--if you like being alone that is."

"I don't know if I could handle being this far away from the rest of the world. But it is serene out here--I can see why you love it so much."

Julian led the way inside the large cave following the bright light of the only flashlight available. Even in such a short amount of time spent exploring, he knew every inch of the rocky cavern.

"Watch your step, Emily," Julian instructed as he walked us deeper inside the fissure. "It's a little slippery sometimes."

I took his word for it.

"How far into it are we going, Julian? It's pretty dark."

"Not too much farther--we're almost *there*. I promise."

"Where, Julian?"

"You'll see," he teased.

We walked a few more feet and then Julian got excited. "Here, Emily, right here! This is my favorite spot."

Julian reached inside his pocket fumbling for matches. When he found the box, he struck a match lighting a large, white candle. And then another--and another.

"Julian! Wow! It's lovely--the crystals on the cave's ceiling are beautiful! Hey, where did the candles come from?"

"I brought them in so I could have light--I like to study in this spot. I get a lot of reading done. Hold on just a minute--I've got some oil lamps too. Give me a second."

Julian let go of my hand in order to find the lamps. Then he carefully lit all three. The cave was suddenly luminous. I couldn't believe how beautiful everything was--the staggered crystals and smooth rocks. Julian had done a wonderful job making the atmosphere cozy. In fact, the ambience was romantic.

"Here, Emily, sit down. I brought these pillows in a few weeks ago. And some blankets. I sleep out here sometimes. It's my little oasis."

"It's incredible, Julian! This place is spectacular. Aren't you scared out here though all by yourself? What about wild animals?"

"This cave is safe," Julian laughed. "I've never seen anything wild inside here before. Besides, there are no animal droppings. Haven't you noticed?" he joked.

"Oh, well, I guess I haven't. I'm sure it's safe then. Besides, I don't think you're scared of anything, Julian."

"That's not true, Emily. I'm scared right now."

"What are you talking about?"

"Um, Emily, I brought you out here so we could talk. I, um, well..."

"What is it, Julian?" I was very curious as to why Julian seemed so nervous. He was practically stuttering. I've never seen him quite like this before.

Julian had no idea where to begin. This was going to be even more difficult than he'd imagined. But it had to be done. Emily needed to know the truth about Julian--Max--and *their* hybrid family. It was the only way she'd ever be able to judge the brothers on an equal playing field. Julian could never be as good as Max--but perhaps she could see them in the same light and try to understood why each brother was the way he was. Julian was convinced Emily would see him differently if she understood his past...

"Emily," Julian cleared his throat, "remember when I told you I was a bad guy? That I'd done things that perhaps were not entirely under my control."

"Yes. I told you that people are responsible for their actions--and they can choose whether to be good or bad. But I don't think you're bad, Julian, I just think you make bad choices sometimes..."

"Emily, I need to tell you something. You'll find it difficult to believe at first. But it's true. Everything I tell you today is true. I would never lie to you." Julian looked at me with honest eyes.

"Okay. You're scaring me, though. Is everything okay?" I began to feel uneasy.

Julian covered me with a fleece blanket he'd hidden behind a rock. He evidently wanted me to be comfortable. Apparently, we might be in the cave for awhile.

"Um, you know today when I left school early?"

"Yeah," I responded--grateful for the cover.

"Well, I went home. To talk to my dad," Julian muttered--suddenly too scared to finish. He looked towards me for encouragement.

"Go on, Julian. Don't stop now," I urged.

"Well, after you showed me the ring Max gave you--I recognized the pattern and the initial on top of the purple stone. My father has a ring similar to that one."

"Really? Hey, that's weird. It's an unusual ring--an heirloom I think. It's been in Max's family for awhile. His father left it behind when he took off. Samuel wanted Max to have it. At least that's what Katie thinks."

"Emily, my father's name is Samuel Knight--just like Max's father. And my mother's name is Katie--*Katie Snow.*"

"Huh?" I was flabbergasted. *How could that be?*

"It's true. Max and I are brothers. We're a family. Katie is my mother."

"What are you talking about, Julian? I don't understand..."

"I know. I don't, either. But it's true--I wouldn't lie to you. I was born here, Emily--in Beckley. My parents used to live out at the cabin together. After Max and I were born, they moved into the house on the tree farm. Katie was a nurse then and my father was an artist. He painted the sign on their property. Like I said, we used to be a family."

"What are you talking about?" My voice was edged in disbelief. "Max never told me that. I don't believe you." Now I grew increasingly uncomfortable.

"Max didn't know he had a brother. My parents split when we were young--very young. My father took off with me while Katie and Max stayed at the farm. It's complicated."

"I don't know what to say, Julian. I mean, Katie's never mentioned you. She said Sam ran off when Max was young. She never said why--and I didn't ask. What's going on? What happened today?"

"Emily, when I was about a year old, my parents-- well--they decided it would be better if Max and I were raised separately. I know it doesn't make sense. I'm confused as well. But my mother decided that she and

Max should be together and my father should take me away--I know it's difficult to understand. I'm sorry..."

"None of this makes sense, Julian. Katie's a great lady. Why would she send you away? She loved Samuel--it just doesn't make sense. You're not making sense. We should leave Julian. Take me home, seriously, I want to leave now."

"Emily. Please sit down. I need to tell you everything--it's the only way..."

"The only way? I don't understand, Julian! What are you saying?" I shrieked.

"Emily, Max and I are *different*."

"I know you are! Max is sweet and kind. He'd never hurt me Julian! He doesn't lie! I don't know what you are trying to do right now. But you and Max are not brothers. Katie would never have sent you away. Never!"

"Emily. Please, I know you're upset. I just think you deserve to know the truth--the truth about my mother and my brother. And me!"

"I know the truth, Julian. Max and Katie are wonderful people. They would have told me about you. And Katie never would have turned her back on her son! Never!" I was furious as I lashed out at Julian.

"I know it's difficult to accept. But it's true. Fifteen years ago, my mother *and* father agreed to separate our family--all because of *Max*." Julian's voice hardened and his tone grew harsh. Whenever Julian spoke about Max he grew cross.

"What are you talking about, Julian? I swear, you aren't making any sense to me. None of this makes any sense!" I screamed.

I was livid. *What is he trying to do? Turn me against my boyfriend? I knew I never should have come here today. Never!*

"Emily. It's complicated," Julian pleaded. "But there's more. What I'm about to tell you is difficult but true. Please hear me out. Okay?"

"Okay, Julian. Just hurry up. I'm ready to go home. I don't want to be here with you anymore. I want to leave,'" I snapped.

Julian took a deep breath before starting. "Okay, here goes. My father and Katie met when she was twenty years old. They bought the house on the tree farm-- Katie was a nurse then. When Max and I were a year old, they split. Katie and Dad agreed it would be better to take me far away from Max so he could live a normal life. That's when my dad and I took off. Eventually, we ended up in Chicago. Max never knew about me and I never knew about him. My parents wanted it that way. They said it was best..."

"Best? For whom? I don't get it, Julian..."

"This part will be hard for you to believe. I don't even know how to say it. But I need to be honest with you, Emily--Max and my mother certainly haven't been," Julian scoffed.

"Spit it out Julian! Come on!" I was in his face, yelling.

"Emily, my parents are *hybrids*--and so are me *and* Max."

"Hybrids...What the heck are you talking about Julian? What is a hybrid?" I scoffed.

"My family, we are...half-human and half-vampire. *Hybrids*, Emily."

"Ha! Is this some sort of a sick joke? It's not funny, you know. Not funny at all!"

"It's no joke, Emily. Believe me, I wish it was. We are vampires--all four of us."

"I don't believe you!"

"I'm sorry. I really am. I wish it wasn't true--I wish I were human--like you. But I'm not. I'm so sorry, Emily."

Julian reached out to me, but I backed away. "Don't touch me! You're a liar, Julian! You're right about one thing though--you are the bad guy. You will always be the bad guy!"

"Emily. Please, I won't hurt you. I would never hurt you. I just need for you to understand me. That's all. You don't have to worry. I would never hurt you or your family," Julian pleaded.

"How can you tell such lies? How?"

"If you don't believe me--perhaps I should show you. Come outside with me. I want to show you--*I need to show you.*"

"Show me what, Julian? That you can fly around like a bat or something? It's that why you like this cave so much? Cuz you're a vampire! Where's the coffin, Julian?" I smirked.

"Please, it's not like that. The myths--most of them are a joke. We don't turn into bats--and we can live just fine in the sun. I'm as much human as anything else. My heart beats and blood flows through my veins. *I can die.*"

"So what you're trying to tell me is that you are a vampire and you live a perfectly average life. You're normal Julian--for a hybrid that is. Am I supposed to believe that?"

"I know it sounds weird. But if you'll come outside, I can show you things--I can make you understand what I am--what Max is..."

"And why has Max failed to mention the fact that he's a vampire to me?" I stammered.

"Because he only found out today--that's why."

"So Max has been a vampire--or hybrid--or whatever ya'll are for sixteen years and only found out about it today. Ha! That makes absolutely no sense Julian! None what- so-ever!"

"I understand your skepticism. Max has been raised to live as a human. He's never *fed--never changed.*"

"OMG, Julian! Just listen to yourself! You're insane! Take me home...right now!" I demanded.

"I'll take you home, Emily, I promise. But I have to show you first--show you what I am. *Who* I am. You need to know."

"You're crazy! Stay away from me, Julian! I'll find another way home. Just stay away from me!"

"Emily, please. Calm down. Just for a few minutes. Please," Julian begged.

"No! I will not calm down! You just told me my boyfriend and his mother are vampires! I will not calm down! I'm leaving. Give me the flashlight--I'm out of here!"

Julian's nails lengthened and he grabbed my face despite my objections. "Just watch, Emily. Please, look at my wrist."

Julian dug deeply into his flesh and the fresh blood poured down his pale arm.

"Oh my God! Stop it, Julian! Stop right now! You'll hurt yourself!" I pleaded. I was becoming hysterical and about to faint.

"Watch, Emily. I'm okay. Watch closely. Please!"

I stared at the oozing wound as it unexpectedly began to heal. My eyes were deceiving me, how else could I explain the gash mending before my eyes. After the skin reconnected--no deep cut or even a scar, Julian ran his fingers across his smooth skin in order to convince me. His wrist was as good as new.

How could that be? It's not possible! "I don't understand, Julian..." I stuttered. "Is this some sort of trick?" I couldn't believe my eyes.

"It's not a trick, Emily. I told you, I'm a vampire. I heal quickly.

I quickly backed away, fear spreading through my trembling body.

"Emily, please. I would never hurt you. You have to believe me. Please!"

"Stay away from me Julian. I don't know what you are trying to accomplish here, but I want no part of this. Take me home. Right now! I mean it!"

"Do you believe me, Emily?"

"I don't know what I believe. Max has never fooled me like this. I don't know what you want. But I'm not buying it..."

Just then Julian disappeared. I gaped in surprise. "What the...Where are you Julian? Where did you go? Please, you're scaring me!"

"I'm right here, Emily. Behind you. Turn around."

I spun around only to find Julian standing directly behind me. Just like that, in a puff of smoke--so to speak--Julian had vanished. Reappearing in seconds.

"I, I, I think..." I was about to pass out.

"Emily! Please..." Julian caught me just before I hit the ground. I moaned while floating inside his arms.

"Julian..."

"I've got you. Emily. It's okay. I'm so sorry..." Julian stroked my face trying to reassure me. I was limp as a dishrag in his tight, caring grasp.

"Julian, I don't understand," I groaned. "Please, tell me what's going on? I'm really scared."

Julian held on securely to my trembling body. He showed that he felt terrible for scaring me. "I never wanted this to happen. I had hoped you would understand--that you wouldn't be afraid of me--that you would believe me. I guess that I was wrong--very wrong. Emily," he cried, "I'm sorry. I never meant for this to happen. I just wanted you to understand--why I'm the way I am sometimes. Oh God, please forgive me," he whimpered.

I was struck by his earnest emotions. I had certainly never seen Julian cry before. I turned towards him, tenderly wiping tears from his cheek. "It's okay, Julian. I'm sorry I didn't believe you. I just...well...I've never...I don't know what to say. I'm confused."

"I know you are. And I'm sorry. It's all true though. I'm a vampire--I mean my family--we're hybrids. But I would never hurt you--you must believe me."

"I do, Julian. I don't know why, but I believe you. It's just scary--I mean, I've never known a vampire before. You have to understand how new this is to me. But I definitely believe you now. What did you just do?"

"It's called shadowing. Vampires and hybrids have the ability to shadow--or disappear whenever they want or need to. Only some hybrids can shadow, however..."

"What do you mean? Can Max and Katie shadow?"

Julian didn't seem to want to answer that burning question. He did anyway.

"Well, um, no. Max and Katie are different, Emily. They can't shadow."

"Why?"

"Um, it's confusing. I, uh..."

"Tell me Julian. I don't care if it's confusing. I want to know everything now. *Everything.*"

There was no turning back. Julian had to elaborate. He owed me that much. "Hybrids and vampires who shadow--well--it's an ability they gain, after they've *fed*." Julian looked apprehensively at me.

If I hadn't been scared before, I certainly was now. "*After they've fed?* What do you mean?"

Julian suddenly looked like he wanted to take it all back. But he couldn't, of course. He was in too deep. "Um, vampires have to feed--they've no other choice. And they can shadow almost immediately after being turned. Some hybrids, however, like Max and my mother never feed--they are able to live entirely as humans. They exhibit some of the qualities of vampires and hybrids--but they can't shadow. Only hybrids that drink blood can disappear."

"So Max doesn't drink blood?"

"No. He and Katie don't feed."

"But you and your father--ya'll feed?"

Julian cleared his throat. "Well, yes and no. We have fed--but since moving back to West Virginia, we've decided to live more as humans. It's complicated, Emily. I don't want to scare you any more than I have. We've fed--and we can shadow--but we are living as humans now. I promise, I will not hurt you. You and your family are safe, Emily," Julian pleaded.

"But you've fed, Julian. What does that mean? Please, don't hold back now. What does that mean?"

"It means I can't take it back, Emily. I've tasted human blood--it means a lot of things. I'm sorry. Like I said, I'm different from Max. But my instincts--my vampire instincts took over at an early age. Max's human instincts were--*are* stronger than mine. We were raised differently--if I could change things--I would."

"It's okay, Julian. I'm not afraid. I'm just trying to understand. So how are you different from a vampire?"

"Vampires are *created* by other vampires. Hybrids are *born*. My parents are hybrids--each had one human and one vampire parent. Hybrids are unique. We live, make choices--some easier than others, and die..."

"And vampires? Exactly which myths are true?"

"Vampires are created by other vampires when bitten--victims always survive their attacks--whether they want to or not. When hybrids feed off humans, however, humans do not change--they die. Unless a hybrid does not drain them of all their blood, that is--which rarely happens of course. *If ever.*"

Chills suddenly ran up and down my spine. "You mean, vampires and hybrids drain their victims of blood--*completely*?"

"Yes. It doesn't matter who does the biting--when humans are victims--they are usually always depleted of blood. But like I said, when they are bitten by vampires, they are *reborn* themselves as vampires. It is not always an instantaneous birth. It can take weeks for humans to fully transform."

I just couldn't believe what I was hearing. *Rose had been drained of blood--not a drop of the fluid remained inside her precious body. Had a hybrid or vampire bitten her?*

Julian noted my confused expression. "I know I'm upsetting you. I'm sorry. I just thought you should know everything about me, Emily."

"I know that now, Julian. Um, tell me more. I don't understand the whole vampire thing. I'm confused," I stuttered--too distraught to focus.

"Well, like I said, vampires feed because they have to. They need blood in order to survive--they crave blood, in fact. Once they've turned--a process that can take days or even weeks--they become immortal--nearly impossible to kill. There are a lot of pure blood vampires in the world, Emily--they've been around since the thirteen hundreds. Still, vampires are an elusive breed. They tend to blend in--and prefer living in larger cities where it's easier to go unnoticed--easier to feed. Vampires are notoriously mysterious creatures. For the most part, they look like humans--like me I guess you should say. They are pale with dark eyes. Vampires have fangs that are retractable. And unlike many legends suggest, sunlight has no effect on them--on us. Not surprisingly, vampires are difficult to kill. In order to die, they must be decapitated--and the body parts burned. It's the only way to be sure, I guess. Other than piercing their hearts and burning them," Julian droned.

I stood there in shock, barely hearing him speak. All I could think about was Rose.

"Julian, I need to tell you something. Be honest with me. I'm scared..."

"What is it, Emily? What could you possibly need to tell me?" Julian quizzed.

"My family...we...well, we moved to West Virginia because..."

"What? What is it?"

"My sister...Rose. Well, she's dead."

"Rose? You never told me you had another sister. When did she die?"

"Rose has been dead for nearly three years Julian. She was four years old when *it* happened."

"What happened?"

"A horrible man snatched her away from us. He left Rose's body near an interstate--inside a ditch. She'd been *drained* Julian...of *blood.*"

Julian's eyes widened. "What?"

"When the police found Rose, her body was intact--in remarkable condition in fact. But Rose's body was discovered bloodless--the coroner had no explanation. Could she have been bitten by a *hybrid*, Julian?"

"I don't know. I mean it's possible. Tell me more. Tell me everything."

"There's not much to tell. A horrible man snatched her from the parking lot and ran away with her body. She was found nearby. She wasn't broken or abused--just drained. Oh, and she had two small holes on the back of her neck--underneath her hair."

"Vampire bites--or hybrid bites. Could've been either. I hate to ask this, Emily, but how longer after you found her was she buried?"

I hated thinking about it. "Well, she was found hours after being abducted. And then her funeral--well--she was buried three or four days after being murdered," I gulped back tears. "What is it, Julian? What are you thinking?"

"Most humans turn well within a week. It's probably nothing..."

"What are you saying, Julian? Rose was dead. I saw her! She was dead when we buried her!"

"I'm sure you're right, Emily. Rose was probably bitten by a hybrid--she *can't come back*."

"Come back? I saw her, Julian! Dead. It's not possible...Rose is gone..."

"It's okay, Emily. Please, don't cry. I'm sorry you lost her." Julian placed his arms around my shoulders. He looked as if he wanted so much to kiss me--to make the pain go away.

"Julian--tell me the truth. Could Rose come back? Is it possible?"

He hated answering my question. But Julian couldn't lie now. It wouldn't be right.

"Well, um, like I said, if Rose was bitten by a hybrid--the answer is no. She's dead. I mean--you saw her. You buried her, Rose definitely died that day. But..."

"But what?"

"Well, if Rose was bitten by a vampire--then...yes, she'll be reborn, Emily. There's no way around it."

"But we buried her. How?"

"It doesn't matter. I mean, I hate to say it. I know it's upsetting. But if Rose is a vampire, she'll..."

"She'll what?"

Julian held on tightly to me. He didn't want to talk about it anymore. It was too much for me to comprehend--too disturbing.

"Go on, Julian. Tell me. If Rose is a vampire...what does that mean? We buried her!"

"It won't matter, Emily. She'll find a way out...Rose will escape..."

"What! Oh my God! What are you saying, Julian! It's not possible! We buried her! She's in the ground...she can't escape!"

"There's only one way to know for sure. I need to go there--to Rose's gravesite. It's the only way to be sure."

I sobbed, sheltered inside his arms. I just couldn't believe any of this. *Rose is dead. She's not a vampire. We buried her.*

"Emily. Where is Rose buried? I'll go there. And if she's not inside the coffin...I'll find her. I'll bring Rose back to you. I can take care of her, Emily. I know what she needs. I'll find her...I promise!"

"I can't believe this. My baby sister--a vampire. This isn't real. None of this is real. It can't be."

"I'll find her, Emily. It's okay. My father and I can take care of Rose. It'll be okay. I promise."

"How can you promise such a thing Julian? My sister's a vampire. She's better off dead! I hope she's dead!"

"Emily, let me take you back home. I know you're upset, but the quicker I get out of town, the sooner I can find out whether or not Rose is a vampire. I'll leave in the morning. I will find out the truth--I promise. I'll take care of this. I'll fix this. I promise."

"You can't leave, Julian. What about school--what about your father?"

"He'll understand. And who cares about school. Besides, you are more important than history class, you know."

"I don't know, Julian. I just don't know..."

"Well I do. I'm going to Dallas and I'm going to discover the truth about Rose. That's final, Emily. I have to do this--I want to do this. Okay?"

"Okay." My weak body trembled.

"Come on. Let's get out of here. I need to get you back. Do me a favor, don't tell your family yet. Let's wait until we know more."

"Okay, Julian," I sniffled. "And thanks for doing this. I appreciate it. I really do."

"I know you do, Emily. I know."

Don't you want to know if I drink blood? Edward Cullen.

Chapter 34

Max...

When Julian and I returned home, another visitor sat inside our living room, waiting coldly.

"Max--how long have you been here?" I sputtered, guiltily hesitating when piling through the front door--Julian trailing closely behind me.

"Long enough. Hello, Julian," Max glared.

I had never seen Max so full of hate before. He looked as if he wanted to kill his brother. Perhaps he did.

"Max," Julian politely nodded. He was only civil because he did not want to upset me any further. I'd been through enough today. However, he wanted to rip into his twin brother's flesh as soon as Julian spotted Max sitting anxiously on the sofa.

"What are you doing here, Julian?" Max quizzed behind clenched teeth.

"Having dinner with Emily's family. And then we're studying of course. We have a project due in our English class. We're partners, Max," Julian chided as calmly as he could manage.

"I know about the project, Julian. But where have you guys been all of this time?" Max pried--still glaring.

"We went for a ride on Julian's motorcycle. It wasn't a big deal Max. Really. I'm okay. Um, why don't you eat with us? I'm sure there's plenty. Mom won't mind," I stuttered--hoping to thwart a potentially nasty fight. I quickly looked at Julian.

"It's okay," Julian reassured. "I'm gonna take off anyway. We'll finish the project later. I've got some things to do." Julian vacillated for a minute before elaborating in front of Max. "I'll um, see you tomorrow. Maybe we can finish this assignment another time?" Julian glanced at me with a strange look in his eyes. I understood immediately what he was implying.

"Okay. Um, thanks for coming. Thanks for *everything.*"

"No problem. Apologize to your mother for me. I'll eat with you guys another time. And say hello to your sisters. Okay?"

"Okay. Hey, Julian--*be careful.*"

"I'll be fine, Emily. Don't worry about me. Don't worry about *anything,*" Julian countered. Max was still staring.

"Goodbye, Julian. Have a nice evening," Max scoffed. "And don't worry about *Dallas. I'll* protect her. *I always do.*"

Julian looked at his brother with wicked eyes. He hated Max. And Max hated him. But Julian refused to upset me further. "Well, I guess I'm out of here. Goodbye, Em..." Julian managed, wishing we were alone.

I sensed he longed to grab me and kiss me deeply. He wanted so much to be with me tonight. Too had his brother was spoiling that idea.

Julian knew it would be awhile before he saw Dallas again. It would take him a couple of days just to drive to Texas. And then he'd have to find the cemetery where Rose was buried. His father would object, of course, to Julian desecrating a grave. But it didn't matter. Julian's mind was made up. He would do anything to right the wrongs Emily and her family had endured at the hands of vampires. Even if it meant finishing Rose off by dismembering her body so she would no longer suffer or roam the earth as a killer.

Max paced the floor of the empty room nervously. He was eager to discover what his loathsome twin brother had revealed to the only girl he'd ever cared for. Emily had walked Julian outside to his motorcycle--a fact that deeply angered Max, and her family was out of sight. All alone, Max didn't know what to think--or do. *Should I tell Dallas about my family? Or has Julian beaten me to the punch?* Anxious, his rigid body was tense and hard; Max wasn't used to feeling like this. Anger was a relatively new emotion for Max whose mother Katie had protected him for most of his sheltered life. Katie didn't want Max to *turn*--that would be disastrous. She encouraged her son to remain calm, avoid aggressive emotions or situations, and to stay out of trouble. It was always best for a hybrid to remain unruffled and collected--never giving in to the harrowing actions of their ominous darker side.

"Max, hey. What's up? I wasn't expecting you tonight," I stammered   apprehensively as I reentered the house.

"I know," Max shuffled to his feet. "I was just thinking about you a lot, I guess. I've missed not seeing you for the last couple of days. *How are you?*"

Max eyed me suspiciously. I'm sure that I looked funny. *Could he see that I had been crying?*

"I'm okay. I've just got a lot on my mind...I mean, I'm trying to finish up this English project. I'm covered up with school work. I'll be okay though. How's your mom?" I asked awkwardly--aware of his pejorative stare.

"She's okay. So tell me, Dallas--or would you rather I call you Emily like Julian does?"

"Dallas is fine, Max. I've grown used to it, you know."

"Okay. You and Julian were gone for awhile. I've been waiting here for about an hour. Where did you guys go?"

I thought for a few minutes before finally answering. Then I decided to be truthful. "Julian took me to a cave Max. He likes to study out there. He wanted to show me around--that's all. No big deal."

"Oh. So did you guys get much studying done when you were there?" Max's inquisitiveness was nerve-wracking. He'd never been so nosy before. And Max had never looked so intimidating while we were together. I felt slightly threatened.

"Of course not. We didn't go to the cave to study. Julian just wanted to show me around. I told you, Max, it's no big deal. Why are you acting this way?"

"I don't know. I'm sorry. I just don't like the *guy*. You know that. He's a jerk. I really don't want you hanging around Julian."

"I was wrong about him, Max. Julian's okay once you get to know him. Besides, you have nothing to worry about. I'm with you--remember?"

"I remember. I just hope you do."

"What are you saying, Max? Of course I remember! You're my boyfriend. You don't need to worry about Julian. Besides, he's leaving..."

"What?"

Suddenly, I regretted mentioning the fact that Julian would be taking off for Dallas in the morning--in search of my *dead* sister.

"Where's he headed to? And why?"

I really hated lying. But I decided I'd had enough with the truth. "Um, I'm not sure, Max. He just said things weren't working out for him here. That he needed to get away for a awhile. What difference does it make? You hate the guy. I mean, good riddance. Right?" I pretended not to care that Julian was leaving.

"I guess. So Julian's checking out soon? That's kind of strange, don't you think? I mean, he just got here. What about his *father*--is he taking off too? Max's voice cracked when he said father.

"I don't think so. Samuel's..."

"Samuel? So you know Julian's dad?"

"No. I've just heard Julian talk about him. I don't know much about either of them. Julian keeps to himself--you know that." I hoped Max believed me-- leaving it at that.

I just wasn't ready to let my boyfriend know that I knew he and Julian were vampires--or hybrids--or whatever. There were many other things on my mind-- like whether or not my little sister was a blood sucker and if Julian would find her and bring her back.

Max decided not to elaborate either, even though he sensed something was different between the two of them. He'd barely accepted the truth about himself. How could he explain to Dallas that he was half-human and half-vampire and that Julian--the person he hated more than anyone in the world--was his brother? He couldn't--he wouldn't.

"Max, we've got some time before dinner. Why don't we hang out in my room for awhile. Want to?"

Max grabbed my hand with more force than before. His clutch was almost possessive--as if he needed to remind me that I belonged to him. The two of us headed down the hallway, hand in hand. I was already beginning to feel better. I was giddy to see my boyfriend. I desperately needed Max. And Max needed me, or at least I hoped so. Though neither of us were willing to admit to the other about the troubles facing us, I knew we would need each other in order to make it through the tough times ahead. And times were definitely about to get tougher. *For everyone.*

The End (For the time being)

We are the shadows in the night.
We are the monsters you fear.
We are the angels of blood and death.
You fear us.
You run from us.
You fight us.
Mankind hates us.
Humanity tries to annihilate us.
Evolution has destroyed us.
We are despised.

We are forgotten.
We are fallen.

Konya651— *Deviant Art*

Coming Soon

Blessed with new life, cursed to live it. Such is the life of a vampire. Always to walk in the shadows, never able to walk freely in the light. They cannot live, so they cannot have normal lives as others do. They cannot die, so they cannot return to the heavens nor the underworld from whence they came. Konya651.

Preview of Hybrid II's--Bloodling

Since arriving in Dallas, Julian could think of nothing but Emily. He wanted so much to protect her from the truth. A truth that would destroy Emily if Julian's assumptions were correct. As he sped towards the cemetery, Julian replayed the last moments he'd spent inside that cave with her. The way Emily smelled, the softness of her skin, Emily's sensuous hair, and caring eyes. Julian was in love--but too scared to admit it. *If I'm right about Rose...everything will change. Everything.*

When Julian finally arrived at the graveyard, his hands shook. *If anyone catches me, I'll shadow. I need to be quick. In and out of here as fast as possible.* He looked for Rose's gravesite, eager to get started. As soon as he found it, Julian's hand's trembled even more.

The grey, heart-shaped granite marker, free of weeds and debris, was hard to Julian's acquiescent touch. He stared pensively into the deeply etched words, searching for answers--*Emily needs answers.* *"Where are you, Rose?"* He wondered aloud. *"How do I find you?"*

Rose Elizabeth Reed
September 14,1998-January 31, 2002
Our Beloved Rose, For All Of Eternity
Always In Our Hearts

In an attempt to get to her, Julian clawed at the clumps of rich, dark dirt and thick grass with his bare hands. Julian's nails were razor sharp and every so often, he glanced up nervously, praying the one-hundred acre cemetery remained dark and empty.   Julian wasn't supposed to be there. Visitors were encouraged to honor their loved ones during the daytime and Julian knew why. *He's been here. I can smell him, Julian thought to himself. Are you with him, Rose?*

Three feet below the hardened ground, Julian reached for the tiny coffin--sure he'd find it intact.   He did of course. Then Julian grabbed the metal casket, pulling it out easily towards the messy surface--its weight no match for Julian's unnatural strength.   Julian pried open the cover expecting to find the inside of the coffin empty. *If I'm right, Rose is gone. Her body having long since left the confines of the velvet-lined casket. If I'm right that is...*

While deeply buried, the dusty metal coffin had lost its luster, and Julian's nervous hands shook as he eyed the deep scratches on top of its marred surface. Julian studied the markings curious as to their origins. *Has someone been here, Rose? Oh please be inside, let me be wrong. Oh please God, let me be wrong...*

Acknowledgements

Thanks to my generous publishing company and its wonderful team of editors for making this *Tween* novel the best it can be. Also, thanks for giving this first time author a chance to write--something she loves to do more than anything else in the world. Also, a special thanks to my loving family for putting up with me while writing this fiction story! Also, a special, special, thanks to my daughter Emily and her best friend Emily for telling me what to write about--they love vampires!

As for my small but continually growing *Hybrid* fan club on Facebook--thanks for caring enough to join! I have enjoyed creating *Hybrid* and look forward to its sequel--*Bloodling*. Which reminds me, a special thanks to everyone who likes to read vampire stories--I truly hope you enjoy this one!

J.D. Tynan (whose work I adore--especially *Jill-9*), William Connor Jr., and Samantha Shu--thanks! I appreciate your professionalism and the desire to help a struggling author. May life bring you nothing but success.

I can be reached at reedangie123@gmail.com or at www.angielreed.com.

www.ingramcontent.com/pod-product-compliance
Lightning Source LLC
Chambersburg PA
CBHW052006020726

47501CB00004B/1024